While the Music Plays

DIANE AUSTELL

BANTAM BOOKS
NEW YORK • TORONTO • LONDON • SYDNEY • AUCKLAND

For my husband

CHAPTER 1

SOMETIME IN THE NIGHT Laura Chandler dreamed of her dead husband. He came toward her down a long flight of stairs, his face forbidding as it had never been in life, his arm raised in a gesture of command. She said his name twice, *Robert, Robert,* and found herself running down a narrow corridor filled with moving shadows. Beside her ran Joseph, the family's dignified butler, explaining that now he was a senator he intended to vote for disunion. *The breach can never be healed,* he said, *never healed,* and looking into his calm black face she knew it was true. They came to a sunny meadow and Joseph became Robert leading her along a path of bright flowers, comforting and reassuring her as he had always done.

And then she was awake, meadow, flowers, sunshine, comfort gone, everything Robert said instantly wiped out. But the emotion was still there. She pressed the edge of the sheet against her eyes and sat up. She hadn't dreamed of him or cried over him in more than a year and it wasn't going to start again now.

Thin light was beginning to filter in, touching her bed, the bright rugs on the polished floor, the wide windows overlooking the garden. It was the bedroom of her childhood in the house her grandfather built, very different from the impressive bedroom she had shared with Robert for nine years in Washington. The entire house had been impressive, the kind a senator needed, but comfortable and homelike as well. She had loved that house.

Two years ago she had come back from Robert's funeral and walked slowly through each room. Everything was as it had been when he left for the last time, the same flowered sofas and comfortable chairs, the same lamps on the tables and carpets on the floors, but it was an imposter house, alien because the heart of it was missing. A few weeks later she sold it and went home to Richmond.

Her brother Edward welcomed her. The family home was his now and Millie, his wife, was the mistress of it, but with loving concern they had assured her that she was welcome to stay with them forever.

She turned over and looked at the little clock on the mantel. Almost six. In the first months after Robert died the early morning hours had always been the hardest—it was when the worst thoughts came—but things had been better lately. Why the dream, why all this pain now? The wedding rehearsal last night might have done it, or the prospect of tonight. Everyone who mattered in Richmond was coming to see Edward and Millie Seymour's daughter get married, and Laura looked forward to it with the misgiving she always felt when facing a crowd of politicians. She didn't like most of them and didn't want to spend the evening politely agreeing with their politics.

Six weeks ago, on the day the guns fired at Fort Sumter, Paige Seymour announced her engagement to Alex Wyatt. All over Richmond girls were doing the same, but in this house it had produced a storm. Edward didn't want his edgy, volatile seventeen-year-old daughter marrying anyone yet, not even Alex Wyatt, a good man who could handle Paige when no one else could. But he was an army officer heading into inevitable war. Edward refused permission and battle of a different kind was joined.

Paige cried, pleaded, tried charm, went into a tumultuous outburst that brought the smooth-working household to a standstill. Edward said no once again. Then, calm and dry-eyed, Paige threatened to elope and Edward knew she would do it.

And so tonight she would marry Alex in the lavish wedding she had always intended to have.

For Laura it meant a public appearance—in reality a public performance—something that for all the years she'd done it had never become easy. She was famous, a burden she despised. Tonight some would treat her with exaggerated deference. Others, like her girlhood friend Valerie Hood, would barely hide their envy. No use to tell Valerie she was not a woman to be envied—she would never believe it.

The sun was up, the day already warm, and a breeze was

disturbing the curtains. Outside, Edward's buggy was being brought around to the front porch. It was always ready at least an hour before he left for the newspaper office. From the kitchen came the banging of pots and pans and the cook's voice singing hosannas to the Lord. Time to face the day.

Laura dressed and went downstairs to eat breakfast with her family, the odd mood of the dream shoved to the back of her mind.

I N ANOTHER BEDROOM in the same section of town Chase Girard woke early too, but not because of disturbing dreams. His dreams had been vague but pleasant and his alert, early waking a result of the discipline of army life. He lit a cigar and smoked for a while, considering his duties on this day, and then slipped out of bed.

Immediately Valerie knew he was gone. She opened her eyes and watched his naked body in the lamplight with sleepy pleasure as he slapped cold water on his face and brushed his hair. It was a body younger men might envy and she loved it, dreamed about it, and caressed it every time she got the chance. So many men in their thirties, including her own husband, were growing soft around the middle—she guessed Chase was in his early thirties although he hadn't said. He had told her so little about himself.

She did know he had been "out West," West meaning to her a place where Indians and nature were an eternal menace, where there was no safety, no comfort, often no food and certainly no white women, a life she could not imagine. Because she knew so little she invented stories about him—who he was and what his past might have been—and quickly came to almost believe them. She did not wonder why a career army officer sworn to defend the United States would leave it at this crisis and come South, for so many Northern army officers were doing just that. Besides, men's motives, hopes, fears, and inner lives did not interest her; she was inclined to doubt that they had any.

In her world men and women commonly lived different lives, the women docile and pretty—Valerie strived for the appearance of both—running their households, bearing the children, accepting whatever men chose to give them without complaint. As for the men she knew, the pursuit and increase of wealth was their occupation, politics their passion, and usually the two intertwined. They ate hugely, drank hard, gambled much, whored frequently—except that Jason was careful with liquor by Southern standards and if he was unfaithful he kept it very quiet.

She had never wondered about her husband's innermost feelings and would no more inquire into her lover's motives or deeply held beliefs than she would have asked the Reverend Jacobson whether he really believed in God. It was enough to know that Chase admired and wanted her and above all was *here* at a time in her life when she needed him. She could read anything she wished into his self-possessed gaze and right now he was looking at her with the smile that devastated.

She had first met him a week ago in the lobby of the Spotswood Hotel where in the basement the young men of Richmond, members of the newly formed Richmond Howitzers, were studying artillery theory. In the weeks since the nation had stumbled into war, young men had been pouring into Richmond, eager to join the Confederate army and strike a blow for freedom. Training them were West Point officers, some of them Northerners, who had resigned from the U.S. Army and come South. Alex Wyatt, her husband's cousin, had introduced her to one of them. Chase Girard.

An old friend and a fine officer, Alex said, who had managed to get out of Washington and arrive in Richmond in time to be Alex's best man at his marriage to the Seymour girl.

Valerie, considering this new find, decided that Colonel Girard was certainly the best man she'd ever seen. She looked him over, wanted him, realized that it was a sign from God (since Jason was out of town), and invited him to walk with her to Capitol Square. The walk led to lunch at the hotel. That evening she let him in by the side door and took him to her bed.

Lovers for six nights. She had never done such an insane thing in seven years of marriage although there had been opportunities; she had never even considered it. At least, not seriously. She was taking a great risk—her husband was a possessive and dangerous man—but for her Chase Girard was irresistible. That he was a Yankee made him all the more glamorous. She saw in him no deep concerns about disunion or slavery, but like most of the men she knew, he looked on war as a tremendous adventure to be snatched and enjoyed before it was over. It was all part of the madness of being male.

In the quiet of the still-sleeping house there was a sound at the door, more a brush than a tap. He pulled on blue trousers and said, "Yes."

The maid slid in and in a moment slid out again. With the door closed it was as if the pitcher of hot water and the pot of steaming coffee had appeared on the bureau without human intervention.

He brought Valerie a cup of coffee and she sat up to watch him shave. No beard such as some higher-ranking officers sported, she was glad of that, and his dark hair was short, just below his ears. He maintained he'd been shaggy as a bear out West—no Hallie to bring him hot water out there, he had said with the smile that could take her breath away. As he buttoned the blue jacket of the United States Army, she said, "You'll be the sensation of the wedding in that uniform. I'd offer you one of Jason's suits but it would never fit."

With a smile he said, "I wouldn't take Jason's suit," and she shivered at the implication. He could give pleasure simply with words spoken from across the room. She rolled over onto his pillow with a little moan of content.

He kissed the back of her head. "I'll see you tonight."

"Indeed you will," she answered, muffled in the pillow, and heard the soft click of the door as he went out.

After a few moments spent thinking about last night and the prospects for tonight, she threw back the covers and shouted for Hallie. Instantly the maid popped in. She knew her mistress's moods and temper and had been waiting just outside the door.

Valerie was sitting on the edge of the bed wearing only her high-heeled, backless slippers, her young body still as firm and virginal as if she were not the twenty-eight-year-old mother of a six-year-old son, her delicate face and uncombed blond hair giving her the look of a tousled angel.

"Find my blue muslin, Hallie, the one with the velvet trim. Are the flowers cut? I promised Mrs. Seymour I'd get them to her first thing this morning."

"Yas'm. Micah, he jus' about ready to go."

"No, no—you run and stop him. I want to take them over myself."

B REAKFAST TIME WAS the best time of the day for Laura. Grief had taught her to seize whatever fleeting enjoyment came her way—the morning sun that cheered the dining room; the snowy tablecloth; the shining silver and crystal; Edward and Millie turning to her with smiling, good-morning faces; the maid, Jewel, faithful as the sun, filling her cup. She looked forward to this moment—the sound of coffee gurgling into the fine china cup, black and hot, warming her cold hand, foaming a little against her lips. This was what her life had ground down to, scattered moments of tiny pleasure, usually sensory, always brief.

And there were a few other good things. Her much-loved brothers, still only boys in her eyes, were home for this great day, looking sleek and military in their expensive tailored uniforms. Kirby had his copy of Hardee's *Infantry Tactics* hidden in his lap—Millie did not allow reading at the table. He was only twenty-one, the baby of the family and somewhat spoiled. It was hard to imagine him as a soldier obeying orders contrary to his own wishes or doing anything at all that did not please him, no matter what some officer said. Douglas, three years older, was the responsible one, anxious to conform, trying always to do the right thing. Doug would be perfect for the army but Laura doubted that the army would be good for him; nothing about this war was good.

Millie handed the platter of ham and sausage to Doug without waiting for Jewel to come back and pass it. "You boys clean this up now, every bit of it. You've hardly made a dent and you're both skinny as rakes."

Doug rolled his eyes. "I've eaten half a pig this morning, Millie." But he took another slice of the sweet juicy ham and pushed the plate over to Kirby. Kirby clamped his book between his knees and took a slice of the ham and a sausage as well. It was a rule. You tried to please Millie whenever you could because she was so good and little things made her so happy.

Millie watched them eat dutifully, her pretty, still-young face filled with pleasure and none of Laura's dark anxieties in her mind. She had loved and mothered her husband's brothers since the day she married Edward; she banished worry by insisting that the war would be over in a month or two, as soon as the North realized that Southerners hated them and would never come back into the Union. Because she wanted to, she believed that her two boys would never have to fight.

In this she differed from her husband. Edward knew better, and Laura suspected his concerns were similar to hers. His editorials against secession, published in the family-owned newspaper, had cost him lifelong friendships, and when his own state seceded he had called it a catastrophe. "But it's decided and I have to stand with Virginia," he had said. "I can't go against my own people."

He looked stern this morning, almost somber. It occurred to Laura that she hadn't seen him really smile in a long time and he had once been a man who smiled easily. Paige's marriage, she supposed, and the war. And he might be anxious about her. She resolved to smile more herself, to be cheerful if she could not be happy, and to eat more too. Like Millie, Edward was always worrying about her weight.

In accordance with this new resolve she took a second helping of the sweet succulent ham.

Edward laid down his napkin, looked at his watch and tucked it back in his pocket. "I want to be in the office by nine. Tell Paige . . . ah, there you are, my dear. At last."

Paige slid into her chair looking abashed. "Sorry, Papa. Sorry, Mama. It's the dress . . . Mama, Addie Shaw will have to come over this morning. The neck is too high and the waist is loose. It just isn't right."

"It isn't *perfect.*"

"Shut up, Kirby."

"Paige!"

"Sorry, Mama." Paige shot a hard look at Kirby. She had taken a lot of teasing about her worries over the food, the flowers, the dress, the music, but beneath it all was the knowledge that Alex was going away and might not come back, whatever Mama said about cowardly Yankees. Papa did not think the war would be easy or short. Neither did Alex and he was a West Pointer who knew about war. She did, indeed, want their wedding to be perfect, an ideal memory that would sustain them no matter what came after.

Like Doug she had the auburn hair that sometimes appeared in the family and at the moment no discontent in her face. Laura thought, She may never be as happy again as she is right now.

Paige waited until her father had taken his leave in that formal way he had, watched the boys disappear as soon as the front door closed behind him, and outlasted her mother, who loved to settle in for a good gossip after breakfast. When Millie finally decided to leave, Paige called after her, "Please send for Addie, Mama—something *has* to be done about that dress," and moved to the seat beside Laura.

"It really isn't right. Addie knows perfectly well what I want but she's stubborn. If you would talk to her she'll be so tickled she'll do the neck over and tell all her friends she had a fashion consultation with *Mrs. Chandler.*"

Laura's eyes crinkled. "I can see my tombstone now. 'She didn't know much but she did know how to dress.' "

Paige giggled. Her face was a softer version of Edward's, but when she laughed it was apparent that she was Millie's child too. "Remember when I came to visit and you decided I was old enough for a grown-up dress? It was pale blue satin with six flounces in the skirt and what I thought was a terribly plunging neckline. You let me go to your party for all those people and introduced me to the Vice President. Oh, it was exciting!"

It had been one of those onerous, politically necessary parties, a huge gathering of ambitious people. The insincerity had flowed as freely as the wine; everyone had smiled and maneuvered and lied, and the evening had left Laura wondering if there was still some small corner of the world where integrity came before self-interest. "I remember.

Run upstairs and get ready for Addie. I'll talk her around before we come up."

Alone at the table she sat listening to the sounds of the house while the kitchen maid cleared the table. This room always soothed her. It was the heart of home—the view of the side garden beyond the French doors, the sideboard where her mother's silver tea service sat in a place of honor, the rosewood table that was so cosy for the family but could be opened to a great length for guests. Here the Seymours had always gathered, here childhood memories of her parents were clearest. Sometimes it seemed that from the corner of her eye she caught glimpses of her beautiful mother, or sensed her father's presence in the room. One day soon she would find a place of her own and face the world again. But not yet, she was not ready to leave home yet.

Elvina, the new maid, stole awed, respectful glances as she worked. Until this morning she had not been allowed out of the kitchen and this was the closest she'd ever been to greatness. There were so many stories about Mrs. Chandler, all of them fascinating, and what she didn't know she imagined. Unable to read, she had listened over the years while others read aloud newspaper accounts of this lady's doings. The most beautiful lady in Washington, the papers said, her dinners and receptions perfection, her clothes so exquisite that other ladies copied them. This ideal woman was sitting right here, close enough to touch, gazing out at the garden in a way that puzzled Elvina. For one so blessed, Mrs. Chandler didn't seem as happy as you might expect, but she had turned out to be as pretty as they said and remarkably gracious and easy to please.

Laura would have been grimly amused if she'd known the girl's thoughts. Life in Washington had taught her how to impress people. You held your head high, walked like a queen, and after a while they believed you were one. At the same time you avoided resentment by showing a flattering interest in them. You smiled a lot and, even when not smiling, kept a pleasant expression on your face no matter your private troubles, worries, or state of health. It was shallow, counterfeit, the part of Washington life she most disliked. No one saw her shyness or self-doubts. Her public self—a famous senator's famous wife—had been a performance given for Robert's sake, a role played so long it had become second nature. Her real self she hadn't thought about in years.

Coming home had made it easy to continue that way. She never knew the dismay Edward and Millie felt when they saw her descend the train steps two years ago. Always slim, she had lost fifteen pounds since Robert's funeral and was wraithlike in her thinness. Black mourning emphasized it and the fluttering black veil made her pale face seem almost transparent. Once home she had built a wall around herself. She received few visitors, accepted no invitations, made no formal public appearances. Yet as soon as the first year of mourning had passed, men with sufficient social connections began to call, ostensibly on Millie, and even took the first steps in courtship.

Millie championed the cause of those she considered worthy. Because he was an old friend and her doctor, she especially favored Byron Rollins. "He's such a nice man, quite good-looking. Come down and meet him, honey. You'd like him if you got to know him."

Feeling badgered, Laura had settled onto her bed with the obdurate look Millie knew well. "I don't care if he's *Launcelot*, I don't want him pestering me. Not one of these men who comes sniffing around cares about me for myself, it's all because of what they think I am. Please, Millie, let me be."

"You don't eat enough to keep a bird alive, that's why you're so snappish," Millie answered. She went downstairs and urged Byron Rollins to try again another day.

Slowly Laura regained the lost weight, her color improved, and Millie, never one to look beneath the surface, announced that she would soon be back to her old self. "It's being home that's done it, Edward."

Edward nodded. "No doubt." It was always easiest to agree with Millie.

Later that evening he had gone looking for his sister and found her curled up on the sofa in the library, staring at a fire that was almost out. Her head was bent, her shoulders curved down as if guarding against a blow. The book on her lap was unopened. He knew what she felt and it broke his heart.

She had always touched his heart for she was in a way his first daughter. He was the one who had had to tell the child she had been that their mother was gone from them, and then only a few months later that their father was dead too. How did you explain to a seven-year-old that mothers could die in childbirth? How did you convince her that her father, so strong, so reliable, so expert with guns, could discharge a rifle accidentally? On the day she found her father lying on his bedroom floor in a pool of blood with part of his chin torn away, she had screamed until Edward picked her up and carried her, whimpering and shuddering, out of the room. After that she did not speak a word for five days and he knew he had to find someone to help him. He was forever beholden to Millie for being the woman who had done it.

"What are you reading?" He was beside her before she knew it and she jumped a little.

"Oh, something by Mr. Thackeray." She handed it to him. "They say it's his best but somehow I can't get into it."

Edward glanced at the book, laid it on the table, and sat down next to her, thinking back to the time she had left this house at barely seventeen. She had gone with Robert Chandler to Washington armed only with intelligence, a trusting heart, and joy in her new marriage. It was the intelligence that had saved her, along with a resilience and strength of will that Edward hadn't known were there. So many wives of powerful men were driven away by the intense demands of the capital city, back to Vermont or Massachusetts or Alabama to live lives for the most part separate from their husbands. But not Laura. She turned out to be agile, quick-witted, and determined to stay. She came home only when her reason for staying was gone.

In the past Edward had known how to comfort her when disaster struck but she wasn't a child now, she was a grown woman. More than anything he wanted to help her begin life again, and he wasn't sure he could.

"It will pass, Laura"—he knew he was already on the wrong track—"and your Christian faith sustains you. You have a long life ahead and there will be other loves."

She didn't believe it, it was the worst thing he could say. "Yes," she said, "of course."

He talked a while longer, finally said good night and went to bed wondering if he'd left any cliché unspoken. She watched him go with a smile in her eyes. Every word he spoke was a wound because there was nothing to be said that didn't hurt, yet she had never loved him more. He was still a shining example of everything a man should be. In some ways he was kinder than Robert, for Robert had had a toughness at the core and no serious self-doubts. Edward had many. He easily forgave the failings of others but never forgave his own.

He did not come close to guessing her real thoughts or how she looked at her life. Growing up, she had gone over and over the tragedy of her parents, had asked *why* so many times and never found a satisfactory answer. When Robert died, as cruelly and suddenly as her mother and father, she saw clearly for the first time that life was balanced on a knife edge; nothing and no one could ever be counted on to last. It was a mistake, she decided, to hope for happiness so she would not even try for it. Instead, she would ration emotions wisely, feel nothing deeply, allow no one too close, and eventually the pain would go away and she would find peace.

Never once in the two years since that talk with Edward had she asked herself if a better way of living might be found. All she wanted was to get through each day. Faced with Paige's wedding tonight, she asked only to play her part well and then go back to life as it had to be lived now, without meaning but also without pain.

Extra help had been brought in for the day and there was much banging of doors and bustling of servants through the entrance hall with boxes of flowers and extra chairs. A loud disagreement was in progress between Bella, Millie's personal maid, and Joseph, who was both the butler and Edward's valet. Joseph and Bella did not like each other and carried on intermittent warfare that grew bitter at times. Joseph didn't like Laura's maid, Jewel, either but found it impossible to get a good quarrel going with her.

In the ballroom, a beautiful room that had seen many

weddings, an altar had been set up and Millie and Jewel were at work arranging the flowers around it. Millie was gifted with flowers and Jewel, imaginative and intelligent, had learned from her. Tonight all the public rooms of the house would be filled with flowers from Millie's own garden and the contributions of friends and neighbors, and Paige would come down the curving staircase to Alex just as Laura had come down to Robert eleven years ago, a seventeen-year-old girl with no real understanding of what lay ahead. Laura's mind moved back to that night and for a little while she allowed herself to remember.

ADDIE SHAW, the seamstress, was an observant little woman with careful, curious eyes in a round, pink face and only a faint lilt in her speech to remind others of Dublin, the city of her birth. The magic she could work with fine cloth, lace, and ribbons took her into wealthy women's homes where there were the art objects, French furniture, and rich fabrics that nourished her artist's soul. There she also indulged her enduring passion for gossip.

The Seymour ladies were her favorite clients. The house itself did her heart good—high-ceilinged gracious rooms, Italian marble mantels bearing Meissen porcelain, walls painted creamy white or covered with the apricot silk brocade she loved to run her fingers over when no one was looking; a wide, sweeping staircase with a walnut banister so highly polished that it reflected light; huge rooms and cosy rooms that made the sprawling house both grand and comfortable; servants so efficient and well trained that food was served and chores accomplished without apparent effort. That was what it was like, being rich. Addie understood very well why the wealthy clung to their wealth and didn't blame them at all. She only wished she could be one of them.

A thoroughgoing snob, she had followed the distinguished Seymour family with interest since she stepped off the boat at the Richmond wharf, an ambitious teenager who was clever with a needle. Her first important patron was Laura's mother, Margaret Seymour, tall, striking, an ideal advertisement for Addie's spectacular gowns. Margaret impressed her as did Margaret's husband, Thomas, for they were true American aristocrats. Their forebears had fought alongside General Washington to drive out the accursed English, had helped write the Constitution that said everyone except slaves was equal (Addie sometimes mixed up the Constitution and the Declaration of Independence but understood the basic philosophy very well), and one of their ancestors had been a governor of Virginia. They seemed to have everything—the parents devoted to each other; Edward, the eldest son, just home from Princeton and preparing to study architecture in Europe; pretty little Laura, who looked so much like her beautiful mother; Douglas, surely the sweetest-natured child in the world; and then another baby on the way.

In the midst of work on the new wardrobe Margaret would need after the baby came, Addie learned that money, power, and an impeccable pedigree could not always save you, for when Kirby, the last child, was born, Margaret Seymour died. As Addie described that terrible day to her friend Rosemary Malone, "Himself went a little mad with grief, threw the doctor out of the house, told the minister to take his platitudes and go straight to hell, locked his bedroom door and wouldn't come out, wouldn't talk to anyone, not even his children. I felt sorry for the son. Edward is a good boy, only a year older than me, and he had to tell the children. Douglas didn't understand—he's only three—but Laura did. When Edward told her that her mama'd gone to be with the angels she screamed 'You're a liar, you're a liar!' and pounded him with her fists and there he was, poor boy, holding her off and saying 'I'm so sorry, so sorry,' as if it were his fault when, after all, he'd lost his mother too."

Rosemary, who loved a good tragedy, had clicked her tongue and murmured, "A true shame, that. Then what happened?"

"For a while I thought the house would tumble down with her screaming and Dougie joining in to keep her company, but we finally got her quieted down and into bed. Later on we tiptoed in and there she was, all cuddled with Jewel, that slave child they gave her. Those two children had their arms around each other, fast asleep. I asked

Edward if I should move Jewel and he said, "No. Let
them be."

"Ah," sighed Rosemary.

"The father's finally gone back to work as a man should.
All will be well now, I'm sure."

But all was not well. Less than a year later Addie had
cause to weep again for the Seymour children when
Thomas Seymour shot himself while cleaning his gun.
Edward, only twenty-two, took on his father's responsibilities. He was, Addie told Rosemary, a truly good man who
always did the right thing. When he married Millicent
Hampton, Addie created a wedding dress so exquisite that
she once again had a Mrs. Seymour as her patron and in
later years the daughter, Paige, as well.

But the best thing about the Seymours was Laura. Since
the night of her mother's death Addie had watched her
grow from a grief-stricken child given to temperamental
outbursts into a young woman of considerable beauty, with
another gift even more rare—she had style. Anything she
wore enhanced her looks and not only because her slim
body showed clothes to advantage. Her eye for design, for
line and color, was infallible and she could do it for other
girls as well as herself. "From now on," her friend Valerie
told Addie, "Laura is going to pick out every stitch I wear.
You can help, Addie, but Laura decides."

Once again Addie made a wedding dress for a Seymour
lady and, puffed up with pride at being invited, saw Laura
marry Robert Chandler, the senior senator from Virginia, a
dynamic man who looked more like a President than the
President himself, in Addie's opinion. Many people thought
he would be President one day but, as Addie reported to
Rosemary, that cut no ice with Edward Seymour. She had
overheard the sharp disagreement between Laura and her
brother. "*He* bellowed at her—and he's such a soft-spoken
gentleman—'You're seventeen, he's forty-eight! He's a fine
man but good God, Laura, thirty-one years? Isn't it possible
that you're flattered by the attention of a great man, even a
little dazzled? Your feelings will change as you grow older.'
She said, cool as a cucumber, 'Of course I'm dazzled, by his
mind, not his position. He talks to me, Edward, about
ideas, not the nonsense most men think girls want to hear.

He's kind, he makes me feel safe, he *loves* me. What more could a woman want?' Let me tell you, Edward had nothing more to say after that."

Laura became an exemplary political wife, Addie noted. Prominent women began to emulate her and newspaper stories describing her clothes, her jewels, her classic elegance, brightened the lives of ordinary women. No one read about her more avidly than Addie Shaw, for business as well as pleasure. She was kept busy stealing ideas from Laura's gowns for wealthy Richmond women who had little to do but keep up with the latest fashions.

Then suddenly, after nearly a decade in the harsh light of national politics, Laura was home again, shockingly pale in her widow's weeds, Addie said, pleasant when you spoke to her but absentminded and remote. "It certainly puts the lie to those who said she only married him because he was a senator," she stated with satisfaction. "I always maintained she loved him dearly, Rosemary Malone."

Rosemary came quickly to her own defense. "I never said she didn't, Addie. Sure, and he was a handsome, good man. I heard him speak once and it all sounded grand though I have no idea what he was talking about. They say she doesn't go out at all, not socially, that is. Perhaps she's one of those who'll mourn forever."

Perhaps she is, thought Addie, waiting for Laura in the entrance hall, but what a waste it would be. Many of Addie's ladies treated her as little more than a servant but Laura gave her the respect due an artist, so she hadn't minded the last-minute summons this morning. It was Adam, Jewel's son, who had brought the message. Before coming to America Addie had never seen a black person and in spite of years spent in Virginia was still not used to them, particularly one like Jewel who talked like a white lady and gave herself airs. It galled Addie to realize that Jewel had a better education than she did. However, Jewel's son was a good little boy with a joyful nature and an appealing grin. Who could help liking Adam? She produced another cookie from her pocket just for the pleasure of seeing him smile and he whirled off as Laura came toward her with arms out in welcome.

"Addie, this is so good of you. Paige wants the waist

nipped in just a trifle and the neckline lowered an inch if you can manage that."

"I can manage it but I shouldn't. A wedding dress should be modest, as I've told her many times. Your dress was up to your neck, I recall."

"I know, but that was in the *olden* days, Paige says. Let's humor her even though we know better." As they started up the stairs the door chimes rang. The hallway was deserted.

Laura said, "I'll get it—Lord knows where Joseph is. You go on, Addie, and I'll be up directly."

Valerie, her arms filled with flowers, was on the front porch, accompanied by two servants burdened with every blossom in her garden and a great package of greenery, "just in case you need it."

"This is wonderful, Val! Bring it all into the ballroom. Millie and Jewel are . . . well, they were here. They must be out in the garden. Wait here and I'll go look."

"No," said Valerie. "Boys, put everything over there by the altar. Micah, you go find Miss Millie and show her what we've brought." She pulled Laura into the hallway and said in a low, tense voice, "I've got to talk to you. Let's go up to your room."

In Laura's bedroom Valerie looked around with a smile. "I haven't been up here since you got married and left home. Same furniture, same books—remember how we used to come up here on rainy days? You'd make up stories and we'd act them out, you and I and Jewel. We were pretty good too, but we never had the nerve to perform for an audience. Do you think I can fool an audience now?" She turned and looked at Laura. Her cheeks were a hectic pink.

"What is it, Val? What's wrong?"

Valerie sat down on the bed and put her hands over her face. "Nothing! Everything. Oh, Laura, I'm in love."

Not for one moment did Laura think she meant her husband.

"Who, for heaven's sake?"

Valerie sat up straighter and smoothed her hair. "Chase Girard, Alex's best man. You must have met him."

"Yes, last night at the wedding rehearsal." Laura sat

beside Valerie and looked into her shining eyes. "Surely you haven't . . ."

Valerie threw herself back on the bed, stretched her arms toward the ceiling and giggled. "Oh yes I have. And Laura, he's so *different*! Laura, with Robert did you ever pretend? Sometimes . . ."—she lowered her voice—"sometimes I pretend I'm making love to a Spanish pirate!"

Oh, Lord. Laura glanced around the room as if there might be someone in it who could overhear. "Where do you meet?" she whispered.

"He comes to the house after everyone's asleep and I let him in. Nothing to it."

"Have you lost your mind? Sit up and listen to me, you idiot. Jason will kill him. He'll kill *you*."

"He won't find out."

"Oh, really. Who knows now?"

"Only Hallie."

"Hallie and every other servant in the house. And all their friends. Have you told this man anything about Jason?"

"Of course I have. What kind of person do you think I am? It doesn't matter—anyhow, it hasn't stopped him. I think he likes to take chances."

Laura was silent, thinking of Jason Hood. A man of enormous vanity, handsome in a narrow-eyed, thin-lipped way, slight of build but well muscled and athletic, a ruthless duelist who had killed seven men over trivial disagreements, a patrician gentleman obsessed with his personal honor. He never overlooked a slight no matter how unintended and seemed to search for opportunities to demonstrate his physical courage. The thought of his rage if he even suspected his beautiful wife of infidelity made Laura go cold.

She asked, "How long have you been . . . seeing him?"

"A week. I met him the day after he got to town. Alex introduced him."

"When will Jason be back?"

"Oh, not for a long time."

"Valerie, it's got to stop. He could come home any day. Don't see Colonel Girard again, don't even look at him, and pray that everyone who knows keeps quiet."

"I told you—I'm in love! It's a little risky—maybe—and

you know what? It makes it more exciting! Now don't look like that. You were always the reckless one who got us into trouble. What's happened to your spunk?"

What's happened to your common sense? Laura thought but she didn't say it. Valerie was "in love" with a good-looking stranger she'd met a week ago and she believed she could hide it from her husband. And here they were, she and Valerie, sitting in this room on her bed sharing confidences as they had when they were girls. Here they had decided to be belles, or try to be. Here Valerie had taught her the most effective ways to ensnare men, methods she claimed to have learned from observation of older, established belles but which Laura believed must be inborn. Watching the many romances going on around her, she had decided that there was much intense flirtation but very little love. All Valerie's strategems were clever. They were also dishonest—but approved. Southern society expected you to appear brainless when you were not and to flatter men into believing they loved you when they didn't.

Laura had worked hard at it all during her sixteenth summer with considerable success, but when summer ended she told Valerie she had decided not to be a belle.

"Not be a belle?" Valerie had said, dumbfounded. "Why of course we are!"

"Just me, Val. You do what you like. I don't enjoy it as much as I thought I would. Pretending I like boys I really don't care for. Pretending I don't know anything so boys can tell me things. Flirting with just about anybody so long as he wears pants. Don't you think it's a little—well—silly?"

When they parted on that long-ago day it was with hugs and kisses and promises of undying affection, but even then Laura dimly realized that she had, without intending it, demeaned the one thing Valerie was good at, the one thing that gave her a sense of self-worth—attracting men. After that their friendship had never been quite as warm and there were no more confidences until today.

For some reason, perhaps her own unadmitted fear, Valerie needed to share with someone this darkest, most dangerous secret, but what could be done to help her? Nothing at all except to hope that her servants were loyal, Colonel Girard was clever, and Jason Hood's self-love so

great that he would not see what was going on right under
his aristocratic nose.

CHAPTER 2

THE SEYMOUR MANSION, high on a hill
overlooking the James River, was a favorite place
for parties. Chief among its attractions was the
great ballroom, the largest in any private home in Richmond. On this June evening the room was at the peak of its
beauty. The crystal drops of the wall sconces shone like diamonds against creamy white walls and the dark oak floor
had been polished to mirror brightness. The ballroom's
oval design and carved Corinthian columns lent a special
grace to any occasion and tonight, because the crowd was
so large, the double doors on both sides had been thrown
open so that people could move through the adjoining
rooms with ease. The wide French doors leading to the
garden had been removed, opening the house to the soft
night breeze off the river.

As Paige maintained, plunging necklines were the
fashion and much bare skin was in view. Ladies who would
have been disgraced by a show of legs could wear gowns
that revealed their shoulders, backs, and a good part of
their breasts and still remain ladies. The incongruity
occurred to no one.

When Laura and Millie came downstairs the guests were
assembled and waiting. Paige was now buttoned into her
dress, her long train was arranged, her attack of nerves
calmed, and she stood with Edward at the top of the stairs
waiting for the moment to start down. Millie took her place
near the altar beside Kirby and Doug, and Laura slipped
into a spot at the back of the room. Now the painful part
was coming, the stirring music and the age-old vows, but
she was ready. None of it was going to touch her.

The musicians gave the signal and Paige and Edward
began to move slowly down the stairs. Paige had always
been pretty but on this evening she was exquisite, a princess
who seemed to float rather than walk down the curving

staircase, her white satin dress as low-cut as she had wished, her enormous bell-shaped skirt spreading out around her. Behind her veil she smiled at Alex, waiting at the altar, and he could not keep the smile from his own face. He was eighteen years older than Paige, a square-faced, compact man, magnificent in a new gray uniform with colorful sash and gold epaulets. Colonel Girard, his friend from West Point days, stood beside him, a little taller but somehow not as impressive in black evening clothes.

Seeing the difference, Laura thought with some bitterness, The military look does give a man an edge, and how we women love it. We should be scared to death.

Her eyes moved on.

Millie was watching Edward as intensely as Paige watched Alex—amazing after all these years—and Edward, hiding his real feelings well, appeared happy as he handed over his high-strung daughter to the man she was determined to have. Doug, hands clasped behind his back in the same way Edward always stood, was intent on the ceremony, but Kirby rocked restlessly onto the balls of his feet and back again, his eyes wandering from girl to girl as the imperishable questions were asked and answered. To shut out the vows Laura fastened her attention on the altar itself—candles, blossoms, lush greenery—but it did no good. The candlelight cast over the man and woman standing there a resplendence that brought her close to tears.

And then it was over, thank God.

Paige and Alex turned to their guests with that particular flourish of triumph a bride and groom always have, and everyone smiled, applauded, congratulated the happy couple, the parents, the family, and themselves, for life was good, they were all friends in this safe, lovely house, and tonight they were going to have a wonderful time. The altar was carried out and the orchestra moved into its place, the great Austrian crystal chandelier was lowered, lighted, and raised again to spread subdued radiance over the crowd.

It was a fun-loving crowd, rich, sociable, engaging, and not unduly oppressed by the presence of so many men in uniform. Impending war did not yet mean shattered bodies and shattered lives; for the moment it only added zest and piquancy to life. So they danced reels and polkas and melodic, swaying waltzes, toasted the newly married couple with French champagne, and clustered around refreshment tables loaded with the imported delicacies they were accustomed to.

Elsewhere in the city lived ordinary people who worked hard at a variety of jobs and there were areas of deep poverty where children went to bed hungry every night. The town was a thriving slave market and Locust Alley, just down the hill from the handsome, respectable Exchange Hotel, was a center of prostitution. But only the upper class attended Paige Seymour's wedding, people of mostly English descent whose hard-driving forebears had fought Indians, grown wealthy on tobacco and slaves, thrown out the British government, and then settled down to lives of pride, ease, and comfort. The men were fast-shooting, hard-riding, and hard-drinking, jealous of their personal honor, easy to offend; the women were charming and soft-spoken. All of them ignored the ways in which their wealth had been accumulated, pretending that it had somehow fallen onto them out of the sky, bestowed by a generous Providence because they deserved it.

They were sturdy, good-looking people, ruthless and unbending beneath elaborate good manners, with a high percentage of beautiful girls and handsome men. The middle-aged women were attractive too. Their husbands, now soldiers in an army that was camped nearby, were back in Richmond for this great occasion and had brought with them more amorous intent than they had felt in years. Many wives were looking forward to an exciting evening after they got home tonight.

As always at large gatherings—especially weddings—of people who know each other well, there were highly charged emotions churning just beneath the courtesy. Relatives both close and distant had brought old, unresolved grievances along with their wedding gifts. There were men present whose dislike for each other went back to childhood; girls who wished to be married and were not struggled with unacknowledged jealousy; long-married couples contemplated their own marriages with pain or satisfaction; and, of course, the parents of the bride were giving up their daughter forever.

In addition, those present were divided in another way. Dominant was old Richmond society, snobbish, insular, inbred, and tradition-bound, wary of newcomers no matter their credentials. To these people a Northerner was a complete outsider. Southerners from other states were received with varying degrees of warmth, South Carolinians being most acceptable. But Virginians were the cream. People in other parts of the South might pride themselves on their family trees, but Virginians, they liked to tell everyone, were the real founders of the country; Virginia's First Families were the elite of the elite.

The other group present tonight had been greeted warily when they first arrived in town. "Washington people," one social leader had remarked with disdain. It was true. Richmond was now the capital of the Confederacy, and most of the Georgians, Alabamans, and Mississippians pouring into town to run the new government were until recently United States senators, congressmen, or other Washington officials. They and their wives, used to power, privilege, and deference, were shocked to find themselves not completely acceptable in Richmond. President Jefferson Davis himself was from the wilds of Mississippi and had been a senator and a secretary of war in the old Union. No one intended that when his wife, Varina, got to town she would be allowed to control the social life of the city even though she was the First Lady of the Confederacy.

Among the men the division was based not only on social but political grounds. Some thought the war need not have come, was now being handled badly, and that Jeff Davis was a fool. The Vice President, Alexander Stephens, detested Davis so heartily that he had declined to come tonight because Davis would be present. Other men were passionately loyal to their President and convinced that the war would soon be won. So far on this happy evening the animosities remained submerged. Men with strong differences limited the talk around the punch bowl to subjects they could agree on, and the Richmond and Washington ladies complimented each other and tacitly declared a truce in the interests of having a good time.

Laura's eyes passed quickly over the crowd, attaching a name to each face, recalling interests, jealousies, feuds, weaknesses. She was the only woman present with a foot in both the Richmond and Washington camps. Every former U.S. senator or congressman in the room had at some time sat at her dinner table in Washington, eaten her food, drunk her wine—and sometimes a great deal of it—danced with her, flattered her; one or two had made advances that could have led to disaster if Robert had found out. She knew their foibles, prejudices, the back-door dealings and scandals that attached to their names, and respected very few. She was friendly with most of their wives. But she was also Richmond's own, the child of one of Virginia's most illustrious families. It was a circumstance that made her welcome everywhere.

Always aware of her looks when in public, she knew that black mourning, intended to make a widow inconspicuous, would cause her to stand out in this brilliant assemblage of rich jewel colors. Be interested, she told herself, happy but not too happy. With a warm smile developed after years of practice, she moved into the crowd and began to do her duty by her family.

"Jane, how wonderful to see you—yes, we must, we really must. Ah, Senator, you are just the *worst* flatterer! Jason, we're *so* glad you could come tonight—we'd heard you might not be home in time." She hugged Valerie and moved on, measuring her pace, pausing but never quite coming to a full stop, sparkling a little more for some people than for others.

Next came some ritual compliments and hand kissing by members of the Confederate cabinet. And then, the President.

Jefferson Davis had been in town only a few days. He looked much the same as when she had last seen him, two years ago, in Washington, sharp-featured, haughty, a man of immense dignity with doubtless the same high opinion of himself and the same unalterable conviction that he was always right.

For him she produced her warmest smile. "Mr. President, how good to see you."

"And you, ma'am. Winnie has missed you sorely."

"I've missed her too. When will she be joining you?"

"She and the children are coming as soon as she can close the house. I'll be much relieved once she's here."

And that was true, Laura thought. Jeff did not do well without Varina. He needed his wife in a way few men did.

From the corner of her eye she noticed again a man watching her across the room and she turned slightly. It was Valerie's lover, Colonel Girard. She had met him at the wedding rehearsal last night, a pleasant man whom she had instantly decided was a shade too charming. She had learned long ago to distrust very charming, noticeably handsome men. They were usually selling something.

Or it could be simply that she did not admire these Northern officers who were coming South. They had gotten their education at West Point and had sworn to defend the United States—"taken the king's shilling," Robert would have said—and now they were here, bringing their training and expertise to a rebel cause that threatened to destroy the United States. She knew the reasons they did it, belief in states' rights being the one most frequently given, but it still seemed dishonorable to her—although she was careful never to say so. How shocked her family and friends would be if she did.

She had been circulating for close to an hour, refused several dances, made vague promises to ambitious hostesses which she would not keep, had a chat with the attorney general, Judah Benjamin, one of Robert's closest friends. It was enough for now. She found a bench in a shadowed alcove a little removed from the crowd and sat down, thinking over what she now knew about Chase Girard that he did not dream she knew. She couldn't blame him really—Valerie had made herself available. The foolish girl had been lured into real danger but he was at even greater risk, and who could tell which of them had done most of the luring.

She shifted her thoughts. There was Doug coming in from the moonlit garden with Rebecca McCauley and they were both so flushed and bright-eyed that she wondered if he'd asked her tonight. He had already told the family he wanted to marry her: ". . . if she'll have me." Rebecca was a plain, quiet girl and no one had known she was more than a friend, but they politely hid their surprise, all but Millie who said in an aggrieved tone, "You can't be serious. Why, you could have the prettiest girl in town!"

Doug flushed deep red. As a child he had always tried hard to please Millie, the only mother he'd ever known. Now he was a man, sure of what he wanted, and he understood Millie well. Out of love and gratitude he forgave the insult to Becca and turned it into a joke. "Ah, Millie," he said, "you're the prettiest girl in town and Edward already has you."

Watching him—broad-shouldered, auburn-haired, a little awkward in his movements but splendid in his grand new uniform—seeing the glances other girls gave him, Laura thought, You *could* have any girl you want, you sweet dear oaf, but you seem to need Becca so that's how it must be.

Kirby, on the other hand, was doing exactly as Millie wanted, giving all the girls a chance. He had danced with every accredited belle in the room, shown no pity for the few wallflowers, and was now waltzing with Valerie Hood. Lean, dark, still very young, he was giving the dashing Mrs. Hood the benefit of all his charm and she was smiling up into his eyes as if he were the only man in the room. It was Valerie's patented admiring gaze and she gave it to every male she met, from boys barely past puberty to grandfathers. When she walked into the room with her husband this evening, she had given Laura one flickering glance, lifted her shoulder in a slight shrug, and then devoted herself exclusively to him. Now that he was busy talking to President Davis she was spreading her wings and allowing Kirby to flirt with her.

It had grown hot in the house despite the night breeze sweeping in through the open doors. Laura placed a pleasant smile on her face and snapped open her black fan, grateful to be entirely alone for the moment.

Colonel Girard, apparently deep in conversation with Attorney General Judah Benjamin, saw the smile. His eyes had been on her most of the evening since the ceremony ended for she was the riskiest part of his assignment. So far

all was going well. He had been welcomed in Richmond
because he was Alex Wyatt's friend and also because people
instinctively trusted him. It was a gift as inborn as the color
of his eyes, this ability to walk into a group of strangers and
immediately win their confidence. He seldom thought
about it—it was simply a facility to be used when needed,
just as he would use his height to reach a high shelf.

Like Valerie, most people judged him to be forthright,
looking for adventure, and not given to deep thought. He
was in reality a reflective man who at the moment was wondering why a career in the army had ever seemed like a
good idea. Richmond was the last place he wanted to be.
As he had watched Mrs. Chandler move among the high-
spirited people in this room, her black mourning a dark
counterpoint to the springlike colors of the other women,
it occurred to him that many of these laughing, vivacious
women would soon be in mourning too, and if he had the
gift of second sight he would be able to pick out which
ones they were.

Earlier in the evening a pretty young girl had informed
him earnestly that the South was very strong in resources,
stronger than the North, and her husband was eager to go
off to fight for the right. Then she laughed. "But I do
believe we women are more passionate for the cause than
our men. If my husband hadn't decided to volunteer I
would have insisted. Of course, there will never be actual
war. Once the Yanks see our soldiers in the field they'll lay
down their arms and it will be all over."

She was living in no deeper a dream than the three members of Jeff Davis's cabinet he had talked to this evening,
mature, experienced officials who all believed that the war
they had started would never lead to serious conflict. The
legal right to secede, they assured him, was guaranteed by
the Constitution; therefore, the North would have to let
them go without a fight. They were, all of them, having
such a good time tonight, people dancing on the edge of a
precipice, not knowing that their civilization was crumbling
beneath them, determined to keep on dancing as long as
they could.

As for Laura Chandler, she was fascinating to watch.
Like an accomplished actress she knew exactly what to do

when she was center stage. For the matrons and eager girls
who crowded around her, for the respectful men who asked
to be introduced, she radiated that magnetic charm all
public figures needed to be successful. She also kept them
at a little distance and did it without giving offense. The
people who sent him here had said there was substance
behind the beauty, that she could help him, and perhaps it
was true, yet how could a woman who had always been
dedicated to her appearance, her parties, and the clothes
she wore have any deeply felt beliefs? How could he guess
what went on in the mind behind the sweet mask she kept
firmly in place?

Well, didn't they all wear masks? He, for example, had
done his smiling duty by the bride and groom, had danced
with the mother of the bride, the bridesmaids, several other
ladies, had had a man-to-man, just-between-soldiers chat
with young Doug Seymour and a much more important
talk with Judah Benjamin. Now it was time for the business
that had brought him to Richmond and it was going to be
hard work. During their few minutes of polite conversation
last night at the wedding rehearsal, he had sensed that the
reserved Mrs. Chandler, unlike most people, had not taken
to him.

He began his approach to her in the manner he would
stalk a skittish wild creature—he circled the room in a
direction away from her. When he finally came upon her in
the secluded alcove, it was with the friendliest of smiles and
a cup of punch held out.

"I thought you might enjoy this."

His eyes were so intent that for a moment her guard
went up, but his manner was agreeable, his tone courteous.
She accepted the punch and, having done so, felt obliged
to ask him to sit with her.

"We've met before last night, ma'am, some time ago in
Washington."

Slight embarrassment showed on her face. Her memory
for faces was good and she did not recall him at all. "I'm
sorry . . ."

"You couldn't possibly remember. It was a large reception at your home and we were introduced in the receiving

line. I hadn't been in Washington long and it was a memorable evening for me."

He had a winning smile. She said, "I do recall an army officer . . . Did you stay after the reception to talk to my husband?"

"Yes, I had that honor."

Now she remembered him, not from the receiving line but from a moment after the reception, when everyone had left. He had walked down the hall with Robert and gone into the library.

He watched her face as she placed him—as he had hoped, the slender connection with Robert Chandler seemed to open a tightly closed door just a crack. At close range she was very pretty—glossy dark hair, fine skin, and the unusual eyes that everyone commented on—but there was something missing that had been there two years ago, a quality that had made her unforgettable. A light had gone out behind her eyes, and more than anything, he felt a sense of pity. He took a breath. Now to bait the hook.

"As I said, the evening was memorable for me. I had the great honor of meeting you"—a modest compliment, the kind she heard all the time—"and I had an interesting discussion with Senator Chandler about what war would mean if it came."

Her eyes flashed up. "You talked about the war?"

"We talked about the possibility, or rather, he talked and I listened. He had a number of concerns and he thought I might be of some small help. He—how shall I say it?—he clarified my thinking on a number of matters."

"He always did that for me too."

At that moment the orchestra played a chord to get everyone's attention and then launched into "Maryland, My Maryland," a song as popular in the South as "Dixie"; even though Maryland hadn't actually seceded, Southerners loved the melody. Paige climbed halfway up the stairs, leaned over the banister and tossed her bouquet. There were shrieks and laughter from the unmarried girls as they scrambled for it, and Laura turned to Chase Girard.

"I'd like to continue our talk. Would it be possible for you to call on me tomorrow?"

"Ma'am," he said with that particularly attractive smile

she had noticed before, "you can't imagine what a pleasure that would be."

THE BRIDE AND GROOM left in a shower of rice and flowers, and the party rolled on. While Jason Hood, who seldom danced, continued his talk with President Davis, Valerie waltzed with a number of men and finally worked her way around to Chase. Once she was in his arms she whispered, "I never thought he'd be back this soon. He *says* he didn't want to miss the wedding! Do you believe that?"

"I don't know. Does he like weddings?"

"How can you laugh? What are we going to do?"

"We'll manage."

The tender smile mollified her. "Where did you get the new suit?"

"I found a very fast tailor."

"Well, it's most becoming. I must say, you did get friendly with the Widow." Valerie, whose feelings for Laura were a mixture of fondness and envy, sometimes referred to her behind her back as "the Widow" or "the Keeper of the Flame." "I hope you were impressed. What did you talk about?"

"Her husband."

Valerie giggled, and as they swept past Jason and Jefferson Davis, she gave them her best smile.

YOU ACTUALLY ASKED him to call? What got into you?" Jewel undid the last of the buttons and Laura stepped out of her dress.

"I thought you'd be pleased."

"I am. You should have done it a long time ago. We could do with a few gentlemen calling at this house."

"He's not that kind of caller. It's hardly an assignation."

"Well, it ought to be. He looks to me like the kind who could cheer a lady up. Sit right there and I'll brush your hair."

Laura sat obediently and Jewel took down her hair and began to brush it with smooth, even strokes, a ritual they went through every night. Watching her in the mirror, Laura decided she did not like the direction of her remarks, and to deflect her she said lightly, "It's no use thinking about Colonel Girard. He's taken."

"Oh? Who?"

"Never mind."

"If you won't tell I guess I'll never know. 'Course, I could use my powers."

Powers were a mysterious force that had to be given, not taught, and given only to those with a bent for it. Jewel's powers had been passed on to her by the fortune-telling woman on the plantation where she was born. "It come from far back," she had told Laura when they were children, "from de other place. It do tell secrets but I cain' ast too often or it gits mad."

Many times as a child Laura had watched in fear and fascination while Jewel performed her magic, a secret activity that no adult ever knew about. Laura's eyes began to sparkle. "Go ahead. Use your powers."

"You sure? I ought to have some chicken bones—" Jewel pulled a few strands of hair from Laura's hairbrush and laid them in the china dish containing her hairpins. "Have you got an old love letter from some really desperate lover? I have to have a letter."

Laura dug in her drawer. "How about this note from Ellen Mercer inviting me to dinner?"

"You turned her down, didn't you? It'll have to do. Let's roll it up tight and tie it with a ribbon—here, red's best."

Jewel laid the letter on top of the hair and the hairpins, lit a candle and turned out the lamp. Softly she began the old moaning chant that never failed to bring a tingling sense of alarm and danger. The moving light of the candle flickered over their faces. Jewel touched the burning candle to the paper. The flame caught and curled upward into the dark, a shifting, inconstant light. She passed her hands across the low flame three times and her face changed and went blank, her chant descending to a hypnotic minor key. Slowly the paper, ribbon, and hair curled into ash, and the hairpins turned red-hot, then faded to black.

Jewel closed her eyes. "There is a princess with golden hair and eyes the color of the sky locked in a tower by a wicked king . . . but a prince is climbing to her balcony . . . he calls 'Valerie, my love . . .' "

Laura exploded with laughter. "Oh, you witch! You already knew."

"You don't trust my powers? Be careful or they'll get you." Jewel lit the lamp and blew out the candle.

"How did you know? You were out in the garden all the time she was up here running on."

"I don't listen at keyholes. Well, I do but not for anything Miss Valerie has to say. My powers told me. 'Course, when she introduced him to Mr. Jason tonight she gave that man a look—oh, my. Anyone could see it."

"I hope not. Maybe only you and me because we know her so well."

Jewel resumed brushing. After a few strokes she murmured, "You could have him in nothing flat if you wanted," and Laura answered quickly, "Oh, Jewel, you don't—" and stopped.

Jewel did understand, too well. She, too, had lost a husband and in a worse way, for Robert's heart had failed, he had been taken by God and nothing could have prevented it, but Ishmael had been taken, needlessly, by a man. The marriage had come about because Jewel had a privileged position in the Seymour household. Edward had planned to buy the man for her, but when he made an offer to the owner Ishmael already had been sold South. Jewel's wild despair still burned in Laura's memory. A slave sold to one of the Louisiana sugar-cane plantations never came back. Those places were notorious hellholes where strong men often died within two or three years. Ishmael was lost forever and Jewel, only sixteen, was pregnant.

Laura thought, We're both widows . . . she has Adam but even a son can't make up for the loss of the man.

She reached up and touched the maid's hand but Jewel had drawn into herself and her face showed nothing.

"Get to bed, missy. You've got a big social engagement tomorrow." Jewel smiled to show there were no hard feelings, straightened the dressing table, emptied the china dish of the remains of her powers, and hung Laura's dress in the wardrobe. At the door she paused. "Good night, Miss Laura. Sleep tight."

She said it every night but tonight the words struck Laura with particular force. After she turned out the lamp she lay thinking back to the time when they were little children and Jewel was her friend and her playmate. Jewel had been her comfort when her mother died, and on that day when she saw what was left of her father lying on his bloody bedroom floor. Through the years, in good times and bad, she had been simply Laura or, if Jewel was feeling especially affectionate, Lolly. And then they left childhood behind. Laura became Miss Laura and the friendship dwindled to mistress and maid. For all the ease, intimacy, and laughter between them, there was a gulf that could never be bridged, for Laura owned Jewel and could dispose of her as she wished.

Downstairs music was still playing for guests who lingered, reluctant to have the evening end. Laura turned over in bed and then back again, unable to find a comfortable position, and finally, troubled about many things, fell asleep.

A FEW OF the younger couples were still dancing in the ballroom or had disappeared into the darker part of the garden, but several men were gathered in Edward's library for a last drink and serious conversation. Edward, so young and untried when he took over the *Courier*, had established a reputation for fairness, good sense, and unswerving integrity, and over the years his home had been considered neutral ground for many meetings. Even those who disagreed with his opinions never questioned his motives or his honor.

Edward raised his glass. "Gentlemen, to the cause." It was a safe toast.

Everyone drank, and then Jason Hood said, "But you don't think we have much chance, do you, Edward?"

The others remained silent. Jason didn't like Edward— just why no one knew—but had never been able to taunt him into a duel.

Edward looked into his whiskey as though he might see the answer in it. "We have a chance. That's why the North is so worried. What we do with our chance may decide the issue. Or it may simply depend on luck."

Judah Benjamin, the urbane and witty attorney general, remarked in the pleasant tone he used for all pronouncements, "I believe we shall win—it would be difficult for me to perform my duties if I did not—but contrary to some of us in this room I foresee a long and bloody conflict. And we may well expect a servile insurrection."

That was the great fear, the terror no one wanted to think about. A slave uprising, with the armed men away at war and unable to protect them.

"I don't expect that," said Edward. "Our people are gentle and loyal. There isn't one of our servants I wouldn't trust with my family."

Jason Hood twisted in his chair and stood up, unable to contain himself. His wealth was built on tobacco and cotton plantations and the work of many slaves, the kind of man Northerners imagined was a typical slaveowner. In reality he was unusual for not many Southerners owned so many slaves or so much land. He had great economic power, a kingly way of life, a beautiful wife, and he intended to keep everything he had. For that reason he yearned to become secretary of war and effectively take control of the army that was now protecting his possessions. His present position as assistant secretary he considered only temporary.

With conviction made fierce by the thought of his endangered property he spat out, "There wouldn't be a war but for the abolitionists. Every sane person, North or South, knows that our Negroes are happy and both races are prospering. But those fanatics talk about raising half a million men and that means a bloodbath. Well, gentlemen, they'll get it."

Edward was tempted to ask when he planned to take up his rifle and join the army but decided not to. Instead he offered his guests another drink.

When Chase Girard left the house later that night he stood on the front porch, looking up. He had seen those same stars over California three years ago and for a moment wished he were there now. During this long evening he had smiled, flattered, cajoled, and suppressed every honest feeling he had. He despised these arrogant Southerners, so full of self-love and with so little reason for it. They saw no flaws in themselves or the slave system and seemed to honestly believe their culture was superior to any other. Good men were going to die because of that belief. He didn't belong in California but right here in Richmond, the heart of the rebellion. Here he could do some good and he intended to use Laura Chandler to help him do it. If, as he hoped, she had absorbed her husband's powerful convictions she could be the heart of the intelligence network he intended to set up.

Tonight he had been successful beyond his expectations. He had been accepted by these people and heard influential Confederates speak their real hopes and fears, he had been given an early morning appointment with Judah Benjamin and best of all a luncheon engagement with the reclusive Mrs. Chandler. He smiled at the thought and went down the steps to his waiting horse.

CHAPTER 3

"IT'S SUCH A LOVELY DAY, Colonel. I thought you might enjoy eating outside." Laura opened the door that led to the garden thinking, Where they can't overhear every word we say.

Jewel was at the top of the stairs, leaning over the banister and grinning. Elvina and Cookie were shamelessly peering past the dining room door, and Bella, who never did such menial labor, was slowly polishing the already spotless table in the hallway.

This morning Laura had woken with a sense of happy anticipation, a feeling almost forgotten, but now she was irritated with Millie, whose curiosity was red-hot, with the servants, with this man, and most of all with herself. She didn't want to spend the next hour or so making polite conversation. There was nothing he could tell her about Robert that she didn't already know. What had possessed her to invite him? His charming smile? The thought almost caused her to slam the door as they stepped out into the yard.

And now, what to talk about? Not the weather. She

could do better than that. "I'm so anxious to show you the garden," she said with her gracious hostess smile. "Let's go this way."

They walked down the gravel path on the far side of Millie's treasured roses, past fruit trees and cascades of purple wisteria covering the red-brick wall, and stopped at the gazebo with its intricate scrollwork and sweeping view. Below the hill the James River flowed and no sounds from the city intruded. The sun was soothing, the breeze scented, and from somewhere a mockingbird obligingly delivered several intricate arabesques for the visitor.

It had been a good idea to bring him out here while she thought about what to do with him. They started back along the broad central path. It led through the arbor, heavy with blossoming vines, and past the lily pond.

A little silence had fallen so she said, "Only a few weeks ago the camellias and azaleas were in full bloom and the dogwood was grand this year." She stopped to read the bronze sundial's weathered inscription. " 'Old Time is still a-flying and this same flower that smiles today tomorrow will be dying.' Oh, dear, how sad. But it all does go so fast."

Around them was a profusion of roses, crimson, white, deep pink, glowing with health and life.

He said, "These magnificent roses will last all summer. My mother grows roses too. She'd love to see this."

"Where is your home, Colonel?"

"Philadelphia."

"I've visited there. I think of it as such a Union city—Independence Hall and so forth. It surprises me that a Philadelphian . . ." She let the question hang delicately.

"That a Philadelphian would fight for the South? There's a lot of Southern sympathy in my hometown. My mother has cousins in Charleston and my father doesn't like Lincoln. But I'm here for other reasons." Good manners prevented her from asking what the other reasons were and he did not explain. Instead he pointed toward a low brick building on the far side of a clipped hedge. "Is that another part of the house?"

"The servants live there."

"Ah. The slave quarters."

"We don't think of them as slaves."

"Of course not. Forgive me."

Jewel had placed a table under the trees and, Laura noted, set out the best china and silver. She came with Joseph glowering behind her, both of them bearing trays.

Enough food for thrashers, Laura thought in mild annoyance as they spread out an enormous lunch. Jewel had gone directly contrary to her orders to keep it simple.

"I hope you're hungry, Colonel," she said with a sharp glance at Jewel.

"Ravenous, ma'am. I had an early meeting with the attorney general this morning and missed breakfast."

"I guess I know what a man wants," Jewel informed Joseph as if he were the one who objected. She picked up the empty trays and handed them to him. He followed her back to the house, silent and scowling.

Chase watched as he stepped inside with a loud bang of the door. "Your butler seems unhappy today."

"Oh, pay no attention to Joseph—he hates to work with Jewel. That's probably why she made him do it."

Her eyes lit with amusement and he wondered why he had felt sorry for her last night. This was the Laura Chandler he remembered, the woman who so astonished him in Washington. Black became her—it set off her skin and eyes—but her good looks didn't depend on clothes or the way she wore her hair or even the freshness of youth. It was bone structure, the harmony of brow, cheekbones, jawline, that so pleased the eye, an unearned gift given to her at birth.

Unlike many Southern women she never pretended helplessness or ignorance. Beneath her soft drawl she was as direct as any Northerner. Clearly, she didn't suffer fools or opportunists gladly. If he presumed too far she would graciously throw him out. And so, he must probe cautiously.

They began to eat. He said, "I'm a Northerner but I've spent time in the South and one thing always puzzles me. The relationship between the master and the—ah—servant. It's often so free and easy and yet . . ."

He'd deliberately gone back to that touchy subject. She said, "With Jewel there's a reason. She was given to me when we were five years old. We grew up together and were tutored together. It wasn't generosity on my family's part. I refused to do my lessons unless Jewel had lessons too." She smiled in reminiscence. "I made quite a scene and they had no choice. She was my best friend then. But we grew up. In the South that changes things."

"She's a handsome woman."

Tall, slim, light-skinned Jewel, with her oval face and dark brown, almond-shaped eyes, was more than handsome, she was beautiful, but in the South white men did not comment on the attributes of servant women, at least not in the presence of white women.

"Yes," Laura agreed in a tone that said the subject was closed.

"Perhaps I shouldn't say this but aren't slaves sometimes manumitted? Why don't you free Jewel?"

He had said he shouldn't say it and then gone right ahead and done so. It was an outrageous remark for a guest to make, completely out of line, and yet she felt no outrage. The same thought had been in her mind.

"I said she was given to me and she was, but I was a child at the time. I don't hold the papers. My brother actually owns all our people. I could suggest it to him but I haven't done so."

"I've been very impertinent. Please forgive me and put it down to a Northerner's clumsiness."

"I'll do that," she said, her eyes gleaming, and he smiled too. He was, she thought, too blunt yet exceedingly likeable. "Will you stay in Richmond long? I suppose you'll be leaving for the army soon."

"Perhaps not. Mr. Benjamin thinks I may be more valuable arranging for supplies and ordnance to be shipped in from the North. We're already in desperate need."

"Is such a thing possible? We're at war."

"Almost all things are possible where money is involved."

"I believe I've heard Robert say the very same thing. Oh, it's all such a muddle. Sometimes I wish I could be like my sister-in-law. Millie hates Yankees, she's certain the South is utterly right and there won't be much of a war as soon as the North realizes it. For my brother Edward, once Virginia seceded his decision was made, though he thinks there's going to be a long, hard fight. For me it's not so simple. I wish . . . You talked with my husband. Anything you can tell me would mean a great deal."

"I only spent a couple of hours with him. You know his thinking better than I."

"But you were particularly talking about . . . if war came. I promise I won't be bored even if I've heard it before."

Chase considered his next words. Because she wanted to believe, he could tell her almost anything and she would believe him if it were not too far from what she knew of Robert Chandler. But in this case the truth would do.

"He opposed secession. He thought the South would eventually collapse even if the North let it go without a fight. He believed that war would be a calamity for both sides . . . but you know this."

"Please go on."

"He told me—I think it was a recent decision—that if war came he would stand with the North."

There was a sigh, just a slight exhalation of breath from Laura. The humming of the bees was loud, making the garden hush deeper.

"I never knew for certain. Did he say why?"

"He believed the Southern system is rotten at the core and that slavery must end. 'To save our souls,' was the way he put it. He said anything that could be done to end it must be done."

She sat for some time saying nothing. A low muttering rumbled in the distance and she looked up. The sun was still bright, the sky a gentle blue.

"Just artillery practice, ma'am, at the camp outside town. You hear it because the wind is in our direction today."

A shiver passed over her. "War," she said, as if the meaning of the word had just become clear to her.

Jewel came down the path with her light, swinging walk and they fell silent while she cleared the table.

When she was gone Laura said, "He never told me. I knew he felt strongly about it—he freed all his slaves as soon as his father died—and yet I'm amazed. He loved Virginia the way one does love home. It's hard to imagine him going so far as to stand against it in war."

"Perhaps he loved his home in a way the rest of us don't see."

She looked up quickly. "Perhaps," she said and poured the coffee.

As he was leaving he respectfully, almost diffidently asked permission to call again and she answered immediately, "I'd be pleased to have you call."

After the door closed behind him she started up the stairs, ignoring the servants clustered in the hall, but halfway up she stopped at the sunny window overlooking the front yard and watched as he walked down the brick path to the street. He had spoken of matters that never should have been mentioned, things most Southerners would have found unforgivable, and she had planned to say goodbye at the end of the meal and forget him. But he had told her that Robert intended to oppose his own people for the sake of a principle and then had said, "Perhaps he loved his home in a way the rest of us don't see." That was the moment she decided to see him again.

At the gate he paused, looked back at the house and then up directly, it seemed, at the window where she stood. Quickly she stepped back. When she looked again he was gone.

She went on to her bedroom, thinking that now she understood Valerie's infatuation. There was more to him than appeared on the surface. Yet how could Valerie look at another man, no matter how attractive, if she loved her husband? Since she didn't love Jason, how could she go on living with him?

Yesterday Valerie claimed to have found a great love, and if that was true, she was to be pitied. Loving someone completely was the most hazardous bargain you could make with fate, bringing more grief than the heart could bear. It was a dangerous mistake, one that she, Laura, would never make again.

Restless, disturbed, she paced her room, wondering why after all these months her thoughts had started down this hurtful trail again. Thoughts of the past were not allowed in her life—they brought nothing but pain. She sat down at her desk, dug through the top drawer, and found several letters she had put off answering. Occupying the mind and hands was the only way to pull out of such an odd mood.

Her thoughts wandered from the letter she was trying to reread, back to the man. His company was really very enjoyable. There was nothing wrong with having as a friend someone she liked and could talk to who was already occupied with another woman and unlikely to make demands. She opened a fresh bottle of ink, took out writing paper, and began a long-overdue letter to Robert's sister, Caroline.

R OBERT. FORCEFUL, SUBTLE, sophisticated, daring in political maneuver, shrewd in negotiation, a formidable enemy, a reliable friend. All this she learned later, but in the beginning she knew only that he charmed her as much as she charmed him, his intellectual energy fired her imagination, his body pleased her. She was barely seventeen and had never had so much as a crush on anyone before, but she knew only days after meeting him that she wanted to be Robert Chandler's wife. When he asked her to marry him she quickly said yes. It was two weeks to the day after they first met.

She went with him to the capital city expecting to love it, determined that he would never regret choosing her. And then she discovered busy, brutal, shamelessly cynical Washington, so different from home as to seem on the other side of the moon.

"It's like coming out of a warm bath and jumping into the Arctic Ocean," she told Robert's sister, Caroline Merritt. "Behind all their smiles these are the coldest people I have ever met."

Caroline, the widow of Langdon Merritt, the Supreme Court justice famous for his dissents, had lived at the pinnacle of Washington society all her adult life and knew it as she knew the lights and shadows of her own heart. "Here only a month and you've learned your most important lesson," she said, her smile and gentle Virginia drawl softening her words. "Everyone in this town is after something, so never accept *anyone* at face value. Always ask yourself— who is the person, where is he from, what axe is he grinding? And don't be impressed by anyone, no matter what job he has at the moment, not even the President. These people are a very ordinary lot when you get to know them, different from the folks back home only in the degree of their ambition."

"Oh, Caroline, that's a sad thought."

"But true. Now, my dear, keep your shoulders back, your head up, and a sweet smile on your pretty face. And be brave—you are going to do just fine."

Maybe so, Laura thought, looking into Caroline's encouraging eyes, but at that moment she felt hopeless, not brave. Only a month ago she had been on her honeymoon—in a haze of delight because she was with Robert. Nothing in life could ever go wrong again, she had believed, which proved how fatuous, how stupid, how unbearably *young* she had been. Time, Caroline pointed out, would take care of that last failing and experience would take care of the rest, but at this moment Laura couldn't see how she would get the experience since her courage was entirely gone. She had made a mistake of mammoth proportions by deciding to give a dinner party at the wrong time and inviting the wrong people. In Richmond it might have been funny in a painful way. In Washington it had affected the outcome of a Senate vote and that was no laughing matter.

It had come about so simply. While shopping Laura had met an amiable lady who turned out to be the wife of John Pryor, the influential senator from Georgia. Hoping to add to her circle of friends, she had invited Mrs. Pryor and her husband to a small dinner party on Saturday evening, her first since arriving in town. Her next mistake was to neglect to tell Robert about the additional guests.

When Senator and Mrs. Pryor walked in a half hour late, Senator Stoker of Connecticut, Robert's close ally and a man with a sharp tongue, remarked, "Well, Johnny, still out of step, I see."

John Pryor, a man with the permanently flushed face of the hard drinker, turned an even darker red. Robert quickly intervened with the only distraction that would work—a large glass of bourbon—and the bad moment passed.

From then on the party—Laura's first contribution to Robert's career—proceeded like a dream. The experienced staff had turned out an elegant meal, her shining china, crystal, silver were magnificent, her flower arrangements exactly right—and she was doing very well in the small-talk department, something she had never been especially good at. At home she hadn't paid much attention to how Millie brought off the dinner parties she and Edward gave, but either it wasn't hard to be a hostess or she, Laura, had a gift for it. Everything fell into place if you planned well.

All during dinner she devoted herself to the ladies, leaving Robert to deal with the gentlemen, so she had no idea what was wrong when John Pryor shouted, "*Why?* States' rights, by the Lord Harry, that's why! And may the goddamned federal government rot in hell!"

Pryor then shoved back his chair, picked up the silver pot that had unfortunately been left beside his plate, and poured a quantity of steaming coffee into Senator Stoker's lap.

After the doctor left, after John Pryor had been carried home with a bruised eye and a broken nose and Senator Stoker had walked gingerly to his carriage in a suit borrowed from Robert, after the smashed china and crystal had been swept up by the two wide-eyed maids and the damaged chair removed, Robert had watched Laura rush upstairs, then quickly followed.

She was in their bedroom, sitting on the end of the bed in petticoats and camisole, carefully examining one of her new silver shoes. The exquisite gown she had designed herself for this evening lay heaped on the floor, a blue cascade of luminous silk.

He said, "Darling, don't look so tragic—we'll laugh about it in the morning."

She raised her head and burst into tears. "It was *my* fault, my idiotic, bird-witted fault! What did I think I was doing? The stupidest woman in Washington would know better than to invite a Southern politician to spend an evening with an antislavery Northerner—no, *I'm* the stupidest woman in Washington and I *didn't* know. Oh, Robert, I'm so sorry!"

He sat down beside her and took her in his arms. "Hush, honey, hush now. John has a filthy temper. He'll send his apologies in the morning—wait and see."

But the next morning John Pryor did not send apologies.

He struggled into the Senate chamber with a large bandage on his nose and ostentatiously voted against a bill Robert had been working on for more than a year, a bill he had agreed to support.

That evening Robert talked about the rejected bill in a dispassionate way, saying it was not a great loss, that he would introduce it again in the next session and it would pass then.

But he looked tired. That particular tightness around his eyes that she was already beginning to recognize was an indication that he'd had a bad day. She said, "Robert, what is it about states' rights that brings out the monster in perfectly decent men?"

His eyes gleamed. "First of all, John Pryor isn't a perfectly decent man—I wouldn't trust him from here to that door. He didn't change his vote because of last night, he undoubtedly made a deal with someone else. As for states' rights, it's an old argument. Who's going to hold the power—the men who run the states or the men who run the central government? Southerners mostly want the states in control. It suits their interests."

"But you're a Virginian and you don't think that way."

He glanced away and the tired look came back. "Yes, I'm a Virginian but I don't see us as a passel of principalities, hanging together as long as it suits us and opting out if we get our feelings hurt. We're one country, together for the long haul—or we ought to be."

"Last night John Pryor said someday the South would pull out, just walk away, and if anyone tried to stop them they'd fight. If that happened would you stay with the Union or—" She stopped, unable to speak the word.

"If we do our job right I'll never have to make that choice."

They changed the subject but her mind continued down a new trail, examining ideas that had never occurred to her before. He had said, If we do our job right—*we* meaning the barons of the Congress who decided the fate of ordinary citizens—and as he said it he smiled the jaunty, confident smile that had won him thousands of votes. It was his vitality and force that drew all eyes to him in any roomful of powerful men and made others believe that he knew what to do. If she could develop just a little of his self-assurance she could do wonders too.

At every gathering from that moment on she watched and took note of how the most successful Washington wives conducted themselves and became friends with most of them—it was easy, she found, to make a friend of a woman whose husband was allied with Robert or wanted something from him. She learned how to soothe the vanity of ambitious, self-seeking people, she learned skepticism, she learned to talk a great deal while saying little and how to charm men while never allowing them too close. She mastered the most challenging task of all—putting together a guest list that was interesting but not explosive. When she began wearing gowns with a dropped sleeve other women of fashion had it copied by their dressmakers. They copied her swept-back hair too, and the cunning way she used ruching to emphasize her long, slender neck. By her twentieth birthday she had developed a reputation for beauty and high style that brought her even more friends. "Everyone loves a winner," Caroline remarked with sardonic approval.

It was all done for Robert, the glittering receptions for the mighty and the intimate dinners where powerful men discussed the course of the nation. It was heady, exciting, unreal, and sometimes the shyness she had almost conquered overtook her and she yearned for a simpler, less calculating way of living. She wished they could go back to Virginia. But it was not possible. This was her life, their life, and it always would be.

Robert maintained that she smoothed his path with other men because they liked her. "They'll listen to an attractive woman in a way they won't to another man. A senator who enjoys an evening in our home may be more willing to work with me the next day."

There was truth in what he said, she knew that. They had become partners in important work, especially close partners because to her sorrow there were no children.

Varina Davis, Jefferson Davis's strong-minded wife, became a reliable ally in a town where allies were essential, for she and Laura had much in common. She, too, had married a powerful, much older man when she was very young and had devoted herself to his interests. Jeff Davis, the senator from Mississippi, was a narrow-minded man, too inflexible and autocratic for Laura's taste, but if handled carefully he could be a pleasant dinner guest and sometimes he could also be influenced. After some intense discussions he agreed with Robert that secession from the Union was not the answer to the South's problems, and it pleased Laura to think that the easy talk in her drawing room had contributed to his change of heart.

Then, at first almost imperceptibly, the mood of the country began to change. Sectional squabbling that had been going on since the beginning of the nation grew more vicious. Men who had once agreed that disunion was a bad idea spoke openly for secession and claimed slavery was good for both blacks and whites. Robert Chandler was one of the few Southerners who still spoke for the Union. He often came home in the early morning hours too exhausted to sleep after long meetings with his fellow Southerners, meetings that had ended in hostility and recrimination. "They're a mulish lot," he told Laura bitterly, "determined to have their way no matter the cost."

His hair in the lamplight seemed suddenly much grayer and his face lined as it surely had not been only a few months ago. With a little chill she said, "Then give it up, Robert. You've done all you can do, more than most."

He only smiled and shrugged and she resolved that soon, before the present session was over, she would talk him into going home for a while. The hills and fields of Virginia would rejuvenate him; they always had. Two days later he collapsed on the Senate floor and died before she could get to him.

The outpouring of grief astonished her. There were hundreds at the funeral. Letters came from people all over the nation expressing sorrow and the conviction that the country had suffered an irreparable loss. His many friends spoke of him with tears in their eyes. His bitterest enemies assured her that he was the finest man they had ever known, the man they had believed would be the next President. A senator who had publicly damned him as a "nigger-lover" and a "traitor to Virginia" made a two-hour speech in which he proclaimed that Robert Chandler was a tow-

ering figure ranking with those other great Virginians—
Washington, Jefferson, Madison . . .

At that point Laura had thrown the newspaper aside and
looked around the room, puzzled. In the days just after his
death she often found herself in one of the rooms of her
own home, wondering why she was there. At first she had
been sodden with grief, her only anchor the prescribed
forms that must be observed. The funeral, the receiving of
condolence callers from two to four each afternoon, the
meeting with the lawyers. Robert had been a wealthy man
and she was his only heir, alone now and a wealthy woman.

Alone.

On the sixth day after the funeral she ventured for the
first time into his office. It was the place where he had
written all his speeches. How many times had she sat on
the old mohair sofa and listened while he tried them out on
her? She sat down at the desk and pulled out the household account books. The bills must still be paid and there
was no one else to do it, no one but her. Dry figures, she
discovered, distracted her, helped blot out for sometimes
as much as a minute or two the unbearable fact—Robert
was dead. She came to look forward to the time spent in
that office with only papers and books, nothing human to
love and lose.

As the days passed she spent more and more time there,
inventing tasks, carefully filing papers of no value, taking
down hundreds of books, dusting them, rearranging them,
climbing the ladder to put them back on the shelves. On
one afternoon almost two weeks after the funeral the maid,
Dina, rapped on the open door, announcing her presence
hesitantly.

"Sorry to disturb you, ma'am—there's a lady come to
call?" Dina often modestly presented statements as questions. "A Mrs. Johnson?"

Laura was sitting on the floor, skirt and hands dusty,
surrounded by books. Mrs. Johnson. Wasn't there an
undersecretary of state named Johnson? Mercifully, the
condolence calls had tapered off but she still had to receive
graciously anyone who came—for Robert's sake. Anyone
who cared for Robert was her friend.

She cleaned her hands, brushed off her skirt, and met Mrs. Johnson in the small parlor.

The visitor was tall and dark-haired, perhaps thirty-eight or forty, with fine dark eyes and a smile of uncommon sweetness.

She said, "Thank you for seeing me, Mrs. Chandler," and accepted the seat offered.

Laura sat down in the chair opposite. The small carved table between them barely kept their skirts from brushing. It was here that she and Robert had often shared after-dinner coffee and read throughout the evening. She searched her memory for the first name of that under-secretary and broke her rule of expressing only vague generalities, never guessing about someone she could not recall. She said, "Your husband is Loren Johnson, I believe?"

"My name is Pauline Johnson." The lady paused. "My husband has been dead for many years."

"Ah," said Laura.

"I felt the need to come, to express my sympathy, Mrs. Chandler. I greatly admired the senator—we were long-time friends."

Oh, Laura thought. Of course. Naturally there had been women during the years before their marriage, women who had loved him—it was to be expected. But she felt cold, stone cold.

Pauline Johnson went on. "I wouldn't have come here though, I would have written my condolences except for my problem. Robert always paid the rent on the first of the month. I had only what he gave me and now . . ."

"I've never heard of you. You could be anyone who read about my husband in the papers. I don't want a scene but if you don't leave now there will be one." Laura started to rise.

The woman held out her hand in a gesture of appeal. "Please, Mrs. Chandler. I know you have a houseful of servants and I don't want trouble. But I am destitute and Robert promised . . ."

"You are not mentioned in his will. If you doubt me speak to my lawyers."

"Oh, no, I don't doubt you. But he did promise . . . see here?"

A chasm opened. In it were unimaginable horrors.

The letters lay there on the table, a small packet tied with a blue ribbon. Laura picked them up.

She read rapidly, taking in every word. The first letter was dated more than a year before her marriage. The second, three years afterward. The third, two years ago. The fourth, only last month.

Why would a man of Robert's experience write such words down on his own stationery and sign his name to it? Why was the house so silent? Why was she so cold?

She raised her head. Her eyes were chips of steel. "You have other letters?"

"Yes. I kept everything he wrote."

"One thousand dollars. For all of them."

"He promised ten thousand! It's right there in that letter, the one you just read. I don't like coming here but what can I do? I need it to live. He was an honorable man, he would want me to have it."

Honor, what is that? Laura had once asked Edward. "Honor" was a word much used by Southern men. She couldn't remember Edward's answer.

"I'm sorry for your troubles"—her voice was laced with irony—"but I cannot, at the most, give you more than fifteen hundred. You might come back with more letters, endlessly."

Mrs. Johnson looked away nervously. "I would never do that, I swear before God! If I had ten thousand dollars"— she glanced at Laura's face—"or even eight, I could invest it, I could live. I don't look to be rich, just to live."

They settled finally for four thousand nine hundred dollars—as the bargaining went on it had become a point of pride with Laura to beat the woman down to less than half—and then Pauline Johnson left.

Laura sat down and listened to her heels clicking on the marble floor, heard Dina's murmured "Good afternoon, ma'am," heard the front door close.

For a while she simply sat staring at nothing, the structure on which she had built her life knocked out from under her. She had believed her husband was a great and good man, he had been her reason for being, and now she knew he had lived a lie. It was common enough in Washington—men of power always had wives but a majority of them had mistresses as well. Their connections were by no means always based on money or sex alone. Power was the great attraction, the stimulant that drew women like bees to honey. Even fat, homely, boring men had to fight off the ladies, Laura's friend Varina Davis, secure in her marriage to Jeff, had once remarked with her loud, sardonic laugh.

And Laura had laughed too, believing her marriage was just as secure. His betrayal was so brutal, the hurt went so deep that she didn't ask herself any of the reasonable, justifiable questions: How could he—when she loved him so much? Why did he—when she tried so hard to do everything right? Why—since he was not only a powerful man but brilliant and handsome as well—had she never wondered about those many late nights?

Evening came and shut down the day. She sat in her chair until she could no longer see her own hands and then went upstairs to her room.

She did not sleep, but during the long night the hurt went away and cold anger took its place. Anger, she discovered, was easier to bear than sorrow. It stiffened the spine, kicked out sadness and despair and replaced those weakening emotions with the energy needed to do what must be done. In the morning she dressed, drank two cups of coffee, and left the house. At her bank she convinced the manager that she didn't need the advice of her lawyer and that it was quite safe to carry five thousand dollars in cash on her person because she was going directly home.

Then she pulled down her veil and took a hack to the agreed-upon inn out on the Alexandria road. Pauline Johnson was waiting. At a table in the back of the room they completed their business.

After the woman left Laura rose to leave too, and a sudden gust of anger, a different, fiery kind of anger, shook her so hard it forced her back into her chair. She wanted him alive so she could claw him with her nails, beat him with her fists, pound him into grief and regret as painful as hers. When she was able she got up and went home, the letters in the large bag she had brought.

Before the fire in her bedroom she read each one of them, in order, as he had written them. It appeared that the affair had begun two years before he and Laura met, stopped then, and resumed shortly after their third anniversary. She began to read letters new to her, the ones Pauline Johnson had held back.

By the time she was finished her thoughts were on her own failings, not Robert's. Never once did he fault her or complain about her in those letters, indeed he never mentioned her name, but now, too late, she could see some of her mistakes. She had expected him to be an ideal man, always wise, always strong, always right; it was an expectation he couldn't fulfill. She believed their marriage was perfect but no marriage ever was. He coped in the wrong way, but Robert, like most men, shied away from self-examination. He didn't like talking about his feelings. And so he had taken the easier, less prickly path. He had told a few lies and kept on the side a woman and a place he could go to and be as ordinary and imperfect as he wished.

But he had also opened the world to her, taught her much, helped her grow up. Memories crowded back. The laughter and love in the early days, the intense late-night talks, the triumph when he won the most bitterly fought election of his career. And the evening two nights before he died. She had looked up from her book to see him gazing at her across the room. He said, "I love you, Laura. I couldn't do without you." Had he known, had he been saying goodbye? Not likely, not Robert. He never gave up, never expected the worst. He said it because he meant it.

She laid the letters on the fire and watched them burn. If there really were no more there would be no further demands for money and no threats to publish things better kept secret. She had done all that could be done and it was out of her hands. After the anguish of these last days nothing had changed except that she knew herself and Robert a little better. The hurt had diminished, the outrage was wiped out. All that was left was sorrow.

Within the month, ignoring Caroline's pleas that she do nothing in haste, she sold the house that was no longer home and boarded the train to Richmond. On that long lonely ride she took a hard look at her life and the many losses in it. Once again everything she loved had been taken from her in the most cruel and unexpected way. There was nothing to do about it except try never to feel anything too deeply again.

CHAPTER 4

ANGELA FLYNN WAS the only real friend Chase Girard had in Richmond, an old friend whom he first met years before in New Orleans. She had lived in town for five years in an unpretentious house in a modest section of town, and while she was not on intimate terms with her neighbors she was unassuming, refined, always ready with a wave or a smile, and they liked her.

Her next-door neighbor had had several chats with her over the back fence and passed on the word that Mrs. Flynn was the widow of a hardware dealer in Raleigh. The neighbors decided that the hardware store must have done well, for while Mrs. Flynn dressed simply in dove grays or dark blues the fabrics were of the finest and her deluxe carriage was drawn by a spanking pair of matched bays. In her quiet way Angela Flynn had excellent taste.

She was a short, thin little thing, not pretty, the neighbors agreed—she was too sharp-featured for beauty—but with the kind of looks that grew on you when you got to know her. Her most striking feature was her hair, an uncommon blue-black always worn low on her neck in a simple, shining coil. She may have married an Irishman but she was surely one of those black-haired Creoles, her neighbors decided; she had once mentioned New Orleans as a fine town for restaurants and that proved it.

In fact she came from Welsh immigrants, Celtic people with hair as black as the coal they mined, and had never been married. She had become Mrs. Flynn because she liked the sound of it. Her mother was long dead. Her father was a hardscrabble farmer who had been brought to God at a Methodist prayer meeting and when she was growing up had frequently tried to remove the sin from

Angela and her little brother, Sam, with his fists. She decided early that beatings and poverty were not good things and ran away to New Orleans at the age of fourteen, a bright, ambitious, iron-willed girl intent on improving her lot in life.

She soon learned two bitter truths: money did not come easily even to a good-looking, clever girl, and men who paid girls for the use of their bodies usually had something wrong with them. Whether they were the offscourings of society or gentlemen of wealth and breeding, they were always unable to love or give of themselves. To them women were commodities to be used and sometimes—if the man felt enough guilt and self-hatred—to be beaten or even killed.

Angela suffered more cruelty from customers than she had from her God-fearing father and after one especially savage beating would have bled to death if a young soldier had not stumbled over her in an alley outside a saloon near Bourbon Street and gotten her to a doctor.

Chase Girard had saved her life, the doctor said after he sewed up her wounds and set her bones. Angela, who never forgot a hurt, never forgot a kindness either. She and Chase did not become lovers and that made it possible for them to be friends. From him she borrowed enough money to leave the house she worked in and buy a stylish but tasteful gown and a pretty pair of shoes on the understanding that she would pay him back if her plan worked. Four years later the protector she had acquired lent her the money to give her a start and she was now the owner of a parlor house that catered to the cream of Richmond's male society.

When Chase suddenly appeared in Richmond and came to her with his proposition, she gave him a flat, cold no. "I adore you, lover, but not enough to get hung for it."

"If anyone hangs it will be me. You know too much about the high-toned gentlemen of this town to even be picked up. Who would dare?"

They were sitting in her office, a dark room where the heavy velvet draperies were always pulled shut even in the daytime. She poured them both another cup of coffee and gazed at him with hard, curious eyes. "If you really believe that why are you doing it?"

"Orders. I'm a soldier."

"They couldn't order you to do this."

"They asked me nicely, then. It's worthy work, holding the Union together. I took an oath to defend it. And I recall some years ago you broke a bottle of good whiskey over the head of a South Carolina gentlemen who said the flag was only good for mopping floors. You nearly killed him."

Angela shrugged. "I must have been drunk at the time." She made a handsome profit selling liquor but never touched it herself.

"You were mad as hell and I don't think your politics have changed. I need only two things from you. Pass on any talk you hear from your genteel clientele and introduce me to your father. I need a way to get information out of town."

"Is that all? I'd rather ask General Beauregard for his battle plans than talk to my father." She tilted her high-backed chair, planted her feet inelegantly on an open desk drawer, and considered the risk involved.

Unlike most women, she saw behind Chase Girard's smiling eyes a thoughtful, sometimes moody man who had never found anyone or anything to care for deeply. It was a failing they shared. She had no faith in God, governments, or people. Never having had a loving relationship with a man, she did not believe in the possibility and did not feel deprived by the lack. Men were savage, greedy, childlike beasts, users every one, and she despised them all with the exception of her brother, Sam—sweet little Sam whom she hadn't seen in fifteen years—and Toddy Beckell, the peevish, elderly black man who played piano in her establishment when the orchestra wasn't present. The only other man she had ever liked or trusted was the man who sat in her office, waiting for her answer.

The liking and the trust were the reasons she was taking him to meet her father today.

"I don't know what he'll say. Sometimes he speaks to me, sometimes he doesn't, but he's heart and soul for the Union—it's the only thing we agree on. He says this is a rich man's war and they couldn't fight it without a lot of poor suckers willing to go out there and get shot."

"Smart man. I see where you get your brains."

"Not smart enough to figure how to make a living without breaking his back. One year I became overwhelmed with Christmas spirit and offered him help, but he wouldn't take it, the fool. Said it was tainted money—turn off right ahead there. It's a mile or so down the road."

Richmond lay only a few miles behind them but the rolling open fields and dark tangled woods seemed far from the city's hustle. They turned off the main road into a narrow, rutted lane and Angela's buggy, brand-new, with fine leather seats, silver trim, and excellent springs took the bumps easily.

Chase said, "This is exactly what I'm looking for."

"A buggy? Since when?"

"Since I met an attractive lady who might like to go for a drive in the country."

She looked at him with fond admiration. "Found somebody already. How long have you been in town? Did you say a week?"

"I found somebody the day after I got here. This is another lady, very elegant and used to nothing but the best. She might possibly be interested in helping us. If I can talk her into it."

"That rich spinster woman who flies the flag every day? Miss Rutledge, is it? I thought she was already in."

"She is. This is someone else."

Angela ran her fingers lightly over the smooth leather seat. She loved the good leather, the shining silver trim that her stableman polished daily, she loved all her costly possessions accumulated over the years. They were the concrete proof of her success, evidence of her security from the storms of life. "A real fine buggy is hard to get hold of these days. They're not being shipped in from New York. I got this one through a friend and he might help you out but it'll be expensive."

Chase shrugged and smiled. "Money is no object since the government's paying. This lady could be worth every dime." To the left, down a slight incline, was a small house and a tumbledown barn. "Is this it?"

"Yeah. Makes me sick every time I see the place." Angela

sighed and squinted her nearsighted eyes. "There's dear old Pa coming out of the barn. You're going to love Pa."

The man stopped when he saw a trim, shiny buggy clatter down the slope. The buggy pulled up before the barn and a well-dressed man got out and helped the lady down. She stood in the dust of the yard, holding her skirts up a little.

"Well, Grizelda." The nanny goat came up to her, nuzzled her hand and leaned against her. "Friendliest critter on the place," she muttered and walked toward the man who still stood watching. A few feet from him she stopped. "Afternoon, Pa."

He stared at her with ice-blue eyes as cool as her own, a lean, small man with hard times and hard labor written on his callused hands and sunburned, furrowed face. His hair, blue-black like hers, was graying but his thick brows were still completely black and added to the fierceness of the eyes that traveled to Chase, looked him over and moved back to her.

"Your manfriend?"

"No, Pa, just an acquaintance. He's a soldier come to talk to you. His name is Chase Girard. This is my pa, Chase. David Rees."

David Rees inspected Chase again, this time more thoroughly. Like most Southern small farmers he had struggled against the land all his life for a bare living. Unlike many he was intelligent enough to see that the large landowners and the slave system were what kept him poor. He had figured out long ago that the purpose of the Rebellion was to maintain that system and hated the Confederacy accordingly. "If you've come for my boy you don't need to bother. You've already got him. If you've come for my mule I'll see you in hell first."

"I don't want your mule, Mr. Rees. I'm a Union soldier. Mr. Lincoln sent me."

The stony face relaxed a little. "You're for the Union, are you? You know Mr. Lincoln?"

"I met him once. He wasn't the President then. I heard him speak and shook hands with him afterward."

Rees thought that over for so long while they all stood in the hot afternoon sun that Angela irritably snapped open her parasol and sat down on the low fence that separated the barn from the house.

Finally her father said, "Well, Mr. Girard, you don't look like a soldier in those fancy clothes but I tend to believe you." He held out his hand. "I guess you can shake with me too." They shook hands soberly, and after more thought Rees said, "You can come inside if you want."

In the small house where Angela had grown up and her mother had died, her father pointed at the table where the family had eaten every meal. "Sit there." He sat, too, leaned back and folded his arms. "What's Mr. Lincoln want with me?"

"Information about the Rebels—what their army is up to. I can get that information in Richmond but I need a way to send it out, I need someone who can move around without suspicion, maybe go right into the Union lines. Will you help me?"

Rees stared at his hands while he thought. "Sounds risky."

"It could be, yes, sir."

"You're an army man, you say. What's your rank?"

"Colonel, at the present. My permanent rank is major."

"A high-up officer. You in the Mexican War?"

"I was at Buena Vista." Chase smiled. "So was Jeff Davis."

"I thought about the army but I had a family." David Rees sat in silence, looking back on his young manhood. Slowly he said, "I've listened to these damned Rebels yammer for the last twenty years and I've got no use for 'em, no use for traitors and that's what they are. You bring me the goods and I'll take it where it needs to go."

"It may not always be me. It may be a lady or sometimes a Negro."

"I've got no use for Negroes either. They take work away from white men and they don't belong in Virginia, never should've been brought here. I read where Lincoln's going to send 'em back to Africa after the war. You think he'll do that?"

"I don't know what will happen. I do believe the Union's worth saving."

Rees pushed back his chair without comment and went out into the yard.

Angela stood up to watch while he pulled up a bucket of water from the well.

He came back in with the bucket of water, found battered tin cups in the cupboard and set a bottle of whiskey on the table. Carefully he poured an inch of whiskey into two cups and water into the third and said, "The Union forever!"

The three of them solemnly drank.

Angela said, "Pa, what did you mean about Sam? He hasn't gone and joined the army, has he?"

"He has. Stopped by here a month ago, passing through. Now he's out there running around with the Rebels, the damned fool. I told him to go back to New York and stay there but he's hot for the Confederates. Can't see he's fighting against his own interests. I thought I taught him better than that."

As they left Angela hesitated and then said, "Pa, if you hear from Sam tell him to stop by and see me when he's in the neighborhood."

He didn't reply.

Chase helped her up the high steps of the buggy and they headed back to town. She was silent for some time but as they were entering the city she said, "Do you know, today my father was the nicest he's ever been to me."

CHAPTER 5

AS THE WARM SUMMER DAYS passed, Washington and Richmond, only a hundred miles apart, struggled to form armies that could fight a war. In Richmond the work went on out of sight in small, quiet government offices, and most civilians were able to ignore the prospect of serious fighting. Even when word came that Federal troops had moved into Virginia and Northern newspapers were demanding that Richmond be taken quickly, few except those directly involved in war plans understood the threat to the city. Those who did

understand chose not to frighten the ladies, and since there
had been no big battles or bloodletting it was easy for the
ladies to shut their eyes and continue to shop, give parties,
and gossip.

Some of the very best gossip was inspired, surprisingly
enough, by the quiet stay-at-home widow, Mrs. Chandler.
They all knew Laura—the older ladies remembered her as
being quite shy as a child—and they all knew that she never
received gentlemen, however respectable. Now news spread
that the Yankee from Philadelphia had not only been
invited to a private lunch but had called again and spent
almost an hour with her. The next time he called, only two
days later, he had brought a gift. Perfectly proper since she
was not an unmarried girl, but still . . . The ladies who
hashed this over would have given their souls to know what
the gift was but none of the Seymours' servants had gotten
close enough to see and Jewel, the only one who might
know, wasn't talking.

"It wasn't flowers and it wasn't candy," Ellen Mercer
told her friends gathered at the Spotswood Hotel for lunch,
"it was a small package but it couldn't be jewelry, not at
this stage." The other ladies agreed. Colonel Girard was a
gentleman.

In fact, it was a book—a small, exquisite book of draw-
ings of native Virginia flowers—not so costly that Laura
couldn't accept it but an unusual book that had taken
time and effort to find in one of the many downtown
bookstores.

"It's lovely, Chase. Thank you."

She had taken the book to the window where the light
was better and he could not see her face. He said, "You're
not pleased."

"Of course I am. It's just that you've gone to so much
trouble . . ." She put the book down and turned to him
with a smile. "Let's go out back. I'll show you where some
of these flowers grow."

They walked through the garden, past the roses and
the lily pond, past the summer house with its cushioned
benches, and at the far end she opened a gate in the brick
wall. Here Seymour land began to curve down in a gentle
slope. Below was the river, smooth, powerful, deep enough

for large vessels, deep enough for Federal warships if they could fight their way upriver, a fact that didn't occur to Laura. A sudden surprising lightheartedness came over her. The day was bright, the countryside green and tranquil, the company pleasant, and for no reason at all she felt like laughing. A breeze had sprung up, blessing the warm summer afternoon. She drew in a breath of the sweet air.

"I love this spot, my favorite thinking place since I was a child. From here we can see . . . oh, I don't know how far! Coming here was the thing I missed most when I lived in Washington. Follow this path and watch your step. See the tiny blue flowers and the pink and yellow ones? I'll match them with the book and learn all the names."

He said, "Washington is a strange place. I've felt safer in the wilderness."

"The streets are dangerous. Most men carry a gun and never go out alone at night."

"I wasn't thinking of the streets."

"Oh. Yes, the people can be dangerous too. I was raised to worship Our Form of Government"—he noticed that when her smile was genuine dimples appeared at the corners of her mouth—"and when I got there and saw what really went on I was so disillusioned. My sister-in-law, Caroline, helped me learn the rules—there are rules, you know."

"Yes, I know."

"I learned how to cope but I never really liked it. Here, let's sit on this rock."

The stony outcropping was smooth and flat. Below them, following the twists and turns of the river, was the Kanawha Canal where barges were hauling iron and coal to the great spreading Tredegar Iron Works. There in plain view lay the two reasons Richmond had to be defended, the reasons the North wanted the city so badly—coal and iron from nearby mines and the Tredegar, capable of producing cannon, ammunition, and other war materiel, making Richmond a booming manufacturing center in a region that prided itself on the absence of factories. But Laura saw only the greenness of trees dotting the riverbank, the many little islands in the river, the bridge, and the James River Valley, the most beautiful land in the world because it was home.

She looked happier today than he'd ever seen her, for she had set aside the great-lady pose—he was convinced it was a pose—and allowed her real feelings to show just as she had back at the house when he gave her the book. She almost refused the gift and then changed her mind. At that moment a decision was made in his favor, but it was one thing to be accepted as a friend and another to be allowed a glimpse into her mind. He now knew her well enough to realize he didn't know her at all. She hated the war. Did she hate it enough to act against her family and her friends? If he approached her his life would depend on where her allegiance lay, and prudence suggested he give up the idea and work with the people he had, people whose loyalty he could count on.

But the safe way had never been his way. Beneath her outward discipline he thought he saw a rebellious streak, a willingness to break the rules. The next task was to find out how far she would go.

F ROM THE UPSTAIRS window Jewel had been watching ever since they left the house. The third floor gave her a view not only of the river and the country beyond but the path and the rocky ledge they were sitting on. She wondered if that Yankee had any idea what a favor he had been granted. Laura never took anyone there, not even girlfriends when she was growing up. It was her private place where she went to think or simply watch the river flow, and the only person she had ever allowed to go with her was Jewel. There they had sat on many long afternoons discussing life and their most secret ambitions, love and the imaginary men they would someday marry—one girl pink-and-cream and privileged, the other brown-skinned, dark-eyed, with no privileges at all except those given by the white girl, with only the relative good fortune of having been bought by a kindly family.

Because Laura insisted—and Edward was willing—Jewel had been allowed to sit with her during her lessons. Her tutor was a demanding scholar who believed that every civilized human being, male or female, should be versed in Latin, French, literature, and mathematics. The result was that both girls received an education usually reserved for boys. Then, at fourteen, Laura was sent away to school to be "finished," married Robert Chandler when she was barely seventeen, and became a different person.

But, Jewel thought, the old Laura, the real Laura was still there somewhere, passionate, venturesome, and bold. This new man had unsettled her, and who could tell—maybe he would find the real Laura and bring her back again. The entire household was fascinated by the drama of it.

Miss Millie was coming up the stairs—the whisper of her taffeta skirts announced her. She was dressed for an important social engagement although she hadn't left the house all day and didn't plan to. It was her way. Every morning she groomed herself for Mr. Edward's eyes; he might not be home until evening but she was ready for him at every hour of the day. It was sweet and loving and probably a mistake in Jewel's opinion, but while Miss Millie had her whims and crotchets she had her problems too, and Jewel felt for her. The frightened little slave child who had come to this house so many years ago had been mothered by Millie in much the same way Millie mothered the white children of the family. Jewel owed her a great deal, loved her in a way, and sometimes suffered for her. She noticed the fragrance of lavender before Millie spoke.

"What are they up to, Jewel? I couldn't see a thing downstairs."

"They're out there sitting on Miss Laura's rock."

"On her rock? Oh, my. Did she accept the gift?"

"I expect so, ma'am. Colonel Girard looked pretty pleased when they came out of the parlor."

"Do you think she really likes him?"

"I'm sure I don't know, Miss Millie."

"Um." Millie craned her neck. "Now they're walking on. Oh, I can't see them now. I expect you to let me know if you find out anything interesting, Jewel."

"Yes, ma'am."

As soon as she heard Millie's door close on the floor below Jewel left the window. Joseph, who had just sent a delivery boy to the rear of the house, turned away from the front door and saw her coming down the stairs. Even before Edward bought him eight years ago Joseph had heard of the Seymours' pretty maid who thought she was so grand and rejected every man she met. He had come into the household convinced that he was the man to change her mind but she turned her nose up at him too. Every time he looked at her he felt a sense of rage. He hated everything about this haughty woman, her stuck-up way of talking—pretending she was almost white folks—her slanting eyes and delicious full lips, her swaying, seductive walk and the high, pointed breasts that seemed to taunt him.

"Afternoon, Joseph," she said and walked right past him, out the French doors and into the side garden.

He stormed down the hall to the kitchen, and Elvina, seeing his face, ducked out the back door.

Jewel was looking for Adam. Her bedroom was on the third floor of the main house but Adam slept in the separate servants' quarters. He was not there. She stepped outside and saw him coming from the direction of the stables.

"Where have you been, boy?"

He looked into her lowering face. "Uh, Mama. I was just—"

"You were down at the stables."

He glanced around nervously. It was plain bad luck, running into her now. By rights, she ought to be working up at the house at this time of day. "No, I—"

"Don't lie to me, don't you *ever* lie! I have told you and told you, stay away from those worthless, no-good stable-hands. You hang around them, you'll end up talking trashy like them and I won't have it."

Adam hated displeasing his mother because he loved her dearly and also because she was a terror when she was mad.

"I won't be like them, Mama, I promise. I just like horses, that's all."

In fear and anger and fiery protective love she broke off a stick from a bush by the path and shook it under his nose. "You see this switch? Next time I catch you down there you'll feel the strength of my arm!" She dropped the switch, held him tight against her, and kissed the top of his head passionately.

Then she marched him back to the kitchen and told the cook to find him some chores to do.

*   *   *

THE FOLLOWING WEEK Chase called on Laura again but this time instead of coming in the house he insisted she step outside to see a surprise. On the graveled drive was a buggy, brand-new, with silver trim and handsome silver lamps. She walked around it exclaiming politely, knowing that in a few moments she was going to have to make an important decision and wondering what she wanted it to be.

It seemed that every time she saw this man she had to make a new decision, that he was gently but firmly pushing her in the direction he wanted her to go, not at all what she'd intended with that first imprudent invitation to lunch. So far he had only come to the house. Now he was about to ask her out for a drive and, if she accepted, it would put the two of them on a subtly different footing. What was worse, the entire town would know it. And not just know, but gabble their heads off.

He pointed to the luggage rack. "There's a picnic lunch in the basket—fried chicken, an excellent wine, and it's a beautiful day for a drive."

He let the implied question lie while the silence lengthened, waiting with a little smile as if, she thought in some aggravation, he knew every difficult consideration she was struggling with. Still, it was a nice smile and she did like him. Let the town talk. If she found him pleasant company it was nobody's business but her own.

She said, "What a good idea. I'd love to."

ON A GRASSY BANK they spread a blanket and she laid out the picnic lunch. There was considerably more in the basket than chicken and wine and she exclaimed over each dish as she took it out. "Ah, angel food cake. I truly love angel food. And peaches in June! Well, almost July."

He watched her with real pleasure. She had turned out to be the most enthusiastic, undemanding woman he'd ever known, able to get enjoyment from the simplest things. It made this courtship—for in a way that's what it was—pleasant work. With her he saw what he might not have noticed otherwise: the clarity of the water on this quiet stretch of the river and its translucent blue-green color here near the bank, the piled-up white clouds to the northeast, fair-weather clouds that, she said, "You could eat with a spoon." Even the cold chicken seemed tastier than usual. She had decided to ignore gossip and do as she pleased and that confirmed his judgment of her—she would go her own way whenever she chose to.

She had a hearty appetite, too, he noticed, as she offered him the last piece of cake and then ate it herself when he refused. It was refreshing in a time when most women prided themselves on eating like birds and then tended to faint from hunger and overtight lacing.

A small flat-bottomed boat drifted by. The two boys in it waved as they went past, and Laura said, "I always wanted to do things like that, but being a girl, I couldn't. Kirby and Doug ran all over town, fished out here, learned to swim and hunt—they're both so good with rifles—and I envied them. Of course, they had a problem I didn't have. Living up to Edward."

"He's a fine man."

"Yes. I won't say everybody likes him. He ruffles a lot of feathers with the *Courier*. But just about everybody trusts him. The boys were so young when Papa died that Edward is really the only father they've had. Imagine being the sons of the most respected man in town. They couldn't get into the kind of mischief most boys do for fear it would embarrass Edward."

"It hasn't seemed to hurt them."

She made a little moue and frowned. "Doug is almost *too* responsible—and I expect he'll be getting married soon. I'd like to see him fly a little first. And Kirby . . ." She shook her head and laughed. "Kirby is too much of a high flier. But maybe I'm worrying about the wrong things. With the war, well, God knows what's in store for them. Edward says there may be a battle before long."

"I think there'll be a big battle quite soon."

"Would you tell me why? I've looked at the map but military strategy is beyond me."

He had been leaning back on one elbow watching her face and he sat up. "Have you heard of Manassas Junction?"

"Isn't it a railroad junction up near Washington?"

"About twenty-five miles southwest. Railroad lines are always military objectives, especially junctions like Manassas. Beauregard has an army up there of close to twenty-two thousand men and I hear Joe Johnston is over at Winchester with about half that many. There are some Union troops around Centerville—look." He laid out forks and spoons on the blanket. "Here's Manassas, here's Centerville a little to the north. Another Union force is up at Harper's Ferry and here's Johnston in the Shenandoah Valley. Johnston can get to Beauregard fast. Do you see why?"

"He's got the railroad."

"That's right. If Washington decides to go after Beauregard—"

"Do you think they will?"

"I think they must and so does everyone else I've talked to, because the people up north are screaming to get down here and take Richmond. Their army isn't ready, all they've got are some untrained troops, mostly militia, but it won't be the first time public opinion has forced a battle."

"It sounds to me like you think Beauregard can beat them."

"In war you never know, but if I were a Northern sympathizer I'd be worried."

"My brothers are still in camp but they think they'll be sent to Beauregard soon. If we were to lose this battle, if the Union did take Richmond, the war might be over and the men could come home."

"That's true but most Southerners don't see it that way. They expect to win."

She looked up at him, her eyes crystal-gray in the clear light. "Thank you for the instruction. I'll come to you whenever I want to know what's really going on."

They sat for some time in silence as the sun dipped, watching the shifting, quivering colors on the water. The clouds to the west drifted and straightened into long trails, spreading streaks of crimson and coral and lavender across the sky. Then just above the point where sky and land met the sun blazed through and for a breathless moment turned the world to gold. And then it was down. The colors blurred and began to fade.

She packed away the dishes and tossed the remaining crumbs to the ducks that had come to rest near the shore. In the soft blue light of early evening they rode back into town.

T HE SMALL PARLOR was the place where Millie liked to spend her evenings. The richness of the furnishings, the dark woods, the heavy velvet draperies drawn against the night gave her the sense of being sheltered from the outside world, a feeling she often needed. Here in this snug room she sewed or read and sipped her after-dinner coffee and hoped that instead of going into his little office to write or study his maps Edward would join her. Tonight he had.

Millie raised her eyes from her novel. Oh, but he was handsome, sitting there frowning a little, absorbed in some competitor's paper. She had loved him so long, ever since she was ten years old and fell out of the apple tree and broke her arm. On that memorable day her strong, good-looking cousin had picked her up and carried her back to the house, scolding her all the way for climbing the tree in the first place, and she had told him he was her knight in shining armor. He had shouted with laughter but she meant it and her feelings had never changed. She had jumped at the chance to marry him after his parents died, not caring that he didn't love her in quite the same way she loved him. Not desperately. She wasn't sure Edward ever felt *desperate* about anything. But he had loved her and there had been happy days for them. Where it had all gone to and why was something she didn't fully understand but she lived in the hope that one day it would return. Meanwhile, she took her happiness where she found it. For now it was enough that they were sitting together companionably in this cozy room, and as the evening passed he would comment on what he read and she would reply and it would seem just like the old days. She returned to her book.

Joseph's voice in the hallway, and then Laura's. Edward glanced at the clock.

Laura sailed past the door, backed up and came into the parlor. "There you are!" She took off her bonnet and smoothed her hair. "Sorry I'm so late—we stayed to watch the sunset. I hope you didn't wait supper."

Edward laid down his paper. "We didn't," he said with a slight smile.

"I'll have Bella bring you a tray, honey."

"Oh, Millie, don't bother—we had a huge lunch . . . ah, there's coffee. Enough for me?" Laura poured herself a cup and sat down on the hassock near Edward. "We had the best angel food cake! I don't know where it came from—some marvelous bakery Chase found." She picked up the paper at Edward's feet. "The New York *Tribune*—how do we get these papers?"

"I wouldn't get it much quicker if I lived in New York," Edward said. "The blockade's mostly talk right now—they've got over three thousand miles of bays and inlets to cover. But they'll get better at it, I'll bet my hat on that, and then I may have to do without Northern opinions."

" 'On to Richmond!' " Laura read. " 'Slay the Rebels in their lair.' Chase says there's going to be a big battle soon. He says they're not ready any more than we are but public opinion will force it."

"I think he's right. We want it too, you know. 'Throw the oppressors out of Virginia!' I hear that kind of talk all the time."

"Chase says it'll probably be up near Manassas and if he was for the North he'd be worried. He thinks Beauregard can beat them because we're defending and it's easier to defend than attack. You know, I *could* eat. Don't bother Bella, Millie. I'll just get something in the kitchen."

There was a stillness in the room after Laura left, as if some unique energy had gone with her.

Millie looked at Edward. "Well? Do you think anything will come of it?"

"I have no idea."

"Bright eyes, I must say. 'Chase says, Chase thinks' . . . I never heard the like from her."

Edward went back to his paper.

"I asked Jewel what she thought and all I got out of her was her enigmatic look and 'I'm sure I don't know, Miss Millie.' "

"She was probably telling the simple truth. Laura wouldn't discuss it with Jewel or anyone else. In any case I hear Colonel Girard's affections are engaged elsewhere."

Millie's round blue eyes grew rounder. "My gracious! Who?"

"Oh, it's just gossip." Edward gave up and laid down his paper again, annoyed with himself for the slip. "I doubt there's anything to it. Laura could never be serious about him anyway."

"Why ever not? He's the nicest man. Everyone says so."

"Just so. Haven't you noticed that when the best thing you can say about a man is that he's 'nice' there isn't much to him?"

"I thought you liked him."

"I do, everyone does. A man worth his salt ought to have a few enemies. Like your husband." He cast a sardonic eye at the newspaper.

"Is the government mad at you? Have you been criticizing President Davis again?"

"He deserves criticizing."

Millie abandoned politics and went back to the more interesting subject. "I can't see why Laura couldn't be serious about him. He's just about the most attractive man around and he's single. You worry about her so much, you ought to be pleased she's interested in someone."

"I'm more than pleased to see her out and doing again. He can come around here any time he likes, but Laura will never settle for him. What kind of soldier deserts his country in time of war?"

"Why, Edward, lots of Yankee officers are coming South because they know we're right. Captain Dunbar is from Boston and you think he's a perfectly honorable man."

"Captain Dunbar believes a state should have the right to leave the Union if it wants to. I doubt that Chase Girard has even thought about it. Oh, I don't mean he's not honorable—I shouldn't have said that about desertion. But I've had a number of conversations with him and I don't think there's a serious thought in his head. After Robert Chandler, Laura would never be satisfied with him."

*　　*　　*

JUST BEFORE DAWN the next day, after a long, sleep-less night, Valerie came to the same conclusion. The previous afternoon her close friend Susan Armistead had come to the house with news so interesting that it couldn't wait until their weekly lunch.

"There she was, riding out of town with him in his brand-new buggy. It isn't a rumor, I saw them with my own eyes less than an hour ago. You know her best, Valerie. Do you suppose she's decided to get married again?"

Valerie maintained her smile. Susan suspected nothing; she was too slow-witted. With crushing calm she drawled, "Really, Suzie, it's a long leap from a buggy ride to marriage. And I do think that in these times with our soldiers risking their lives for us, you could think of something better to do than shop and go to teas and pass on silly gossip. Why don't you go volunteer at the hospital? I hear they're training nurses."

Susan was so appalled at the thought of having to bathe or bandage a strange man that she mumbled, "Oh, I couldn't—I know I'd get sick or faint," and didn't think to point out that shopping, teas, and gossip were Valerie's chief occupations too.

Ten minutes after Susan left the house Valerie got a second shock. She was sitting at the far end of the garden tearing her handkerchief into shreds when she saw Jason coming down from the house with the smile on his face that he gave only to her. After that she was busy expressing joy at this unexpected homecoming while trying to think of a way to send a warning to Chase. The anguish and the fear didn't return until late that night after Jason was asleep. As the slow hours passed, gusts of rage at Laura's duplicity alternated with the conviction that it was foolish to be upset—there couldn't be anything between those two. They were friends, that was all.

When the clock in the hall struck four she could stand inaction no longer. Quietly she eased out of bed, went into her dressing room and lit a lamp. The long mirror reflected her face, tense, white, wide-eyed, as familiar as the palm of her hand for she had spent much of her life before a mirror, studying it. She liked her right profile best and consciously turned it toward any observer whenever possible. Her hair was pale gold, her eyes large, dark blue, and especially effective when used in a sidelong glance she had perfected after long practice.

For her time and her world Valerie was not especially vain, she had simply recognized early a fundamental truth about Southern attitudes toward women. Just as in men personal honor and the ability to shoot straight were valued above all other qualities, so physical beauty in women was admired more than less obvious qualities of mind and heart. It was true to an extent in all cultures but seldom so intensely as among Southerners. Valerie knew very well that her worth as a human being was determined by her ability to attract and hold the admiration of men. Jason would never have married her if she had been a plain girl. Chase was bewitched by her beautiful body, not her mental powers.

She did not wholly understand the man who had so recently swept into her life and turned it upside down; shrewdly she sensed that there were areas of his life she knew nothing of. But she believed he did not like intellectual women, he liked pleasure and women who were happy and uncomplicated. And Laura preferred serious men who talked about states' rights and the Constitution, men like Robert Chandler. It was almost a certainty—there couldn't be anything going on.

As the sun rose on another hot summer day she came to a decision. This afternoon she would talk Laura into going out to camp to watch the evening review of the troops—everyone would be there for it had become the fashionable thing to do—and while they were together she would make certain her instincts were correct.

THE TROOPS HAD been assembled on the parade ground and politicians, businessmen, and ladies of the highest social rank were looking on from landaus and carriages, an enthusiastic audience prepared to cheer their soldiers and enjoy the evening show.

It was a colorful show. Zouaves from Louisiana were lined up in their baggy striped pants and brilliant red jackets, a rowdy lot notorious in Richmond for brawling,

frequenting brothels, and accosting ladies in the better
parts of town. The Texans were dashing too, in their own
way—tough, rangy, hard-looking men, many wearing
buckskins, a kind of dress not seen in Virginia in a generation; next to them the aristocratic South Carolinians were
almost painfully stylish in their expensive tailored uniforms.

Several regiments of Virginians were present, including
the Richmond Howitzers who recently had been studying
artillery theory at the Spotswood Hotel, and the state ban-
ners of Georgia, Arkansas, Mississippi, and Alabama units
snapped in the light breeze. In fact, every state flew its own
flag instead of the Confederate flag, declaring to the world
that these warriors bowed the knee to no central government; it was the reason they were here. An assortment of
uniforms proclaimed their individuality too—dark blue not
much different from the U.S. Army's uniform, light blue,
butternut, and even gray, the official Confederate army uniform. Guns had been decorated with flowers and ribbons
fluttered from the tips of bayonets.

It was as if these men had dressed up in costumes and
come to an enormous party to have a good time. Regimental bands played lustily, often in competition with each
other, and dogs excited by the hubbub raced through the
ranks barking wildly. Behind the troops a vast cluttered tent
city trailed off into woods that were outlined against a sun
that was almost down.

It was a vivid scene and Valerie, sitting in her carriage
with Laura, exclaimed, "Aren't they gorgeous!"

Laura, remembering the martial sharpness and élan of
the U.S. Army units on parade in Washington, said, "They
surely are colorful," and wondered how these disorganized
individualists could ever fight a war against a real army.

With a hoarse shout followed by more shouts and
encouragement in the ranks, a scuffle broke out between a
Zouave and an elegant South Carolinian. The patrician
gentleman, like many other rich young men, had brought
with him his personal servant and wanted the servant to
hold his rifle for him. He also wanted the Zouave to move
over. An officer had hurried over and was trying to settle
the dispute tactfully—no officer, no matter how exalted his

rank, dared speak roughly to a Southern gentleman for fear of immediately finding himself on the field of honor.

When order was restored commands were bawled out and the men went through their drill with fair competency; Southerners would cooperate with their officers but only voluntarily and only if convinced it was essential to a good result. The performance ended, the troops were dismissed, and soldiers began to hunt through the watching crowd for girls who were waiting for them.

Valerie's eyes, searching, searching, lighted on Doug Seymour with a girl clinging to his arm, pausing to speak to a well-dressed civilian. The civilian removed his tall beaver hat and she looked at Laura with an odd smile. "There's Chase with Doug and Becca. What do you think of him now you know him better?"

Laura thought, What does he see in her? She said, "Very nice. I understand why you like him."

"Do you?" Valerie poked at her coachman with a gloved finger. "Micah, go get us a drink of something cool, lemonade, I think, and don't come back telling me there isn't any."

Micah answered, "Yas'm," and went off, as was often the case, on an impossible assignment.

As soon as he was out of earshot Valerie turned on Laura, her eyes as hard as a hunter preparing to gun down a deer. "You can't have him, Laura. I don't intend to give him up." The moment the words were out of her mouth she knew how ridiculous they were, for her best friend, hurt, astonished, was looking at her as if she'd lost her mind.

In fact, Laura felt no hurt at all. She had at that moment just discovered that she truly disliked Valerie. Why had she come out here to be insulted? She would get coldly and silently out of this carriage, find someone else to take her home, and never again spend time with this vain, silly girl who attracted foolish males for no discernible reason. She wouldn't deny or explain a thing. And then she went ahead and did so.

"How can you say such a thing to *me*! Never a day or a night goes by that I don't think of Robert and wish he were here. I could never . . ." She passed her hand across her forehead. "I suppose you're talking about yesterday. Everybody seems to be. It was just something to do, an afternoon away from the house . . . I'm sure he'd rather be with you but he can't, not very often. If they're gabbling about me, think what they'd say if you'd gone with him, think what Jason would say! I hardly know the man and as far as I'm concerned he's entirely yours."

Valerie leaned back against the carriage seat. "You really think he'd rather be with me?"

"Of course. I'm not much fun."

"Does he ever mention me?"

"Certainly not. How could he? I envy you, Val. I wish I could feel the way you do about someone but I can't."

Valerie touched her hand, thoroughly chastened. "I'm sorry, honey. I don't know what got into me. Let's walk for a while—you look pale as a ghost."

The parade ground was now a mass of civilians and soldiers and a number of young men noticed the two young women climbing down the high steps of the carriage, their wide crinolines blowing up in the light breeze and no servant to assist them. Several rushed forward to help, the women caught at their billowing skirts, and Valerie laughed and thanked them. The men watched them walk off, wishing they could have arranged a formal introduction.

Valerie glanced back quickly at them and then straight ahead. "Nice, aren't they? Oh, there's Mrs. Davis." She smiled, waved, and whispered, "What a cow. She dresses to the nines but I'll bet her waist is thirty inches without her stays. I hear she's expecting again, poor thing. Imagine, a baby every other year."

Some little distance away was Varina Davis's carriage where she sat with Ellen Mercer, one of the ladies included in her newly formed social circle. Immediately after arriving in town with her three children, Varina had organized a group made up of women friends from Washington, the wives of men who, until war began, had held high positions in the federal government.

It was a necessary move because Richmond's established social leaders looked down their noses at the Mississippi wife of their President, calling her their "Western Belle" in a compliment with a faint derogatory tinge. They were courteous but aloof and Varina could not afford social isolation.

Only thirty-four, she was young to be the First Lady of a new nation, but intelligent and vital, a woman who intended to be a success. She was also pretty and plump and always tastefully dressed. Her interest in fashion was one of the things she and Laura had in common.

She waved and Laura said, "Let's go over, Val. I haven't called since she came to town and I should have."

"Well, I've called and a more boring afternoon I never spent. All she talks about is how smart Jeff Davis is and how everybody picks on him. You go on. I'm going to look for Jason."

She doesn't have the least intention of looking for Jason, Laura thought, watching Valerie move purposefully across the parade ground. She walked toward the Davis carriage, angry, resentful, more deeply offended than Valerie dreamed. Why be deprived of an honorable friendship because people liked to talk and Valerie was jealous and obsessed? It was funny when you thought about it, the way they had quarreled over Chase, as if possession of him was something to be decided between the two of them. That girl had a hide like an elephant—she didn't even realize how impertinent and rude and downright tactless she had been and her apology didn't make up for it.

She climbed into the Davis carriage without waiting for the coachman to hand her up, nodded at Ellen Mercer, said, "It's good to see you, Varina," and sat down.

Varina laughed. "I don't think so. My, what a furious scowl."

"Oh—forgive me." Laura cleared her face quickly and laughed too. "It *is* good to see both of you. It's just . . . there are times when Valerie Hood irritates the life out of me."

Ellen followed Laura's gaze to where Valerie was chatting with Doug, Becca, and Chase Girard. Something must have been said that amused her for she tossed her head and laughed and her dancing earrings flashed in the fading light. Ellen remarked in a considering way, "She can be aggravating and I doubt a sensible thought ever crosses her mind but isn't she pretty!"

"Do you think so? Well, yes, of course she is. How do you like living at the Spotswood, Varina?"

Varina's eyes widened in amusement but she said, "It's great fun, the crossroads of the world. Eight of us have a table for lunch every day and often one or two gentlemen join us. You must come and contribute to the conversation. I hope this outing means you'll soon be back in society?"

She knows about the picnic too, Laura thought. "I'd love to come to lunch and I will one day soon, I promise."

Across the field she saw Jason Hood talking with his close friend George Armistead, and far to the other side of the crowd, only a pace or two from a line of cannon, Valerie was whispering something in Becca's ear and Doug was deep in conversation with his current hero, Chase Girard.

Doug Seymour had only two ambitions in life at the present time—to marry Rebecca McCauley and to become the best officer in the Confederate army, or if not the best, at least a very good one. He admired Chase enormously and liked to talk to him because he was a professional soldier, had actually been in battle and knew what it was to hear a bullet that was meant for you flying past your ear. And he was willing to give time to a young inexperienced fellow. So many real soldiers could not be bothered. The first thing Doug had done when his unit was dismissed was to find Becca. The second thing was to search out Chase.

He had finally located him talking to some Richmond Howitzer boys and looking over the small cannon which were, for now, all they had to practice with. Big guns were at this very moment being manufactured at the great Tredegar Iron Works down by the river and someday, no doubt, they would have all they needed. But for now heavy cannon were still sparse in the army.

"Small potatoes, aren't they?" Doug said, looking at the cannon. "We can't do much damage with them."

"Sure you can, with well-trained men and tight discipline. Good evening, Miss McCauley."

Becca murmured a soft-voiced reply and gave Doug a quick glance. She did that often, as if assuring herself that he was really there and really hers, and he smiled back so lovingly that passersby were struck by it and smiled themselves.

Doug said, "Well, what did you think of the review? Are we any good?"

"I'm impressed by how far you've come in a short time. Washington would be worried if it knew."

"That's good to hear coming from an expert like you. We sure are training hard but discipline's our weakness. Everybody thinks he's in his own private army. Not like the Federals. We don't even all have the same uniform."

"The Federals have their problems too, and uniforms don't mean much in a serious fight." Chase looked out over the crowd. "Those men look like a tough lot to me."

"Some of them are hard-bitten, all right. I never knew there were such types in the world before I joined the army. Oh, good evening, Mrs. Hood. You have met Becca, haven't you?"

"Indeed I have, at Paige's wedding. How good to see you again, dear." Valerie spoke as to a young girl from her eminence as a married woman but in fact Becca was only a year younger, a certified old maid until, Valerie thought not unkindly, Doug Seymour took her off the shelf.

In the thin gold light that always hung over the land just before twilight, Becca's plain features seemed softer, her small nose less sharp, her light brown hair darker and richer. Valerie needed no flattering light yet her face appeared even more delicate and her smile sweeter.

Watching them, Chase had a quick, unexpected sense of regret which came and went so rapidly that it was almost impossible to examine. There had been a number of women like Valerie in his life—not as many as his brother officers believed and none so beautiful, but still, more than he'd ever expected when he was a young and innocent boy. In every case there had been some circumstance that made a permanent connection impossible. Other army officers married, some disastrously but many happily in spite of long separations and comfortless army posts. His own love affairs were always intense, enthralling but temporary, and at rare moments he wondered if there was something missing in him, a lack that made him incapable of lasting devotion. He was too realistic to imagine that he hadn't yet met the right woman.

His attention was caught by Laura, descending from the

Davis carriage and coming toward them across the open field, her black veil fluttering around her face. The professional part of his mind noted her friendliness with the wife of the Confederate President; she could tell him so much if she wished. Some other part of him knew that she was the most uncommon woman he'd ever met, capable of many things including lasting devotion, a woman he was not certain how to deal with. It was an unfamiliar feeling for him. She could be reached—everyone was vulnerable in some way—but as yet he had no idea how to go about it.

CHAPTER 6

BOOKSTORES WERE LAURA'S particular weakness. She loved the feel and heft of the books, the endless bountiful surprises inside them, the smell of paper and glue and dust, and her reading tastes were catholic. Novels, journals, biographies—she might turn to any one of them depending on her mood. She relished an hour or two in a good bookstore searching for some overlooked, underrated treasure.

This morning Millie had sent word at breakfast that she had one of her headaches and would be in bed all day. Laura, after visiting her in her darkened room, agreed to go downtown to get the new bonnet that was waiting at Mademoiselle Margot's and incidentally to pay Mademoiselle the balance of a rather large bill without mentioning it to Edward. She hesitated outside the shop and then decided to first walk over to the next street and spend a little time in O'Halloran's Book Emporium.

"Morning, Mr. O'Halloran. Isn't this a grand day?"

"It is now I've seen your lovely face, Mrs. Chandler."

She paused beside the counter. "Sure, you're full o' the blarney, O'Halloran, but I like the sound of it."

Tim O'Halloran had the round, broad-lipped look of an Irish peasant and was a man of great erudition. He had known Laura since she was twelve years old.

He said, "Y'do have the Dublin accent down pat," and she laughed.

"'Tis a gift. Do you have anything new for me?"

He leaned on the counter. "A shipment came in from London last night. There ought to be something good there though I have not yet opened the crates. No tellin' how many more we'll get. The war, you know."

"The war—yes. I'll check again next week. Today I'll just browse."

Slowly she walked down the aisle, running her finger along the titles, standing on tiptoe to see the books on the highest shelves. She was in a cheerful frame of mind. Tonight was to be another first for her. A new comedy was opening at the Marshall Theater and she was going with Edward and Millie and Chase. War and uncertainty hung over them all but on this hot summer day the future seemed somehow bright. Much later she remembered hearing the bell on the front door announce another customer, but at the time it barely registered. She pulled out a book, read a few pages and looked through the fine illustrations. She considered buying it, then laid it on the shelf to come back to later and moved on, wanting to discover something irresistible.

She turned into the next aisle, pulled out a large book of lithographs, and saw Chase on the other side. They said "Good morning" at the same moment and laughed.

She said, "Are you looking for something special?"

"I think I've found it." He came around to her side with a surveying map of the Virginia colony dated 1728.

She examined it carefully. "Randolph Collier, Surveyor. I wonder who he was and if he was the immigrant in his family, I wonder what he was looking for when he came here."

"A better future, I suppose. That's what we're all looking for."

"Aren't we Americans a funny lot? We're so new in this country that things a hundred years old seem ancient to us. This is a treasure. Edward would love to see it. And we have a little book that might interest you. I'll show it to you tonight."

When Chase paid for the map Tim O'Halloran moaned, "You've found the gem of my collection. It shouldn't have been out there—my clerk made a terrible mistake. And he's got the price wrong."

"Pay him no mind," said Laura. "He always cries when you find something worth buying. I'll be back, Tim. If there's a really good book in one of those crates, put it aside for me."

"You have no finer feelings, Mrs. Chandler. Look out for this woman, Colonel Girard. She'll break your heart. She broke mine years ago."

She kissed her fingers to him and she and Chase went out into the noonday sun, walked south and turned into Franklin Street. Just ahead a crowd of men gathered in front of a store building were jostling each other in a effort to pass through the open door. One of the men noticed them, courteously removed his hat and bowed, a well-fed man with splendid chin whiskers and hard, smiling eyes, his prosperity proclaimed by fine clothes and the heavy gold seals that rested against his brocade waistcoat.

He said, "Good day, Colonel. Shall we assist Mrs. Chandler across the street? Unless you've come to buy, this is no place for you, ma'am."

George Armistead. A man Laura had regarded with contempt since the day he sold Jewel's husband south. She said, "Thank you, no. Chase, I'd like to go inside."

Chase gave her a doubting look, then took her hand and, ignoring the grumbling of men not inclined to be generous, persuaded them to allow her passage through the crowd. "Your pardon, gentlemen, the lady would like to enter. If you'll excuse us, sir . . ."

Laura followed with a sinking sensation that reminded her of nothing so much as the dread she felt at funerals when honor, decency, and consideration for the living compelled her to look upon the remains of someone she had not deeply loved or perhaps even known well but whose lifeless body was still a painful sight (the pain of looking on those she loved was of another order entirely). Today, for some unnameable reason, she felt that same sense of duty, an obligation to finally look upon a terrible sight which she had successfully avoided for so many years.

It was a dark, low-ceilinged room. With an odd tingling sensation she saw in front the auction block, smooth and polished by the many feet that had stood upon it, and on each side, benches where the slaves to be sold on this day sat waiting, women and children on one side, men on the other. All were clean, neatly dressed, and well shod, for no matter how ragged their condition when they arrived at the great slave market that was Richmond, their owners always invested in new clothing. Well-dressed slaves brought a higher price.

Most of the white men present had come with a serious intent to buy, and since the rule of the marketplace was buyer beware all slaves were being inspected carefully regardless of assurances by the sellers. Both male and female slaves removed their new clothing when ordered to and stood naked while potential buyers moved among them feeling the muscles of arms and legs, looking over the skin for sores or marks from a whip (such marks were taken as indicative of bad temper), examining teeth, eyes, and ears for signs of defects.

"Reminds me of a horse market," Laura said in a low voice and then added, more to herself than the men she was with, "and they don't seem to mind at all."

"They don't," said George Armistead, who had taken advantage of the path Chase created and gotten into the room ahead of other buyers. "After all, they are trained to obedience and they don't have our modesty. I not only look them over, I find out why they're being sold, what skills they have and where they were raised. Susan needs a maid now that her old nurse is gone and I want a girl off a good plantation with sewing skills and the ability to dress hair. I told her she ought to pick the wench herself but she doesn't like to come down here, doesn't like the nudity. There's a likely looking girl just brought in. Excuse me, ma'am, sir. I believe I'll take a closer look."

He moved to the far side of the room where the girl stood with a child in her arms, seeming scarcely to notice as a customer turned back her lips and ran a finger over her gums and teeth. She was tall, dark complected, comely, and very young. Without knowing she was doing it, Laura held her breath while the girl put her child on the floor as George Armistead commanded, unhooked her dress and let it drop. George and another potential buyer walked slowly around her, feeling her arms and legs, examining her breasts. If either man harbored a licentious thought it was not evident in his face. They might have been viewing a naked baby.

George returned, smiling. "She's just the ticket. Says she was a lady's maid down on Roseview plantation and her mistress died so her master decided to sell her."

There was a stir in the back of the room and John Tabb, the auctioneer, came through, calling out to friends, stopping to shake hands, making a joke or two, back-slapping like a master politician running for office. He was a stout, short-legged man with rusty hair that straggled to his shoulders, gold rings on three fingers of each hand, and a wide-based stance that gave him a decided swagger; a man who by his dress could have been a barkeep or a backwoods planter but who understood how to work a crowd.

"Gentlemen," he began in a stentorian voice, ". . . and gentleladies," he added with a smile at Laura, the only white woman in the room, "what a fine lot we have for you today. You've looked 'em over, you've seen their quality, ever' one of them good boys and girls sold by need or maybe death of the owner—no fault of theirs. I'm gonna start off today with one of the best. Come here, boy . . ." An exceedingly tall, broad, heavily muscled man came forward, smiling. "Name's Jonas, twenty-two years old, never been whipped. See them teeth, see them muscles, that's *strength* you're lookin' at, folks. Did you ever see a likelier looking boy? He can chop cotton with the best of 'em but he's smart too, knows how to wait table, looks fine in livery, you wouldn't be embarrassed having him serve in your dining room. Pick up that table, boy. Show these good gentlemen what you can do."

Jonas picked up the heavy wooden table used for recording sales and effortlessly held it over his head with one hand.

"What do you think of that?" John Tabb looked around in satisfaction. "You can put that table down, boy. Now I'm gonna start the bidding and I don't want no insults. We're going straight to business. Who'll say eight hundred? Thank you, sir, but he don't expect to get this fine boy for that, does he, gentlemen? Who'll come up to nine?" His voice dropped into a rapid, hypnotic chant that to Laura was only an unintelligible babble. But the final bid was clear. ". . . last call . . . going, going . . ."—the gavel cracked—"*sold* for thirteen hundred and ninety-five dollars to Judge Talbot. You made a good buy, sir."

The auctioneer's eyes passed over the crowd, assessing his buyers' mood, and went on swiftly. "Now comes a real bargain, sirs. Look here at this prime piece—twelve years of age, smart as a whip and big for his years too. Stand up boy. This lot'll grow up to be worth eleven, twelve hundred by the time he's sixteen but I'll start him at four fifty." Two men moved forward, interested, and John Tabb added for their benefit, "Good hands, learns fast, agile as a whippet. Let's see some tumbling, boy." The boy did several cart-wheels and came up smiling. After five bids during which the auctioneer's voice and beringed hands never rested, he bellowed out a sale of six hundred thirty dollars.

The hot, crowded room was blue with cigar smoke. George Armistead brought a chair and urged Laura to sit, but she shook her head and watched two male field-hands, young and strong enough to bring a good price, sell quickly.

On the opposite bench five women slaves waited, none over thirty, two with three children each, and at the end of the bench the young girl with the baby that George was considering as a maid for Susan. The auctioneer waved a hand toward them. "Now there's a sight for you, sirs. Ten breasts among 'em, fit for a lot of use before they're through." The gentlemen laughed. Hints or jokes unacceptable in other circumstances were expected at auctions even if ladies were present—it established a jolly mood—and although they laughed the potential buyers looked the women over with cool detachment.

George leaned around Laura and whispered to Chase, "This your first auction?" Chase nodded. "Well, sir, watch this. The women with children may fetch better prices than the men. Proven breeders, you see. That's where the money is."

The auctioneer gestured the young girl onto the auction block and turned to his audience with a beaming smile. "How about this, gentlemen? Handsome, ain't she? Only sixteen and already showed what she can do. Bend over, Sallie." The girl leaned forward so that her loose cotton dress hung down and her breasts showed plainly. "Good for a lot of babies, gentlemen, and soft hands too. Stand up, girl, and show 'em your hands. She can sew, cook, do most anything; those hands won't snag the cloth if your wife wants a dress or two stitched up. Good-tempered, never whipped, always been a house servant. I'm gonna start her and her young one at eleven hundred—two for the price of one and lots more to come—and I expect good bids. Who'll give me eleven hundred?"

The first bid was nine hundred and John Tabb, deeply offended, sputtered, "You expect this fine girl and her child for free? Why, she's produced a girl here." He pointed at the baby. "Gonna grow up to be a good breeder herself, and by the time she's three or four she'll be worth more than a mule. Now who'll make it nine fifty? Thank you, sir." He smiled at George Armistead and began to roll his words out more rapidly. "There's a man knows a good servant, somebody here better make it a thousand or he'll steal her. Ten *fifty!*" He launched into his chant and when he finally cracked the gavel, George, the victor, paid fifteen hundred ten dollars and took possession of Susan's new maid and the child that would soon be as valuable as prime livestock.

As he passed her with a friendly goodbye Laura saw, or imagined, that the girl looked directly into her eyes with a kind of recognition. Chase asked, low in her ear, "Would you like to leave?", and she could only nod and follow him out of the dim, hot, smoky room into a world of bright summer sunshine, a world she had always believed was sane. She closed her eyes and took several long, deep breaths.

It was well past the noon hour. He said, "It's late but we could get lunch at the hotel."

"No."

They walked without speaking, past the bookstore, past the millinery shop and Millie's forgotten bonnet, Laura moving so rapidly that her hoop swung up with every step. They passed St. Paul's church. Ahead was Capitol Square, a popular gathering spot in the heart of town, a place of shade trees, grassy slopes, and many benches along the curving brick paths. At the entrance to the square she slowed and looked at him.

"Do you know Adam? Of course you do," she answered herself. "That child doing cartwheels could have been Adam. He loves horses," she added as if it were a fact of great importance.

He said nothing. A man coming toward them lifted his hat and murmured her name in respectful greeting but she did not hear. She said, "What did George mean, 'Breeders are where the money is'?"

"I can only tell you what I've heard from my cousins in Charleston. They have a large rice plantation and own, I believe, about a hundred and forty slaves. Breeders—are you sure you want to hear this? I notice my cousin never speaks of it in front of his wife."

"No one's ever spoken of it in front of me either. Yes, I want to hear."

"He simply meant that breeders are slave women who have proven they can bear children."

"I understand that. Why are they more valuable than a strong fieldhand?"

"Fieldhands produce the great staple crops—tobacco, cotton, rice—"

"And that's where the money is."

"Not anymore, not in the old slave states like Virginia. But in the Southwest where the land is still cheap and fertile the staple crops do pay and they need slaves, a lot of them. Here in Virginia or the Carolinas or Georgia it's good business to produce slaves for the Southwestern demand, where the price is always rising. You can see why girls and young women would be especially valuable, more valuable than a man who produces a cotton crop."

She said slowly, "They produce crops of slaves."

"You could put it that way, yes."

"That girl—Sallie—she was sixteen and her baby was at least a year old." That meant she was only fourteen when she was gotten pregnant.

He spoke as if he had read her thoughts. "They often start them at fourteen or even thirteen if possible. Slaves are a risky investment. They can get sick or die and the women have the additional danger of childbirth, but still it's considered the best way to wealth. My cousin believes female slaves are the best inheritance he can leave his children."

He could have said more but decided to let her think that over.

She was silent and except for a certain lack of color her face showed nothing. It had been a conversation touching on subjects usually avoided between ladies and gentlemen but possible because they were talking not about their own kind but about slaves. His manner was as matter-of-fact as if he'd been discussing the cultivation and sale of tobacco leaf or the fact that mules were at least twice as valuable as horses. He showed no disapproval, no opinion at all. Well, she thought, probably he didn't disapprove. He had come here to give his services to the South, she had known that all along . . . and yet she had expected better of him.

But who was she to criticize, she who had lived all her comfortable life in a society whose lifeblood was slavery, in a city that was one of the great slave markets of the South, in a family served and supported by slaves, and had managed during all those years to avoid any real knowledge of how the system worked? Who was she to judge him when her own and her family's complicity went so deep?

She took another long, deep breath. "Well." And then, "I must go straight home or we'll never be in time for the theater."

"My buggy's just over on Bank Street. I'll drive you."

T HE FRONT DOOR swung open before they reached it and Joseph greeted them with a smile. He had seen the buggy pull up and had hurried to get to the door before they did. He liked the family to think he was close to omniscient about their comings and goings.

"Good evening, Joseph. Is Mr. Edward home yet?"

"He's in his office, Miss Laura, but Miss Millie, she hasn't come back from shopping."

"Shopping?" Laura's brows rose. Shopping, along with her roses, was Millie's chief occupation and it sometimes led to cold disagreements with Edward. It was the reason she had wanted to settle the millinery bill in secret. "I guess she got over her headache. Come in the library, Chase. I want to show you that book."

The library, serene and silent in the late afternoon light, contained more than a thousand books, among them many hard-to-find volumes and old manuscripts assembled by three generations of Seymours. It was the pride of the family, a fine collection in a region not noted for bookish people. The most valuable were kept in locked glass cases. Laura unlocked one and took out a book of illustrated maxims, leather-bound, printed in Edinburgh in 1709.

"Edward treasures it."

"I see why."

As Chase turned the fragile pages they heard chimes sounding beyond the closed double doors, then Millie greeting Joseph, followed by Edward's voice, loud and echoing in the entrance hall. Laura looked up in surprise. Edward never raised his voice.

"What is all this? Put those boxes down and open them, Millie."

"Edward, not here—"

"Open them." There were thuds as several boxes dropped on the floor. "A dozen pairs of gloves? You have drawers full of gloves you've never worn. Five boxes of lace handkerchiefs. And what's in here?"

"I need a new bonnet."

In the library neither of them spoke. They could not leave to avoid overhearing because there was no way out except through the entrance hall. Laura stared at her hands.

Then, Edward's voice. "*Seven* hats? Are you out of your mind? How many dresses have you ordered?"

"Only . . . a few. I need them, Edward. It isn't as if we can't afford—"

"We can't afford thousands of dollars spent every year on anything you happen to see in the stores. *Five* women wouldn't have time to wear what you buy. I believe it's a sickness, Millie. See Dr. Rollins or I'll talk to him myself."

"I'm not sick, I'm just—oh, Edward, it's the way I cope. I see something nice, I buy it and for a little while I feel better."

"What in God's name do you have to feel bad about? You have a daughter any woman would be proud of, closets full of clothes, a beautiful house, servants who wait on you hand and foot—"

He stopped and there was complete silence. Then, quietly, Millie's voice, filled with pain. "Oh, Edward."

Again there was silence and it stretched so long that Laura wondered if they had gone to another part of the house. At last Edward spoke and he sounded not angry but tired. "Go to your room, Millie. No. No more. I'll have your supper sent up."

In the library they could hear her crying as she ran up the stairs and then the firm closing of the front door. With her eyes down Laura put the book away and locked the case. She didn't want to see what expression was on Chase's face. They went into the hall to be told by a blank-faced Joseph that Miss Millie had been felled by a severe migraine and Mr. Edward had been called to the office. He was picking up boxes filled with Millie's purchases and stacking them on the hall table.

Chase turned to Laura. "I should leave."

"Please don't. I'll go check on Millie and be back directly. Joseph, could you serve supper for us in half an hour? Colonel Girard and I are going to the theater."

She flew upstairs. Outside Millie's door there was the sound of quiet sobbing and Bella's murmuring voice. She opened the door and went in. Millie was huddled on the bed, her knees drawn up like a child, her hoops billowing, her face buried in the pillow. Bella was trying to undo a long column of tiny buttons at the back of her dress.

"Come on, Miss Millie, let me get dis dress offen you. You gonna feel better if you take off dem stays."

"Bring some cool water and a cloth," Laura told her and sat down on the bed. "Turn over, dear, and blow your nose." Gently she pulled Millie's hands from her face and Millie let her do it.

Her cheeks were blotchy, her eyes swollen. She mopped her eyes and blew her nose and Bella, clucking softly, washed her face. Bella was a dark brown woman, six feet tall and big-boned, with a genuine fondness for her mistress. She had come along when Millie left home to marry Edward, a gift from Millie's parents. Between them, she and Laura got Millie out of her dress and corset and into a wrapper. Millie sat on the bed, eyes closed, rocking and whimpering.

Laura said, "Honey, don't take on so. Edward was too harsh but—"

Millie stopped rocking and opened her eyes. "What do you know? You don't know anything." She resumed rocking and said to herself, "Bella knows, Bella knows."

Laura thought, It's more than a scolding that's done this. She looked across the room at the maid but Bella was at the wardrobe, absorbed in brushing the dust off the huge hem of Millie's skirt, hearing nothing, hearing everything.

Softly she said, "I must go, dear. I'll barely have time to eat before the theater."

Millie's eyes flew open. "Is Colonel Girard here? Did he—"

"He just came. He's waiting downstairs. I'll tell him you're indisposed."

Millie sat up and blew her nose again. "I don't think you should go without me, Laura. You can't go on running around town with this man unchaperoned."

"Oh, Millie, that's funny. I'm twenty-eight years old. In Washington I went to the theater with gentlemen many times when Robert was working and no one thought a thing of it."

"This isn't Washington. Everyone's talking already."

Laura kissed her sister-in-law, said, "Get some sleep," and closed the door softly. Even as a little girl she had understood that Millie and Edward were not alike. Now she could see just how ill-matched they were. Millie was no fool but she lived always on the surface of things, ignoring what she didn't want to see; Edward never ceased to read, to probe, to question everything, especially himself. Laura went downstairs wondering for the first time whether Edward would have married Millie if he hadn't been saddled with his little brothers and sister all those years ago. Maybe Millie wondered too.

S OMNOLENT, ARISTOCRATIC RICHMOND was now, without question, a wartime city, raucous, brawling, overflowing with strangers, not unlike that other hustling boomtown, Washington City, a hundred miles away. As in Washington, sharpers, speculators, and other men on the make pursued profitable deals in every saloon, restaurant, hotel, and government office. Soldiers, many of them farm boys away from home for the first time, swarmed through the city in search of pleasure; they were easy prey for professional gamblers and were cheated regularly at games of chance. They would be cheated again when they tried to use guns and ammunition that failed in battle, boots that fell apart in the first rain, cannon that exploded when fired—this because the government, like all governments, frequently failed in its duty and was easily swindled by contractors who considered the war an event being held for the sole purpose of making them rich.

Street crime was less lucrative but just as common. Store burglaries were frequent, assaults with guns and knives left bodies for the police to pick up every morning, and a short street called Locust Alley was already noted for its glamorous and costly parlor houses. Down dark side streets, no more sordid in purpose, were cheaper brothels staffed with seedier prostitutes—sad, sometimes diseased women whom poverty-stricken soldiers could afford.

Soldiers were not the only men searching for pleasure. Civilians liked gambling and women too. Song-and-dance shows drew big crowds and the Marshall Theater presented dramas, concerts, grand opera, and, tonight, a comedy.

The play was a good one, cheering and energizing the audience, and when the curtain came down many decided it was much too early to go home. Laura and Chase walked to the restaurant a few doors down the street. They took a table in an alcove that seemed to offer privacy near the back of the large room and Laura stripped off her gloves.

There had been a little stir, a murmur, when they entered. Many of the other patrons knew Laura, many had met Chase or at least knew of him. They nodded and smiled and spoke, some even stared, these people she had known all her life. They were wondering . . . and as Millie would say, *So what?* Let them wonder. It was her first night out in so many years and she intended to enjoy it.

She smiled at him across the table. "I like this place. It reminds me of a time . . . I must have been quite young because I was with my parents. We'd been to an entertainment at a theater—I don't know which one—and afterward they bought me ice cream, a huge dish it seemed to me. And I ate every bite." It all came back with surprising clarity, the mood of that long-ago night: the thrill of the theater, the lights and colors of the restaurant, the many sounds and smells and loud-voiced strangers around her, and she, Laura, so small, so safe with the two people who loved her best. In almost a whisper she said, "I was very happy on that night." And then a little pink crept into her cheeks. It was in poor taste to reveal one's deepest feelings to any but the closest friends.

She said quickly, "Funny, isn't it, what makes a child happy. Ice cream!"

"A big bowl of ice cream and a spoon always made the world look better to me. My folks used to take me and my brother to a fish house on the river for special occasions— my memories of it are very happy ones. Richard and I make it a point to go there at least once whenever I'm in town."

"And it will be a long time before you see your family again."

"It may be quite soon. Philadelphia factories are booming now and I know a lot of people there. I hope to make some arrangements soon that will benefit us."

Arrangements. He meant guns, armaments, supplies. She said, "And you really believe it can be done? Surely the authorities will be watching out for that kind of thing."

"They will. And they'll trip over their own feet. You know how incompetent the Federal government can be."

She didn't like that at all. "I can't agree." Flatly, cooly, no polite equivocation. "I've known many competent Federal workers—worthy, intelligent people who work hard and accomplish a great deal for their country. Sometimes they give their lives for it. My husband, for example. All big organizations stumble and make their share of mistakes— take a close look at large businesses. And how about your own army!"

"Not my army anymore. You're right—armies make mistakes that get men killed needlessly. But that's not the point. People down South are fed up, Laura. They don't want the Federals poking into their business and telling them what to do. They want to separate, they want a divorce."

Her flare of indignation was fading. It was after all only an evening out, not a political campaign. She said, "I know what they want. I honestly don't know who's right. A long time ago, when things hadn't gone so far, Robert said he didn't see us as just a passel of principalities staying together when it suits us and running away if we get mad. He thought if we, all of us, were going to survive we needed to have a marriage that lasts."

Their food arrived. She smiled to take any remaining sting out of her words and then, to put the evening back on a friendlier footing, she began to recall some of the funny lines from the play, delivering them as the actors had.

He watched her changing expressions. "You should go on the stage."

"I planned to, once—really, I did."

"Why didn't you do it?"

"I couldn't. That is, I grew up."

"Well, you're good at impersonation and you have a fine memory. Someday maybe you'll find a way to put those talents to use."

"You're teasing me." She smiled, but felt flattered. Actually, she thought, I am quite good.

Just inside the entrance to the restaurant there was a noisy disagreement. Then a voice, unpleasantly loud and harsh, boomed across the room. "Out on the town for a big evening, are you, Chase? What will your other lady say?"

Alex Wyatt was striding through the crowded restaurant toward their table. Alex, home on a short leave, had taken his new wife out to dinner and the evening had not been a success.

People turned to look. The same diners who had stared at Laura and Chase now stared at Alex and murmured to each other. Paige, trotting behind him, grabbed at his arm but Alex shook her off.

He stopped abruptly at their table and glared at Chase. There flashed into Laura's mind the memory of Senator Pryor's eyes just before he poured the burning coffee over Senator Stoker and then beat him bloody in her elegant, civilized dining room. Alex, too, had that look of rage about to break loose. And Chase just sat there watching him. She waited for a fist to fling out, or worse, a gun—Alex was wearing one. But all he did was pinch her cheek hard and announce to the room, "Ain't she a sweet little widow? Rich too. Chase, you devil."

"Go home, Alex, sleep it off. Don't embarrass the ladies."

"You accuse me of embarrassing my wife and the great lady here? I ought to call you out for that."

"Alex, please, for pity's sake . . ."

"Yes, Paige, for pity's sake." Alex threw himself into a chair and stared at Chase. "I see you're not in uniform. Not gonna be either. Found yourself a cushy civilian job, I hear, and I'll bet you'll make money at it. Everybody but me'll make money out of this war." He leaned forward, stared deeply into Chase's eyes, and said slowly and distinctly, "I hate war profiteers, especially when I'm going to be out there where the Minie balls are flying."

Paige sank into the chair beside Laura and under the table Laura reached for her hand and held it in a tight grip. Paige's father never drank to the point of drunkenness nor had any man, ever, in her presence, and now she sat here in public with an irrational drunken husband on her hands. Not only was she mortified, she had not the faintest idea of how to deal with him.

Alex leaned on both arms and stared around the table, his face flushed, his eyes unusually bright. "You know, ladies, things are quiet right now but it won't last, it won't last." He turned to the room and roared, "I know the U.S. Army. They're gearing up and when they get ready they're going to beat the crap out of us if they can. Maybe they can, I don't know."

He slumped down further in his chair and ran his thumbnail over the surface of the table. His eyes closed.

Paige leaned close and murmured, "Let's go home, sweetheart. You're tired."

"I'm drunk's what I am. Chase knows I'm drunk."

Paige urged him up and headed him toward the door, knowing every eye was on them, her face hot with humiliation. Alex went with her like a docile child.

* * *

CONVERSATION ON THE ride home was not too difficult. Laura had experience at appearing at ease while inwardly burning. This day, begun so well, had been filled with ugly realities she didn't want to look at, and she was embarrassed that the man beside her knew too many things about her family that she wished he didn't know. He was only a casual friend, after all, who shouldn't have had to witness such intimacies. Some kind of apology was in order. They talked about the play but when they pulled up at the front gate she turned to him with a rueful smile.

"Well, Chase, you certainly have seen the worst side of my family today."

"Don't give it a thought. Alex will be full of remorse in the morning. He always is."

He was pretending she meant only Alex, who was his friend too, giving her an honorable way to ignore the embarrassing quarrel between Edward and Millie.

She accepted the offer. "Does he often drink like that?"

"Not on duty but on leave, yes. Most soldiers do, out of boredom or fear. The worst times are always when you're waiting, knowing what's ahead. That's what he's doing. Waiting."

"He's afraid?"

"You heard him. He knows the U.S. Army. He means the U.S. government."

The moon had been hiding during the ride home but the clouds were now shifting and moving apart. Her face in the white moonlight was unreadable. It was her social face, perfected over the years, but this afternoon in the dim smoky auction room he thought he'd seen repulsion and outrage. She hadn't mentioned it again but her fierce defense of the Federals this evening heartened him so much that his gambler's spirit took over.

He relaxed the reins and turned to her. "Laura, Alex is right. The North won't let the Union break up without a fight to the death. There are men in the United States government who started planning for this years ago. I am one of them."

Her mind, never slow, did not grasp what he said. "I'm sorry. I don't—" She stopped, confused.

"I didn't resign my commission when I came South. I'm an officer in the United States Army."

Her mind stumbled. This was a man she had spent considerable time with during recent weeks and thought she knew rather well. Now, although his face was no different, she had the eerie sensation of looking at an absolute stranger.

She heard her own voice saying, "Do you mean . . . you're a *spy*?" and knew how fantastic the words sounded. She might as well ask if he were from Mars.

But he left her in no doubt. "I was sent here for information that will help the army. Richmond is my duty post."

She sat scarcely breathing, trying to understand how such a thing could be. "Why tell me this? If I reported it they'd hang you."

"Because I don't believe you will. As I told you, I'm leaving town in a few days and before I go I want you to promise to help me."

"You want me to—become a *spy*?"

"Yes."

"Why me? Can't you find anyone else for this—this business?"

"You have something no one else has. You're welcome everywhere. Varina Davis is your friend."

She thought that over and said slowly, "I see. What have I ever done to make you think I'd betray my friends? And my family! My brothers and my niece's husband are Confederate officers."

He looked past her. "It's a terrible thing I'm asking. We'll all do terrible things before this is over. For myself I'd rather be in battle, bad as that is." His eyes came back to her. "I'd never seen a slave auction, either, before today. For the first time I understand clearly what your husband meant when he said slavery has to end to save our souls. The North is guilty too, the whole country is guilty. We have to do what we can and you can do more than most."

The wind had increased and the gate opened and shut repeatedly, a lonely sound in the night. Beyond it, set far back from the street, the great house loomed. A lamp in the front parlor window sent a slender beam into the dark but upstairs all were sleeping.

She said, "I'll do this much for you. I won't report you."

"Think about it, Laura. I'm going north at the end of the week. I'll come by Friday evening for your answer."

She climbed down from the buggy, hurried up the path and went into the house without a backward look.

CHAPTER 7

AT LEAST ONE PERSON in the house was still awake. Jewel was waiting for her with the lamp lit and the bed turned down.

"I told you not to stay up."

Jewel shrugged. "I like to tuck you in."

She began to unbutton Laura's dress and Laura pulled away. "I can do it myself. Go to bed."

Jewel continued to work on the little jet buttons. "I'd like to shoot the person who decided teeny-tiny buttons were a good idea." She lifted the somber black dress over Laura's head, untied her hoops and began to unlace her stays. "Didn't have such a good time tonight?"

"It was very pleasant. Truly, I want you to go to bed. I can brush my own hair."

Jewel opened her mouth to speak, took another look at Laura and changed her mind.

The moment she was out of the room Laura sat down on the window seat and stared out into the night, the familiar furniture of her mind in shambles. Strange how you guided your life by assumptions, appearances, and what you wanted to believe. A *spy*, my God! The very word made her tremble. A spy in the heart of Richmond, right under the government's nose. Meetings with Benjamin, that subtle, intelligent man, meetings with Davis himself. They would hang him higher than Hamen if they found out. Tonight he had put his life in her hands, a burden she wouldn't have touched with a ten-foot pole if she could have avoided it.

He certainly was good at what he did. Such a decent, open-faced, trustworthy, uncomplicated man, so devoted to the Southern cause. The rapt attention in his face while other people confided in him, the deep interest that drew them out. They talked and talked while he occasionally expressed concern or amazement—and listened. What a cold-blooded performance! How could she who had spent a decade in Washington learning to recognize deceit have been so easily taken in? Why had she allowed him to come so close? Because he had handled her so well, that was why—never alarming her with a word or gesture out of line and yet so attractive, such a pleasure to be with. And she had thought he liked her—in spite of Valerie, she actually had thought that.

She pulled the pillow from behind her head and threw it across the room. It hit the mantel and a vase toppled and shattered. She took off her slipper and sent it sailing after the pillow. He had deliberately cultivated a friendship that meant nothing to him—blandished was not too strong a word—all with the intent to use her. She cared nothing, absolutely nothing, about who he loved but oh, how she hated being *used*!

And yet . . . and yet, what did he want to use her for? Not personal gain. He had risked his life tonight. It had been a mad thing to do. And what had he said? *To save our souls*. He could be lying but he wasn't. Those were Robert's words, she knew it as certainly as if she'd heard them herself, words that required her to set aside shock and fear and wounded vanity and consider his proposition seriously.

As she had come in tonight the rooms in this house lay in shadows, but she knew them all like the palm of her hand. Everything about them spoke of large amounts of money tastefully spent. As she ran up the stairs she had passed the portraits of her ancestors. Grandfather William, Great-grandfather George, Great-great-grandfather Elijah. Noble men all. She knew their faces as the artists had portrayed them, she knew the stories about them and their many admirable accomplishments. But who were they really? What had they done in the dark corners of their lives to begin the Seymour dynasty, acquire wealth, increase it and bring the family to its present eminence? It wasn't all based on hard work and greater ability than lesser men as the family myths maintained. Enormous wealth never was. As in England, as in every other country in the world, so it

was in the United States—money and power were always
built by slash-and-burn ruthlessness and, in the case of the
Seymours and other Southerners like them, on the backs of
black slaves.

Tonight, here in her bedroom, she had not once looked
directly at Jewel for fear of seeing that other girl, the child
with a child who was Susan Armistead's new maid, looking
back at her out of Jewel's eyes. Chase had followed her into
the bookstore this morning and pretended surprise at
meeting her, he had deliberately guided her toward that
slave auction, she was sure of it. The selling of men and
women and children was a hideous thing, she despised it,
but it was not her fault. She hadn't invented the system, she
was not accountable for what her family had done, she had
never bought a slave in her life.

In her agitation she began to pace across the room and
back, twisting her hands without knowing it. To save our
souls, Robert had said, he would stand with the North, but
would he have actually betrayed family and friends to do it?
Betrayal was such a terrible thing. But owning people body
and soul was terrible too, a sight she had averted her eyes
from all her life.

We are guilty, I am guilty, she thought. Was what Chase
asked of her monstrous, not to be considered, or could
living a double life with the people she loved best be honorable because it was done for a noble cause? It was an
impossible question and she could not think it through, not
now, not tonight. She would store it away in some far
corner of her mind, go to bed and sleep, and the answer
would no doubt be clear in the morning. Problems that
seemed insurmountable at midnight were often resolved in
the bright light of day.

The next day dawned bright enough but nothing was
resolved. Everywhere she looked as she came down the
stairs to breakfast the house reproached her. The polished
banister she ran her hand along, the walls covered in silk
brocade, the cream-colored woodwork that never collected
soil in its carved niches, the exquisite French furniture
cared for so beautifully, the endless airy rooms upstairs and
down, the flowers that were always fresh, the tables that
never bore a speck of dust, the beds made, clothes washed

and ironed, meals cooked and served, dishes cleaned, silver polished, gardens trim and tranquil—what did such perfection cost to buy, how much human effort did it take to maintain?

The *Courier* was chiefly a forum for the Seymour family's views, not a substantial source of income. It was profits on the crops at their plantation, Pine Hill, that supported their way of life, crops sown, tended, harvested by slaves; all the flawless service given each member of the family every day was performed by slaves.

What about our people? she thought. Elvina, trying so hard to serve breakfast unobtrusively, a pretty, bright girl no more than fifteen or sixteen: where was she born, who were her parents and where are they now, what does she fear, what does she hope for? Dignified, devoted Bella, no children, no man: does she really care for nothing but serving Millie? Cookie out there in the kitchen, always smiling, producing simple meals and masterful company dinners with equal ease, tasting every dish and growing fatter by the day: she could poison us all but instead she feeds us. Joseph, so smooth and efficient, seeing nothing he isn't supposed to see, always smiling when he isn't on his dignity or glaring at Jewel as he is doing now.

And what about Jewel—had she ever found another man to love? What are her hopes for Adam, what does she hope for herself? Who are these people we live with in such intimacy? What in God's name did we think we were doing when we brought them here, what are we going to do now?

She muttered "Excuse me," and left the table, thinking that she would somehow feel better if she got out of the house into the open air where she could breathe.

O NCE AGAIN JEWEL was hunting for Adam. He had eaten supper in the kitchen while she served the family, but when she came out with the last of the plates he was gone.

"Elvina, you seen that boy of mine?"

"I hasn't caught sight of him." Elvina looked over her shoulder, worried. Jewel had immense status in her eyes and she didn't want to displease her.

"I's seen him, I shorely has," Joseph remarked calmly.

"Well, where is he?"

Joseph grinned in the familiar manner he knew would annoy her. "Whut you gonna give me if I tells you?"

He got nothing but a cold stare. Then, because he knew his piece of information would upset her even more he said, "I seen him go into Mr. Edward's office. Far's I know he's still there."

The dining room was empty, the hallway deserted. Jewel knocked firmly at Edward's door. She heard his voice, hesitated only a moment and opened the door. They were poring over a map so big that it hung over the edge of the desk.

"Ah. Jewel. Well, come in. Adam and I are having a geography lesson. He wants to know where our troops are stationed."

"What are you doing here, boy? It's past your bedtime."

Edward laid a hand on Adam's shoulder. "He's learning something, Jewel. That's more important than a little lost sleep."

"He's not supposed to bother you, Mr. Edward, and he knows it. I've told him many a time."

"He doesn't bother me—as I've told you many times." He smiled at Adam. "You're always welcome but you must mind your mother too. Run along now but come back tomorrow evening. Come just a little earlier and we'll finish with Beauregard and go on to Johnston."

Adam nodded, his eyes down, and slid out past his mother as if he expected a lift on the seat of his pants, the kind of swat she had given him when he was little and did something naughty. He almost hoped she would. Better a swat, better a good hard licking than the icy disapproval that was his lot these days.

With the door closed Edward said, "You must not be so hard on him, Jewel. He's a good boy."

"Thank you, sir. He's good but he needs to be strong too. Colored folks have to be strong in this world."

Edward sat down and gazed at her in a speculative way. "Everyone needs to be strong in this world. Do you think a little kindness from me weakens him?"

Her lips set in a stubborn line. "Forgive me, sir, but it could. He won't get special treatment outside this house."

"It's not special treatment to help him learn. Miss Millie and I have talked it over. We've decided to free him when he's eighteen and he needs to be prepared for it. Once he's free he can work for me or not, as he wishes. If not, I'll set him up in a business of his own. Does that please you?"

Sometimes favored slaves were freed and helped to get started; it had happened before in other white families—and everybody in this household loved Adam. But she had never allowed herself even to hope, for fear of disappointment. In a soft, surprised voice she said, "Yes, sir, it surely does." She stood for a moment, looking at the prospect of freedom for her son and not knowing what to do. She said very low, "Thank you," and went out, shutting the door gently behind her.

As soon as he was alone Edward leaned back in his chair, taking time to rest and think before tackling the next verbal missile he intended to launch at his government. The *Courier* was a morning paper and each day's editorial had to be in the printer's hands by eleven the previous night.

This homely book-lined office where he did much of his work had been his father's. The scars on the old desk were the evidence of years of work by his father and his grandfather. Here all the Seymour enterprises had been managed for decades, here he had been summoned as a young boy for minor infractions of the rules—he never committed major infractions. And here Thomas would explain the reasons for the rules, mention his displeasure and his expectation that such behavior would not happen again. It rarely did, for Edward loved his kind, strong, forceful father as much as his father loved him. He was the heir to the dynasty and although it was never quite put into words he knew exactly what was expected of him.

And when the time came years earlier than he expected he put aside his dream of becoming an architect and assumed his father's role, both at home and at the *Courier*. His mother's cousin Esther Clay had offered him a way out—"Let me take the children, Edward . . . your parents would want you to have your chance." It hadn't even been a temptation. They were a family, he and the children, and they would stay together.

The first years were arduous but satisfying. His immediate

task was to convince the men who had worked for Thomas Seymour that Edward was his father's son, a man they could respect. Like so many young men searching for instant maturity he grew a mustache and a short, trim beard as black as his hair. The beard seemed to help, which bore out something his father had once told him. "Appearances are everything, son, outward appearance and a manner of authority can win respect when trueness of heart goes begging." Edward, very young and a little worried by his father's cynicism, had asked earnestly, "But Father, what about honor?" and Thomas had replied, "Ah, honor. That's for us to know inside ourselves. The men I'm speaking of don't care."

The talented, experienced writers and editors who worked for him at the *Courier* came to respect him for his breadth of mind, his lack of arrogance, and his desire to learn. The men of power in the town approved of him too, for his affability and reasoned approach to the most volatile issues of the day, and for the manly way he faced up to his obligations without turning to drink or whoring around. Some few also wondered if all that temperance and self-control might not one day lead to an explosion.

It did not. He became a good writer and in later years began to write many of the *Courier*'s editorials. He struggled for years to find a good overseer for Pine Hill, one who would treat the workers decently and still turn a profit; he never found a man who entirely satisfied him but Pine Hill did make money. He invested with success in several major industries in New York and Pennsylvania and steadily increased the family's wealth as his father would have expected him to do.

He rarely thought of the dreams he once had had—personal freedom of a kind he'd never known, adventures in Europe far from the strictures of the society he had grown up in. And he completely put out of his mind the graceful, powerful buildings he had wanted to build. He didn't think of himself in a self-pitying way but believed he was lucky. An adoring wife, a pretty little daughter, his sister and brothers growing up well, the esteem of men whose opinion he valued—what more could anyone ask?

Yet beneath those satisfactions was an aching emptiness that grew with the years.

He remembered with great clarity the moment he began to love Jewel. For years she had simply been the child who helped them all because she helped Laura, so wounded and so alone. And then—it had happened only a little while after Laura went away to school and Jewel was spending more time serving the family—Kirby told one of his awful seven-year-old's jokes at the dinner table, funny because it was so terrible, and they all laughed. Edward turned away from his little brother to share the moment with Millie, saw Jewel laughing, too, as she set down the platter of roast lamb, and for an instant his breath stopped. Jewel was no longer a child, she was a woman and she was beautiful.

The realization stunned him. After that evening she became the obsession of his life. Her dark oblique eyes smiled in his imagination during sleepless nights, he saw her graceful walk even when she was out of his sight, her humor and her quick mind delighted him, and her body . . .

He stopped going to Milie's bedroom for it was impossible to make love to her; he wanted only Jewel. And that first time he took her—even after all these years the grief, guilt, and joy it brought burned bright in memory. He, who never went to brothels as so many of his friends did, he who had always looked with contempt on men who exercised the *droit du seigneur,* he was sleeping with a black slave—a very young black slave. It had been a terrible thing to do to Millie; she had raised Jewel and loved her almost as a daughter. Now he could admit to himself that it had been a terrible thing to do to Jewel too, for in reality how could she refuse him regardless of the many times he assured her that she could?

He believed she eventually came to care for him in a way. Certainly she loved Adam who looked like a Seymour—or it seemed so to him. His sense of guilt told him that everyone ought to see it but people often were blind to what they didn't want to see. She must have been very upset to march in here this evening, something she rarely did.

He passed his hand across his eyes as if to wipe away his thoughts, folded the huge map, set out paper, pen, and ink and began work, much too late in the evening, on the next day's editorial.

He was less than halfway through when the door opened a crack and Laura peeked in. "If you're too busy I can see you another time."

He leaned back in his worn leather chair, the one he had brought home when it became too shabby for the office. "It's a good time for a break. This isn't going well."

He looks tired, she thought. She sat down in the chair opposite him, wondering how to begin. "What's the editorial about?"

"That fool, Davis. He lives in a dream world."

In spite of the ominous words she almost smiled. Edward could scarcely say Davis's name without adding "that fool." She said, "The day Virginia seceded most people were happy. You weren't happy at all but you said you would stand with Virginia. Why, Edward, when you believe the war is such a terrible mistake?"

He looked surprised. "I told you then. Virginia is home. I can't go against my kin."

"That's the whole reason?"

"Isn't it enough? I would be dishonored if I did."

She considered that and said, "The Old Union used to be almost a religion in our family. It was you who taught me to love it. This argument with the Yankees—isn't it all really a fight over money? Isn't it because we don't want to let our slaves go?"

An expression passed over Edward's face so brief and pain-filled that she wondered if she'd actually seen it. He looked down. "This is home, that's what I care about."

"Thomas Jefferson wrote something that I've never forgotten although I'm not sure what he meant. 'I tremble for my country when I reflect that God is just.' I wonder if this war is what he foresaw, if maybe all our chickens aren't coming home to roost. I wonder"—she hesitated—"why he never freed his slaves." It was as close as she dared come to asking why Edward, who had always said slavery was a huge blunder, had not freed the Seymour family's slaves.

"He wasn't a rich man, Laura. Without slaves he'd have lost Monticello and in a way that place was his life's work. He wouldn't have had the leisure to give all he did to this country. Those may not be the best reasons but they're human reasons. He was a great man but he was human, after all." He pushed at the papers before him in an absent, irritable way and they fluttered to the floor on her side of the desk.

She picked them up and handed them to him. "I guess when all's said and done, human reasons decide everything," she said softly, and kissed him good night.

A T TWELVE-THIRTY, just after the tall clock in the hallway chimed the half hour, Edward left his office. On the second floor he hesitated, looking down the long hall to the narrower stairs that led to the third floor. Up there in a room overlooking the rose garden Jewel slept. More than anything he missed talking, really talking to her as he used to do. She would listen and sometimes laugh, on occasion she would give him her unvarnished opinions. She read the same books he read, she understood his thoughts better than Millie ever had, and when she was in a disputatious mood she would argue with him. She had done so tonight in the kind of subtle confrontation they seldom had these days.

He had not gone up to that third-floor room since Laura came home from Washington. It had begun after she went away to school, it continued during the years of her marriage. Her homecoming helped him end it, as he should have done years ago. Laura did not know; she never would find out if he could prevent it. Millie's pain was a hairshirt that chafed him daily. He could not bear the thought of what would be in Laura's eyes if she found out.

He turned away from those narrow, tempting stairs and went into Millie's bedroom. She was sitting on the edge of the bed examining her fine complexion in a magnifying mirror. She had been cheerful at breakfast and full of gossip at their evening meal.

How does she do it? Edward thought. It's as though yesterday never happened. She didn't deserve to be as unhappy as he made her but he was unable to mend their lives or give her what she wanted. All he knew was that he stood at a crossroads, denied what he wanted most, unsure which direction to go.

And Millie, as always, was unaware. An intelligent woman, at times even witty, her way of dealing with painful reality was to ignore it. She had accepted Edward's proposal knowing why he made the offer and then convinced herself that their marriage was happy and fulfilling. She had gone through every crisis in her life smilingly assuring herself that no problems existed. When once in exasperation Edward remarked that she lived in a world of dreams, she replied, "Why, of course I do, dear. It's always best to look at the beautiful side of life. Things turn out well when you do." She had been pretty as a young woman and she was pretty now, her eyes deep blue, her hair still without a touch of gray. Her figure remained almost girlish—she believed that a woman who kept her looks would keep her husband and devoted herself to that end.

Maybe she's right, Edward thought, maybe it's best to pretend.

CHAPTER 8

ON FRIDAY EVENING, the day before he was to leave town, Chase came to the house. He sat in the small parlor, listening for half an hour while Edward denounced the government's latest blunder, drank two cups of coffee—real coffee was at a premium but still plentiful in the houses of the rich—and then Laura invited him to walk with her in the garden.

Millie waited only a few moments. She tiptoed to the window and moved the draperies just enough to see out. "Edward, come here. Did you ever see a more romantic couple? The way he looks at her! And she can't take her eyes off him."

Edward looked out. They were outlined in the light of a full moon—a man, his head bent, a woman looking up, with a tension between them that was not the product of Millie's imagination. "Yes, Millie, they look romantic. Close the draperies now or they'll see you."

They did see the appearance, then the disappearance of light from the parlor window. She said, "I know no one can hear but let's go on a little farther." She moved down the path to the point where it curved around the lily pond.

It had been a bad week for her, a week of coping with a torrent of emotions, all tricky, all hurtful, and all the fault of this troublesome man whom she wished she'd never heard of. He had torn the blinders from her eyes, forced her to look at things she didn't want to see and then proposed action so stupefying that after days to think it over she was still numb.

At another level she burned with disappointment. He had charmed her, and Valerie or no Valerie she had believed she attracted him too. The truth was so embarrassing that although her answer had been ready for two days, she let him wait and—she hoped—suffer. Regardless of her promise he couldn't be sure she wouldn't talk. But he seemed as much at ease tonight as if he sat safe in Washington instead of in the home of loyal Rebels, only a mile from the house of the man who could order him tried and then hung. It was exasperating, yet somehow admirable.

The faint breeze had died. The thick, oppressive heat of the summer night pressed on them. She sat down on the low brick wall that circled the lily pond and dipped a finger in the murky water. "I found out just this year that waterlilies don't float magically on the surface of the water the way I thought. The gardeners plant them in pots and set the pots on the bottom of the pond so they *look* like they're floating. Imagine, flowers that fool you."

She isn't happy with me, Chase thought. It had been a bad week for him too. He had followed his usual routine—meals in the better restaurants, evenings with friends in luxurious saloons and gambling parlors, and faro for an entire evening in the company of Judah Benjamin—alarmed whenever a friendly hand was clapped on his shoulder, relieved when he went to his hotel room at night and did not find the provost guard there waiting for him. He even met Valerie at a small inn far outside the city, an afternoon that was not entirely successful. Valerie, always quick to detect what directly affected her, sensed she did not have his complete attention and let him know of her displeasure.

Each morning he had woken wondering if he should

leave town that day, tell Washington the task was impossible and demand a combat assignment. The worst they could do was strip him of his rank, send him into the army as a private and put him in the forefront of battle, something the soft-spoken man he worked for was capable of. In battle he could fight and have a chance of surviving. Here if he were caught there was no chance at all. It must be the way civilians felt when trapped in the middle of a war, surrounded and helpless, and he didn't like it. Life was often difficult or downright unpleasant but he had no desire to leave it soon, especially not at the end of a rope because he had bet on Laura Chandler and bet wrong. It had been a grim half hour back there in the house with Millie's coffee and Edward's politics, but the provost marshall, General Winder, had not come for him and he now knew with intense relief that whatever the answer Laura was about to give him he had not bet wrong.

She said, "I've thought about what you said—well, truth to tell, I haven't thought about anything else since that auction you dragged me to. You certainly destroyed my peace of mind."

"I'm sorry I couldn't think of a better way."

She shrugged. "My peace of mind deserves to be destroyed. Growing up in my family it's all been so easy. Our people, our slaves—there, I said it—our slaves have been kindly treated, at least I always believed we were kind. None of us approves of slavery. Even Kirby, who never thinks of anything but hunting and girls, doesn't like it although he needs four or five servants to keep him happy. You'd be surprised how many Southerners wish it would just go away. But what would happen to our way of life if it did? What scares us is having to change. We'll fight a war to prevent it."

"Even if it destroys the nation."

"I know." Her voice was low and troubled. "Have you noticed the portraits in our house?"

"I noticed. Handsome people, interesting faces."

"The man and woman in the parlor are my parents, the four in the dining room are their parents. The portraits in the hall and on the stairway wall are Seymours, Hamptons, Whitneys, Kirklands. They fought alongside Washington

and handed the country on to us, to me. I love the Union.
I always have."

"Then you'll work with me?"

She looked up. "No."

It was so unexpected after all she'd said that he started to
marshall his arguments. She cut him off. "I'd have to live a
lie every moment, pretend and pretend. It would take
strength and nerve—you have it and maybe I do too. I'd
also have to do something you don't. Use my family's love,
cheat them, lie to them, use the friends who trust me.
That's betrayal any way you look at it. Betrayal is what I
can't get past. But"—she smiled—"I wish you good fortune and a safe passage through this thing."

Her smile was marvelous—sweet and honest, and he
wasn't used to honest women. Now it was his duty to use
all his gifts of persuasion to talk her around, but he would
be ashamed.

He said, "You're right, of course," and surprised them
both. He took her hand and kissed it.

IT ASTONISHED HER to discover that she missed him.
Without her noticing he had become a presence in her
life. Now that he was gone she could not think on waking,
"Maybe I'll see Chase today," and be buoyed by the
prospect. There was no reason to try out new hairstyles as
she had recently begun doing, because he would not see
them.

Again and again at odd times, especially at night just
before sleep, her mind turned back to that last moment in
the garden—the warm, humid air of the summer night, the
perfume of roses, the sense of being cut off by the darkness
from the rest of the world, the unexpected, tender kiss.
Hand kissing was a social courtesy and could mean much or
little, depending. This time she wasn't sure what it meant
but she thought of it often.

One thing pleased her. She not only knew who he really
was, as Valerie did not, she knew where he was, something
Valerie didn't know and mourned over frequently. She also
knew that he would certainly come back; she didn't tell
Valerie that either.

A week after he left town another in a series of notes

came from Varina Davis inviting her to lunch at the Spotswood Hotel, and this time she accepted. She wanted to make a change—not become a spy, God in heaven—but do something interesting, different. Lunch with Varina and her ladies wouldn't transform her life but it was a beginning.

The Spotswood was the best hotel in town, built around an inner courtyard with crowded public rooms on the first floor and private rooms above, the temporary home for many government leaders including Jefferson Davis and his wife. That made it for the time being the heart of the Confederacy. Not only did the highest of high society congregate to eat, to gossip, to hear the latest news, but major decisions of government were made there. So far the war news had been good. Only a few scattered engagements had taken place, a battle in West Virginia and another in faraway Missouri. And there'd been a small fight at Big Bethel down on the Virginia peninsula that resulted in a Confederate victory. Everyone was greatly cheered.

Even here at the center of the Confederate government there was little serious talk about the war. Most of what Laura heard over lunch barely rose above the level of tittle-tattle about power fights within the government or social struggles among the women. These women—all old Washington hands—kept up with current gossip and made contemptuous fun of poor, foolish Mary Lincoln, her taste in clothes, her extravagance, her foibles. There was light-hearted fun in everything they did, many parties and dinner-dances and shopping expeditions. Life during a war, they discovered, was exciting.

True, General Beauregard, the hero of Fort Sumter, was up in northern Virginia near the little village of Manassas calling for more reinforcements as Union troop strength facing him grew greater. But everyone knew that those troops had no stomach for a serious invasion. They didn't dare face Southern soldiers in an all-out fight, they were there only to defend Washington. Yankee politicians were scared to death that the Confederate army would capture the city and force senators and congressmen and old Abe Lincoln himself to run for their lives. So far, for the South, war was not terrible at all.

The women were right in thinking that Washington greatly feared invasion, for the city was an enclave completely surrounded by Maryland and Virginia. Maryland, while it had not seceded, was a hotbed of Southern sentiment, and Virginia was enemy territory. So many troops had been pulled in to defend the capital that it had become the main Federal encampment and in early July a small force of Union soldiers had crossed the Potomac into Virginia.

Laura was one of the first to know that Beauregard had demanded even more reinforcements because the word came in to Edward at the *Courier*. That evening she had dinner with the attorney general, Judah Benjamin.

He was a charming, popular man who was never seen without a smile on his face, a lover of good food and fine wines as his rotund body suggested, and by far the most intelligent man in the Confederate government. He had spent many evenings in Laura's Washington home.

She said, "Judah, my brother says there's been skirmishing up around Manassas. Is there a chance of a real battle? With all the talk in the Northern papers about coming right down here to Richmond—"

"Dear lady, we are perfectly safe. General Beauregard has been reinforced and now has twenty-two thousand men under his command. General Johnston has eleven thousand. If the Federals try to move forward we'll drive them out of the state."

Good Lord, Laura thought, Chase was right. How thoughtlessly this clever man dropped critical information about troop strength.

Judah helped himself to more dessert. "We are a resourceful people. In fact, our people are our greatest asset. You are acquainted, I believe, with Colonel Girard?"

"Yes, a delightful gentleman. I understand he's going to try to get supplies for us from Northern factories though how such a thing can be—"

"Ah, there are ways and he will find them. With such men and"—his smile broadened—"the support of ladies like you we cannot lose."

"Do you think the Yankees will attack soon?"

"The President thinks they may not attack at all, poorly

trained as they are. I'm not so sure but in any case it can't happen for several weeks."

When Edward came home for his midday meal the next day, she learned that battle had been joined at Bull Run River near the little town of Manassas. So much, she thought, for Benjamin's predictions.

Leaving her lunch on the table, she ordered the coachman to take her directly to the Spotswood, where any news would be heard first. Edward had said bitterly that the President, unable to keep his fingers out of the pie, had hurried up to Manassas to harass and second-guess the generals. That meant Varina Davis would know the outcome of battle as soon as anyone because Jeff Davis would see to it.

Throughout that hot July afternoon Varina's friends waited upstairs in her room, fanning themselves, stoically suffering tight, high-necked basques and whalebone corsets, occasionally pacing the corridors when inaction became too much to bear.

It could all end today, Laura thought with a surge of hope. If the Federals break through they'll be in Richmond by tomorrow and Doug and Kirby can come home. I don't even know if they're in this battle. Oh, God, let them not be in it!

Others were thinking quite different thoughts. If they lost today, all would be ended—their golden dream of a new nation, their way of life with its comforts and beauty. And what of honor? A Southerner was nothing without honor and if they lost they would be only rebels, outcasts, with everything gone, perhaps even their lives; the brutal, uncivilized Yankees might do terrible things to people they considered traitors.

Judah Benjamin arrived. Inconclusive dispatches had come to the War Office and the attorney general had hurried to the hotel for he, like Laura, realized that Varina Davis would have the first word from the President. He was right. She came into the room, white-faced, holding a telegram. "A great battle has been fought . . . the President says it is a great victory . . ."—they all looked at each other—"but dead and dying cover the field . . ."

Their husbands were safe, Varina assured each of them, but Wade Hampton was wounded and Colonel Johnston was killed as were Colonel Bee and Colonel Bartow. Bartow was leading his men into the hottest part of the fight and died gallantly at the head of his regiment. He and his wife were well liked and Mrs. Bartow was just down the hall. She had to be told. Varina went out into the corridor, pale but composed, to do what must be done. Laura watched her go, despair at the news of the Federals' loss hidden as it must be, her grief for Mrs. Bartow sharp and personal. From down the hall came a low cry and she closed her eyes. Only she, of all the women in this room, knew what it really meant to lose a husband.

She went home that evening to find the house blazing with light, the front door standing open, and the servants gathered in the hall listening to Edward read the latest dispatches. In the parlor Millie sat beside her daughter. Downtown the streets had been filled with cheering, joyous crowds but in this room there was a cold and frightened silence. Paige had come home to wait for news of Alex; he was serving with Colonel Thomas Jackson and Jackson's brigade had been in the thickest part of the battle. That was all they knew. She looked at Laura with dry, desperate eyes, reached out and took her hand.

All during the long evening they sat with her, Millie occasionally stroking her daughter's hair, Laura thinking of her brothers, so hopeful, so young, and of Alex, drunk, announcing to a roomful of diners that the U.S. Army was going to beat the crap out of them. Alex was with Jackson. Kirby and Doug were with Bartow's brigade and Bartow was dead. She hadn't mentioned that to the family. She tried to conquer the fear, push it away, beat it down, and continued to hold Paige's hand.

For the next few days there was euphoria in Richmond. In the first real confrontation between North and South, the Confederacy's valiant soldiers had licked the mighty Yankees, had sent them not just in retreat but running pell-mell back to Washington where their leaders cowered. The South had beaten them, probably once and for all, and soon the Confederate flag would fly over the Federal capital, proclaiming to the world that liberty had triumphed. Church bells rang throughout the city, thanksgiving services were held and Richmond celebrated.

And then the dead and wounded began to pour in. Homes became hospitals filled not with gallant young soldiers in dashing uniforms who complimented the ladies and sang songs around the piano, but bloody, dirty men with terrible wounds who suffered and died before their eyes. For the first time the real cost of war was made plain and criticism of the commanding generals began to mount. Why hadn't Beauregard and Johnston chased after the Yankees when they had them on the run? The South could have occupied Washington by now if the generals had had more gumption. Perhaps, people began to say, it was going to be a longer war than they had thought.

But if the South was dissatisfied with its leadership and shocked by the cost of battle, the North was stunned. Their army had marched out in spanking new uniforms to crush the enemy and they had lost in the most humiliating way possible. Many soldiers had fought bravely but most were new to the army and untrained. Frightened and confused, they had thrown down their rifles and run away, stumbling over congressmen and other civilians and their ladies who had brought picnic baskets and come out to watch what they were sure would be a rout of the foe. Something was fundamentally wrong with both the army and the government and whatever it was had to be corrected quickly or the Rebels would get away with their schemes. Grimly the North settled down to the job of staightening things out and then going after the Confederates again.

L IKE OTHERS IN RICHMOND the Seymours opened their home and desperately wounded men were brought into the house. They lay on cots and pallets in the library, the two parlors, and the beautiful ballroom where such a short time ago Alex and Paige had danced on the night of their wedding. Wounded men were upstairs, too, in guest bedrooms and even the attic. Laura, Millie, and the maids, unskilled and untrained, bathed these strangers who were now their own, fed those who could eat, and spooned laudanum and morphine into the mouths of those whose pain was unendurable. Even Paige, who had looked like a sleepwalker the first day after the battle, attempted to help although she was absentminded and sometimes forgot what item she had been sent to fetch.

Military funerals were beginning to take place and the somber, depressing death march was heard all over the city. Word came that Mrs. Bartow was in a bad way. As her husband's cortege passed by the hotel with his warhorse and empty saddle she had collapsed and still was unable to leave her bed. When Paige was told this the color left her face. She and Laura were standing on the front porch listening to Addie Shaw recount the story of Mrs. Bartow's tragedy, and Laura reached out to her, thinking the girl was going to faint. But she was staring at the front gate, the cords on her neck standing out in sudden strain, and in the next instant she was flying down the steps and into the arms of the filthy soldier hobbling up the path. She turned back to Laura, tears streaming down her face, and called in a triumphant voice, "Alex is home!"

It was a bayonet wound in the thigh and, Dr. Rollins said, not as serious as it might have been. He ordered bed rest for Alex, strengthening food, and—he smiled at Paige—the ministrations of his wife.

A tide of relief rolled through the house on Alex's return. Everyone's step was lighter, everyone was happy for Paige, but it was a tentative, uneasy happiness that was to become familiar in the months ahead. They did not dare be truly happy for the fates of Douglas and Kirby were still unknown. Then, a week after Alex arrived Doug came home. He was dirty, unshaven, hungry, and tired but he was unharmed, sent home with dispatches from General Johnston, and he brought the news that Kirby was ornery as ever and all in one piece. For this time at least the Seymour family had escaped destruction.

AT THE DINNER TABLE one hot August evening Edward remarked casually, "I'll be leaving early tomorrow. I'm going up to Manassas."

"Manassas?" Millie said with dismay. "Why, Edward? It must be a terrible place."

"That's why. I'm a newspaperman. I ought to see what I'm writing about."

"You couldn't pay me to go there," Millie muttered, but

Laura said, "I'd like to go with you, Edward." At his expression she added firmly, "If you don't mind."

"I'm going, too, Papa."

Alex took in the headlong determination in Paige's eyes. "Sweetheart, it's not a good idea."

Edward, thinking that he was probably already licked, said in his most authoritative manner, "No, Paige. Laura shouldn't go but I can't very well forbid her."

"You can't forbid me either. My husband nearly died there. I have every right." Paige gazed at her father, cool but resolute.

Edward and Alex exchanged a look. Edward said, "It's a long trip and we'll have to stop over. Both of you, be ready to leave the house by dawn."

HENRY HILL WAS a small area for such a frenzied fight, high rolling land that must have been lovely once. Decaying horses were the dominant fact of the battlefield and the stench clung to the hair and skin of those who walked over it. Bloody clothing, stray boots, canteens, knapsacks, discarded equipment, wagons burned and broken apart, personal belongings lay strewn everywhere. The red clay earth had been trampled into a muddy morass by men and horses and heavy gun carriages and was now drying under a burning August sun. Bull Run itself was a narrow, peaceful stream, its banks covered with tangled vines and brush. Overhanging trees reflected in the water. It was said that this small pleasant stream had run red with blood.

Some distance away a few people were poking in the rubble or simply standing and staring. The only sound was the faint rustle of a breeze moving through the remains of once-beautiful pines now mangled by canister and grape. In the eerie silence Laura imagined she could hear shouting and the shrieks of horses, the quick rattle of rifles and the incessant roar of artillery, and then the moans of wounded men and the terrible silence of the dead that spoke as loud as any scream. Before he died a young soldier she had nursed in Richmond muttered of the deafening gunfire, the acrid powder smoke rolling like thick fog, his fear at the sight of the charging enemy—vivid, graphic words she wanted to forget and could not.

This was madness, she thought. There were mounded graves everywhere, some of them very large mounds, but whether they were mass graves she was afraid to ask. The summer flowers and new green grass already springing up seemed not hopeful but deeply sad. Life was renewing itself but only with grass and flowers; for the broken men under those mounds life was not renewed. She stumbled over a cannonball and in falling found under her hand a small book, muddy, damp, bloodstained, a journal kept by some luckless man. Inside was a folded sheet of paper addressed to Lucy—a letter someone's wife or sweetheart would never read. Carefully she refolded it along the exact crease and slipped the book into the deep pocket of her skirt.

Edward and Paige were walking back toward her, moving slowly over the uneven ground. Paige's face was strained and Edward . . . On Edward's face was a look Laura had never seen before. When she felt calmer, when she was home and time had passed and the pain of today had diminished a little, she would take that look out and examine it and determine what it meant.

The trip home was arduous, the road rutted and scarred by the passage of many military vehicles. Twice the carriage axle broke and the makeshift repairs forced the horses to a walk. During the trip Laura decided she did not want to read the journal that was now hidden in the bottom of her bag, it was meant for Lucy, not her. But as soon as she was home and behind the locked door of her bedroom she took it out and read the name inscribed on the inside cover: Jesse Ashford, Captain U.S. Army. That was all. No regiment, no address, no hometown, no way to find out where he had lived and send his thoughts home to those who loved him. With only a slight hesitation she unfolded the letter written on a sheet torn from the journal and began to read.

Lucy, my dear one,

We move out tomorrow and are very busy but I must snatch a few moments to write you my thoughts. I regret more than I can say our last words on parting. We were both tired and anxious. I did not mean what I said and I know quite well that you didn't either. It preys on my mind that if I should die in this battle that is coming you would reproach yourself. For my sake you must not. I know you love me and I know how much. You have been at my side through all the years and lived the hard life of a soldier's wife without complaint. I hope this letter is unnecessary and I can tell you myself, but it may not be. Southerners take well to the military and are good men in a fight. No battle with them will ever be easy. We have worked hard with our recruits but the time has been too short to train them well. I can only hope the Rebels are as unready. Kiss the children once more for me and tell them I love them. How I wish

That was all. A hasty, heartfelt letter from a devoted husband to a loyal wife, a loving attempt to ease grief and guilt, filled with fear well controlled. A career officer probably, interrupted and unable to finish as true a love letter as ever was written. She put the letter into the book and closed it, then sat for a while with it in her hand, not looking at it.

Another time she would search through it for some clue that would help her send it home to Lucy Ashford. But not tonight. She would read no more tonight.

CHAPTER 9

PHILADELPHIA HAD CHANGED in the four years Chase had been away. Horse-drawn trolleys on rails now rattled down the cobbled streets, a great new park was in the planning stage, and since war had come, the peaceful tree-lined streets pulsed with energy. A welcome prosperity had descended on the city. The many arms and ordnance factories were already raking in profits and the naval yard was working around the clock, bringing smiles to the faces of merchants who fed and clothed the new workers that poured into town. So far, Philadelphia decided, war was a good investment. However, war also brought a dilemma no one had expected to face. This Northern city, the cradle of the nation, was pro-Southern.

Close ties to the South went back to colonial times and many Philadelphians believed slavery was a fine idea. No one wanted to fight a war to end it. There were already too many blacks in the city, everyone agreed—more than in New York where anti-Negro feeling was venomous, more than in most cities in the country—and over the years there had been several bloody race riots. If slavery was abolished Negroes would come pouring in, competing with white men for jobs and causing more trouble. The tiny group of abolitionists in the city was considered a menace.

The blacks already present were hard to ignore. They seemed to be everywhere, clustering in ramshackle housing in the center of the city, within walking distance of the great mansions they worked in. White theaters, churches, concert halls, and libraries would not admit them and they could not ride the trolleys although there was some talk about providing separate cars for "coloreds." It was essential, whites believed, that blacks be kept separate in every area of life for that was the only way to deal with a people so different.

So when white Philadelphians were faced with a war that could bring emancipation, they hesitated. War was an expensive and dangerous enterprise at best and a war against their own interests would be folly. Yet they loved the idea of liberty for here in their city it had come to fruition. Here, at great risk, the ringing words of the Declaration had been read out and signed, here the flag had been made, here the Constitution, the soul of the nation, had been painfully worked out and agreed to. For this they were willing to fight, and if many thousands of Negroes were freed in the process, well, they would deal with that when they had to.

Nowhere was the bitter choice more evident than in the Girard family. For Chase this homecoming was on the surface the best in many years. His parents were happy, believing his story that he had come to his senses at last, was out of the army and engaged in a business enterprise that could not help but be lucrative in wartime. It pained him to see the disillusion in his younger brother's eyes but he dared not tell Richard the truth. He could not tell anyone.

And Richard, who had always revered his brother, manfully swallowed his doubts and pretended to believe that in leaving the army at a time of danger to the nation Chase had done the right thing. There had already been sharp words between Richard and his parents over the war and he was determined that nothing should spoil this family dinner; it might, after all, be the last time they would all be together. So when his mother spoke up on the tender subject he kept silent.

Isabel Girard was a woman of some compassion, generous toward her servants and without any desire to own slaves herself. But close family was involved and her Charleston cousins were dear to her.

"Jane and Melva are the sweetest women in the world. I've never seen unkindness from either of them. Southerners only want the freedom to live in their own style and I strongly believe they should be allowed to do so." Isabel's comments were directed at everyone at the table but her eyes were on Richard. He was passionately pro-Union and she feared he might lose his mind and join the army just when she no longer had to worry about her older son. Her husband, William, said Richard was much too sensible but Isabel was not so sure.

William Girard cleared his throat. He always did that before making a pronouncement and everyone waited deferentially. He was a banker whose financial ties to the South were important to his business and for him business was all—or almost all. In his own way he loved the Union as much as Laura Chandler did and for similar reasons. His ancestors, too, had helped found the country and he believed in the Constitution as he believed in God.

"The Union," he said, and paused. "It is a grand thing and I love it dearly but I want the Union my forefathers handed down to me, a nation meant for the white race. Freedom for the Negroes, yes, eventually, but *not* equality."

He glanced around the table. His sons were politely atten-
tive. His daughter-in-law, Audra, looked as if she had swallowed a chicken bone and was trying to keep from
coughing rudely. He went on. "Never forget how close we
are to the border. Free Negroes pouring in can swamp this
state and we'll have that dog, Lincoln, to thank for it. If the
South wins we'll be stronger for it and go on as we always
have."

It was too much for Audra. She loved her husband and
tried not to offend his parents but she was an intense
young woman from an abolitionist Boston family and had
learned social concern at her mother's knee. Her in-laws
did not know that she attended meetings of the Pennsylvania Anti-Slavery Society, a radical group whose leadership included two Negroes, but her Unitarian conscience
had often startled them.

"I can't agree," she said with flat certitude. "Freedom is
freedom and if it is withheld from one group of human
beings it diminishes freedom for everyone. Masters are
harmed as much as slaves. They are involved in something
so immoral that it destroys them."

When she could speak Isabel said in a tightly controlled
voice, "My cousins and their husbands are the most moral
of people and their servants love them. You should not talk
of things you know nothing about, dear."

"I do know about them, ma'am. I've talked to escaped
slaves and they have told me their stories. No doubt kindly
masters do exist but that isn't the point. Slaves are still
slaves and can be bought and sold, beaten at the whim of
the master, used in any way"—she looked around the
table—"*any way* the master chooses."

There was dead silence. Everyone knew exactly what she
meant. Stories were always circulating about white masters
using their female slaves for sexual purposes, so shocking an
accusation and so impossible to discuss in mixed company
that it was referred to, if at all, only obliquely. People who
were pro-Southern vigorously denied it as an insult to high-
minded Southern gentlemen, but who could ignore the
many light-skinned, even blue-eyed Negroes? What other
explanation could there be than the obvious one?

Isabel and William, speechless with outrage, glared

across their dining table at the shameless, disrespectful younger generation, Audra red-faced but defiant, Richard looking as if he wished himself anywhere else but determined to back up his wife.

Chase reflected that this little scene would be interesting to watch if the family involved were not his own. Such scenes were taking place all over the country between family members who did not want to hurt each other but could not help it. In Richmond he had witnessed an explosion so violent between a Confederate army officer and his son that they almost came to blows; it had ended with the son storming off to join the Union Army.

Isabel was gathering herself for a counterattack, and to draw fire away from Audra, Chase said mildly, "There may be something in what Audra says. I'm acquainted with a Southern lady whose family has owned slaves for generations. Only recently she told me slavery is a great evil which must end. She believes we will all suffer if it doesn't."

Isabel, not wanting to quarrel with the son who at the moment pleased her most, bit back a sharp retort but Audra refused to let the matter rest. With serene conviction she remarked, "That shows all Southerners are not uncivilized."

The evening ended with cool goodbyes and promises to meet again at some unspecified time, but before Richard left he asked Chase to meet him for lunch the next day.

In the morning, armed with a letter of introduction from his father, Chase went to the office of Henry Graham, a man with great influence and social prestige, the descendant of a signer of the Declaration of Independence, and at the present time a United States congressman. At the end of an hour's conference in the hushed, elegant office, Mr. Graham agreed to commit treason. He would accept a consignment of uniforms and rifles Chase had arranged for and send them South in one of his shipping company's vessels.

"There'll be no difficulty running the guns into a Southern port because," Mr. Graham chuckled, "the blockade is notoriously ineffective."

Chase shook the man's hand, joined him in a drink to seal the bargain, and after a few more moments of pleasant conversation, went out into the busy city street.

He had believed that by now he was unshockable but Mr. Graham's cheerful treason was staggering. It was a shipment sent for the purpose of establishing Chase as an agent whom the Confederate government could rely on, and it would get past the blockade because U.S. Navy gunships would allow it through. But Henry Graham didn't know that. Contrary to his oath of office, the oath every military and civilian officer took, to support and defend the Constitution of the United States, Congressman Graham intended to give all the aid and comfort to the enemy he could manage. Walking away from Graham's office, Chase wondered how much active treason there was in this City of Brotherly Love.

Yet Philadelphia gave the appearance of a devoutly Union city. The Stars and Stripes flew from every public building and uniformed men swarmed through the town— soldiers heading South to defend Washington, new recruits who had patriotically volunteered after the defeat at Bull Run, sailors off ships in drydock at the navy yard. Girard's Bank had been faithfully flying the flag since Fort Sumter, and when Chase walked in at midday Richard was at a desk piled high with papers, hard at work, wearing a remote expression that had kept underlings from disturbing him all morning.

He looked up and a smile transformed his face. "Is it noon already? What do you say we go to that seafood place over on the wharf?"

The seafood place was a tradition for them. Sunlight slanted cheerfully through tall windows and outside river traffic bustled past and seabirds swooped low over the water.

Richard ate chowder and talked of family and friends and wondered what had happened to his brother in the years since he had seen him. When Chase came home the last time, resplendent in the dress uniform of the United States Army—brass buttons gleaming, epaulettes and sash gold-fringed, saber at his side, proudly wearing his new major's leaves—he had been to Richard the flawless example of all that a man should be. And now there he sat in a business suit looking like a banker, like their father. How could he leave the army at this of all times, when the nation's very life was at stake, when the chance for honor and glory had never been so great?

Chase had always been an ideal older brother who protected and challenged the admiring boy who followed him everywhere. Barely into his teens, Richard had seen him go off to the military academy against his father's wishes, risking disapproval in a way that won Richard's awed respect, and come home in his uniform to proud, forgiving parents. That uniform had intrigued and dazzled Richard, but instead of following Chase into the military he married young, went to work in the bank as his father wanted, and over the years read the letters Chase wrote from exotic places like Mexico and Arizona and California.

Often, in the secret places of his heart, Richard wondered if he had been a fool. Life was short and precious and he had never engaged in an adventurous or foolhardy act. He had trudged through the university and gotten his degree, he went to the bank every day and home to his wife and children every night, and he wondered . . . What would it be like to ride across open plains at a full gallop, never knowing if hostile Indians were over the next ridge, to travel through country that only a few white men had ever crossed, to stand on a cliff and gaze at the great rolling Pacific and know that on the far side was China, to see cities like Washington, the center of power, and New Orleans where, they said, the women were astonishing.

Richard thought about women a good part of the time. In all his life he had never been with anyone but Audra. She was pretty and charming, with a wide-ranging mind, and he loved her devotedly, but he did sometimes wonder what another girl, any other girl, would be like.

"Chase, how does it feel to be utterly free?"

Chase looked at him with a frown, not liking the direction of that remark. "Why ask me? I've been in the army for fifteen years. That means I've been in prison."

"But you've seen so much, you've been everywhere."

"Prison, Richard. They owned me. They could send me anywhere, anytime, to do anything. I haven't called my soul my own since I was a boy."

"What about the women? The Mexican girls and those

Creole women in New Orleans? And the Indian squaws . . .
are they different?"

Chase looked up, amusement in his eyes. "My life isn't
as exciting as you think. Now and then I come across a girl
I like. I met one recently—a gorgeous woman, charming, a
little vain, very blond."

"Blond," Richard murmured, contemplating the picture
Chase painted.

"And married. I don't know how long it can last."

Richard's smile sparkled suddenly. "Maybe she'll run
away with you."

"Maybe. As far as exotic experiences are concerned, the
army charges a high price to teach you about foreign lands
and customs."

"It's not that I don't love Audra . . ."

"I know. You think you've missed something. But what
do I have? No wife, no children, no home, and I probably
never will."

"What about the Southern lady you mentioned last
night who disapproves of slavery? Do you like her?"

"Yes. She's remarkable."

"Pretty?"

Chase thought of Laura and smiled. "She's a widow.
Old and fat but I admire her mind."

Richard took a breath. "I have some news. I've
joined up."

Chase set down his coffee, realizing that he had been
expecting this. Richard was thirty, old enough to know
better, but he didn't. Most men didn't until they were in
the army and into battle and then it was too late. He said,
"How long are you signed up for?"

"Three years, though I figure the war will be over long
before then. This is only temporary. I don't mean to make
a career of it."

"How does Audra feel?"

"Well, she's a little worried, of course, but proud. She
says it's what every honorable man must do . . . oh, but I
don't mean . . ."

"I know you don't."

"Chase, honestly, I don't think less of you. I understand
better now how you feel. You were at Buena Vista, you've

fought your war and put in your time. What you do now is nobody's business but yours."

"Come," said Chase. "Let's get out of here."

They walked back to the bank and said goodbye. Coming out were three army officers, one of them a friend Chase had served with in the Mexican War with a major's leaves on his shoulders. The man looked at him, then past him, and Chase said, "John? How are you?"

The man stopped but gazed at him with cold eyes. "Well, Chase. What are you doing here? I heard you'd gone South."

"I'm in town on business. Let me introduce my brother. Richard, this is John Bartlett—Major Bartlett, now. Congratulations, John."

John Bartlett did not reply. He nodded briefly at Richard and walked on without introducing his friends or saying anything more. It was discourtesy all the more insulting because there was no anger in it, only disdain.

Richard looked after the man, astonished. "What was that all about? What did he mean, you'd gone South?"

"No telling. The army's a rumor mill as you'll find out."

"I ought to—"

"Forget it, Richard."

Slowly Richard's flush faded. He invited Chase into his office but Chase said he had to catch the three o'clock train to New York. Richard hesitated, looked down at his feet, said, "Well—goodbye." Then, in spite of the people hurrying past, they embraced, two grown men who had loved each other since childhood, knowing they might never see each other again.

After they parted Chase walked over to the waterfront and stood for a long time gazing out at the traffic on the Delaware River—navy ships, merchant ships, ocean-going vessels of all kinds coming upriver from Delaware Bay or heading out to sea again. His train left at five, not three o'clock, but he feared that with a few more minutes in his brother's company he would have told him everything. The contempt in John Bartlett's eyes had been nothing compared to the questions and the pain in Richard's.

When he had been asked to fight in a secret war he had known it would be dirty but, he had thought, no dirtier than murdering men in battle simply because they happened to be born in a different country. He had not expected the personal cost to him and those he loved. He had lost Richard's respect, whatever Richard said to the contrary, and he had used his father's trust and his connections. William had no idea what his real business with Henry Graham had been this morning.

He was lying to everyone he cared for, yet in the beginning it had seemed the right thing, the only thing he could do. He had been distanced from his family and his home for a long time; the army for all its shortcomings had provided comradeship and the respect of other men that came from sharing the same problems and dangers. Now there was neither comradeship nor respect. He faced the enemy alone, an outsider without one friend he could talk to honestly.

And so, why do it? The answer had been clear to him since the moment he accepted the job. He had advanced in the army faster than other capable officers because he had the gift of making people like him, but behind the charm he was a discontented man unable to attach himself to one woman, one place, or anything else that mattered. In the defense of the Union he had at last found something that gave meaning to his life, a cause that, if it came to it, might be worth dying for.

CHAPTER 10

AS SUMMER WORE ON the heat became crushing in Richmond, but it was the same every summer, wet, sultry, oppressive, and Southerners understood it. They moved more slowly and did nothing that was not essential. The wealthy with business to conduct did it early and then retreated behind the drawn curtains of their large homes, ate light midday meals, and rested through the long, slow afternoons. Those who had to work in offices or stores sweltered all day at their jobs and chose the shadiest streets to walk along. Outdoor laborers drank copious amounts of water and endured as best they could. Toward nightfall the city cooled.

On an evening in early September when people were trying to imagine that the temperature was dropping a little, Millie decided to have a party. The last of the wounded soldiers had recovered or been moved to Byron Rollins's new hospital and it was now possible to have a few old friends over for dinner, to talk, to laugh, to forget for a while that there was such a thing as war. She gave orders to Joseph and a menu to Cookie, cut flowers and arranged them in the morning and spent the afternoon resting.

Laura, too, retreated to her bedroom, but not to rest. Instead, she took off her dress and loosened her stays, and in chemise and petticoats sat down in a chair by the window and began to read Jesse Ashford's journal. It turned out to be not a daily diary of events but another self Jesse talked to when he was troubled or simply reflective.

She had scanned part of it when she first came home from Manassas, reading quickly, a little nervously, fearful that by intruding on the man's thoughts she might stumble onto something too intimate to be read by a stranger, hoping for some clue that would tell her where his home was and where his wife might be reached. She had found no mention of a town or even a state. Today she read it through slowly and carefully and as the afternoon passed the man Jesse Ashford had been became clear.

He was a Union Army officer, a reading man who liked William Blake and sometimes quoted him; he was a loving man who cared deeply for his wife and their two sons; he was of a logical turn of mind with a strong sense of duty; he was religious enough to believe that God had a plan for him. And he was a Southerner. As she read she felt not an intruder but a friend listening to ideas he would have spoken if he had known her.

"Today another letter from Father, more bitter than the last. I must come home, he says, or I am a traitor. I have explained the oath I took and my obligation to the United States but it falls on deaf ears." There was a recounting of a disastrous visit to his parents' home ending with: "They caught Marcus today. Four nights, three days he had been gone but the dogs found him in the swamp. They whipped him, a bad beating, and there was nothing I could do to stop it. I watched every blow. It would have been cowardly to turn away. I took a salve to him tonight and talked about the old days and the fishing on the river but he wouldn't look at me. I can't blame him."

Later on, another entry: "What will Lucy do if I die? I don't want her and the boys living with Father, though he would doubtless take them in. More than anything in life I want to be with her, with them, and I fear it will not be. Oh, how I fear. Every experienced soldier I know fears greatly."

And finally, the last entry: "Father writes to say that Maynard and Daniel are now with Beauregard and I must resign immediately and join them. If I do not, he says, I will be fighting for the country that kills them and it will be as if I fired the bullets. I have had the same thought myself and it gives me pause. Am I doing right or am I betraying my own? After much searching of mind and heart I have come to this conclusion. There is no easy way for any of us. If by some miracle I could stay out of it and avoid a choice I would be the worst of cowards, dodging and hiding while braver men take their stand on one side or the other. My brothers have made their choice. I must make my own. How I wish it could be otherwise."

It was the first time Laura had read that passage. The word "coward" leaped at her and she sat for a long time, struck to the heart.

Jewel tapped on the door and when she got no answer opened it and peered in. "You planning to go down to dinner, by any chance?"

Laura jumped up in a quick guilty way and tucked Jesse's journal back in the drawer. "I don't know where the time went to! Come on in and help me get myself together."

She seldom attended Millie's dinner parties but tonight the only guests were Ellen and John Mercer, a congenial, sociable couple, and thin, nervous Grace Weston and her husband, Lowell. Lowell Weston was an ambitious, ill-tempered blowhard in Laura's opinion but one she could usually ignore. On this night he made it impossible.

"If I didn't hate the North for so many other reasons,"

he said, taking over the dinner-table conversation, "I'd hate them for their self-righteousness, those sanctimonious hypocrites. Emerson, Greeley . . ."

"That Stowe woman," Grace put in with languid distaste.

"Yes, her. What do any of them know about slavery? We know it, we live with it, and I tell you it has to go—they're right about that. I can't afford it any longer. Every dime I make out of my plantation goes back to support it. Those Africans don't earn their keep. I feed, clothe, and doctor them and then *I* am accused of inhumanity! How would those squeamish New Englanders like to come down here and live with a raft of lazy, slovenly children? They'd find it damned unpleasant, by God. I don't know why we keep on with it!"

Laura leaned forward a little and looked down the table. "Why do you, then?"

Lowell, wrapped up in his own words, seemed more surprised than irritated. "That was purely rhetorical, my dear. We all know why. Better they were never brought here but here they are. Someone has to take care of them and we are elected. I inherited my people as you did, Edward. I didn't choose this burden but I can't abandon them. They're quite helpless."

"Indeed I've tried to teach them," said Grace in her faded, elegant drawl. "They like the Bible stories and usually can learn the Commandments. I tell them that God loves them just as much as He does us—that before Him they are *entirely white*—and that comforts them. I've even taught several to read a little but they soon lose interest."

Lowell gave his wife's hand a pat. "Grace has the patience of a saint but how many of us do? I confess I'm peevish with them at times."

Laura glanced at Joseph, working at the long sideboard. He had opened another wine bottle and was filling each glass with his usual flourish, his face completely blank. Was the mind behind the dark, impassive face filled with hate or quite disinterested? What was Jewel thinking, so pretty, so graceful, blandly serving the third course? You wouldn't know a war was going on that might remotely affect them in some way. Hallie, Valerie's maid, was violently patriotic, waved her little Confederate flag when the soldiers paraded through town, called them "our boys," and wept tears of joy when word of the Manassas victory came in. Elvina, the kitchen maid, feared the wicked Yankees and ran through the house shouting "Glory be!" when the news arrived.

They are like us, Laura thought, seeing the world in their own individual ways and dealing with it as best they can. Like us.

After the guests left, after the house was quiet and Millie had gone to bed, Laura went to Edward's door. His bedroom, in contrast with the rest of the house, was defiantly shabby, decorated in what she had once called "early Edward." His bed, the table, chairs, even the rug had all been in his boyhood bedroom. And his desk, now covered with papers—did he sometimes sit there writing his innermost thoughts in a journal, like Jesse Ashford? Would she want to read them if he had?

She had not been in this room since before she went away to school, but in the old days she and Edward often sat here late at night in these big chairs, just the two of them, drinking hot chocolate and talking about anything that was on their minds. Or at least, what was on her mind. Edward always listened more than he talked.

She told herself there was no reason to be nervous, but she was nervous. It was such an explosive subject, almost impossible to discuss with anyone these days unless you knew exactly where that person stood. He was not only her older brother, he was almost her father, the man who had held their little family together regardless of personal cost, loved and sustained her through childhood, guided her toward womanhood with a steady hand, but no straightforward, honest talk on this slippery subject had ever taken place between them. How could she look into his quiet eyes and challenge the system he had accepted and based his life on? How could she even hint that he might be wrong?

"Edward"—oh, this was hard—"I've never talked with you about handling my inheritance . . ."

"I have your portfolio here." He started to rise, to go to his desk, and she said quickly, "No, no. You've done a wonderful job. I'm very pleased, Robert would be pleased.

It's not the money I want to talk about, it's . . . other assets."

He sat down, puzzled.

"At least, I think of them as my assets although techni-cally . . ." She took a breath. "Jewel was given to me for my fifth birthday and even though you hold the papers I con-sider her mine. If I understand the law correctly any child of hers is mine too. Edward, I want you to manumit Jewel and Adam."

He stared at her. "That's the last thing in the world I expected you to say."

He looked so astonished, so completely taken aback. She should never have thrown a bombshell in his lap like that without first preparing the way. She should have presented facts, logic, led up to what she specifically wanted slowly. She started to speak and he asked suddenly, "Do you mean now? Tomorrow?"

She jumped at the opening he gave her. "Why not tomorrow? I should have done it years ago. You heard what Lowell Weston called our people—lazy, slovenly children who have to be taken care of. Does that describe Jewel? She's bright, capable, she's as well educated as I am. Adam is still a child but he's her child. He should be with her, they should both be as free to live their lives as we are."

He listened with a frown of concentration and when she was finished said, "Well, suppose we gave her her papers tomorrow and told her that she's free to walk out of this house, take Adam and go anywhere she wants, do anything she wants. Where would she find shelter, how would she earn a living?"

"She can sew, she's a good cook."

"She is indeed, but who would hire her and pay a decent wage when they have slaves to do the job?"

"Well, she could . . . she could be a tutor, teach children just like Dr. Russell taught me."

"Dr. Russell was a Princeton graduate, a doctor of phi-losophy. How many families would hire a freed slave to educate their children? I don't know of any. Free Negroes have a difficult time of it, Laura. Most get only menial jobs and live hand-to-mouth. Believe me, the world outside these walls is a hard, hustling place—there's no quarter given ever, not for anyone. Especially not a black woman with a child to support." He stopped and the soft hooting of the owl who liked to perch in the chestnut tree near the stable was the only sound in the room.

She said, "Not too long ago I saw something I'd never seen before. I went to Tim O'Halloran's to look for a book and down the street a little way a crowd had gathered . . ."

Edward sat forward. He knew that part of town.

She ploughed on. "I went into this place—"

"Alone? You shouldn't have done that."

"People I knew were there. I went in and saw things I didn't know existed in this world, but I should have known." She raised her eyes to his. "I felt filthy."

"I saw an auction once with Father. I was fifteen. He didn't buy that day. He said he'd never bought a slave at auction and advised me to buy only from friends. Since he died I've bought two, Joseph from Dr. Miller, and Elvina as a favor to Mrs. Gibbes. She needed the money." Laura started to speak and he made a little gesture of the hand. "One thing more. I've promised to free Adam on his eighteenth birthday. We'll hire him to work for us or help him start a business if that's what he wants."

"Jewel knows?"

He smiled. "She was pleased, I think."

"She never said a word to me."

"I should have told you. But I knew you'd approve."

"Yes—yes, of course I approve. But why wait? What about Jewel? It's wrong to keep her a slave. It's *wrong*, Edward."

He looked down, his face unreadable. "I know. She never should have been a slave but she has been all her life, it's all she knows. If we freed her now she'd be adrift in a country at war. If we wait—the war will be over before long. When things settle down, when we've established our new nation on a sound basis, then we'll release her and she can do as she wishes."

Gently, Laura said, "Let's be more definite than that. We'll free Jewel when Adam is eighteen. Not a day later, whether things have settled down or not."

Edward looked into her eyes and understood her clearly. He said, "As you wish, of course."

This was the moment to say good night and leave. She had pressed him as far as she dared, they had both made concessions and come to an agreement that really pleased neither of them. Which was, she supposed, the definition of compromise. But she couldn't go to bed and sleep well tonight without asking one more question.

"You said 'when we've established our new nation.' Didn't you once believe the war would be long and the Confederacy might lose in the end?"

"I did at first. They're rich up North, they've got an industrial base we don't have and a powerful navy—we don't have that either. But to win they have to come after us on our home ground and destroy us completely. I don't think they can do it. We have shorter supply lines and we know our territory—the roads, the woods, the rivers. It's always easier to defend than attack. You have to have three times as many men for an assault." Edward smiled in self-derision. "You see what an expert I've become since I started studying tactics. If you read the newspapers in from London and Paris, you'll see that the best military minds in Europe agree with me. No one thinks the North can conquer us. Remember this, we are fighting for our homes and our freedom. The Yankees can't match us because they aren't fighting for what they love."

"They're fighting for the Union," Laura said in a low voice. "Edward, every day I look at the faces of those people on our walls, the ones who helped set up this nation, and I wonder what they'd think of us now. Would they approve or would they consider us traitors the way the Yankees do?"

"They would approve. They did the same thing—broke away from an oppressive government for the sake of liberty. We've started another American Revolution."

I N HER OWN BEDROOM, by the light of her bedside lamp, she read again the words of Jesse Ashford that had moved her so.

If by some miracle I could stay on the sidelines and avoid a choice I would be the worst of cowards . . . My brothers have made their choice. I must make my own.

Strange how words written on paper by a man who in all

likelihood was now dead could speak to you mind to mind, soul to soul, and change your life. Unlike Jesse Ashford and Chase Girard, unlike all the men on both sides, she could stay safely out of it and avoid a choice. Because she was a woman she could sit here in Richmond doing nothing to aid the Southern cause but nothing against it either.

That was the easy way, the coward's way, and in the deepest part of her mind she had known it on the night she refused Chase's proposition. Jesse Ashford forced her to acknowledge what she had known all along. Her brothers, all three of them, had chosen their path according to their own sense of duty. Her beliefs were different from theirs and she had to choose her path too. Edward claimed the Confederacy was fighting for freedom. But how could she believe that when she and he together could control how other human beings lived their lives? Mind and soul, she believed in the Union. It was the best hope ordinary people, white and black, had ever had for real control over their lives. That made it worth fighting for.

Chase said she could make a difference. If that were true her own sense of duty and honor required that she try, and she would do it with the only weapons a woman had: looks and charm, and the intelligence God gave her.

E ARLY THE NEXT MORNING she told Joseph to bring down from the attic the trunks she had brought home from Washington. Alone, she opened them and took out dress after dress—costumes that summed up her life as it once had been: shopping, teas, receptions, dinners, one elaborate gown ordered for a White House ball she had not attended. She sat down and stared at the piles of lace, muslin, taffeta, velvet on her bed. Moiré, why had she chosen so much moiré when she didn't even like it? Why in God's name had she ever thought she needed so many clothes? Well, they were a treasure now. Along with every other luxury and necessity cloth of all kinds was scarce and already Southern women were learning to make do and make over. These dresses were not so old or out-of-date that a change of neckline or sleeve would not rescue them.

From the top of the pile she took the glistening, paper-thin taffeta with the huge skirt, a deep blue taffeta that brought out chestnut lights in her dark hair and reflected in her eyes. She had worn it only once, to an inaugural reception at the White House. The woman she had been on that long-ago night was the one who made Washington believe she was a paragon of charm and allure. If that woman could mislead those worldly sophisticates she could fool Richmond in more fateful matters. It was essential if she was to accomplish what Laura had decided she must.

Just before dusk Addie Shaw arrived and together they examined every dress and agreed on what changes should be made. Neither of them remarked on what Addie's assignment meant but when she left Laura swore her to secrecy, thus assuring that the word would be out immediately—Laura Chandler was reentering society.

CHAPTER 11

IN SPITE OF wartime shortages, lavish parties continued. Exotic food and fine liquors could still be obtained by those who had the cash and Richmond was a city of great wealth.

Hostesses, thrilled that Mrs. Chandler was now available as a guest, sent invitations to musicales, dinner parties, and on one occasion a ball. Laura accepted them all. A few eyebrows rose over the fact that she had come out of deep mourning so suddenly, but most women felt that life had changed, speeded up, and there was no longer time for such niceties as half-mourning. The men thought it was fine too. Slow, stately courtships were out of fashion. The times were fast and romantic, the girls swept away by the glamour of young men in uniform, the men, fearful that life would end for them before it began, ready to jump into marriage without thought. It was not uncommon for a man and woman who knew nothing about each other but their names and outward appearance to fall in love and marry in three weeks.

Soldiers in town on short leaves immediately looked for pretty women to court. A number of young officers, hoping to impress Laura, came to dinners at the Seymours' house and stayed for amateur theatricals or singing around the piano. They soon realized that the lady wasn't interested in lowly captains or lieutenants. She favored higher-ranking military men and politicians who held important posts in the government.

Millie tried to discuss it. "She's just a different girl, Edward. She's gone all shiny and vivacious. *Edward*. What do you make of it?"

From behind his newspaper Edward said, "Yes, she looks lovely," but Millie knew he wasn't really listening. These days he seemed farther away than he had ever been, struggling with the decision she feared most. She pushed the bad thought out of her mind and put in its place the recent sudden change in Laura. When the aggravating girl finally came out of mourning she'd done it with a vengeance. Colonel Girard seemed to be completely out of the running—regrettable because he was such an obliging, attractive man—but it was his own fault for being gone so long. As Edward had predicted Laura was going to settle only for a man of substance.

Her most persistent caller was General Matthias Riley, a forceful, supremely confident man respected by other men for his physical strength, his athletic ability, his valiant charge in support of Jackson at Manassas that had helped bring victory and won him his stars.

His present rank pleased but did not surprise him. From his days as a humble Academy plebe he had planned to be a general, to rise to the top, to be the best at anything he did. He wasn't going to be like his father, poor and obscure all his life. Albert Riley still lived in the little Kentucky town where Matt had grown to manhood, still believed and lived every word of his worn Bible, still served as pastor of his tiny church. Reverend Al, his parishioners called him, a good man, a father Matt loved dearly, but it had been his mother's brother, the congressman, who handed him his chance. Uncle Nathan, who had connections, had gotten him the appointment to West Point.

Because of that stroke of good fortune Matt had lived an interesting, sometimes exciting life. He understood the military mind, loved the army's ways and prospered in it, but had no particular regard for the U.S. Army as such.

When the Confederacy stood up bold and daring as the original American revolutionists and declared independence, there had been no hesitation in his soul, no tortured examination of conscience or questions of duty to the army or the Federal Union. On hearing the news of secession, he wrote out his resignation, headed south and never looked back.

He had a long and varied romantic history. His was a rugged kind of attractiveness, high-browed, heavy-jawed, his blond hair shoulder-length, his mustache luxuriant, his bright blue eyes flashing with good humor and determination. Like many officers in the Southern army, he expressed himself in his dress—the elaborate uniform, the dashing feather in his hat telling the world he was an ideal Confederate warrior. He had fallen so suddenly and deeply in love with Laura Chandler that almost against his will he had begun to hope for an outcome unthinkable in the past. Marriage. Life was short, love was sweet, who better for a permanent partner than lovely, luscious Laura. The musicality of the thought tickled him and then he frowned. Luscious—although she certainly was—did not quite suit. It smacked of a hedonist, a voluptuary. His impressions of her, his feelings for her were mostly on a higher plane.

Eventually she would marry him, he didn't doubt it, yet he was shy in her presence. Ladies often turned out not to be so ladylike when you got to know them but Laura really was as fine as she appeared to be. Above all he yearned to impress her, charm her, overwhelm her with his masculine ardor and devotion and do it quickly, before he had to go back to the damned war and leave the field to other men. He wanted her committed but so far hadn't gotten beyond squeezing her hand.

He was low in his mind on the evening he ran into a friend in the saloon next door to the Excelsior Hotel. The friend—a young captain who wanted a promotion— suggested that the general might do well to take Mrs. Chandler riding in the country. Out there they wouldn't be interrupted by the other men who hung around the house and he could press his suit with more success. The captain also knew someone who had a carriage he might be willing to lend.

"Excellent, excellent!" Matt smiled at the captain. "I wonder why you're being so helpful."

"I want to see you succeed, General."

"Decent of you considering you saw her first."

"I soon found out I didn't stand a chance. But a war hero like you—how can she resist?"

Matt realized the captain was right when Laura came floating down the stairs, exquisite in a lilac gown of some slithery fabric that he could not identify but believed would feel wonderful if he could get his hands on it. He loved women like this, soft, round, sweet-smelling, marvelous women who were so delicious and hard to get. He loved the pursuit and he loved the capture. She had dressed to please him and was coming to him with the smile he loved.

"I happen to have a carriage and driver today, Laura. Would you enjoy a drive in the country?"

"You are good to me, Matt. Where did you get the carriage?"

"A friend, a good friend." Captain Blake was indeed a fine fellow or, more likely, had a return favor in mind. And why not—it was the usual way one got ahead. Matt held Laura's arm longer than necessary as he helped her up the carriage steps.

It was one of those haunting autumn days, the breeze cool, the woods turning orange and gold, the sun promising to last forever, that had sadness as well as beauty in it. Winter in all its cruelty was not far away.

Laura said, "It's hard to say goodbye to summer, isn't it? When the world starts to turn cold it's like losing a friend."

"What's this? Doldrums on such a grand day?" Matt patted her hand. "We'll have none of that. After all, if winter comes won't spring be along before we know it?" That wasn't quite right but it was close. Laura, being a bookish person, knew all about Shakespeare, and he liked to dredge up quotations on occasion to show her he was not your ordinary soldier.

She thought, I should have known better. An optimist and man of action if ever there was one, Matt never spoke of his inmost feelings and didn't care to hear about anyone else's. She shifted quickly. "You're right, never mind dark days. They'll be short and sweet."

His spirits rose at sight of her smile. They were approaching a section of the James he knew well, an ideal place for a romantic moment. He pointed. "Just beyond those trees there's a spot you'll find very pleasant." He ordered the driver to stop.

It was the bend of the river where she and Chase had eaten peaches and chicken and angel food cake and watched the water eddy and flow onward in the changing light.

She said, "No, not there. A little farther on there's a better path."

At the river's edge she picked up a stick and sat down. He sat beside her, as close as her voluminous skirt would allow. Here the riverbank was several feet high, the water below deep.

She held the stick over the water and laughed. "See, I'm fishing!"

It charmed him, everything about her charmed him. She was adorable, sitting there with her imaginary fishing pole and laughing up at him, her wonderful eyes seeming to change from gray to blue according to the light. Seize the moment, seize it now when the enemy's defenses are down. Take her in his arms and convince her with mouth and hands that she wanted him as much as he wanted her.

She said, "When I spoke of winter I didn't mean to sound sad. I was thinking of our soldiers without shoes and blankets when the snow comes on. They're certain to be in battle before Christmas. With all the cold-weather illness, it will be so hard. Mrs. Davis is terribly worried about the President's health. She said there'd been some trouble between him and General Beauregard but just what it was she didn't mention."

There went his opportunity. A sober discussion of the war wasn't what he had in mind but it was a chance to impress her in a different way. A good general takes what fortune offers.

"Beauregard is upset too," he said. "He and Joe Johnston are sitting out there at Fairfax Court House with forty thousand men ready to go and Washington just across the river defended by the incompetents who ran away from us at Manassas. They told the President that if he'd give them twenty thousand more troops before the Yankees reorganize, we could jump across the Potomac and take the city like that." Matt snapped his fingers to show how easy it would be. "But Davis said no—I was there, I heard him. He doesn't understand strategy and he thinks he knows it all, a dangerous combination. He says if the troops need action let them invade Maryland. Mind you, that's exactly what the Federals are expecting us to do. Davis and Beauregard had a big fight over that."

She looked at him as if he were tall as God and understood the mysteries of the universe. "But what do you think they should do?"

It wasn't possible but sometimes he thought her eyes turned violet. Many a man would give his right arm to be sitting here at this instant with this glorious woman hanging on his words. His voiced dropped confidentially. "I can tell you what they're *going* to do. They should attack Washington but they can't because Davis won't let them. They won't cross the river and invade Maryland—it would be foolish in the extreme. So they'll sit where they are until spring while the Northern army gets ready to fight. There is one hopeful thing though. I have it on the best authority that Beauregard has been kicked downstairs—second in command to Albert Sidney Johnston, the finest soldier I ever knew. How's that for good news?"

Laura drew in a long deep breath. "It's wonderful. Matt, I can't tell you how glad I am to hear this."

S HE CAME HOME with such an air of suppressed excitement that everyone in the house noticed and wondered. Finally, at dinner, Millie asked the question. "You might as well tell us, Laura, before you explode. Did General Riley propose today?"

"Oh, Millie, where do you get such ideas?"

"From you. You look like the cat that got into the cream and I don't appreciate being snickered at."

"Did I snicker? I apologize, honey—but it is funny."

She giggled again, excused herself, and went out into the garden, into night air that was brisk on her skin, and paced along the path, trying to hold down a rising sense of triumph. She had learned the details of a strategy session—

in fact, a violent disagreement—between the President and his commanding generals, she knew what the plan was for the coming months and who the new commanding general would be, and it hadn't been hard, it had been *easy*! She had forgotten what a good actress she was. Maybe, as Chase said, she should go on the stage. The information Matt Riley had disgorged so willingly could save lives and oh, how she wanted to tell Chase about it. If only he were here, if only she knew if there were other people in Richmond who were his people. But she didn't know. She would have to wait, contain herself in patience and hope he came back soon. At the very least she now knew she could do it.

At the end of the garden she opened the gate. In the dim light someone sat hunched on her rock.

"Why Adam, does your mama know you're up so late?"

"Yes, ma'am." Adam's eyes dropped. "No, ma'am."

She sat down beside him. Everyone liked Adam but she was especially fond of him because he was Jewel's child. Not so much a child anymore—he would soon be thirteen—but he retained the appealing, happy innocence that he would have to lose one day. Adam still believed the world was good.

He gave a long, shivering sigh, and she said, "What is it? Troubles?"

"Oh . . . Mama . . . she picks on me. Always bawling me out for something. She don't . . . doesn't like me going down to the stables. She says I'll get to talking like a stablehand but I like to be around horses, that's all."

"Your mama just wants you to speak as educated people do, as she does. She loves you and wants the best for you."

He looked out at the river shining darkly in the night. "If she loves me why does she whip me?"

"She whipped you for going down to the stables?"

"For asking Mr. Edward if I could be his coachman when I grow up. She said I wasn't to beg favors from the white folks. I told her I wasn't begging, I was just asking, but she whipped me anyway." He rubbed at his cheek but raised his head to show he wasn't crying.

Laura said, "I've known your mama almost all her life. She's a good woman but strict. I don't know why she was so upset but she was and maybe she just made a mistake. You have to forgive her."

He looked at her directly. "Miss Laura, I try to be good. I try hard because my daddy's gone and I'm all she's got."

"I know. Go on back to the house now. She'll be looking for you."

"Yes, ma'am." He slid off the rock and trudged slowly up the path.

She sat alone for a while thinking that but for a vicious system that should have ended long ago Adam would have his daddy and Jewel her husband. Maybe the information prised out of Matt Riley today would be a tiny step toward finishing something that never should have been started in the first place.

ALTHOUGH MRS. JAMES DAVENPORT was not the wealthiest woman in town she was one of the cleverest and had convinced Richmond years ago that an invitation to her small but handsome house was a mark of final acceptance into high society. Before the war the only outsiders included in her exclusive circle were distinguished writers, artists, statesmen, and visiting European nobility. Now that war had come Mrs. Davenport felt that it was not a lowering of standards to invite a few politicians and military officers. Rather, it was a contribution to the cause.

Matt Riley was one outsider who received her simple cream-colored card and on a cool evening in late October he presented it at her front door. Once inside a quick glance told him that only the most important people in town were present, the inbred group that had always run Richmond along with the politicians who now governed the Confederacy and a few high-ranking military officers who were fighting for it. They were all in great good humor—smiling, chatting, eating delicacies from Mrs. Davenport's munificent buffet. He was glad to be present too, not to eat or social-climb but because he knew Laura would be here.

And there she was across the room, laughing at some remark another woman had just whispered in her ear. The blue dress was new. How had he failed to notice before that her dark hair, tonight coiled into an amazingly intricate arrangement on her neck, had a faint reddish cast to it? The white rose behind her ear was dashing and the light in her eyes when she saw him something quite new . . .

But that smile was not for him. Someone else had gotten to her first, a civilian who had entered just before him and was now taking her outstretched hand and saying something complimentary about her dress. It was obvious that's what the bastard had done because she touched her skirt and looked at him in a way Matt did not care for at all.

He asked abruptly, "Madam, who is that man—the young, healthy-looking fellow who isn't in uniform?"

"That's Colonel Girard, one of our Yankees. He does something for the government, don't ask me what. Would you like to meet him?"

"Perhaps when he's finished his tête-à-tête," Matt said bitterly and Mrs. Davenport suppressed a smile. A short square-shaped woman with iron-gray hair and a deceptively open face, she had an instinct about people that seldom failed and although she cared nothing for politics she loved man-woman intrigue. With this interesting triangle filed in the back of her mind she took General Riley into her richly furnished drawing room and introduced him to the most distinguished guest she could find.

THERE WAS A SPOT near an open window a little removed from the crowd. Chase said, "I always did think you looked wonderful in that color."

"Remarkable since you've never seen me in blue."

"Oh, but I have. The night I first met you. You were wearing this exact shade but in velvet, wasn't it?"

"How could you possibly remember that?"

"I told you it was a memorable evening for me."

"Yes. Well. Was your trip successful? Where all did you go?"

"Home, for one place."

"What a happy time for you. Or I should ask, was it happy?"

"Happy. Painful. You know how it is with families. I understand our last conversation better now that I've done some betraying myself."

General Riley, who had been eyeing them, was now

moving in their direction with a purposeful expression on his hard, handsome face. Behind her smile Laura murmured, "I've gone back to an old habit—I ride every morning before breakfast. Meet me tomorrow about seven just out of town on the Petersburg road. Matt, how good to see you. I want you to meet a friend of mine."

T HE COUNTRY SOUTH of Richmond was heavily wooded rolling land and the many small rivers were green and smooth, the movement of the strong current scarcely visible. Early as it was the autumn sun had overcome the night chill and after a brief canter they let the horses walk.

"I just started riding again this week, the first time I've been on a horse since Robert died," she told him. "I don't know why because I love it."

It was the first time, too, that she had mentioned Robert without strain in her voice. Chase said, "You are a beautiful rider. I don't know how you ladies manage a sidesaddle. I wouldn't want to attempt it."

She laughed at the thought of him or any man trying to ride with one leg hooked awkwardly over the horn of a sidesaddle. "You get used to it, especially when you've never known anything else. I was put on a pony when I was five and taught to jump. I wasn't frightened, didn't have the sense to be, I guess, but I should have been—I don't think I'd do that to a child of mine," she added, more to herself than him, and then went on. "At twelve I was expected to join the hunt and I tried it. I loved the excitement, the danger, the flying over fences. The hounds baying and the sound of the horn gave me goose bumps, but then the dogs got the fox. First I threw up, then I announced that I would never hunt again and I never did. When I told Robert about it he said I'd never make a politician because I loved the pursuit but I couldn't go for the kill."

"Couldn't or wouldn't?"

She thought that over. "Wouldn't. I could for someone or something I loved—at least, I believe I could."

"I believe you could too."

They were still some distance out of town. The woods

thinned and there was an open stretch where the stream curved near the road, a good place to stop. They dismounted and watched the horses drink.

The sun climbed the sky. Somewhere a mockingbird trilled a series of complex melodies that never once repeated. It occurred to her that she was happy sitting here with him in the morning hush with the light glinting sharply on the water.

She shaded her eyes with her hand and used its protection to glance at him. His face was as it had always been and yet altered in some subtle way—more clearly defined, less bland. She wondered if it only seemed so because of what she knew about him now or if she was seeing him clearly for the first time.

A breeze disturbed the tree they were sitting under and a few leaves showered down. She brushed them from her skirt. "Have you ever known an army officer named Ashford? Captain Jesse Ashford? I believe him to be a Southerner."

"I don't think so. Why?"

"Oh, I happened across the name." Another leaf drifted onto the surface of the water and moved erratically downstream, catching once on a floating branch and then traveling on. She took a breath, more excited than nervous over what she was about to say. "Beauregard and Joe Johnston have forty thousand men at Fairfax Court House." His eyes shifted sharply to her face. "They had a bitter fight with the President because he refused to give them twenty thousand more and let them attack Washington. They won't invade Maryland anytime soon, they can't move before spring. I also heard that Beauregard is being demoted and Albert Sidney Johnston given command of the army."

He made no attempt to hide his surprise. "What changed you?"

"I had second thoughts—a lot of thoughts. The reason I gave for turning you down sounded fine but it wasn't really. I was doing what I've always done, shutting my eyes and fooling myself. My brothers . . . you . . . all the men I know, you're fighting for what you believe in. Well, I love my own people but I hate what they're doing. I want to fight for what I believe, just like the men. Can you understand?"

"I understand. Most people wouldn't be so hard on themselves or so honest."

The approval in his eyes sent a little thrill of satisfaction through her.

"Is what I told you any help?"

"It confirms what we've heard about Albert Sidney Johnston."

Her face fell. "You already knew. I hoped it would be valuable."

"It is. When the same story comes in from several different sources, the army can begin to believe it. The rest is news to me. Where did you get information like that?"

"From General Riley." She dimpled. "I've led him on terribly, poor man."

"I noticed. Don't expect a plum like that often—he was out of his mind to tell anyone what he told you. And remember, the weaknesses of the men running the war, quarrels in the high command, anything that gives us an idea of their thinking can be as important as knowing they won't attack Washington."

"I know President Davis fancies himself a military expert and he's not. Edward says he'd rather run the army than be President and he interferes with the generals all the time."

"That's the kind of thing I mean. Anything that helps or hurts their ability to fight. Factory production, work stoppages. And of course troop movements, enlistments, complaints you hear from soldiers." He smiled. "Battle plans are very nice, too, but we really don't expect that more than once a month. Can you spare an hour this afternoon? I'd like you to meet another lady—someone you can contact if you can't reach me."

THE HOUSE RAMBLED over the crest of the hill in haphazard fashion, the product of several generations of unorthodox, nonconformist Rutledges, each with differing ideas of architectural beauty and the money to indulge their fancies.

As they walked up the path Laura said, "Fiona Rutledge—

amazing. How can she be part of this network of yours?
Everybody knows she's a Unionist."

"Yes, isn't it wonderful? Who would suspect crazy
Fiona?"

Fiona was considered crazy by most of Richmond. She
lived alone with only her servants in the odd, magnificent
Rutledge mansion, a frail-looking spinster who wore her
graying blond hair in unfashionable sausage curls around
her pale, sharp-featured face and said exactly what was in
her mind whenever it pleased her. Her pedigree was as long
and lustrous as Laura's own, she was enormously rich, and
she was the town crank. Her devotion to the Union and
contempt for the Confederacy were well known. She
abhored slavery and said so at every opportunity. On the
Fourth of July just past she had flown the Stars and Stripes
from the tall flagpole in her front yard as her family had
done all her life.

It was the last straw for Richmond. She had freed her
own slaves long ago and that would have been all right if
she hadn't talked about it so much. She had searched out,
bought from their present owners, and freed the children of
her former slaves, somewhat excessive but she was so rich it
meant little to her. However, the sight of the Old Flag
snapping in the breeze up on that hill was more than Richmond could stomach. She was crazy, she had to be.
Someone to be pitied and ignored.

Laura had known Fiona from childhood and could
remember her as a pretty woman, but she had aged and did
nothing to soften or improve her appearance. She cared for
nothing but her cause. Tradition-bound in a way she would
have despised if she had recognized it, she served a large,
elaborate English tea every day—to herself if there were no
guests, and these days Fiona had very few guests. Her maid,
Maria, set out the Georgian silver teapot, the fine china
cups, the tiny sandwiches, the scones, crumpets, and cakes,
and then, instead of allowing her visitors to eat, Fiona took
Laura's hand, held it tightly, and gazed deep into her eyes,
her own eyes brilliant.

"My dear, I can't tell you how happy I am that you are
one of us. We shall prevail. Never doubt that for a
moment." She released Laura's hand and went on in a

voice that was clipped in spite of her soft Southern speech.
"Now. I keep three servants and they are completely loyal.
There will be many ways they can help. Anything I see I
will report, of course, but too many doors are closed to
me—you will be welcome where I am not. Colonel Girard
has set up contacts for me. You get the information and I
will get it through the lines. Also," she added with a con-
tented smile, "there is a room in this house, a hidden room
that is undetectable. If we need to hide people we can
do it."

After leaving Fiona they drove down to the canal that
paralleled the river and walked along the broad towpath.
It was a popular place for walking, especially for young
couples.

She said, "I think Fiona is a fanatic."

"She's also smart and capable. We have to rely on
fanatics. Not many people can look at the risks realistically
and still be willing to do it. You are unusual."

"So you tell me. I've known Fiona all my life. She and
my mother grew up together and Mama was willing to put
up with her although even then she was considered a little
peculiar. She believes all Negroes are good and all whites
are bad, except abolitionists."

"She's like my sister-in-law. Audra is an abolitionist and
declares herself at every opportunity. If she lived here no
one would suspect her just as they won't suspect Fiona—
she's too obvious. You don't have that protection."

This section of the towpath was bordered by a low wall
and they stopped to sit and watch the boats trundle slowly
by. Sunset was the best time along the James, flowing
smooth and silent around the many rocks and islands that
dotted it. The gold light on the water, the hush, the sense
of being a great distance from the city that was in reality so
close always soothed the spirit. Time seemed to slow and
stop and they sat, not looking at each other, not speaking.

Another couple stopped to look at the view and when
they moved on she said, "No one will suspect me either.
I'm a Seymour. This is home."

"That's your greatest danger. You feel safe but if you're
caught you'll find there's no one so unforgiving as a former

friend. Never let down your guard, for all our sakes. Never trust anyone."

She said, "I'll be careful," and gave a nod as if agreeing to a business deal, a contract as binding as if written on paper, signed and sealed.

As they walked back along the way they had come she buttoned her tight, stylish jacket against the river wind. Today she had stepped over a line into unknown, perilous territory, accompanied only by him, and she wasn't afraid, not of getting caught. There had been moments though, especially just now sitting by the river, when her thoughts had gone in directions she didn't like and made her aware of other hazards. But thoughts were slippery things, darting out of nowhere into the mind. Desires were the same—one couldn't be held responsible for them. By the time they left the towpath and climbed the steps to the street she was convinced that she had not felt or thought anything of importance. She was only anxious to leave him, to go home.

It had been a tense day for him too. He was not always at ease with her. She was too quick, too different from other women he had known, complex in ways that would be fascinating to unravel but made her dangerous. Any man who truly loved her would be caught forever.

Luckily he was not that man. Valerie had sent word that Jason was safely out of town and she expected to see him tonight. He had not wanted to go but now, after the time spent today with Laura, he did. Thank God for uncomplicated, selfish, desirable Valerie, too shallow to give everything but giving all he needed. The affair with her was the most foolish he'd ever embarked on considering his other risky business, but he didn't regret it. Not yet anyway. At this moment, watching Laura settle herself in his buggy, he gave thanks for Valerie's existence and wished Jason Hood was dead.

CHAPTER 12

DURING THE WINTER of 1862 nothing went right for the Confederacy. It was all because of mistakes made by the generals, everyone said—that posing little Napoleon, Beauregard, and vain, spiteful Joe Johnston—or the President, who fancied himself a military genius and constantly interfered. People who did not like Jefferson Davis said he ought to go out with the troops as he wanted to and do his struggling country a favor by getting captured.

On a dark, depressing day in February 1862 a crowd gathered in Capitol Square in a heavy rainstorm to watch his formal inauguration. At the end of his impassioned speech they managed to shout, "God bless our President!", but on every mind was the news that the forts of Henry and Donelson on the Cumberland and Tennessee rivers had fallen and the great river roads into the Deep South were now open. A young, newly promoted brigadier general no one had ever heard of, Ulysses S. Grant, had refused to negotiate and demanded the unconditional surrender of the forts, ominous words for a people who had never believed that Yankees would really fight. Southerners hoped that the new head of the army, Albert Sidney Johnston, would set things right. He'd better accomplish something soon because the growing scarcity of basic necessities was making life more difficult with every passing week.

In Tennessee on a clear, bright April morning North and South savaged each other in a vicious battle which the North won, but at a shocking cost in lives. For the South it was a disaster. Southern losses were equally great and lost, too, was the life of Albert Sidney Johnston. Then, at the end of the month came another blow—New Orleans, the exotic city at the mouth of the Mississippi, fell to the Union.

Laura sat in the terraced garden of the Confederate White House with two other women of Varina Davis's social circle, listening to their predictions of disaster and thinking her own thoughts. Varina was upstairs putting her new baby son down for his nap in the mansion recently provided for the President and his growing family. It was a large house, not as splendid as that other White House in Washington but roomy enough for the four Davis children and for the entertaining Southerners expected their President and his wife to do. Today in the garden the horse chestnut trees Varina loved were in full flower and the dogwood blossoms were pink and white clouds over their heads.

"We are lost—that's my opinion," announced Ellen Mercer in her flat, authoritative way. She was a clever, observant woman and when she spoke her friends listened. "The Yankees have got New Orleans. That means they've got the Mississippi and they've just about cut us in two."

Laura, who was performing Varina's hostess duties, offered more tea and asked, "Is that what John says?" John Mercer was a colonel in the army and an aide to Jefferson Davis.

"That's what *I* say. Read the newspapers, look at the map. It gives me a headache just thinking about it."

Grace Weston spoke up. "My husband says as long as we hold Vicksburg we can hold the Mississippi. Oh, why don't the Yankees go home and leave us be! We need a new general, someone who can chase them back where they came from."

"We need a miracle," Ellen said and accepted a second piece of cake.

"They say General Lee is very fine." Laura gave Ellen a bright inquiring look. "Do you ever hear him mentioned as a possibility?"

"John says he's the best general we have and ought to replace Joe Johnston. He's in town now—I saw him riding by the other day. He lifted his hat and smiled in the most charming way. Some people think he's the finest man alive but—I don't know. He's so dignified, almost majestic. With a man that cool and reserved how can you tell what makes him tick?"

As suppertime approached the other women went home to husbands and children but Laura stayed to listen to

Varina's moans about the household help. "Horace, our butler, has left. Just ran off and abandoned us, the ungrateful wretch. That talk about emancipation in the Northern papers has them all riled up. You never see them reading the papers—as far as I know Horace can't read— but they always seem to know everything. What goes on in their minds? How can they be so disloyal?"

"I often wonder what the servants really think about the war but they never give a hint. I'm amazed that most of them are as loyal as they are."

"Laura, you do have peculiar ideas. Why shouldn't they be? They're well housed and cared for, they never have to worry about where their next meal is coming from, and *our* servants have the privilege of serving the President. What else could they ask? Sometimes I think they're more trouble than they're worth, especially now when Banny is unwell." "Banny" was Varina's private name for her husband.

"I'm so sorry. What is it this time?"

"His dyspepsia plagues him and he has headaches every day. There's been so much bad news and he takes it very hard. No matter what he does his enemies are always after him, criticizing and second-guessing. It breaks my heart to see him wounded so unfairly."

"And my brother is one of the critics. It's good of you not to hold that against me, Varina."

"We've been friends too long for that. I know you have nothing to do with what Edward writes."

"Maybe I can help with the servant problem. Let me find a good butler for you."

"That would be wonderful! I don't want Banny troubled with little things when so much is on his mind, and he does notice if the house isn't running smoothly."

Laura put on her bonnet before the entrance-hall mirror and Varina remarked in a musing voice, "Sometimes I wonder what it's like to look into a mirror and see real beauty looking back. Does it make troubles easier to bear?" She was standing slightly behind and to one side of Laura and their two faces reflected in the gilt-framed mirror. Varina, a pretty girl in her youth, had become a plump, handsome woman, oval-faced, full-lipped, her eyes dark, heavy-lidded, and intelligent.

They gazed at each other in the mirror. Laura said, "If you mean me, then no. I only see me, the same me I've always been. Someone I don't always like very much." She touched Varina's hand. "Don't be sad. Times are hard right now for all of us one way or another, but you have your children and the man you love. I don't have either. Try not to think too much about what may happen next week or next year."

Varina made a little grimace of apology. "I know I'm lucky and I need you to remind me of it once in a while. I wish I could do something for you."

"Then give me your opinion. What would you think if I went to work? Not just sewing haversacks for the soldiers or visiting the hospital but a real job in an office."

"Work? In an office?"

"Mrs. Bartow is working in a government office cutting Confederate bonds."

"Yes, poor dear, for five hundred dollars a year. Colonel Bartow left her with nothing, she hasn't a penny to her name. What a sacrifice she made for the cause."

"I can't do what she's done but I can make a small contribution. We're short of manpower and clerks are needed. I could free a man for the fighting."

That idea appealed to Varina. "What a good thought! And you are so clever with figures. Perhaps the Treasury?"

"The War Department would be more interesting. If you would ask the President . . . ?"

"I'll speak to him tonight but you may not be happy there. Jason Hood supervises all the clerks."

Laura shrugged and laughed. "Oh, I can deal with Jason. You just watch, Varina. Give me a little time and he'll be eating out of my hand."

She hurried home in the deepening twilight and sent a message asking Chase to come immediately, a message that did not reach him for he was out very late that night.

He began the evening at Fanshaw's, the toniest gambling house in town. There were more than forty such luxurious establishments in Richmond catering to the wealthy (and countless other gambling hells in tumbledown buildings where poorer people could lose their dollars as quickly as the rich) but Fanshaw's was the most popular. It offered crystal chandeliers, silk-lined walls, mahogany tables with velvet benches, fine china, and dignified waiters who served imported wines and whiskies, French champagne, and food fit for gourmets. And upstairs top-drawer prostitutes were available to finish the evening in grand style.

Judah Benjamin, recently elevated to Secretary of War, was a connoisseur of wines and loved good food and the game of faro. He found all he liked best at Fanshaw's and had invited Chase to dine with him there.

"We were pleased with the uniforms and the rifles, Colonel Girard. We wish there could have been more of them but they did come through the blockade with no difficulty. I knew Congressman Graham in Washington—a fine man and a good Confederate." Judah helped himself to more filet mignon, hard to get these days but available at Fanshaw's. "Sadly, it's the only shipment you've arranged for us in some time."

"It's a touchy business, Mr. Benjamin. Up North they're looking for people like me behind every bush. I'm met with suspicion everywhere."

"I understand. We watch constantly, too, and sometimes make mistakes. It's embarrassing when we arrest an innocent person but then a case like Arthur Osborne's makes it all worthwhile."

During the last month while the depressing news of Shiloh and New Orleans was coming in, the people of Richmond had been heartened by the capture and trial of a Northern spy. It proved to them that at least some government officials were doing their jobs right. Arthur Osborne, an attractive Englishman who had made a number of friends in Richmond, had turned out to be not English at all but a Pinkerton detective, a spy who was important to the Yankees. Lincoln's government had tried desperately to save him, even threatening to execute some of the Southerners they held if he were not released. The threats had had no effect. His woman accomplice was imprisoned and early this morning Osborne had been hanged. In the afternoon Chase had been at the War Department talking to the chief clerk when Jason Hood came in, uncommonly garrulous, exhilarated, friendlier than Chase had ever seen him. He had just come from the hanging ground.

"Until the last minute the bastard thought he'd get a reprieve. He wouldn't even talk to the minister who came to the jail last night but this morning it was a different story, let me tell you. This morning when he saw it was really going to happen he broke down and cried and begged to be shot, not hanged, and they had to drag him out of his cell. I'll admit he handled himself like a man at the gallows, pale but calm." By now everyone in the office was gathered around listening, most with approval, some few with revulsion, one or two, like Chase, showing no reaction at all. "The noose wasn't quite right and it came off. Osborne fell straight to the ground and had to be taken back up on the scaffold. They did a careful knot the second time and he died fast but they're letting him dangle for a while. Lets everybody know we mean business."

The picture of Arthur Osborne twitching in the sun in a Virginia field had stayed with Chase all day. The satisfaction in Jason Hood's voice told him that if there ever had been an idea of chivalry or glory in this war it was gone now. It had become a brutal, no-holds-barred grudge fight to be won by any means available.

To Benjamin he said, "I hope to get some breechloading rifles from the Sharp and Rankin factory in Philadelphia but so far I haven't found an employee who isn't a Unionist."

Benjamin sighed lightly and his constant smile faded. "Some of our generals don't like breechloaders, but I believe they are the coming thing and we'll need them before we're through. We desperately need niter for gunpowder, too, and fuses and mortars. We need everything." His smile returned and he raised his glass. "To the Confederacy and all those who are loyal to it!"

Chase lifted his glass and they drank together.

From across the room came the soft slap of cards, the click of chips, the steady murmur of voices as bets were placed, then groans or cries of triumph as the cards were turned up.

Benjamin's eyes lit. "Time for a game, I believe. Will you join me?"

It occurred to Chase that of all the influential men he dealt with Judah Benjamin was the greatest threat. If ever anyone saw through him it would probably be this cheerful,

rotund, pleasure-loving man with the sharp dark eyes and
the even sharper mind.

He said, "There's nothing I like better than a good
game of faro but tonight I can't stay. I have an appointment on the other side of town."

I N FACT, he hadn't far to go from the bright-light district but he walked down the dark side streets with his
pistol in his belt. Richmond grew more dangerous daily and
garroting or stabbing were the most popular methods of
murder.

However, the Daisychain, widely acknowledged to be
the finest bordello in Richmond, was warm, comfortable,
and above all safe. It was to parlor houses what Fanshaw's
was to gambling—the best. It not only furnished exquisite
prostitutes, silk bed sheets, velvet draperies, and Brussels
carpets, it provided secrecy, with a secluded entrance and
absolute descretion on behalf of the men whose lives and
careers would be destroyed if they were found out. A man
could go publicly to Fanshaw's and even though prostitutes
were available have it assumed he was there for the gambling. There was only one reason for being at the Daisychain.

Chase entered the shadowed side door and stepped into
a brightly lit room where a party was going full blast. In a
way it reminded him of the ballroom in the Seymour
house. The colors of the walls and draperies were less subdued but the crystal chandelier was just as impressive, the
polished French furniture as expensive, the orchestra—
which was now turning out a fast polka—one that often
performed in the houses of the respectable rich. The young
ladies were remarkably pretty, and a number of the gentlemen present tonight had also attended Paige Seymour's
wedding.

In a smaller room off the main room was a long, polished mahogany bar where men who had left their usual
prudence and discipline at the door could get blind drunk
on the finest liquors obtainable and no one outside be the
wiser. Behind the bar rank upon rank of bottles reflected in
mirrors that stretched to the high ceiling, and the bar-
tender, Frederick, a black man of immense dignity and

many talents, presided with a sympathetic ear and a liberal hand. Frederick's drinks were legendary in Richmond. A man who was still on his feet after three or four was considered to have a phenomenal head.

In the main room one of the girls was singing out of time with the music. Another girl and a customer were attempting to dance around a table placed too close to a velvet settee. The girl's wide skirt caught on the table, she bumped into the settee, fell over it and landed on the floor with such force that her hoop flew up to reveal nothing on underneath. Everyone cheered and applauded and she sat there with a vague grin on her face until her partner pulled her up.

Beside the grand piano Angela Flynn watched with a smile that said she found these antics charming. Her neighbors would not have recognized plain little Mrs. Flynn, for at night at the Daisychain, Angela became beautiful. Her hair, freed from its knot, was dressed in a gleaming swirl around her face and her eyes, enhanced by cosmetics, seemed softer and more brilliant. Purple appeared to be her favorite color. Her slight body was encased in a well-padded gown of violet, heliotrope, and lavender, and the Daisychain's draperies, the velvet-covered chairs, the carpets were all plum-colored.

In a way she had something in common with Laura. She, too, had played a part all her adult life, relying on costumes and a public face to help her. Laura had done it for love, Angela did it for money. These men making fools of themselves tonight, these respected, powerful men who controlled governments and caused wars to happen, never guessed how she despised them. Users all, users of everyone, especially women. And the girls, so young and still so fresh, were simply stupid, imagining that selling themselves was an easy way to make money, all of them hoping a customer would fall in love, propose marriage, and take them into another life. In all her time in the business Angela knew of only two whores it had happened to, both exceptionally handsome, smart, and, above all, lucky. For almost everyone else the trail led rapidly downhill. Every girl in this room was under twenty because most men wanted the perfection of youth. In two or three years they would have to move on to a less select house. Most of them would end up on the streets. At thirty-five they would look fifty, if they weren't dead by then.

Angela, never seeing she was as much a user as any customer, looked forward to a better life too. Her salvation would come not from some mythical rescuer but from money, a great deal of it. Profits produced by the women of the Daisychain.

Someday, when rich enough, she was going to retire to a tasteful, respectable life among her costly possessions and wear only fine silk dresses of dove-gray and dark blue. The only question in her mind was what was rich enough?

When she saw Chase she glided across the room as if the parts under the purple gown were not ordinary hips and legs but smooth rolling wheels, a walk she had developed as a girl after months of practice and was now as much a part of her business self as her friendliness and her startling dresses.

"Hello, lover." She was so short that she had to rise on tiptoe to kiss him. "Come into my office."

The room was lit by only one small lamp. She shoved the papers on her desk aside and sat down in the high-backed leather armchair which she had once pointed out with sardonic amusement was the same kind of judges' throne used in their courtrooms by some of her regular patrons. Chase sat down, too, and they smiled at each other.

She said, "Did you see those clowns out there?"

"Three cabinet officers, an undersecretary of the treasury, a couple of senators, and at least four congressmen. A gold mine."

"All the young ladies are hot for the Confederacy—that is, when they think about politics—so I'm careful, but I hear that Senator Jordan thinks Davis might make a deal with Lincoln if he were approached the right way. After he'd had a few drinks I asked him what was the right way and he—" There was a crash on the floor above, then a woman's scream and loud male voices.

"Fighting! They know I don't allow fighting."

Angela jumped up and as she threw open the door a man wearing nothing but socks tumbled down the wide stairs that led to the many rooms on the upper floors, struggled to his feet and shook his head like a dog shaking off water. He was tall and brawny, a formidable opponent, but the enraged, black-bearded man who raced down the stairs after him hitched up his underdrawers and jumped on him with fists flying. The naked man, everyone noted, was Senator George Watson. The man in the underdrawers with the neatly clipped beard was the editor and publisher of the Richmond *Courier*, Edward Seymour.

Edward had never fought with his fists in his life but his forward velocity was so great that he landed a stunning blow and sent George Watson careering backward into a table. Several whiskey-filled glasses went spinning into the laps of the girl and the man who sat there.

Angela shouted, "Somebody stop them!" She grabbed Chase's arm. "Why don't you stop them!"

"Let them fight it out."

"Fight it out? That's my whiskey, my carpet"—George Watson smashed Edward's face with a blow so hard that the crunch of bone on bone could be heard. Edward clutched at the draperies behind him and they came down—"my *drapes*!" Angela climbed on a chair and shrieked, "Frederick, where the hell are you!"

Frederick, who had been polishing glasses in the bar and ignoring the tumult in the next room, came to the door. "Yes, ma'am?" he inquired mildly.

At that moment Senator Watson gathered himself and caught Edward under the chin with a blow that slammed his teeth together and lifted him off his feet. He went down with a crash and Watson was on top of him, pounding him with both fists and roaring. It took Frederick and Chase together to pull him off. All the other gentlemen had moved to the far side of the room where there was less chance of black eyes that would have to be explained to wives in the morning.

Edward lay still.

Senator Watson, who was beginning to realize what he'd done, allowed Angela to lead him to a sofa and push him onto it. Edward was hauled upstairs to the nearest unoccupied bedroom and deposited on a silken bed. Chase took the pitcher of water from the table and poured most of it on his face. He coughed, blinked, and tried to sit up.

"Stay quiet for a while. You took a pounding, Edward."

Edward sank back on the pillow and blood from his battered mouth ran down his face and dribbled onto the wet pillowcase.

"Oh, God." He shut his eyes. After a time he raised his hand, probed gingerly and mumbled, "My teeth aren't loose."

Chase pulled forward a frail-looking, brocaded chair, tilted back in it and crossed his boots comfortably. "What was it about?"

"I got the girl first and that son of a bitch claimed he was one of her regulars and tried to throw me out. Said he didn't like my editorials either." Edward started to laugh and stopped. "What's wrong with my mouth?"

"He sliced you. You'll need a doctor to sew it up."

Slowly Edward raised himself to a sitting position. "What do I look like?"

"Let's see. Your lip is torn. Your nose is bloody and might be out of line a little. Both your eyes are swelling. In a couple of days you'll look like a very pretty sunset."

"How can I go home? How can I explain?"

"We'll think of something. You were jumped while on a mission of mercy in a rough part of town? Your wife ought to believe that."

"You think I'm a humbug, don't you?"

Chase shrugged. "We're all humbugs."

"I've never been in a place like this before, never even thought about it. Well, I have thought about it but I've never done it." Edward looked around the room. It was lined with mirrors reflecting many Edwards from many different angles. He shut his eyes and sat for a while with his head down. Finally he asked in a muffled voice, "Could I impose on you to get me home? I don't think I can sit my horse."

"I'll find your clothes and borrow Angela's buggy. Give me all your money. You got robbed tonight."

It was just after two o'clock when Chase pounded on the door of a house that was dark and silent. Upstairs in Millie's room a lamp glowed almost immediately, but before she could get down the stairs Joseph came scurrying through the long hallway, opened the door a crack, lifted his lamp and peered out. "Who is dat? Mistah Chase? Mistah Edward! My Lordy, suh, what happened?"

Millie was coming down the stairs, hurrying, hurrying. She cried out, "Oh, my God! Oh, please, Edward, don't faint!", as Edward slumped forward. Chase grappled with his sagging body and hoisted him up. "Send for a doctor, Joseph. Would you lead the way, Mrs. Seymour?"

Laura was just starting down the stairs and Chase, glancing up, saw her horrified face. She turned and ran ahead of them to Edward's bedroom, tearing back the coverlet, ordering Bella to bring more water. When she saw his battered face in the lamplight she gasped, "Oh, your nose, your poor mouth." He moaned a little as she daubed at wounds that had begun to bleed again.

Millie sank to her knees beside the bed. "Edward, are you all right? Oh, darling, who did this to you?" He tried to speak and she said quickly, "Don't talk, sweetheart. Colonel Girard, what happened?"

"I had the great good fortune to come across him just after he'd been robbed. He fought back and they beat him severely."

"They? How many were there?"

"Several men, I believe. Always best to give them your money."

"Oh, yes, what's money? Darling, you could have been killed!"

Bella brought in fresh water and clean towels and took away the basin of bloody water, her passage scarcely noticed in the hushed room.

Downstairs the clock struck the half hour. Moments later the front door bell chimed. Then Dr. Rollins was in the room, making no effort to be quiet, his cool authority lifting some of the fear from Millie's stricken face.

He opened his bag and gently turned his patient's face to the light. "Well, Edward, you've had a high old time tonight."

At the door Chase murmured goodbye to Laura and she whispered urgently, "I have to talk to you. Wait for me in the small parlor."

*   *   *

HE HAD OPENED the heavy draperies and the pale light of dawn lit her tense face. She said, "I'm sorry to keep you waiting so long. Lord, what a night!"

"How is he?"

"Sleeping. The doctor gave him something. Thirty-five stitches around his mouth. We had to cut back his mustache, we couldn't shave it. His nose is broken and the cut over his eye took twelve stitches."

"It may not be as bad as it looks. I've seen worse beatings that didn't leave permanent scars."

"I'm not as worried about his face as I am about him. Is he in trouble? When you told us about the attack he gave you such a look—"

"Tonight he did something foolish and he doesn't want Millie to know. He went down to Bird-in-Hand"—she drew in a sharp breath—"to take home a man who'd come to him for help. He was jumped as he was coming back. If I hadn't taken a short cut to my hotel—"

"Bird-in-Hand!" Even the police didn't like to go into that part of town. "It would be just like him if someone asked for help but"—she shook her head in an anxious way—"lately he hasn't been himself at all. I thought perhaps you might have some idea . . ."

"He seems as always to me. Of course, you know him better."

His bland expression told her she had come up against that male conspiracy which never told its secrets to women. If he did know anything he wasn't going to tell her. She said, "I sent you a message tonight and I'm sure you didn't get it. Varina has lost another servant—her butler, Horace—and I promised to find a new one for her."

He began to smile. "Is that so? I know a man, a free Negro. He has a good job now but he might be interested. Would she take a freeman?"

"She might prefer it. She says it's the Yankee talk about emancipation that's giving the servants ideas and causing all this disloyalty."

"I think the man I have in mind would be very loyal." But would Angela ever forgive him for taking Frederick, even for the cause?

CHAPTER 13

GEORGE RANDOLPH WAS the current secretary of war, the third appointed by the President in less than a year, but Jason Hood, the undersecretary, oversaw daily operations, and because his mood had been so sour lately the people who worked there avoided him when they could.

Frustrated ambition was the cause of his discontent. He had been certain he would succeed sickly, inept Leroy Walker, the unpopular first secretary of war, but instead the President had promoted his bosom friend Judah Benjamin. Jason had always despised Judah for his wit, his imperturbable charm, his Jewish religion, his influence with Jefferson and Varina Davis. When, as secretary, Benjamin so annoyed the army's generals that Joe Johnston complained bitterly and Stonewall Jackson threatened to resign, Jason waited confidently for a call that never came. Instead, Benjamin was made secretary of state, the highest post in the cabinet, and George Randolph was given the War Department—George, whose only achievement was being the grandson of Thomas Jefferson. Jason kicked his chair at the thought of George Randolph and then had to pick it up before he could sit down and prepare himself for the interview he must have with Laura Chandler this morning.

He disliked Laura and had never understood how she'd gotten a reputation for great beauty. She couldn't compare with Valerie. His wife was the most desirable of women just as all his other possessions were the best—his house, horses, land, his reputation as a duelist, all the best and the most. Valerie flirted, of course, and it rather amused him, knowing other men wanted but couldn't get her. It never crossed his mind that she could be unfaithful for, after all, she had him.

Only minutes after he came into the office Laura arrived wearing a modest pale green gown with narrow hoops, knowing Jason would resent her and hoping she could quickly fade into the background and he would forget she was there.

He rose courteously from his desk, expressed his delight in seeing her, inquired after her family, commented on the fine spring weather, and wondered how a woman of breeding could be so unfeminine as to push herself into an exclusively male domain.

He offered her a chair, sat down again at his desk and smiled. "I fear you will not care for the work, Laura. It is dull, routine, quite boring. There's no excitement here and our budget is very small."

"Oh, but I wouldn't want to be paid! And I don't care how dull the work is. I just want to help."

You can help by going home and knitting socks, he thought, knowing he had to put up with her if she insisted. She was Varina Davis's friend. "Most admirable." He rubbed his hands together and said cheerily, "Well. Let's find you a place to sit and get you started."

THE WORK WAS indeed dull, Jason saw to that. During the first week Laura did nothing but file bills of lading. But only a small space had been allotted to the War Department and even the secretary of war himself had little privacy. She could hear almost every word spoken by the important men around her without leaving her desk.

There was still much talk about the hanging of Arthur Osborne and the hunt for spies had intensified. Rumors of spies were everywhere and there had been a number of accusations, none of them proved out so far. Most doubts centered on new people in town, especially women of questionable virtue and rough-looking men. In spite of increasing bitterness and disillusion there was still naïveté in the South and the North and both sides assumed that well-bred, well-spoken, intelligent people must, of course, be on the right side, their side. That was what was so shocking about Arthur Osborne. He had been a gentleman.

Laura had promised herself not to inquire into what Chase did away from her or the wider implications of his work, but although it was the talk of the town he never mentioned the trial or the hanging to her. Finally she could stand it no longer, she had to ask the question uppermost in her mind. Was he, was she—unknowingly—connected with the man who had dangled for a day in that field?

The answer was what she wanted to hear. "He worked for Pinkerton. I report elsewhere. I never heard of him until I saw his name in the papers."

"They say he was very clever, but he was caught."

"He got careless and he had miserable luck. Don't be afraid. You can be careful and still accomplish something. Look at you, calmly planting a spy in the White House right under Davis's nose. Even if Frederick is discovered it would appear that you did it in good faith."

Everything he said was true and yet that night and for several nights thereafter she was plagued by dreams in which some unspeakable, ill-defined horror was visited on Chase and she was unable to help him. She did not fear for herself—the Confederacy still balked at hanging women and she could stand prison, no matter how terrible—but she did fear for Chase if he, like Osborne, were caught.

She decided to occasionally work late into the evening and on one such night, after she promised to lock up and everyone left, she went into Secretary Randolph's office and opened the top drawer of the file cabinet near his desk. It was easy to do. She had seen George Randolph leave the key in the covered dish on the small table under the window. An outsider could easily enter through that window and break open the file, but with all the constant rumors of spies in Richmond George seemed not to have thought of the possibility. It would make no difference if he had for the spy he needed to fear was the charming young woman in the outer office who quietly did such prosaic work, the woman with the unknown loyalty to the Federal Union, his distant cousin Laura.

She found in the second drawer the dispatch that caused a hurried conference and hushed tones in the President's office that afternoon. To her, unschooled though she was in military strategy, it appeared to be General Joe Johnston's plan for the disposition of his troops in the defense of Richmond. Swiftly she copied the parts that seemed most vital, returned the papers to the file cabinet and locked it. Then she rolled her copy into a tight ball, took down her long thick hair and with the paper inside twisted

it into a knot on her neck. As she hastily secured the knot
with the last of the hairpins, there came a sound, the creak
of the wooden stairs that meant someone was coming up.
That sound caused her to fly from Randolph's office, snatch
her short cape from the coat rack and throw it around her
shoulders. She was just tying her bonnet strings as Jason
Hood walked in.

"Laura?" he said, at first showing nothing more than
surprise. And then in a sharper tone, "Why are you here at
this hour?"

"You ought to know, Jason," she replied with equal tart-
ness. "I don't mind drudgery, I'm happy to do anything for
the cause—but if you continue to dump on me every stray
piece of paper that happens to land in this office I may have
to complain to George. Good night." She sailed past him
into the hall, feeling the hairpins slipping from the knot. As
she moved swiftly down the shadowed stairs she called
back, "Be sure to lock up when you leave."

It was with a sense of great achievement that she showed
Chase her precious paper, crumpled but readable. They
were sitting in the buggy above the towpath, as private a
place as they could find.

"I'm sorry about the wrinkles—I carried it out in my
hair—but I think it's quite legible."

He read it swiftly and looked at her. "How the hell did
you get this?" Never before had he spoken to her in such a
manner. His voice, his eyes were cold.

"Why—I stayed late and copied it out of George's file. I
thought you'd be pleased. Isn't it any good?"

"Don't ever, *ever* do this again unless you're instructed
to. You are to listen and report what you hear to me. That's
all. Do you realize what would have happened if someone
had walked in on you?" He took her arm in a grip so tight
that she winced.

She had never seen him angry before. "I knew there was
a risk but isn't that part of the job? If I see something that
might make a difference, shouldn't I go after it?"

"Risk is part of my job. This is just another kind of hazardous duty for me but you're not a soldier." He released
her arm and when she rubbed it absently he said, very low,
"I'm sorry I hurt you but this thing"—he looked at the

paper lying on the seat between them—"it worries me. Don't do it again."

She answered quickly, passionately, "Men risk their lives for their beliefs—you do it every day. You can't deny me the right to do it too. I have no children, no one needs me. I see no reason not to take the same risks you take."

"The reason is that I decide what my agents do. You must follow instructions or I won't be able to trust you."

That hurt worse than her arm. "You don't *trust* me?"

"I shouldn't have put it that way. I trust you. I also must be able to depend on you. Swear to me that you won't do this again unless I tell you to."

She started to argue back, looked into his eyes and decided not to. For some time she watched a barge move slowly up the canal and finally said in a muffled voice, "All right, from now on I'll do exactly as you say. But it is good, isn't it?" For the first time he smiled a little. "Yes, it's good."

S HORTLY AFTER THAT stormy conversation Chase left town. From then on everything Laura heard at the War Department or from Frederick Peel, ensconced in the Davis White House and running the staff with a firm hand, she reported to Fiona Rutledge. It was up to Fiona to get her messages through the lines to the Union general, McClellan. He had landed by sea on the peninsula near Yorktown and was advancing slowly on Richmond. Telegrams were being sent out almost hourly by Jason Hood exhorting, pleading, demanding that General Joe Johnston cease his eternal retreating—the military maneuver he performed best—and stand and fight against the invader.

May arrived, glorious with pink and white dogwood, purple wisteria, and jessamine. Honey locusts and creamy magnolia blossoms perfumed the warm soft air, the sky was a gentle blue, yet fear swept through the city like a fire that could not be stopped. McClellan and the great Army of the Potomac were on the move at last, snaking slowly up the peninsula.

Quietly government offices packed the archives. Plans were made to transport the treasury south and rumors spread that Federal gunboats were moving upriver toward the city. A short ride out of town brought artillery and rifle fire within earshot; the main Federal army was eighty-five miles south but some detachments were already in the surrounding hills. The government, believing as governments always did that the people could not be trusted with the truth, told them there was no danger and exhorted them to rely on God and their leaders, but Congress, following the tradition of parliaments everywhere when threatened, promptly adjourned and ran out of town. That gave the citizens all the information they needed.

They are coming! people told each other and each time the words were spoken fear grew greater. Those faceless soldiers moving inexorably through the Virginia countryside were no longer Americans just like them, brothers engaged in a family feud, but strangers, brutal enemies, come to rape and destroy, to punish in ways unimaginable to decent folk.

Jason Hood declared his surprise that Edward had not sent Laura and the other Seymour ladies south to Raleigh as he had sent Valerie. Laura replied sharply, "I wouldn't consider leaving nor would Millie or Paige. Alex and my brothers are somewhere with the army. We have to be here in case . . ." She took a breath and battled down her anger. "There's going to be a major battle and that means wounded men. Somebody has to take care of them. We can't all run away."

Jason ignored the implied criticism of Valerie. "The President has ordered Mrs. Davis to prepare herself and the children for flight. Concerns for her safety would distract him from the conduct of the war. I'm sure it must be difficult for Edward to leave with his womenfolk in danger."

"Leave? I don't—"

"His regiment is moving out today and I assume he will go with it. His commission came through a week ago."

Laura was out of her chair and flying down the stairs without so much as a polite goodbye. In the streets were masses of people and vehicles moving frantically in whatever direction they thought might mean safety. The elaborate carriages of the wealthy struggled past as did farm wagons and carts, all loaded with food and clothes as well

as odd objects snatched up in haste. At Capitol Square
traffic had come to a complete halt where a wagon had
overturned and spilled its load into the street. A bed lay
upside down, a spinning wheel had landed on top of it,
linens were being ground into the dirt by the frantic hoofs
of horses still attached to the wagon, and a harp rested in
the roadway, incongruously upright as if a harpist were
about to sit down and play it. There were shouts, fist-
shaking, insults and oaths between the two drivers directly
involved but so far no blows had been struck.

Ruthlessly Laura pushed through the crowd watching
on the sidewalk and raced on up Ninth Street to Clay, past
the marble steps of the White House—God knew what was
going on in there—a combination of anger and fear pro-
pelling her. How *dare* Edward do this? How could he
secretly, coolly plan to go to war, of all the idiotic things in
the world, and not tell her? For all his talk of fighting for
freedom he hated the war, he despised the government, he
would have kept his brothers out of the army if he could
have; he was forty-three years old, for God's sake!

At her own gate she halted for a moment, breathless,
then raced up the front steps. Millie, whom she had
expected to find prostrate with hysterics, was lining up the
household staff in the entrance hall, her eyes dry, her
manner calm, almost detached. Paige, her eyes red and
swollen, looked more upset than Millie. There were footsteps in the upper hall and Laura, with a sinking feeling,
looked up and saw what she did not want to see—Edward
starting down the stairs in a beautifully tailored gray uniform with a captain's bars on his shoulders, a sword at his
side, a dark felt hat in his hand. He looked somehow taller,
more muscular and masculine. Oh, there is something
about a uniform, she thought bitterly. I could strangle him!

As he came into the hall he looked straight at her and
the accusations she had meant to make about brothers who
sneaked off to war without even saying goodbye to their
grieving sisters became impossible.

Slowly, he moved down the line of servants with a word
for each. Joseph, Bella, Jewel. When he came to Adam he
said, "Remember, you and I have an agreement, Adam.
You take care of things here at home, do as Miss Millie and

your mother say, and when you grow up you will be my coachman if you still want the job." They shook hands and Edward moved on. Cook, parlor maids, and kitchen maids all had their farewell from the master and the opportunity to wish him well. Then he turned to his family.

He kissed Laura and in the morning light she saw clearly the scars left by the beating he had suffered the night he was robbed, a deep scar near his upper lip, partly hidden by his mustache, a fainter but noticeable scar cutting sharply into his eyebrow. It had not spoiled the symmetry of his face but made it seem stronger.

Paige put out her arms, her young face momentarily old. "Goodbye, Papa."

Edward held her tight for a moment and spoke a few words that no one else could hear. Then Paige watched as her father walked over to her mother, standing a little apart from the others, waiting. Millie's face was utterly still, her eyes wide, her whole being concentrated on him.

He said, "Well, my dear." And then, "I'll write. You write me too."

"Every day, Edward."

He bent to kiss her and her arms went around his neck as if she would never let him go. Then she pulled back and smiled. "Try to keep dry. You take cold so easily. Wear your overcoat and—and don't be a hero." He smiled too. That last was the advice he had given his brothers when they left. Joseph opened the wide front door and he went down the steps to say goodbye to the coachman, the gardeners, the stablehands. His horse, a fine chestnut, was ready. He waved and cantered off down the street.

Later that morning the troops came marching down Main Street. It was not necessary, they could have bypassed the city and moved out more quickly, but it had been decided that a display of military might was needed to reassure and hearten the people. When the bands played the "Bonny Blue Flag" the flags carried by the regimental flag-bearers seemed to flutter even more proudly and an exaltation rippled through the crowds along the sidewalks. These were their best, the flower of their civilization sweeping out to save them. How could such men not prevail?

General Longstreet appeared, grim-faced, unsmiling, the

ultimate warrior. The crowd roared and ladies wept for they all knew he had recently lost three children to a fever, had set aside his personal pain, left his grieving wife and come forth to defend his country. Jeb Stuart dashed past at the head of his cavalry, smiling and waving to the crowd, as bold and assured as everyone had heard, a true cavalier if ever there was one. As the men continued to pass in what seemed like endless numbers, girls waved handkerchiefs and tossed spring flowers that were sometimes picked up and tucked in shirts or under hatbands.

Standing under the green linden trees, Millie saw Edward and cried out. He turned at the sound of her voice, heard through all the uproar, located her in the crowd and rode over. She stood with her hand resting against his leg, her head tilted up, and Laura and Paige moved back, trying in the midst of hundreds of excited people to give them some privacy. He leaned from the saddle, kissed Millie, then spurred to catch up with his men.

The Seymour women ate little that night but sat talking late into the evening about the war, about Edward, skirting some dangerous areas, speaking honestly of others.

"How long have you known, Millie?" Laura asked, her eyes on her moving needles. All the women had taken up knitting.

"He told me last week when he got his commission. I wasn't surprised, I expected it. He's said many times that he didn't feel like a man, safe in the office every day, scribbling with a pen when he should be using a sword. I told him there are a lot of ways to fight but I could have saved my breath. I don't think he even heard me." She sat staring at her hands for several minutes and then said, "I'm going to write to Mrs. McCauley and ask her to let Becca come and stay with us."

Laura and Paige exchanged glances. Becca McCauley, the girl Doug wanted so much to marry, lived in southern Virginia, far from the fighting. Doug had written several times to say that he wanted her in Richmond where he could see her if ever he got a furlough, but Millie had not yet invited her.

She said, "I've been wrong, I admit it. It would be terrible if she wasn't here and Doug . . . That is, suppose he got leave and he had to travel down south to see her. Wouldn't I feel silly!" She gave her quick, nervous laugh. "I'll go upstairs right now and write that letter."

Paige watched her mother leave the room, then got up and looked out in the hallway to make sure she was really gone. She came back and sat down on the hearth. "About time. Mama's been so cold to that girl and Doug let her get away with it. Kirby would have gotten married whenever he wanted and let her stew." She stared into the low fire. "This morning when Papa told me he was leaving I begged him not to go and he said he had to for honor's sake. He said he couldn't live with dishonor. I've heard that kind of talk from men all my life—they fight duels because of honor, they fight this war because of honor—and I never have known what they mean."

"Maybe honor is like love—it means different things to different people. Edward needs to feel"—Laura searched for the right word—"happy about himself and he has high standards. If he fails some test he's set for himself and thinks he's dishonored there's no living with him. He's always been like that."

"And it's more honorable to go to war than stay here and fight with words because—why? It's more dangerous? More uncomfortable?"

"So he thinks."

"What about Colonel Girard? Is he an honorable man? Alex says he should be in the army and that everything he's told us is a lie."

Laura's expression did not change but alarm bells in her mind rang wildly. Paige was a clever, perceptive girl and a red-hot Rebel. Her brows rose in mild surprise. "Whatever do you mean, Paige?"

"Oh, maybe what he does helps but isn't Alex right? When other men are getting killed, shouldn't an experienced officer be in the army instead of living comfortably here in Richmond or traveling around the country? Alex says he doesn't have an ideal in his head. Or he used to say that. The last time I saw him he said he'd do the same if he could get out of the army."

The alarm bells diminished. Laura said, "Chase believes in what he's doing and he takes great risks. Crossing the lines time after time, passing through two armies to do it. Think what the Yankees would do to him if they found out."

"The same thing we did to that spy, Arthur Osborne."

"Yes, they would. It was sickening."

A hard jawline showed suddenly in Paige's soft face. "It didn't make me sick. They should have hung the woman, too, and made a good job of it. The newspapers say Yankee spies are everywhere, trying to destroy us. I say, hang them all!"

Laura fastened her eyes on her knitting. Better that than her niece's merciless young face. Here in the house where she was born she was deep in enemy territory. If Paige found out, if she even suspected, there would be no forgiveness and no philosophical discussions about differing ideas of honor. She would turn in Chase Girard without compunction. She would turn in Laura, too, and no ties of blood or affection would stop her. Laura searched back through the words she had spoken tonight. Her comment about the hanging of Arthur Osborne had been a dangerous slip. Paige would probably put it down to genteel squeamishness, not disloyalty, but it must not happen again.

L IKE MANY SOUTHERN officers Edward was not a trained soldier but he had some understanding of tactics, he was liked and trusted by the men under his command, and in his first battle, at the little town of Williamsburg, he established a reputation for risk-taking that amounted almost to foolhardiness. Who would have thought, some of his fellow officers said, that steady, conventional Edward Seymour was at heart a daredevil?

At the War Department word came that the Yankees were claiming victory although their losses had been great, and that General Johnston was retreating yet again. The wounded poured into the city and ordinary people learned what the government had hoped to keep hidden as long as possible. Johnston was going to make his decisive move to save the Confederate capital on the banks of the Chickahominy River and the river was only twenty-five miles away.

Once again the two armies joined battle and among the

more severely wounded was General Joseph Johnston. He had to be replaced and the man appointed to take command was Robert E. Lee.

In a letter home Edward wrote:

Some of the other officers say that General Lee has so far done nothing to show outstanding ability and they are worried, for they all love Joe Johnston. But I remember Chase saying that Lee is the best general in either army, North or South, and I'm willing to give him a chance. I saw him for the first time two days ago, a man of remarkable composure and dignity, clear-eyed and impressive. I hope for the best. By the way, he has given us a new name. We are now the Army of Northern Virginia.

CHAPTER 14

HALE MCCAULEY WAS one of the great success stories of the South. Starting out a poor boy with nothing but driving ambition and a feel for business that was almost mystical, he had become rich beyond even his own dreams and was now the owner of huge tracts of land in several states. At least two thousand slaves worked on his various plantations—he didn't know the exact number, he told friends, because they were breeding so fast that he didn't bother to count them more than once a year. Although, as he liked to say, his own family background was nil he was accepted warmly at the highest levels of Virginia society. His power and money might not have brought that kind of final inclusion but his wife's name was Randolph. It made all the difference.

Malvern, his plantation in southern Virginia, was the crown jewel of his properties, set above a vast grassy area that rolled from the front veranda down to the river. The rose garden was famous and the formal Italian garden with imported, larger-than-life Roman statuary unique. It was his permanent residence, the castle he had designed for his wife and his daughter, Becca. His princess, he often said with a fond smile.

In spite of the grandeur around her and the constant attention of many servants, Becca had had a lonely childhood. Being an only child, she told Doug when he proposed, was not what she intended for her own offspring. Doug had heard about her growing-up years in some detail and one of his ambitions was to make her life with him better than it had been before.

Malvern had few near neighbors and Becca spent much of her childhood wandering the meadows and fields alone or with slave children as playmates. Her formal education was sketchy. Miss Elder, her teacher, was primarily concerned with correct deportment, not the life of the intellect. She got her real education from the books in her father's library.

Hale found a number of eligible men willing to marry his only daughter. Becca refused them all. Her mother, who understood Becca well, began sending her on visits to Richmond when she was fifteen, but twelve discouraging years passed before Doug Seymour, who had known her for most of those years, noticed that he was happiest when with her, then that he wanted to be with her all the time, then that he loved and wanted to marry her.

Their engagement was a thunderbolt to several hopeful girls. Becca McCauley with her flat chest and retiring ways had turned out to be more of a threat than anyone had dreamed.

The truth was that only a society that placed inordinate value on female beauty of a certain kind would have found her unattractive. She was short and hoopskirts, now at their widest, did not flatter her; she was slender to the point of thinness—bony, some said unkindly—a fact that tight basques and low necklines emphasized. But her complexion was clear except for a few freckles on her sharp little nose, her light brown hair was thick and shining, her eyes large and well shaped, the warm color of old brandy.

She knew how she was regarded but had never told anyone she could have married at a younger age if she hadn't come to the conclusion, much as Laura had, that being popular with men one did not care for was pointless. She was quiet, intelligent, not as shy as people supposed, and still dumbstruck by the fact that Douglas Seymour wanted her as his wife. The thought of actually living at the Seymour house made her stomach sink. Millie Seymour did not like her, she was ill at ease with pretty, vivacious Paige Wyatt and completely overawed by Laura Chandler. But Doug was going to be her husband, come what may. For his sake she was ready to accept Millie's invitation and brave the Seymour lionesses in their den.

Stunned by such determination her gentle mother gave permission and watched her start off on a dangerous ride to Richmond and the war zone.

On the third day of June, as early battle reports were filtering in along with the news that General Lee was now the commander standing between Richmond and destruction, Becca arrived for an indefinite stay.

She got a reception she hadn't expected. Millie could be charming at her social best and she had decided to charm Becca and like her if she possibly could. Paige was a self-assured, popular girl, the kind that Becca had never known how to deal with. Ordinarily they would not have become friends, but Becca was going to be a Seymour. Paige offered friendship and Becca accepted gratefully.

Laura was the greatest surprise. Before coming to Richmond this time Becca had known her only slightly and been too impressed to say much in her company. Living in the same house she discovered that the woman who would be her sister-in-law was unpretentious and generous, with a subtle intelligence, a sometimes wicked sense of humor, and another quality that Becca could not quite put her finger on. She only knew there was more to Laura than the obvious and that she was worth getting to know better.

Two letters came from Doug as soon as he knew she was in town. Becca kept most of her letter to herself. Millie's letter, which she read aloud, overflowed with gratitude, happiness, and plans for a wedding "after this next battle."

" 'Next battle,' " she repeated, took off the spectacles she wore for reading when Edward wasn't there to see, and put the letter back in its envelope. The "next battle" was always the one that might decide the outcome of the

Southern cause and, more important, the fate of their men. They did not want to think about the next battle and could not think of anything else.

On the day Becca arrived the wounded from the last battle were already flooding in. The injured General Johnston was taken to a house in one of the better residential sections but there were many more casualties than after Manassas and most of the wounded had to be lodged either in the newly built but inadequate hospitals or any other structures that could provide a roof, four walls, and a cot. Empty store buildings were taken over, people stepped around wounded men as they entered church on Sunday mornings, old warehouses and even sheds never intended for human habitation housed the injured and the dying. Minié-ball and shell-fragment wounds were particularly savage and little was known about how to deal with them other than to amputate if the wound was to an arm or leg. It was growing more difficult to bring in medicines past the blockade or smuggle them through the lines, and laudanum and morphine stores were declining rapidly as were all medical supplies.

Paige and Becca decided that it was not enough to pass out jars of preserves to wounded men and offer to wash their faces as many young ladies did. Instead they went to the hospital that Mary Elliott, a friend of the Seymour family, had set up in a school building and offered to nurse on a regular basis. Mrs. Elliott viewed society girls with a skeptical eye. Too many who attempted real nursing found it tiring, repugnant, or shocking and quit after time and energy had been spent training them or fainted at the sight of a festering stump and had to be treated themselves.

Paige, who like all very popular people was good at selling herself, convinced this stern-faced woman that she and Becca had sturdy souls as well as bodies and were fearless in the face of messy chores, hideous wounds, and death itself. Mrs. Elliott let them worry for a while and then informed them that they might stay on a trial basis but if they refused any task or, worse, fainted they would be immediately dismissed.

On their first day the greatest number of wounded from the recent battle arrived, hauled in by the wagonload from the surrounding countryside. At first they searched each face apprehensively, for any one of the new casualties could be Alex or Doug, Kirby or Edward. Becca, shaking in her shoes, came close to violent nausea several times but managed to keep control by taking slow, deep breaths and concentrating on the wound that needed cleaning, not the man himself, closing her mind to his pain and to the woman who must be waiting for him. Paige, armed with the tiny bit of knowledge gained after Manassas, was prepared for the groans, the smells, the screams from the operating theater after the chloroform ran out, yet several times she almost dropped a bottle of precious medicine because of the trembling of her hands. After several hours the pressure of work became so great that both forgot everything but the task at hand and simply did as they were ordered, inexperienced, clumsy, frightened but determined. They worked long into the evening and, when they were finally relieved, left rewarded by one of Mary Elliott's rare smiles. They came home exhausted to find a party in progress.

Millie's parties had become more frequent since Edward left. She liked to surround herself with people, especially young people, to play charades, to sing around the piano and even dance if there were enough men, to eat the good fresh food—meat, fruit, and vegetables presently so scarce in Richmond—that Pine Hill furnished.

She nursed the wounded in her own house after Manassas when Edward was safe at home, but now he was at risk she would not take in injured men or go into the hospitals. It was illogical, she did not understand it herself, but, she told her daughter, she could not and would not do it. Every moment of every day she feared the officer who would come to the door or the terrible letter that could not be opened. In order to live at all she had to shut her eyes to what happened to men in battle and how could she do that if she was surrounded by them?

She still spent many hours a week shopping for fancy slippers, gloves and bonnets, merchandise that was increasingly hard to get but could sometimes be found by a determined shopper with money to spend. Such luxury items commanded exorbitant prices and were brought in by blockade runners in preference to more needed items—

medicines, army boots, shovels, or other mundane goods. She spent the rest of her time writing a daily letter to Edward and keeping herself ready for his sudden reappearance. The army was so close by that men did come into town between battles, wives and sweethearts were always being surprised by their unexpected arrival, and Millie went through each day wearing her most flattering gowns, her hair prettily arranged, prepared for a visit that so far had not come.

Throughout the month of June, Laura continued to work at the War Department instead of rolling bandages, sewing for the troops, or nursing. Any bit of information overheard at the office, any scrap of White House gossip passed on to her by Frederick, she immediately gave to Fiona Rutledge. Fiona took the messages to David Rees, who carried them to the Union general, George McClellan. What the general did with such information neither she nor Laura nor David Rees knew.

Fiona had another activity which, far from being secret, was carried out in as public a way as possible and had even been denounced in the newspapers—she visited Yankee prisoners of war locked up in a brick warehouse on Cary Street, brought them food, stationery, reading material, and encouragement. Gave aid and comfort to the enemy, several editorials thundered. Fiona was serenely undisturbed. Federal prisoners had poured into Richmond along with the Confederate wounded and the city was equally unprepared for both. The luckless prisoners were locked up behind barred windows, without beds or blankets and with precious little food in the unheated warehouse confiscated from Libby and Son. Fiona's concern for them only confirmed the general belief that she had lost her mind. How any Southerner could have sympathy for these rapacious vandals was beyond the understanding of most people. They detested her but they did not suspect her.

THE INFORMATION LAURA SENT to McClellan was correct and would have been invaluable if the Northern general had acted on it: Robert E. Lee, although outnumbered, intended to attack instead of defend, to pounce on McClellan's larger force and either destroy the

Federal army or drive it out of Virginia. McClellan, sitting
near the Chickahominy River, always timid, always reluctant to go on the offensive himself, refused to believe Lee
would take such a gamble. While he was deciding this Lee
struck.

Early on the morning of the first day of fighting Laura
awoke to the sound of the guns. It's begun, she thought
and leaped from bed, threw on her clothes with shaking
hands and raced downstairs calling for Joseph. He came
through the hall from the kitchen, natty in his livery, his
dark face as blank as if he didn't know the rolling thunder
they both heard could mean his freedom. He was carrying a
breakfast tray for Millie.

"Put that down, Joseph. Get some help and take a sofa
up to the roof."

"Miss Millie wants breakfast upstairs dis mornin',
ma'am. It's her haid."

"I'll take care of her head. You get that sofa up there."

She ran back up the stairs to Millie's door, knocked once
and went in without waiting for an invitation. The room
was hot already and the windows were tightly shuttered.
Millie was in bed with a sheet over her head. Laura snapped
the draperies back and threw open the windows.

"Morning, Millie," she sang out and pulled the
sheet away.

Immediately Millie put a pillow over her head. "Close
those windows! Go away. Oh, close them, Laura. I can't
stand the noise."

"Nonsense. Up, up." Laura tossed the pillow on the
floor and dragged Millie out of bed.

"I have a headache. I need my breakfast."

"You need a little fresh air. We're going up on the roof."

"To watch? I can't."

"Better than moping down here." Laura brought petticoats and the plainest dress she could find. "Into this. No,
you don't need stays and you don't need Bella. I'll do up
your hair."

With the dress on Millie sat down on the bed and stared
at her bare feet. "I can't watch it, Laura. I'm scared."

"So am I. So is Edward, I imagine. Put on your shoes
and stockings or you'll have to go up there barefoot."

"Don't try to shame me. I'm a coward, so what? I don't want to watch."

"Put on your shoes."

With sulky slowness, overborne by a stronger personality, Millie pulled on stockings and wiggled her feet into shoes that were one size too small. "I don't know what's come over you, Laura. You were the sweetest little girl."

"Come on, my dear, march."

Ahead of them on the stairs to the roof Joseph and Adam were carrying the seven-foot brocade sofa from the front parlor. Getting it through the door and onto the roof was a delicate maneuver and Jewel was ahead, directing them.

"Lift up your end, Adam. Watch the leg, Joseph! If you scratch that leg I'll snatch you bald-headed."

"Yas'm, *Miss* Jewel, anything you sez, *Miss* Jewel," Joseph muttered with heavy sarcasm, but he said it softly.

From the roof of the great house on this high hill they could see spread out before them the lovely countryside, the flame as ranks of cannon fired, the clouds of smoke that soon grew thick enough to obscure portions of the battlefield. Laura and Millie sat on the sofa sheltered by parasols. Adam sat at their feet, excited, trying to follow the course of battle, cheering when he thought the Confederates were winning, turning once to tell Laura earnestly that the Yankees were very bad men to come down here to Virginia and cause so much trouble. Jewel laid a hand lightly on his head. She and Bella and Joseph sat in chairs, watching too, sipping lemonade along with the white ladies who owned them.

They seem disinterested, almost, Laura thought, but does Bella say secret prayers for a Union victory? Is Joseph waiting for the chance to run away like Varina's butler? Underneath all Jewel's sweetness and calm does she hate us? Would she be glad if she knew what I'm doing or would she think I'm a fool? If I told her . . . *Trust no one,* Chase said, and he's right. I can't tell even Jewel.

During the next six days until the battle ended, Paige and Becca slipped away from the hospital whenever they could and joined the little group on the roof. It was during this time that Laura began to see what Doug saw in Becca

McCauley. Paige, quick-tempered and volatile, seemed strong because she was strong-willed, but gentle, reticent Becca had a soul of steel. She sat under her parasol, her eyes fixed on the distant struggle, and remarked coolly, "It looks like the Federals are moving back toward the river. If they go across I believe it means we've won. Doug says a river crossing is the most difficult maneuver of all—they won't do it if they're not forced to."

Laura sat and watched until the sun went down, the sounds of battle died away, and scattered campfires began to sparkle, beautiful in a darkness that concealed pain, desolation, and death. That evening Laura was overcome with a loneliness that was almost beyond bearing. Chase had been gone for weeks and until these battles started she had not realized how much she missed him. He was going to Washington, he had told her when he left, and as always when they said goodbye she wondered if she was seeing him for the last time. So many things could go wrong. The lines between the armies had grown tighter, the war more bitter, and there was no longer any talk of chivalrous enemies. It was dangerous for him to approach the Union lines with their nervous sentries quick on the trigger and dangerous to move through the Confederate army. He had a pass signed by Judah Benjamin himself but Jason and the provost marshall had opposed giving it to him and Laura wondered why. Always, always there was the possibility of betrayal. She sat down on a bench in the garden, staring into the dark, and Millie came to the door and called to her.

"Laura, are you all right? What are you doing out there?"

"I'm fine, Millie. I'll be right in." She took a long breath and went back into the house.

A HOT JULY SUN beat down the next day and within hours the breeze told what could not be seen at this distance. Death was everywhere, for the smell of it was borne on the wind. Yet in spite of the losses that had struck so many families, people rejoiced for the siege of Richmond had been raised. The Army of Northern Virginia had driven the powerful Yankees away, their capital was safe, and they

had a real leader at last, the miracle-worker they needed—
Robert E. Lee. It was true that Confederate losses had been
great and every man lost was hard to replace. It was also
true that the Yankees had not quite been driven from Virginia, for the Army of the Potomac and most of its equipment had moved downriver and still sat there protected by
powerful gunboats of the U.S. Navy. But in the Seymour
household there was a great deal of rejoicing for they now
knew that all their men were safe. Doug wrote to Becca
that some lucky fellows were getting furloughs and as soon
as he got his they would be married.

Many soldiers did get to Richmond on flying visits,
long-postponed weddings were taking place, babies were
seen by fathers for the first time, and the streets were once
again teeming with uniformed men. Military funerals were
taking place too, for young men who would never marry
the girls they loved, for fathers who would never see their
babies. Hospitals were swamped with the wounded and
there was yet another burden for Richmond to cope with—
Union prisoners of war were pouring into a city completely
unprepared to deal with them.

Libby Prison was now bursting and Fiona Rutledge was
a fixture there, arriving in the mornings with her bags of
food, clothing, and little luxuries, irritating the commandant almost beyond endurance. He complained to Jason
Hood, who thought it over and then approached Laura
with a request.

"You are a close friend of Fiona Rutledge, aren't you,
Laura." It was a flat statement, not a question but his tone
was unthreatening and he was smiling—he smiled most of
the time now that Valerie was back in town.

Laura answered cautiously. "Not close. She was my
mother's friend and I've known her all my life. Lately she
seems to have gone round the bend, poor thing."

"So it seems. She's causing no end of trouble over at the
prison, but she's also an old friend of the provost marshal
and he won't forbid her to go there. Do me a favor and go
with her on one of these little expeditions. Watch what she
does there. These bundles she takes in are always carefully
searched but I'd like to know what she says to the prisoners
and what they say to her."

In shocked tones Laura said, "You want me to *spy* on that poor, confused lady?"

"Well, not spy. I certainly wouldn't ask a lady to do such a thing. We've had a detective following her for some time and she seems to be a harmless crackpot, but we want to be certain and you can help. Just let us know if she is doing anything improper. We will do the rest."

Early the next morning Laura went to Libby Prison. Fiona was waiting with her gardener and coachman, guarding a number of large bundles they had unloaded from her carriage. Sentries paced past as if she weren't there. They didn't like her but they were used to her and had been ordered to leave her alone. The neighborhood was rundown and the prison a somber building, dark red brick with small barred windows, gloomy even on the sunniest days. In one of the many ironies of war it had until recently been run and run badly by Mary Lincoln's half brother, Lieutenant Todd.

Just inside the door Fiona and Laura were stopped and told to wait for the commandant. He bustled down the stairs, a heavyset man with a florid face and an expression of exasperation.

"Here you are again, Miss Rutledge. What have you brought today?" He shook out her bundles and dumped a quantity of bedding on the floor. "No fatted calf or caviar?"

"Just blankets and some clothing. They have only the clothes on their backs." Like a schoolteacher reproving a badly behaved pupil, she added, "You don't keep this place properly heated, Captain." It was dark, chilly, and damp in here even on this hot July day.

"Our own soldiers could use these blankets." He looked at Laura. "Who are you? You can't go in with her."

"I'm Mrs. Chandler. I was asked by Secretary Hood to come with Miss Rutledge today."

"I doubt that."

Just as coldly Laura said. "Then send a messenger to the War Department and ask him."

He gazed at her wearily. She was probably somebody. She looked like somebody. "Why aren't you doing something useful? How can you sympathize with these Yankees?

Most true Southerners would like to shoot them. Oh, go on in. Let them in, Sergeant. Get them out of my sight."

This was the officers' prison, and looking around Laura wondered what the enlisted men's prison out on Belle Isle was like. Men were locked in large holding areas, sitting or lying on the bare wooden floor. Except for the most recently captured they were ragged and thin and many looked sick. The place was surprisingly hushed considering the packed room. There was only a low murmur of voices in quiet conversation punctuated by constant hoarse coughing.

Someone saw Fiona and called out, "Good morning, Miss Rutledge!" She passed among them, her eyes sparkling like a girl's, dispensing blankets, giving clothes to those most in need, introducing Laura as if they were at a formal party, and the men responded, courteous, well-spoken, standing a little straighter, flushed with the excitement of this break in the deadly routine, laughing occasionally.

Large, strong hands shook Laura's enthusiastically and she asked each in turn, "Where are you from? How long have you been here?"

The answers came back: Boston. Camden, Maine. Ohio. New York. Seven months, nine days. Since Bull Run, ma'am. Forever, ma'am.

The senior officer, a colonel, showed Laura the stove they cooked on when they could get wood, the tub they washed their clothes and themselves in, the "store" where goods, when they had any, were traded. They were so young, most of them, and many looked so sick.

Beside one of the men she knelt a long time. He looked about Kirby's age but he was blond instead of dark, and very weak. She settled down beside him and asked his name.

"Reuben Heitzen, ma'am."

"Heitzen. Is that German?"

"Pa says it's Pennsylvania Dutch, but I guess we're from Germany way back. My mother is a MacTavish, so there you are."

His gaunt young face lit with his smile and she smiled back. "Very American. And you're from Pennsylvania?"

"Illinois. A little town on the Mississippi River . . . wish I was there now. Mr. Lincoln and Mr. Douglas held one of their debates right there in the park. Pa made me and my brothers go and I was glad I did. I thought Mr. Lincoln had the straight of it." He looked at her in a worried manner. "But these people down South don't seem to think so." His voice broke and he began to cough, a deep, rattling cough, and someone brought him a cup of brackish river water. After catching his breath he sank back, eyes closed.

Laura looked up at Fiona. "This boy should be in the hospital."

"A lot of them should. I've tried but no one will listen to me."

As they parted outside the prison Laura looked at Fiona's capacious bag. "What have you got in there?"

"Letters home. They're not allowed to send out many so I bring them out. The fools"—she nodded toward the prison—"they never search me when I leave, only when I arrive. I lend those nice boys books too, and after a while they return them to me."

"With messages, I suppose. Fiona, be careful. They suspect you. They've got a detective following you."

"I know." Fiona's eyes danced. "Not a very good one— I see him everywhere."

She climbed into her carriage and rode off, a spare, dry spinster with ridiculous curls and the boldness and daring of a pirate.

Laura found Dr. Rollins in his new hospital built a little ways out of town, high above the river on one of Richmond's seven hills. The site had been selected carefully and the hospital was well staffed and relatively clean, the best in the city. Rollins was a didactic man, as certain of his own opinions as President Davis or Jason Hood but more open to new ideas than Davis and kinder than Jason.

He saw Laura come in through the wide front door, speak to the matron, and then smile and wave at him. He had long been attracted to her but admired her loyalty to her dead husband. Of course, she wanted a favor. He was constantly importuned by women who wanted special consideration for some wounded relative or friend and he wondered whom she had in mind. Her brothers had come safely through the last battles and were now at the army encampment not too many miles from town. Whatever it was, he decided, he would grant it if he could, for she was his idea of all a Southern lady should be. Her only flaw, if she had one, was a cosmopolitan quality—which most Southern ladies did not have—that he supposed came from her years in Washington. She had recently set aside mourning and was wearing a white gown sprinkled with green flowers. Its simplicity appealed to him. He disapproved of the many wealthy women who did no work but pranced about in extravagant gowns and enormous hoops and expected life to go on undisturbed while good men died for their sakes.

"Mrs. Chandler," he said with an enormous smile, and bowed. He would have liked to sweep off his hat but he wasn't wearing one.

"Dr. Rollins, it's good to see you." She looked admiringly around the light, airy ward. "This is remarkable, so different from the other hospitals."

She meant to flatter him, of course, but what was wrong with that? His hospital was remarkable and he couldn't help but be pleased that she saw it. "Well," he said modestly, "we are reasonably satisfied. May I show you around?"

After a tour through the ward they went outside into the July sunshine and she raised her parasol as they walked between the many separate buildings of the hospital, a remarkably self-contained place with its own bakery, dairy, and brewery.

Laura gazed at each of the wonders as he pointed them out, making little sounds of approval. "I am bowled over, Doctor. I heard you were accomplishing marvelous things but this is astonishing. Why, it's a little city and all for the purpose of making men whole again."

He was immensely gratified, for the hospital was his life, and he wanted to hear her say more. "Please, won't you sit here for a moment? We've planted trees and placed benches strategically so that our convalescents have convenient resting spots at short intervals. I am a great believer in the benefits of fresh air and sunshine."

She closed her parasol and sat down. He sat beside her, realized he was staring and searched for a sensible remark.

She said, "Doctor—"

"I wish you would call me Byron."

She smiled. "Thank you. Byron, I have a favor to ask . . ."

"I would gladly do anything for you that is in my power."

"This is well within your power but it's a *great* favor. You may be shocked when you hear what it is." He looked amused at the thought that she could do anything that shocked him and then heard her say, "I want you to transfer a very sick soldier out of Libby Prison and bring him here."

He said nothing. He appeared to be too stunned to say anything.

"You see," she said gently, "I have shocked you."

"Not at all, not at all. That is—" He hesitated and then inquired delicately, "Is this soldier a relative perhaps? So many families do have, ah, misguided members. I have a friend whose own son has gone to the North. Broken his father's heart, of course."

"This man is not a relative, not even a friend, unless you can make a friend in fifteen minutes. I met him this morning."

"You were visiting strange men in the prison?"

"It was in connection with my work at the War Department. Jason Hood asked me to go. You do know about my work?"

"Yes, and I venerate you for it. It must be unpleasant in the extreme for a lady to work in a man's world."

Laura thought of the ladies slaving away in this hospital and wondered at the blindness of a man so imaginative when it came to his own work. But he seemed relieved at the mention of Jason Hood. She pushed her advantage. "You know what conditions are like at Libby. He is very young, Byron, and very sick. He could be one of my brothers."

"He is the enemy. This hospital exists for those who have borne the battle for the Confederate cause. Our whole purpose is to send them back into battle, hard as that may seem. How can I give one of our beds to our enemy?"

"He isn't our enemy now, just a sick boy who will die if

we don't help him. You're a healer, Byron. So many will die on both sides and we can't help most of them but we can save this boy. Let's make him well and after the war send him home to his mother."

His stern face relaxed a little. "You should take up the law, Laura. You're a good pleader."

"Would you come with me to the prison and examine him? If you think it's right you could transfer him today." Her eyes, pleading but hopeful, locked on his. There might be tears in them, he thought.

He was forty-two and had been a widower for four long years; he supposed he had no chance with her, but he did like to look at her, almost as one enjoyed a great painting. It was well past noon and there was the possibility that they might have lunch together before going to the prison. If the boy was as sick as she thought, he could, indeed, transfer him before the end of the day.

When Laura went to the War Department to report on Fiona the sun was low on the horizon. A cool river wind was beginning to stir the trees and the lemon fragrance of magnolias made the dusk seem even cooler. The day had been one of sham, maneuver, and haggling that had grown tricky at times. Byron Rollins had had his lunch with her in a private booth at Sanson's restaurant and held her hand while he told her about the struggles and sorrows of his life—that was his fee for examining Lieutenant Reuben Heitzen. He said the boy had pneumonia and ordered him moved to the hospital. That favor had cost permission to call on her, a cheap enough price.

Now she must report her opinion of Fiona to Jason Hood and do it convincingly. Climbing the stairs to the office, she met Jefferson Davis coming down. He looked tense and tired, his thin, bony face a mass of fine lines— unusual for a man in his early fifties—an erect, soldierly figure striving to appear even more military in his inevitable gray suit and dark felt hat, an approximation, if one did not look too closely, of a Confederate officer's uniform. How he longs to be a general, Laura thought, gazing after him. He revealed himself so plainly and never knew he was doing it.

She came to her own office and stopped just inside the

door. Jason had a visitor. His wife. She started to back out, not wanting to talk to Valerie now when she had already doled out all her available insincerity earlier in the day. But Jason caught sight of her and called out in friendly fashion, "Ah, Laura, there you are."

"Valerie, how nice to see you. I'll come back another time, Jason."

"Not at all. I want to talk to you." He turned to Valerie. "I sent Laura on an important mission today. You won't be bored if we talk shop for a moment, will you, my dear?"

Valerie dimpled and hugged Laura. "Of course not. My poor little brain probably won't understand a thing but I'm fascinated."

Your poor little brain is like a steel trap, Laura thought, but you know how to make a man happy. She said, "I have good news, Jason. We needn't waste another thought on poor Fiona. She's harmless as a child. She says Christian love is her only guide and if our cause is to have a happy outcome we must succor the imprisoned and the helpless, even the undeserving. I must say, from my reading of the Bible she has a point, don't you think?"

Jason, who was a prominent communicant of the Episcopal Church, muttered, "Um," but Valerie's eyes sparkled suddenly before she cast them down.

Laura went on cheerfully. "I must admit the thought impressed me so that I talked to Dr. Rollins about a desperately ill prisoner and he agreed that the man should be transferred to the hospital."

"You did *what?*"

"I talked to Dr. Rollins—"

"I heard you. Did Rollins do it?"

"Yes, he did. The man is very ill. I also talked to him about Fiona. He's been watching her closely and takes great interest in her case."

"He thinks she's mentally gone, does he?"

"Not quite that. He believes her to be simply a sentimental old maid inspired perhaps by some thwarted mothering instinct to bring goodies to imprisoned young men. It's sad, in a way, and yet generous and Christian."

Jason sat down in his large swivel chair and fingered his watch fob. Byron Rollins was a good friend and a loyal

Confederate and he had always been impressed by his judgment.

Valerie said, "Darling, I must go. Try not to be too late." When she bent to kiss him he looked up and Laura was struck by his uncharacteristic, gentle smile. As she and Valerie went down the stairs together she considered that smile. His pride in Valerie, his possessiveness and the delight he took in showing her off, had always been obvious. Now she knew that as much as he could love anyone he loved his pretty, flirtatious, unfaithful wife.

On the street as they paused before parting Valerie said, "We must get together more often, Laura. I know I've said that before and haven't done it but everything has been so topsy-turvy lately. You're busy, too, but we can make time for each other. Oh, I do envy you! Imagine, a real job, an important job. Imagine *having* to get up and go to work every day."

"Surely Jason could find something for you to do if you really want it. He never refuses you anything."

"Oh, yes he does. He has absolutely forbidden me to nurse at the hospital. To tell the truth, I'm not too sorry about that—illness frightens me though I'm sure I could do it. He says I would be disturbing to sick men. I told him they're much too sick to pay attention to me but he wouldn't listen." She spoke without guile, not preening but voicing the honest complaint of a woman controlled by a husband who expected from her a certain kind of behavior, one which did not include competence or independence. Laura felt a surge of sympathy for her such as she hadn't felt since they were girls. Valerie had a sharp intelligence that she wanted to use and could not. Laura said the one thing that would cheer her up.

"Honestly, Val, you can't blame him for being a mite jealous. You're even prettier now than before you were married."

"Do you think so? Oh, I have missed you! Are you going toward Capitol Square? Come along, I'll go with you." They linked arms and she lowered her voice although there was no one to hear. "By the way, do you ever hear from Chase? I promise I won't be mad if you say yes—he can't write to me and he didn't mention how long he'd be away. Do you know where he's gone to or when he's coming back?"

"No," said Laura, "I haven't an idea in the world."

CHAPTER 15

WILLARD'S HOTEL WAS Washington's favorite rendezvous. In its elegant lobby, hallways, and bar, gregarious people came to cross paths with those more important, to eat, drink, and conduct business of all kinds. Here diplomats and politicians mended fences, gamblers arranged quiet games, prostitutes agreed on terms with prospective customers, businessmen arranged lucrative government contracts. And although it was not publicly acknowledged, it was here that much of the official business of government was done. On this hot, muggy day in late August the habitués of Willard's had taken refuge in the hotel from the tumultuous streets.

Little more than a month ago Richmond had trembled as the Army of the Potomac assaulted it. Robert E. Lee had driven them off and now suddenly, bitterly, the tables were turned, Washington's back was to the wall and the streets were filled with panicked people who sniffed the sharp odor of gunpowder on the wind and heard the reverberation of Rebel cannon just across the river. The Federal army seemed to have abruptly come apart. Green recruits were being hurled into battle while experienced soldiers were allowed to prowl the streets, unruly, often drunk, contributing nothing to the Union cause. Army draft horses were dying of starvation while fodder waited in storage without the manpower to load and ship it; fighting soldiers were beginning to run out of ammunition and food; and the wounded lay on the battlefield unattended because of the lack of doctors, nurses, and medical supplies. Refugees in carriages, wagons, and on foot poured into the city from Manassas bringing word that the ragged Rebel troops had taken the army warehouse there, supplying themselves with guns, ammunition, boots, and other desperately needed equipment stamped U.S. Army. They were burning as they

came, blowing up vital bridges, pulling up railroad tracks so
that even if Washington did get the chaotic transportation
system organized, there were no tracks for the trains to
travel over.

Rumors flashed through town—there had been a disastrous battle and thousands of men were dead, the army was
broken in a rout worse than the first battle at Bull Run, a
monstrous Rebel army was in hot pursuit and would
overrun Washington within hours. Many people believed
every story, the more horrifying the better, and scrambled
to escape, usually though liquor since it wasn't easy for any
but the rich to find a way out of the city.

Inside Willard's Hotel there was an illusion of safety and
calm. Business was still being conducted and patrons were
enjoying the hotel's lavish breakfast. Chase was just rising
from his table when he saw with astonishment and pleasure
that the tall lieutenant entering the dining room with a
young woman was a man he had last seen in Philadelphia
almost a year ago. His brother.

Richard Girard had traveled upriver on a transport when
the Army of the Potomac was ordered to leave the Virginia
peninsula and come back to defend Washington. He had
been in town only three days. The last year in the army had
taught Richard the truth of his brother's comments about a
soldier's life, and last month the fighting before Richmond
had taught him more. He had learned that war was not
glory and honor, it was confusion, hideous accident, senseless death—it was life intensified and more terrible. Before
the war he had believed that discipline and hard work
would bring eventual happiness. Now he knew it was useless to plan and foolish to forgo the satisfactions of the
moment, for the moment was all there was.

When he got to town he had sought out the wife of a
man in his company, a man he knew and liked who had
died through a long night of a stomach wound. In Washington he sat in the woman's small parlor and told her the
soldier's lie, that her husband had died instantly and suffered no pain. She was young and pretty and had been married two weeks when her husband left. Her grief was
painful to watch. Richard, who had thought he would
never feel anything again, reached out to console her and,

swamped with grief, fear, and a sense of life's hopelessness, they had ended up in bed. He spent the next two nights with her and this morning brought her to Willard's for their famous breakfast. His brother was very nearly the last person in the world he wanted to see.

Chase came up to him with a happy smile, and Richard might have been able to carry it off if both he and the lady had been more experienced. But he stumbled as he introduced her, gave a long, unnecessary explanation of why they were there, and she turned scarlet and said in a suffocated voice that she would leave the brothers to their reunion.

"Not at all, ma'am," Chase said. "I have an appointment this morning. Could we meet for dinner, Richard?"

"I really do have to go," she muttered. "Goodbye, Lieutenant Girard. Thank you for your kindness to—to my husband and me." She hurried through the lobby, her eyes down, her face flaming.

Chase said, "Let's sit in the bar. We can get some coffee there."

Richard looked around the wood-paneled, smoky, luxurious room and then at Chase. "I feel like a fool. I did that badly."

"Don't apologize to me—I ruined your morning. You look fine. How has it gone for you?"

Richard gave him a sardonic smile. "You were right about the army. I saw my first combat down on the peninsula last month and it was enough to last me a lifetime."

"What next?"

"Nobody's told me but I think we'll dig in around here and try to hold off the Rebs, although even if we do there'll just be another fight somewhere else. They're good fighters, Chase. Smart and brave and a little crazy. They're not going to quit and we're not going to quit and it will go on and on. I don't think I'll come out of this alive."

"Everybody feels that way after a battle but it doesn't mean anything. You're just as likely to survive as the next man."

"I'll tell you this—if I am still alive after this is over I'm going to change my life, I don't know how but I'm going to change it." The waiter came, a black man who was new at his job. All the white waiters were in the army. After he was gone Richard said, "All I've done is talk about myself. How are things with you? Do you live here now?"

"I travel around. I do have an appointment to keep this morning. How about dinner?"

"I have to report in. If they don't grab me for something I'll be here." Just before they parted Richard remarked in a reflective way, "You're the smart one, brother, and I wish I'd listened to you. There's not one good thing about a war. If I could I'd get out of the army and make money like you."

THE WAR DEPARTMENT was on Seventeenth Street across from the White House, a small, three-story building with a columned portico. Here was the office of the arrogant, emotional, much-hated secretary of war, Edwin Stanton, the second most powerful man in Washington. Here, too, in a small back room on the second floor was the office of a man not widely known in the city, a slight man with pale eyes and a perpetually worried expression, wearing a rumpled seersucker suit. Most of the workers in the building assumed he was a low-level clerk but, in fact, he reported directly to the President. His name was Theodore Harper. He had no wife, no children, and as far as curious friends could find out, no mistress; his work had always been his life. He loved being close to power, a behind-the-scenes mover of men and events. The war had brought him fulfillment. He was now a master of spies.

He said, "I understand you're impatient to be back in uniform, Chase, and I honor you for it—of course you want to fight for your country and you're doing a fine job of it where you are. The President himself said—"

"Please, Ted, not your Fourth of July speech. I've done everything you asked. Information is coming out regularly, some of it high quality, although I haven't noticed it being used to advantage."

"I know. It's disheartening but eventually . . . You've done a magnificent job. We're very impressed. Miss Rutledge was no surprise but how did you snag Laura Chandler?"

"You ordered me to."

Ted laughed. "I told you to try. I didn't really think you could do it. I met her once back in—oh, fifty or fifty-one. Do you know why she's doing this? I always like to know my agents' reasons."

"She believes in the Union, she's against slavery."

"And? What else?"

With a smile Chase said, "If I find out I'll let you know. You already know my reason."

"You volunteered."

"I was ordered to volunteer. I'm a good officer with combat experience and I want back in, Ted. I'm not going through the whole damn war like this."

Ted Harper tilted back his chair. "You would revert to major."

"Is that the way this great country rewards its faithful servants? What would the President say?"

"Go back to Richmond this time and I'll do what I can for you. If we can hold Lee off, we expect him to pull out and make a move into Maryland. We'll need all the intelligence we can get. Of course, it may be all over in a few days if we don't hold the city."

"You know better than that. If Lee takes this town we'll lose our dignity but it won't finish us. They have to destroy the army to do that and I don't think they can. How close are we to an evacuation?"

"Closer than I like to think about. Mr. Stanton is in a sweat, convinced there are traitors in the army. He's ordered all our reserve guns and ammunition shipped out and his clerks are packing the records this morning. They even came after mine but I refused to turn them over. We've got a gunboat standing by at the navy yard ready to rescue the President and the senior members of the cabinet, but people like you and me will have to fend for ourselves."

Chase walked to the open window and gazed out into the hot August day. South of the White House, next to the slaughterhouse and the stinking canal, stood the squat beginning of what was to be a columnar monument to General Washington if it was ever finished. At present it looked like a sawed-off tree stump. At the other end of Pennsylvania Avenue the Capitol building stood uncompleted too, its dome open to the sky. This malodorous, confused, corrupt city was stumbling through the war, day after frightened day, determined to hold the country together. Some people believed it was worth it. He sighed and without turning said, "Give me a pass, Ted. I'll go back this last time."

VARINA DAVIS HAD grown comfortable in her position as First Lady. She had grown arrogant too, her critics said, aloof, demanding, and overbearing. Her friends maintained she simply expected the deference due the President's wife and her enemies admitted that the welfare of her touchy, temperamental husband was her chief concern. Even when giving a party her first question was, Will it be good for Banny?

So it was with the grand dinner party held at the Executive Mansion in September. For weeks the war news had been good. While Washington cowered behind its fortifications General Lee had handed the Union a second blistering defeat on the Bull Run battlefield near Manassas. Then, instead of attacking the city, Lee had moved toward Maryland and official Washington breathed a sigh of relief, unpacked its suitcases and began assigning blame.

Jeff Davis had been in an optimistic mood when his shabby, impoverished army crossed the Potomac into Maryland. In Maryland, he told Varina, the Rebel spirit burned at white heat; the populace would welcome the army and supply it with everything it needed. So it had been a stunning blow when Marylanders had not greeted Lee with rejoicing; they had not been happy to see him at all. Davis had had a severe case of dyspepsia all week.

For the past two days Varina and her indispensable butler, Frederick, had supervised preparations for the evening. At the last moment Frederick mentioned that he had seen Colonel Girard in town that afternoon and she immediately sent an invitation to his hotel and added a place at the table. Chase was a hostess's delight, a charming single man at a time when they were scarce.

Most of the guests were already present when Laura arrived in a black mood for yet another long, difficult evening spent catering to the peculiarities of Jefferson Davis. This afternoon she had brought over the remainder of the late summer roses for Varina's flower arrangements and waited in the little upstairs room next to the President's study while he talked to his aide, John Mercer. What she had overheard sounded important and she would pass it on to Fiona in the morning, but she was low in her mind, oppressed by loneliness and a feeling that nothing she did was of any real use. None of the Seymour men had written in weeks, but they were surely with Lee and Lee was pressing battle once again. Tonight the smothering blanket of heat that lay over the city burdened body and spirit and convinced her that her work was absurd and the war wouldn't end until everything good was destroyed.

The dining room, where the guests were chatting and circulating, was so large that the long rosewood table, seating thirty people, occupied only a small portion of it.

At the end of the room the triple-sash windows, a uniquely Southern invention, were raised to the top so that they became doors through which guests could pass if they wished. Laura stepped out on the portico into the hot September night.

The columned portico ran across the back of the house and overlooked the garden. Not a leaf on the trees stirred, no nightbirds sang, the air was still.

Laura gave up hope of a breeze and went back into the dining room, lost in her own dark thoughts. The last guests were arriving—Serena Wynn, a girl famous for announcing and then breaking engagements to a series of young men, her latest fiancé, Mason Campbell, wounded at the second Battle of Manassas last month and still walking with a crutch, and Chase Girard.

He saw her from the doorway, staring at nothing with a somber, almost brooding expression, and watched the light come into her face when she saw him.

As everyone clustered around the injured hero, Chase came across the room to her.

She said, "I didn't know you were in town."

"I got in this afternoon. I'm at the Arlington House again."

She gazed admiringly in the direction of Lieutenant Campbell, who was being helped to a seat by several hovering ladies, and murmured, "Harpers Ferry has fallen and

Jackson has come back to join Lee. I heard the President read the dispatch when it came in." Over in Maryland, General Lee had unexpectedly, daringly divided his little army and sent his right arm, Stonewall Jackson, to take Harpers Ferry and safeguard his rear; as always, Stonewall had done his job. Now Lee and Jackson were dug in near the village of Sharpsburg. "They're spread out between Antietam Creek and the town, forty thousand men at the most."

Chase, too, was watching Mason Campbell. "I'll try to get it out tonight but it may not do any good. George McClellan always believes Lee has three times the troop strength he actually has." He glanced at her with a smile. "You're worth three or four regiments, Mrs. Chandler, all the time looking so cool and lovely and innocent."

"I don't feel any of those things."

Varina's dinner was of a variety and richness that impressed her guests for even the wealthy were beginning to feel the pinch of shortages.

Mason Campbell was the centerpiece of the evening. Everyone wanted to talk to and even touch him, for he was so fine, stalwart, brave, representative of all that was best in their world, living proof that in the long run they must prevail. He had been shot in the foot at the beginning of the battle and seen little of the terror and brutality that followed. He was nineteen years old, filled with buoyant optimism and the young man's belief that unlike everyone else, he is immortal. Although he still walked with a crutch, his wound was not severe and he hoped, he told them all at the dinner table, that he would be back with Lee before the next battle.

Byron Rollins asked, "Is it true that the Yankee army we beat at Manassas had more than twice as many men and cannon?"

"They have all the men they want and more where they came from. They have cannon, powder, boots, blankets—or I should say, they did have. When we need supplies we capture their supply depots. We beat them in battle and then take everything we need from the battlefield. We fight them with their own supplies and we win and take more. They'll never beat us and I'll tell you why. They have the foundries and factories but we have the heart." His young face was afire with conviction.

Laura looked at his shining eyes and thought of her brothers, now preparing to fight for God and country over in Maryland, and of other equally idealistic, determined young men such as she had seen at Libby Prison, preparing to do the same on the other side. She applauded Lieutenant Campbell with the rest and glanced at Chase, knowing what was in his mind as certainly as if he had spoken. Boys like this could touch the heart with their innocence and splendid, stupid courage. Without them old men could not have wars.

At the head of the shining dinner table Frederick bent beside Jefferson Davis and spoke a few quiet words. The President excused himself and left the room. Varina urged everyone to continue eating and they tried, straining their ears for they knew not what.

When he returned he stood at his place, his haughty, bony face tight with emotion, his deep-set eyes blazing. "Word has just come. This morning General Lee joined battle with the enemy in Maryland at a little creek called Antietam near the village of Sharpsburg. The fighting has been desperate and bloody all day, the Yankees have hurled themselves on us again and again and we have held. Let us bow our heads and beseech the God of Hosts to bless our enterprise."

CHAPTER 16

IT WAS HOT AT DAYBREAK. They camped the night before in the yard of a man who had taken his family and fled before the oncoming Confederates and when they went to his pump to fill their canteens they found the pump handle broken and the pump destroyed.

To his friend Doug said, "Why do I have the feeling these people aren't happy to see us?"

Brad Ely stared glumly at the pump. "Son of a bitch," he remarked without emotion. The effect the army had had on his language would have shocked his mother. Before the war he had not even known most of the words that now casually sprinkled his conversation.

Doug said, "I saw a little pond down by the stable."

They hurried to the empty stable. The horses had been taken away by the owner as had everything of value that was movable, but the evidence of their recent presence was everywhere including the soles of Doug's shabby boots, boots he wouldn't have allowed his groom to wear at home in the old days.

In the pink light of dawn they stared at the pond, actually a small mud hole, squatted and filled their canteens. The sun would soon be high and even dirty water might make the difference on such a day as this would be.

Yankee artillery had been roaring since first light, preparing for the assault that was coming, perhaps in moments, against the sparse ranks of Confederates entrenched on the steep banks of the Antietam, and Rebel cannon answered steadily. Edward had said yesterday that their position was strategically about as bad as it could be. Doug had not seen him or Kirby since, but he knew approximately where their unit was. His captain, a brave and kindly man, had moved him to his present position without saying why. Doug had protested but it did no good. Brothers always wanted to fight together and the army considered it good for morale and allowed it. But so many families had lost all their sons in one battle that Captain Ferguson had decided on a policy of his own—he separated brothers if he could do it without harming his unit. Doug didn't want to acknowledge the reason he wasn't with his own family today; he couldn't let himself think that he might never see Edward or Kirby again.

The sun was well up when the order came to advance toward town on the double-quick. In a corn field they halted, formed up, and hurled themselves up the rising ground under murderous artillery fire. Doug raced through cornstalks as high as his head, hearing as from a great distance the screams of friends who dropped around him. He flung himself down sweating and gasping behind a rail fence. They were coming, a mass of Yanks, firing as they came. He fired, reloaded, fired. The din was so great he could not think, he could not hear, but he shot those blue-bellies with no sense of killing men, only beasts who would kill him if they could. They were blown away before his eyes, dozens of them simply vanished under the Confederates' lethal fire as if a sweeping blade were cutting them down like stalks of corn. Huge holes appeared in the blue line yet they came on with a frenzied, bestial shouting like the roaring of a violent wind.

Powder smoke stung the nose and eyes and had grown so great that it hid parts of the battlefield. Someone screamed, "Shoot that man!", and Doug loaded, fired, saw the Yankee color-bearer jerk and fly backward and the Stars and Stripes go down. The sight filled him with joy. He would stop them, he would kill them all before they got to him. He tore another cartridge, loaded, fired, then jumped over the rail fence as farther down the line it flew apart under an artillery shell. A voice was cursing steadily; he didn't know it was his own. Grapeshot and canister came down, a thick, deadly rain, but it didn't matter, nothing mattered but load, fire, kill. He shrieked a cry more piercing than ever he had when sighting the fox on the hunting field, never knowing he did it. His friends were shrieking too, he heard it distantly, a terrifying sound to any enemy, yet still they came on. Move back, move back behind the fence, flatten out behind the thin rails and hope the earth will swallow you, for there are no more bullets.

General Longstreet's courier raced up on a lathered horse. He called out, "This position must be held at all costs, it's the key to the line!"

His face pressed into the dirt, Doug heard his colonel shout back, "Tell the general to send me ammunition. I haven't a cartridge in my command, but I'll hold at bayonet point as long as there's a man left."

The order "Fix bayonets!" roared out. A sharp needle stung Doug's thigh but he ignored it, braced himself behind a tree and gathered his strength as a blue uniform hurtled at him. He thrust deep and the blade stuck. He put his foot on the dead man's chest, wrenched it out and braced himself again. They wouldn't stop, they would never stop. He would die today.

*   *   *

KIRBY FOUND HIM under the tree. Dusk had forced an end to battle and men were sitting or lying on the ground too exhausted even to move away from the dead who lay among them, Federal and Confederate, with arms and legs flung out awkwardly or completely gone, faces blank, without the surprised expression that had been there at the moment they were hit. Scattered burning buildings lit the battlefield and the cries of the wounded stirred uninjured men with some compassion left to try to help them.

"Brother?" Kirby said. "Brother . . ." And he embraced Doug.

He opened his eyes and mumbled, "I thought you were dead. I thought everyone was dead."

"Any water in your canteen? I drank all mine."

Doug fumbled at his belt and Kirby took the canteen from him and held it to his brother's lips.

"Tastes good."

"Yeah, muddy but delicious."

Doug opened his eyes again at the jaunty tone, saw Kirby's haggard face and the infinite knowledge there.

Kirby said, "How bad is the leg? You've got this tied too tight."

"Got the bleeding stopped but then I couldn't get the knot untied." Doug fumbled weakly at the strip of cloth tied above the wound in his thigh, and Kirby pushed his hand away and loosened the improvised tourniquet.

"A little seeping, not too bad. I'll try to find a doctor . . ."

Doug grabbed his arm. "Edward?"

Kirby grinned, an odd, crooked grin. "Like me, not a scratch, though God knows why. He tempted fate enough times today."

Doug shifted his weight, sat up a little straighter. "What did he do?"

Kirby sank down on the hard ground, stretched out his feet with a groan and looked sideways at Doug. "He fought like a madman, out in front all the way. I know an officer's supposed to lead but these were damn-fool chances there was no reason to take. Later on we were trying to hold our position, but the Yanks were enfilading the road, pouring it in point-blank. No one could live through fire like that. We pulled back, all but Edward. He ran forward alone, waving his sword and screaming, right into the Yankee cannon. They held their fire until he finally turned back. I guess they knew a crazy man when they saw one."

"I can understand. You get crazy in battle, I found that out today."

"You have any food?"

Doug shook his head. He had thrown away his knapsack and other belongings, not wanting to be encumbered in the heat of battle.

Kirby pulled a package from inside his shirt. "Got some salt pork here. You chew on it and I'll try to find some more water."

He came back with two canteens of creek water and sat down again, groaning. "Lord God, I feel like an old man. Here, take a swig. It ain't brandy but it's wet."

Doug sucked in water. Some of it dribbled down his chin.

"Those Yanks aren't cowards," he said.

"No."

"They're hell-fire, is what they are. Not what we thought."

"I know."

There was silence for a while, not a comfortable silence. Then, "You think maybe Edward really has gone round the bend? They say battle does that to some fellows."

Kirby tossed down a swallow of water as if taking whiskey neat. "Not Edward. But he sure talks crazy sometimes. Last night I was trying to sleep and he was running on to Alex about how all a man really needs is honor and he's going to recoup his honor in this war. That's what he said—'I'm going to atone, recoup my honor, and I know just how to do it.' "

"What in hell did he mean by that?"

"Beats me. What could he have to atone for?" Kirby got to his feet. "Stay put, old buddy. I'm going to scout you up a doctor."

M ANY TIMES during that bloodiest of days in the orchards, fields, and woodlands near the banks of the Antietam, the Army of Northern Virginia had nearly broken. Later, when soldiers were able to reflect, they asked themselves, If the Yankees had attacked one more time would the army not have been destroyed? Would it not have been the end? But by the time they were able to ask the question it no longer mattered. For all the determination, ability, and superlative courage of the Union men, they did not have a leader willing to risk all. Their general, McClellan, had withheld his reserves.

Lee and his battered army rested through the night and the next morning waited for an attack that did not come. Then, having held his position and allowed the army to lick its wounds, Lee moved back over the Potomac into home territory with no sense of ignominious defeat. The bravery, the blood, the death, had resulted in what seemed to be a draw. Both sides had taken enormous casualties; the North claimed victory and the Confederates slipped back into Virginia in dignified withdrawal. Maryland had not welcomed them with open arms but they had held on by the skin of their teeth against all the enemy had thrown at them. What came next no man could say.

Six days after Antietam, to its horror, the South discovered what came next. Abraham Lincoln, the monster, the beast, the tyrant who called himself an American President, had the day before announced his decision—his covenant with God, he had told his cabinet—that all slaves in any state now in rebellion against the United States would on January 1, 1863, be "forever free."

Laura heard the dispatch at the War Department the moment it came in. As soon as she decently could she hurried to the White House, where Jefferson Davis was closeted with Judah Benjamin. Varina, in a cold rage, paced alone in the garden.

At sight of Laura she spat out, "He thinks we fight because of our slaves! He thinks we'll stop if he destroys our property when all we want is *liberty*!" She hurled herself onto a bench under the horse-chestnut tree, her whole body shaking.

Laura sat down beside her. Southerners always insisted they were fighting for liberty, never seeing that the liberty they wanted meant the freedom to enslave another people. "It's a great shock, I know . . ." she began, searching for some sympathy that was neither a lie nor a platitude, but got no further.

"Shock? It's an *abomination*! The man is not mad—I don't allow him that excuse. He is simply vile and without human feeling." Varina gathered herself and with the discipline that was her greatest strength stilled her twisting hands. In a more controlled voice she went on. "With a single dash of the pen he means to wipe out *four hundred billions* of our property, destroy our society, and bring down on us evils far greater than the loss of money. Well, we won't yield, we will never yield."

"Yes. It will make resistance more bitter."

"Oh, you are so right! Do you want to know what Banny says?"

"I'd very much like to know."

"He says that in the long run this will be beneficial. No Southerner will imagine now that we can ever go back to the Union. We can't live with a mass of free Negroes in our midst! Either the slaves will be exterminated, every Southern white will be exiled, or there will be absolute, *total* separation from the United States."

Laura gazed into the flashing dark eyes, wondering how she had maintained a friendship so long with this woman. What did she mean—*"The slaves will be exterminated"*? Did she realize what she'd just said?

She had to get away from Varina now, before her real feelings betrayed her, get out of this house and go home. But even home was no longer sanctuary. It had been in her mind for some time—very soon she must find another home, a place of her own where she could live her life as she pleased.

T HE WEDDING OF Doug Seymour and Becca McCauley was simple, nothing like the elaborate affair Paige had insisted on, but it was charming, everyone agreed. Becca's parents were not present because her mother was ill, but the Seymours and their relations as well as all their friends were there to witness this union and to forget for a little while that there was a war where men were dying.

The church was St. John's Episcopal—Becca's choice—a

small, simple church where late afternoon sunlight glowed through the windows and spread warmth over the faces of guests pleased to be in the presence of such happiness although they knew how temporary it might be. Near the pulpit was the pew where Patrick Henry had spoken out for liberty, the same valuable commodity Varina believed Doug and Kirby were fighting for. Laura pushed the thought out of her mind and her eyes moved on, picking out the people most important to her.

Millie sat alone at the end of the pew. Edward hadn't been able to come home; few leaves were being granted with the army maneuvering for position and another battle probable at any time. Millie was unhappy about it but resigned. Paige was not resigned at all. She sat a little distance away from her mother, nodding pleasantly at friends and hiding the bitterness she had expressed so vividly when Kirby came home.

"I understand about Doug—after all, he is wounded, though not too badly as far as I can tell. But what about you, Kirby? How come you're home and Alex isn't? Since when are they letting men come home just to be best man at their brother's wedding?"

Kirby shrugged. "I know how to work things better, I guess. Or maybe he doesn't want to come home. Lots of pretty girls out there in the farm country, pink, round, corn-fed—"

"Don't listen to him, Paige," Laura interposed hastily, "he's only trying to rile you. Shut up and get out of here, Kirby."

Kirby sauntered out, grinning, with Paige shrieking after him and Becca staring at the floor, nonplussed by such frank talk. She never heard frank talk at home. No one ever teased or told you to shut up or screamed that you were a weak, cowardly shirker; at home everyone was always so polite. They were in her room with Laura's wedding dress, altered to fit her short stature and slight figure, lying on the bed. Addie Shaw pulled it over her head, pinned it in a little more over the bosom, and they all stood back while she looked into the tall mirror on the wardrobe door. The dress was exquisite, it fit perfectly, and she felt nothing but dismay.

"Something tells me I don't look quite like you did, Laura," she said, and Laura laughed. "Why should you? I'm dark, you're fair. Wait till you see yourself with the veil and the flowers. You'll be the most beautiful bride in the world."

And she is, Laura thought as Becca started down the aisle.

The rector straightened his narrow shoulders and cleared his throat. As Millie had pointed out, his sermons were dull as ditchwater but he did nice weddings and funerals. Was that because he could handle the forms but had no guidance to offer for the great questions? Like dishonor, like betrayal. She had thought about going to him or Reverend Jacobson and talking out her doubts and fears in a kind of Protestant confession. They were men of God whose business it was to help people struggle with right and wrong. They were kind, they were decent . . . they were Confederates and she was out of her mind to consider such a thing for even a moment. Chase, Fiona, Frederick, David Rees—she could kill them all just by seeking absolution.

Most of the time she believed she was doing right; Varina's outburst had only added to her strength of purpose. But looking at Doug's wound, she felt guilt roll over her in crushing waves. Had information she sent North driven the minié ball into that good man's leg? It could be. An overheard conversation, the confidence of a friend, could, like a stone dropped in a still pond, ripple out and bring who knew what results. It could cause a Union commander to change his tactics, put a Union boy in position to level his rifle at Doug and as easily hit his heart as his leg . . . This kind of thinking had to stop, it was self-pity of the worst kind.

The rector began the last prayer and heads were bowed. She glanced at the pew to her left one row behind. Chase was there as she knew he would be—the only person in the world she could talk to honestly. He knew the guilt she suffered and talked about his own pain when he lied to his brother. She could tell him anything and he did not criticize or think less of her. She had some time ago decided that she respected and trusted him as much as anyone she'd ever known.

The prayer ended. He looked up and their eyes met. She inclined her head and he smiled. She turned back in time to see her brother lift Becca's veil and kiss her.

THE GUESTS ALL left the church together, full of good spirits. Kirby fell into step beside Valerie. He was a boy whose flippancy and irreverence she had always rather liked but now there was a reckless, almost wild look in his eyes that hadn't been there before. He had filled out too.

Just behind them Laura walked with Paige, who said something rude to Kirby as he passed, and snatches of her low voice floated on the evening breeze. ". . . you're not happy, Paige, well, most folks aren't . . . don't spoil this day . . . it may be the last time for them . . ."

Funny, Valerie thought, observing Paige's lowering face, how upset some women got when their husbands went away. She was more than pleased that Jason had gone out to one of the plantations. Labor trouble, he had said, and the overseer wasn't handling it well. That accursed emancipation thing had unsettled the slaves and too many were running off leaving crops untended. He had been in a foul mood ever since word came that Lincoln did indeed mean to take his property from him. The only problem with his going away was that he didn't do it often enough.

Ahead, walking up the hill beside the bride and groom, Millie was telling Chase some long-winded story, looking for the moment like her old vivacious self. She had developed a staunch affection for him and always seemed more cheerful when he was around. In her presence no one dared question his manhood for being out of uniform as other men, soldiers themselves, sometimes did behind his back. Valerie tended to agree with the soldiers. How else to explain why he was never able to meet her at any of several hideaways she had discovered? Since it wasn't possible that he had lost interest, it must be Jason's constant presence these days. "He's afraid," she told Laura with disgust the night before, "just plain afraid of getting caught—you've missed a whole row there."

Laura threw her knitting aside. "I'll never get this finished. I'm just no good at it."

Valerie, absorbed in herself, went on. "Let me tell you, I

never was so disillusioned and disappointed in a person. It
had to end sometime, of course, but not like this. I've cried
and cried but"—her voice lowered and she smiled—"I've
met somebody else. His name is Hugh Kellogg. He's an
engineer out at the Tredegar Iron Works, a civilian with a
wife and two children—not especially good-looking but
sort of, well, appealing and not, thank God, afraid of my
husband! At least, I don't think he is. It hasn't gotten past
two lunches and a kiss when we said goodbye but it
might."

Laura stared at her. "I thought you were already madly
in love."

"I was. Maybe I still am but nothing ever seemed to
work out and then he was gone almost two months. Now
I've met Hugh and there's no one but you I dare talk to
about it. I suppose it's hard for you to understand—you
don't need someone the way I do."

Laura picked up her knitting, examined it with great
care, and ripped out the last three rows. "Well," she said,
"tell me what you're going to wear tomorrow."

Hugh Kellogg was not present at the wedding; he
hadn't been invited, not being of quite the same social
class. Valerie looked at Kirby as they turned in at the Seymours' gate and, with no idea what he had just been running on about, widened her eyes and said, "I do love it
when a man explains something so clearly that even I can
understand. May I take your arm? That old hill has made
me go breathless."

CHAPTER 17

❧ KIRBY RETURNED TO THE ARMY the next
day, tired because he had been up most of the
night but without the miserable hangover late
nights usually gave him. There had been only enough
champagne to toast the bride and groom, wartime shortages being what they were, but food enough for all—turkey
salad made from turkeys sent up from Pine Hill plantation,
game birds from the woods, and a rich stew made from

river terrapin. There had been a tiny bite of fruitcake as well
and he had relished it. Sugar was almost nonexistent and he
hadn't tasted a sweet since the Second Battle of Manassas—
all of life for him was now related to some stinking, insane
battle, and he wondered why he had ever thought this war
was a good idea and what would happen if he didn't go
back. He would like not to go back, he would like to stay
right here in Richmond and continue what had started last
night.

He had admired Mrs. Hood—Valerie—since before he
could shave but never even in his wilder fantasies had
he imagined that she ever could be for him. But she was.
She was trapped in a loveless marriage, her husband was
cold and cruel and probably beat her—she hadn't quite said
so but he understood her meaning—they had gone out to
look at the moonlight on the river and then there they were
under a tree in a secluded area on a comfortably thick pile
of autumn leaves listening to the waltzes drifting distantly
from the house and making the most amazing love he had
ever experienced. She was astonishing, extraordinary, the
most intoxicating woman he had ever known, and if he
didn't stop thinking about her he wouldn't be able to leave.

After breakfast he had told everyone in the house
farewell except Laura and he had to find her. He couldn't
leave without saying goodbye. But although she had said
not one word of reproach during that distressing incident
in the early hours of this morning, it was hard to face her in
the cold light of day. She was so—not exactly straightlaced
but so proper—that wasn't quite right either—anyway, she
must have been shocked even though she hadn't shown it.

Just before he and Valerie had gone into the copse of
trees he had glanced back and seen her dancing with Chase
on the moonlit terrace. It pleased him to see her happy. She
suffered so much when Robert died, and grew so thin that
at one point he feared he might lose her as he had lost his
parents. Things had been much better lately. Last night she
was the girl he remembered from the happy past, dark hair
shining, her eyes like jewels, her red velvet dress with its
huge skirt seeming almost black in the moonlight and then
flaming into crimson in the light that fell through the ballroom doors. That dress was smashing and he was glad he'd

told her how beautiful she looked earlier in the evening. If he'd said it later she might have believed he was buttering her up.

Thinking it over afterward he realized that he had heard them coming, heard their voices, but it hadn't seemed to matter at the time. Then Valerie gave a muffled shriek, grabbed at her dress, and he leaped to his feet, hauling up his pants, to face the most embarrassing moment of his life. But you would have thought nothing at all had happened; neither Laura nor Chase had blinked an eye. They went on out to the cliff and before long were joined by other guests come out to watch the sunrise. He had tried to do the right thing, helped Valerie get that damned hoop back on under her skirt, tied the tapes for her and brushed the leaves out of her hair. Then that wonderful woman had patted his face and ordered him not to worry, everything was fine. He had never admired anyone so much.

And now he had to leave her with a man she did not love, he had to go. The army shot deserters. All around him servants were busy cleaning up, putting chairs, sofas, and tables back in their accustomed places, and Laura was coming up the garden path. He would go out there quickly. He had to talk to her with no one else around.

She saw him and sang out "Morning!" as if the awful moment had never happened, stopped before him and looked over his uniform, clean and newly patched. "You're going," she said.

"I have to."

"I know." She put her arms around him and kissed his cheek.

"I want to apologize, Laura, it was all my fault. A man of the world would have—"

"Hush." She laid a finger lightly over his lips. "I love you, Kirby, you're still my darling little brother even though I have to look up at you. Come back safe and don't . . . don't take unnecessary risks. I don't believe any cause is worth your life."

His eyes suddenly sparkled in the old way. "Neither do I." They smiled at each other. Then he turned back into the house, said goodbye to Joseph and went out the front door.

Laura stood in the sunlit garden, frozen in pain. He was going back and there was nothing to do about it, no way in the world she could protect him. She couldn't even protect him from her maurauding friends. At that horrible moment last night she had simply averted her eyes and gone on, torn between monumental embarrassment and a violent desire to murder Valerie. He was so young and good at heart and had had the bad luck to be the right age at a time of war. In a vivid flash of memory she saw once again a sweet-faced child running down this very path, bright, wide-eyed, trusting—running to her with arms outstretched.

She raced into the house and stopped in the open doorway, her last glimpse of Kirby that of a vigorous, long-legged young man with shoulders squared and head held high, his cap in his hand and his dark hair with the chestnut lights, the same color as hers, shining in the sun.

I T WAS A LONG, bitterly cold winter. Fuel was scarce and costly and food as basic as flour was priced out of the reach of poorer people. Soldiers in the field, in need of almost everything, suffered greatly. There were few warm overcoats to be had and many were barefoot in the snow. Lee's soldiers saw that their general's dark beard was now white, and there was a weariness in his smile that his officers noted and commented on.

Then, on a dark, freezing day two weeks before Christmas came news that cheered the soul. A great victory had been won by Lee's ragged army only a few miles north at Fredericksburg, won with a slaughter of Union soldiers that stunned even the Confederates holding the high ground above the town. The Union general must be raving mad, they decided, to repeatedly hurl his men across that open field toward heights so well entrenched, mad or crim-inally obtuse. He sent them out again and again in long blue lines, bayonets fixed, flags flying valiantly, roaring their deep-throated "Hurrah!" and racing toward the stone wall where well-protected Confederate infantry and artillery fire cut them down and rank after rank of blue-coated men seemed to simply vanish.

Wounded soldiers returning to Richmond said the battlefield had been blue with the piled-up Union dead and

the next day, after a night when Confederates had gone out
to forage for supplies, the field was no longer blue but
white with stripped, naked bodies. They did not tell civilians what the dead Yankees actually looked like—they did
not say that after a time their faces turned black and shone
in the sun, they did not mention the severed heads, arms,
legs, the vast quantities of blood, the brains leaking out of
shattered skulls, the tortured, fearful expressions on those
who still had faces. Civilians did not want to hear about the
gallantry, the suffering and devotion of brave men on the
other side who, like their own men, had families at home
who loved them; they only wanted to hear that they had at
last won a major victory over the enemy. It gave them a
happy Christmas.

All during the cold days of the ending year, without
telling anyone, Laura had been searching for a house of her
own and it turned out to be an almost impossible task. As
with all wartime cities there was a housing shortage.
Modest but pleasant houses with the particular features
important to her were in short supply. Late in January,
when she had at last found three houses that might do, she
mentioned it to Chase.

"No one else knows I'm leaving—Millie will have a fit
when she finds out—and I want to talk it over with
someone before I decide. Would you come look at them
with me?"

She saved the one she wanted for last. It was small and
not colonnaded as were some of the bigger houses downtown; the exterior was simple red brick, but the lot was
large, keeping neighbors at a distance. "And it gets the
breeze off the river. The rooms are a nice size too."

She led him through the house upstairs and down and
then through the kitchen to the backyard. "This is the best
part. See how secluded it is from the back door to the
stable? The high walls and the vines make it all rather
secret. And it would be possible to go back through the
woods behind the stable and come out on the other street.
If it's ever necessary people could come and go and no one
would know they'd been here. Well, what do you think?"

He had walked over the entire property and now
was standing in the small back garden, smiling at her

enthusiasm. "I think you don't need me. You've already decided."

"Sort of. But what do you think about the whole idea? Moving out, having a place where Frederick or Fiona or even Mr. Rees could come if need be? Or anybody else, for that matter."

At that his gaze became so considering that it was hard to sustain, but she did it. Finally he said, "I think you're old enough to leave home." He looked at the vine-covered walls and the shady path beside the stable that led into the woods beyond. "And the seclusion could come in handy."

"Good. Now I'll talk to Jewel."

B UT TO HER SURPRISE Jewel was not pleased by the prospect. "I thought you'd want to come, Jewel. Adam would come too, of course, and there'd be much less work."

Jewel was leaning into the wardrobe, hanging up Laura's dress, and her voice was muffled. "I don't think I should. Miss Millie isn't going to like this one bit. She'll need me."

Puzzled and a little hurt, Laura wanted to say, You're *my* friend and *I* need you, but she didn't. With as little resentment as she could manage she said, "I won't insist. You can come over anytime you want and I'll be coming here. We'll see each other all the time."

And so, which servant to take? She didn't want more than one on a regular basis—privacy was essential. It had to be someone either too stupid to understand or intelligent but discreet and trustworthy. She chose intelligence. After eliminating Bella, whom Millie would never part with, she considered every female servant in the house and stopped when she came to Elvina.

Elvina, with the Seymours for two years, had learned to cook, mend, and dress hair, was a presentable parlor maid, and best of all, had developed a devotion to Laura that was almost a crush. Heaven knew why but there it was.

Elvina knew why and could have told Laura if she dared. It was due to Laura's simple kindness and interest in her as a person which she'd never experienced before in her short life. Miss Laura was Elvina's idea of a real lady, someone who seemed aware of her as a person with thoughts and feelings of her own, not just as part of the well-functioning machinery of the house. She had long ago decided that if necessary she would die for Miss Laura.

Laura had no idea how deep Elvina's loyalty went but she sensed that here was a good girl, bright and capable, who would serve her well, and so she brought up the subject with Millie, not an easy task. Two days after finding out about her plans, Millie still burst into tears whenever she thought about it.

"I don't see how you can do it, I really don't," she had moaned when Laura told her. "Haven't I enough heartache without you abandoning me too?"

"I'll be ten minutes away. You didn't take on like this when I moved to Washington."

"That was different. I was younger then."

"And you're all of what now? Forty-one?"

"Edward was home then. Oh, Laura, sometimes I don't think I'll ever see him again. How can you leave your family when any moment we may get a letter—"

"Don't do that, Millie, it won't work." Laura spoke with more firmness than she felt. Millie had been her mother since she was eight and knew exactly how to strike a nerve. If you started to feel sorry for her you were lost.

Millie stopped crying and murmured sadly, "Oh, you are cold. Why on earth do you want to move out of your own home?"

"Because it isn't my home—no, don't argue, it isn't. My own home was in Washington. It was wonderful that you took me in when I needed it and I'm grateful but now I want to go. I always intended to eventually."

"Why now all of a sudden?"

Laura thought of her reasons. How flabbergasted Millie would be if she knew. She said simply, "It's time."

When she brought up the matter of Elvina, tears came to Millie's eyes again. "You're taking my servants too?"

"You can do without Elvina very well and I need someone. I could have taken Jewel but I didn't. You can thank her for that. She turned me down for your sake."

Millie moved to the fireplace where a small fire struggled feebly against the cold, blew her nose and stuffed the handkerchief into her pocket. Her back to Laura, she remarked in a dry, cool voice, "Did she really? She'll have to be rewarded for that. Go ahead then, tell Elvina she has my permission to leave."

ELVINA WAS FLATTERED, thrilled, excited almost beyond endurance. Miss Laura, who could have any servant in the house, even Jewel, had chosen her as the only one to come with her to her wonderful new house.

She arrived with one bag containing her few possessions and slowly walked up the path. It was without doubt the most pleasing house in Richmond, beautiful but not over-whelmingly grand, like Miss Laura herself. The parlor and dining room were large enough for the small parties Miss Laura said she might give, the kitchen well arranged, her own room next to the kitchen bigger than the one she had just come from. For some reason she liked her mistress's bedroom in this house better than the one she had had at home. It was large, airy, and it, too, had a window seat that overlooked the back garden, but there the similarity ended. That other had been a child's room, a young girl's room. This, Elvina recognized at some deep level, was appropriate for an adult.

It interested Elvina that Miss Laura was somehow dif-ferent in her own home than she had been at Miss Millie's, happier and more optimistic. In their first week they flew around the little house, working side by side, trying out the sofa here, the easy chairs there, then reversing them and standing back to judge the effect. They installed new cur-tains themselves, Miss Laura teetering on a ladder while Elvina, watching nervously, handed up hammer and nails. They hung pictures, scrubbed and cleaned and polished like furies, and at the end of the week, late on a Friday night, they collapsed onto chairs, looked at each other and laughed.

Chimes rang softly, the new melodic front door chimes. Chase had been told not to come near the place until given permission but he tended to ignore orders. Laura jumped up. "I'll get it, Elvina. You go on to bed."

She stopped at the mirror in the hallway, swiped at ten-drils of hair, and opened the door to the last person in the world she expected to see on this dark winter night.

Matt Riley, his male vanity at full throttle, instantly translated the disappointment in her face into stunned delight. How completely charming she was standing there in amazement with all those little loose curls falling about.

"Never hoped to see me tonight, did you, ma'am?"

"No—I certainly didn't. Come in, come in, don't stay out there in the cold." He was already in the hall unwrapping his scarf, shrugging off his greatcoat. "How did you find me, Matt?"

"Basic reconnoiter. I stopped by your old home and talked to Mrs. Seymour." He glanced around the parlor. "Not too happy about this, is she? I, on the other hand, find it delightful." His tone was full of meaning.

"Come sit by the fire—over there." But he was already seated comfortably on the sofa. He reached out for her hand and she slipped away. "Would you like a taste of brandy to warm you up?"

"Brandy would go down very well. I've had a cold time of it since I got to town this morning. Talked to Davis, talked to Benjamin, talked to John Mercer—he has influence, you know—and they froze me right out."

"Oh?" She was at her father's old liquor cabinet in the dining room. In her hand was the precious bottle of brandy Chase had given her as a housewarming present on the day she moved in. She poured it slowly, closed the cabinet and came back, bringing the bottle with her. This time she sat down beside him. "You mean they wouldn't take your advice? How can they do that? You're a general and you know so much more than they do about things like strategy and tactics—I never did understand the difference."

He tasted the brandy and sighed. "This is splendid! How did you come by such quality in times like these?"

She thought about telling him Chase had bought it straight out of Angela Flynn's excellent cellar and said, "It was my father's."

"Ah. Of course. Yes, it's true—they won't listen to me, they won't listen to General Lee either and they worship him. Pigheaded fools."

He finished his brandy. She poured him another and he sipped slowly, staring into the fire with an odd, absent expression. Without his smile he looked older. Letters couldn't tell you what was really happening to a man, especially if he didn't want you to know. During the last months he had written to her as regularly as a fighting soldier could, oddly touching letters filled with ardor expressed quite formally and always containing at least one literary allusion. She answered each one faithfully, an obligation because he was far from home, in danger, and loved her. Or thought he did.

He said suddenly, "Strategy is a plan to strike at the enemy—the whole shooting match, dear. Not just their army, but their politics and economics and"—he tapped his head—"what's going on up here. Tactics is how we use our forces in battle. We beat them to a pulp up at Fredericksburg because we held the high ground—that's good tactics, you see—and they just kept coming, wave after wave, letting us kill them. That's bad tactics. Hard to believe their generals are that stupid but they are." His glass was still half full. She topped it off and he took a swallow. "I brought a message from Lee to the President today. He didn't want to send it by telegram. But—" He shrugged.

"Did they just refuse to listen?"

"Oh, they listened. They let me say my piece and didn't hear a word, didn't want to hear. Because of Fredericksburg they think we're winning but we're not. No matter how badly we beat them, no matter how many Union dead are on the field, the Federals don't give up. We'll have to fight them again; Lee doesn't know where yet but we'll pick the spot, hole in somewhere around Fredericksburg and they'll come after us. Those woods are the worst fighting ground in the world if you're attacking and we'll beat 'em again, by God. But, eventually . . ."

He swallowed the rest of the brandy and set down his glass. His hair, dark blond when she saw him last, seemed much lighter in the lamplight. He was going gray, she realized with a shock and touched his arm gently.

He looked at the hand, then at her, and some of the old aggressive sparkle came into his eyes. "And here I am talking like a defeated man when I'm an inch away from the loveliest lady in the world."

Before she could think his arms—very muscular, determined arms—were around her and before she could turn her head he caught her full on the lips. The kiss continued for some time. Lord, he was strong. He had her pinned. Her arm was twisted and her neck bent so far back it was developing a crick. No doubt he was an expert and this was a good kiss but she hoped it would end soon. She could taste the brandy, which brought to mind the place it had come from. The town was filled with women who could make convincing love with any man who came along and had the price. How did they manage? They were better actresses than she was.

The pressure on her mouth eased enough for her to get out a squeak of pain. "My arm, Matt . . ."

"Oh, my dear, have I hurt you? Let me see."

"Here," she said in a small voice, rubbing her arm. There was a bruise on her forearm, put there yesterday by a collision with a cabinet she was trying to move. She pushed up her sleeve.

"Oh, my God, what have I done?" He bent and kissed the bruise, a light, feathery brush on her skin. "I apologize, dear. It was brutish behavior. I was—I was overwhelmed by your presence but that's no excuse. I would never hurt you, not for the world. Can you forgive me?"

He looked so miserable, so abject, that she wanted to reach out and pat him. Instead she moved a little away from him and folded her arms to make a less inviting target.

"Of course I forgive you, Matt. It's just that—well—I do bruise easily. My mother always worried about it."

That thrust went straight in and he moaned a little. Too bad to cause him pain but war was war.

Staring straight ahead, he said, "I'm not usually that clumsy but I never asked a woman to marry me before." Her eyes widened in what he hoped was happiness. "Yes, that's what I meant to do. I thought perhaps . . . we might marry before I leave next Friday"—he stole a quick look at her—"or at least get engaged? But then maybe it would be better to wait until I'm home for good. I wouldn't want you widowed a second time."

Except for the age-old wartime appeal of men to women—remember, I might get killed—he was winding down nicely. She waited. He seemed to have run out. She raised her eyes. "I'm deeply honored, Matt, and—and quite flustered. I had no idea—"

She did look confused and he had caused it, jumping on her like that, throwing everything out of kilter when it was going so well. He hadn't wanted to propose by letter; he'd thought his personal charm would carry the day and instead he'd made a mess of it . . . she was saying something.

"You are absolutely right. We should wait. Let's go on writing, come visit me when you can, and then, after the war, Matt dear, we'll talk about this again."

She closed her mind against the sadness in his eyes when he left. He didn't get what he wanted and neither did anyone else most of the time. He killed people, not knowing or caring who would be hurt by each death as did everyone on both sides. She was lucky. She didn't have to kill, just break a heart now and then. He never had told her exactly what Lee's message to Davis was—he wasn't that irresponsible—but she now knew about confusion, anger, and spite at the highest levels, she knew that regardless of Fredericksburg, Lee was worried and that his probable choice of the next killing ground was somewhere in the tangle of woods and thickets not far from the last blood-letting. That information would travel swiftly North to do whatever good it could.

O FTEN, LATE AT NIGHT, people Elvina did not know came to the back door and Miss Laura received them behind closed parlor doors.

A man Elvina knew only as Frederick came with fair regularity and his visits always cheered her. He was tall, brawny, dignified, he was as black as she was, he had a smile that brought joy to her heart and a deep, mellow, unforgettable voice. Whether he had a woman of his own she did not know and could not ask, but she liked the way he looked her over and the smile he gave her when he came in the back way and walked through her kitchen.

Mr. Chase was often at the house when no one else was there. He and Miss Laura would eat a simple supper in the dining room and then go into the parlor, sit before the fire and talk late into the night. Sugar was very dear and hard to get but Elvina always tried to have an extra good dessert

when he was there because she liked to please him. Miss
Laura liked to please him too; Elvina knew it because she
always approved the expenditure of sugar and because with
him she smiled a lot. When they talked through the long
winter evenings you could often hear her laughter out in
the kitchen.

You couldn't hear anything else though, not a word they
spoke. Although she didn't know it Elvina had as finely
honed a sense of honor—a word foreign to her vocabu-
lary—as Edward Seymour, who analyzed its nuances. She
could have listened through the door, overheard their
words and satisfied her curiosity about why they sometimes
laughed and sometimes looked so somber—but that would
not be right. The only time she caught snatches of their
conversation was when she served her pies and cakes and
the biting, sour coffee she made from dried corn or parched
sweet potatoes, real coffee being almost unobtainable now.

On one freezing evening near the end of March they
were in the little parlor in their accustomed places, he in the
big chair on one side of the fireplace, she in the smaller
chair on the other side, close to the fire built with wood he
had brought that evening. Laura hadn't asked where he got
it. Although it was almost April snow remained on the
ground in this bitterest winter in many years and firewood
was in short supply and very hard to get, especially good
oak wood that could provide such a lovely, warm, slow-
burning fire. Toward evening a piercing wind had risen and
was now poking and prodding at the house, moving the
heavy, tightly closed draperies and slipping under doors
and across floors to chill the feet.

She tucked her feet under her. It was a raw dark night;
somewhere those she loved were trying to sleep on the cold
earth under thin ragged blankets if they had any blankets at
all. Fear for them was her constant companion, the war
ground on hopelessly, and yet just now she felt secure and
oddly happy.

One of those moments had occurred again this evening.
Because the dining table was long they sat together when
they were alone and as she was rising her hand had brushed
his shoulder. The familiar disorienting surge of feeling rose,
causing her hands and voice to shake. It was the accidental

touches that did it, not the expected ones, and she tried to avoid them. When it did happen her mind immediately told her it had not, and usually she convinced herself. She had gone on into the parlor and established herself in the small wing chair across from him, close yet far enough away to be safe.

They had been sitting for some time in silence—they no longer had to make conversation—and he was watching the moving orange-gold flames with an abstracted expression. She couldn't guess his thoughts but she liked to study him when he didn't know she was doing it. Long ago she had seen beyond his face to the person beneath. He was both strong and gentle, he was brave, he was kind, an uncommon man, someone she could talk to about anything or be silent with as she was now.

He began to tell her about his trip to Washington as Elvina brought in scalding hot tea made from blackberry leaves, a concoction she hoped would be an improvement over dried-corn coffee. Because her sense of what was right did not include trying not to listen when they knew she was in the room, she heard him say, "Would you like to come too?", and saw Laura look up, her eyes somehow veiled, and reply, "Is that possible?" Elvina left without hearing more.

When the door closed behind her Laura asked, "How could it be done?"

"The trains sometimes run and there are other ways to travel. Benjamin always gives me a pass and I doubt he'd object to giving one to you if we can think up a good reason why you need to go. I think he'd be willing to put you into my keeping."

She looked down at the blackberry tea as a little flush rose in her cheeks, said, "Well, we can try," and as she put down her cup, "My, this is dreadful stuff. You don't have to drink it." She stood up quickly. "A letter from my sister-in-law got through to me last week. She's been ill. I'll get it and read you what she says." She left the room and trotted up the stairs. Elvina had lit the lamp and its rosy glow fell on the bed and the desk under the window. She went to the desk, stood looking down at it, then opened the top drawer and took out Caroline's letter. There it was, the perfect reason for going to Washington with him, but was this a journey she wanted to take? Thinking of it, her hand shook so that she could not read the words.

She did not hear him coming up the stairs, did not know he was anywhere nearby until he was at the door. She looked up in surprise and he said quietly, "I've had about all of this I can stand. If you say no I'll leave and that will be the end of it but if you don't I'm coming in."

Her eyes seemed to darken and her chin went up. Then a tight knot of tension she had not known was there relaxed.

"I can't stand it either."

He came across the room, took the letter and tossed it on the desk, and she went into his arms like a child going home. It seemed marvelous, rare, and yet familiar to be held against him like this in a grip so tight it hurt, as if many times before she had clung to him and felt him tremble, as if here above all was the place she should be. He buried his face in her hair, holding her like a man who at last had what he needed and was not about to let it go.

"I was afraid this would never happen," she whispered. "I didn't know what to do."

"I wasn't sure what you wanted. Now I know."

She pulled back a little, breathing quickly, still holding on to him. "Look at me. I'm shaking."

"So am I."

She had never seen him smile like that and she smiled too, a radiant smile, and reached for the lamp.

His hand came over hers. "Leave it on. I want to see your face."

DURING THE NIGHT the wind increased in violence, lashing at the house, shrieking through the trees, frightening Elvina in her little room off the kitchen. The lovers in the upstairs room did not even hear it. Laura was aware of nothing but him and her own feelings. Chase, who had realized long ago how much he wanted this woman he could not have, simply thought, At last, and gave himself up to her.

At two o'clock, the deepest part of the night, the wind rose higher, slammed open the casement, and icy air suddenly poured into the room. Laura, torn out of sleep, leaped from bed, locked the window, and slid, shivering and laughing, back into his arms.

"That was your fault—I forgot to lock it. My mind was on my hair and my dress and the dinner, all because you were coming tonight."

"That's right, blame me for female vanity. You always look wonderful, dinner is always wonderful . . . everything in my life is good if you are there."

She reached out with the same rising desire, thinking that if she could stop it morning would never come.

THEY WOKE SHORTLY after dawn and watched the light increase, a brighter light than had been seen in weeks. Toward morning the great wind had dwindled to a stiff breeze, leaving behind a clean-swept sky and a hope that spring might one day arrive after a winter that had seemed to last forever.

She ran her hand down his cheek to his jaw in a light caress. He turned his face into her palm, kissed it, and she said with profound content, "That's very nice."

"Tell me what else pleases you."

"Everything. Except that you have to go. Look how light it's getting."

"No I don't, I can stay and have breakfast. As you pointed out when you picked this place, anyone can come and go without being seen."

"If you think I did that for your benefit you're mistaken—you can stop smiling."

"Maybe not but I'll always believe you did." He drew a strand of her hair over the pillow and spread it out like a fan. "What about Washington? Do you want to go?"

"I was going to turn you down. I was afraid this would happen if I did . . . that was a silly reason. Do you want me to go?"

"You deserve a chance for some recognition—you've been so brave and done so much, but now I regret saying anything."

She sat up a little. "Why? Would I make it harder for you?"

"You'd make it easier—at least I'd be happy. But it's

dangerous, Laura. We'd have to cross both armies at some point and they are on the move. There's no way of knowing exactly where they are. One nervous picket on either side can do the job. There are a lot of pickets and they're all nervous. So many things can go wrong I can't even name them all." His arms tightened around her as if he were suddenly afraid. "You are precious to me, not only this body but your mind and your heart. I love to watch you struggle with some high moral principle, earnestly trying to decide what is right. You are smart and funny, the gentlest person I've ever come across, the only woman I know who can still blush. You're already in too much danger and I wish to God I'd never dragged you into this."

Her face was hot, she could feel it, and how could she help it after a declaration like that? "That was a lovely thing to say to me. I want to come with you, Chase. I'm going to come. I think I can help."

They ate breakfast at the small kitchen table, Elvina serving them in her efficient, noisy way, clattering dishes and pans and humming under her breath. She was thrilled by the romance of it all and by a sense that there was more going on in the house than a love affair, something she couldn't put her finger on that lent it all an exciting edge of danger. Mr. Chase was very close to being good enough for Miss Laura and she wished she could tell her mistress that she approved and could be counted on for anything. Of course, such words could never be spoken by a maid to a mistress. She could only give silent support and invent a mission in the backyard in order to give them privacy.

Laura waited until the door closed and then said softly, "I have to tell you something, Chase. I hope I can say it right." She took a breath and plunged in. "I misjudged you at the start. I thought—well, never mind what I thought. I was wrong. It would be easy to love you but I'm not going to and it wouldn't be fair to let you think I will."

He leaned back in his chair and looked at her. Finally he said, "Sometimes loving just falls on us and we don't have much choice."

"I can choose. I've done it before." She picked up a fork, turned it over, put it down. "Love means nothing but pain and loss and I don't want any more of it. I was so little when my parents died. I've never stopped missing them. Then there was Robert. He was strong and good and he knew everything. I decided to love him—yes, I did. It wasn't some outside force that fell on me. When he died and . . . and everything came apart I swore a vow to God that I'd never give so much of myself to anyone again and I won't, not even to you."

His eyes never left hers. She didn't know what he felt. He said, "Would you tell me, just so I'll know, what you do feel for me?"

Slow warmth came into her face. "I admire you, I trust you, I can tell you anything. I'm happy when I'm with you and not so happy when I'm not. You're the best friend I have. The only friend, really."

He had been leaning his chin on his hand, listening with an expression that was almost pleasure. With a smile in his eyes he said, "Well, if you can't love me I guess I'll have to settle for that."

CHAPTER 18

IT'S CAROLINE'S HEART, JUDAH. Just a little flutter, she says, but I would like to see her. I'm her closest relative now."

"Does she still maintain her home on H Street? I remember many marvelous dinners there when Mr. Justice Merritt was alive."

"Yes, and when I left she still entertained often. I suppose that's changed now, with the war and her poor health. I haven't seen her in over four years."

Laura waited with a hopeful smile, allowing Judah Benjamin to summon up memories of the charming Caroline Merritt and her many excellences as a hostess. He was secretary of state now and passports were not handled in his office, but he also had more influence over Jefferson Davis than any other man in the government and therein lay his power. Usually he could arrange passage for friends if he chose.

He made a steeple of his pudgy fingers. "You do realize the dangers."

"Colonel Girard described them graphically—in fact, tried to discourage me—but others pass through the lines all the time. I'll be quite safe with him."

"Indeed. I'll see what I can do, Laura. There should be no difficulty in your case."

But the provost marshal, General Winder, and Jason Hood, whose department issued the passes, were deeply suspicious of almost everyone wishing to travel north. Jason also detested Benjamin, automatically delayed any request he made as long as possible, and saw no reason for Laura Chandler to go anywhere. Her sister-in-law had chosen to stay in the North instead of coming home to family and friends; let her get along as best she could. For good measure and just because he didn't like him, he held up Chase Girard's passport too.

So the April weeks passed, stormy, sunny, fragrant with new blossoms, a spring that Laura knew she would remember in old age when all else was gone. She was happy and Chase was too, and happiness was always brief. It had to be seized on the moment.

The intensity of her emotions astonished her. Before Chase came into it, her life had been ordered and calm, her feelings under tight control; after, she had begun, subtly, to change. Now he was the central fact of her existence. She would not love him, she had warned him of that, but there was a powerful bond between them, one that had been there from the beginning and that she did not entirely understand.

He was changed too, more than she realized. He allowed his feelings to show in ways he never had before. There was a side to his nature that he had always kept well hidden—biting humor and a skeptic's outlook on life—yet always the kindness at the core. She now saw clearly that his gentleness, surprising in a soldier, was the reason most people liked him. When he walked into the house, bringing so much vitality and warmth, it seemed safer to her and more homelike. When he brought boxes of food—hard-to-get necessities and delicacies impossible to buy on the open market—he was so pleased with himself that she laughed too, knowing he was glad to be with her. The food and the luxurious goodies all came from the same source as the brandy she'd given Matt Riley—the Daisychain's kitchen. Only brothels and gambling hells had plentiful supplies of such scarce items now and Angela Flynn, he told her, was fit to be tied.

"She says she's contributed enough to the cause—she means Frederick—but so far she hasn't forbidden the chef to sell to me."

"She's a generous woman."

"Sometimes. Depends on her mood."

In fact Angela was fascinated by Chase's friendship with the glamorous Mrs. Chandler and wished she knew more about it. She tried to get information out of Chase, even offering a tiny tin of caviar worth its weight in gold if he would describe to her what Laura wore at home and just a tidbit or two about what she was really like.

For some reason the picture that leaped into his mind was of her hair, thick, opulent, rich as polished mahogany, tumbling below her shoulders and curling in that unique way off her face. He said, "Everything she wears looks lovely, and she's a very nice person."

"You're not getting any caviar for that!"

"How about some anchovy paste?"

"Oh, get out and don't come back for at least a week. I can't go on supplying you and your ladylove and still have anything left for the customers."

She ordered the chef not to sell him so much as a bag of cornmeal without her permission and watched him go, annoyed, amused, her curiosity even greater, thinking that whether he knew it or not the lady had him nailed.

He knew it very well and had known it for a long time. He loved Laura completely, without reservation, and the fact still surprised him. He had thought he was immune. It surprised him, too, that so much happiness had come from simply being in her presence, eating with her, talking to her, carefully building a friendship; he'd never had a real friendship with a woman before, had believed such a thing was not possible. Now she was utterly his, for the present at least. In a way it was the greatest risk he'd ever taken, far

greater than facing an outraged husband or an enemy soldier, for Laura could break his heart.

It was a power she didn't know she had. To her happiness was temporary, good things were always temporary.
When the war ended, however it ended, her life with him
would end too. Until then there was this time, quiet, tur-
bulent, enchanted, when she could talk to him, laugh with
him, touch him whenever she wished. One day he would
leave her but for now there was this shimmering spring.

They kept up the outward appearance of their usual
lives. Although he was with her almost every night, he
made sure to be seen at his hotel, occasionally dined with
friends, kept close touch with Judah Benjamin and even
spent an evening with him losing at faro.

One late afternoon in mid-month Frederick came to the
house with news that General Lee had once again divided
his army. He had sent Longstreet's corps south and now
had less than sixty thousand men north of the James River.
Frederick had heard President Davis discuss the dispatch
with his wife as he did all matters, significant or trivial.
Chase left at dusk to give the message to David Rees. David
could move through the countryside unnoticed—he was
only a dirt farmer in a battered wagon hauling whatever he
had to sell at the moment to the small towns on the road to
Fredricksburg, but he also had a friend on the other side of
the Pamunkey River who would take the message north.

Laura watched Chase leave with the misgivings she
always felt when he went into the unknown. It had rained
hard in the morning but the sky had cleared. The roads
were muddy but passable and he should be back by eight or
nine at the latest. By midnight she was pacing through the
parlor, the dining room, into the kitchen and back again,
her imagination conjuring horrors that were too likely to
brush aside. Why, oh, why hadn't he waited until
tomorrow as she begged him to, when they could have
traveled out there together, when no one would question a
man taking a lady for a pleasant daylight ride in the
country—at least, no one would question it if it wasn't
raining again tomorrow. In that case the message would
not go out.

He refused to listen—he always did where his work was

concerned—simply smiled, kissed her, and left, his mind already on the problems ahead: the black night, the slippery, narrow road to David's farm, the patrols . . .

Elvina saw her taut face, her hands clenched into fists, her restless pacing, and suffered with her as the night moved on.

At one o'clock Laura sent her to bed and promised to get some sleep soon herself, but instead she sat down beside the banked kitchen fire to wait through the night. He would come in this way when he came back. If he came back. The clock in the front hallway struck the half hour. Two-thirty. If they had stopped him, questioned him, arrested him, she would not hear of it until tomorrow and perhaps not even then; they were sometimes closemouthed about security. Arthur Osborne, the Englishman who had not been an Englishman, came into her mind with a vividness that made her sick and she sat up straighter and tried to think. Her business was to help him if he were accused, yet how could she do it? Her social connections, her family's position, would be nothing in the face of the fear and hatred of spies. The accusation alone could be enough to hang him.

She stoked up the fire and took from the cupboard a small tin of genuine coffee saved for a special occasion, made a pot and set it on the back of the stove to keep warm. She wanted none herself; it was cold outside and she would give him the whole pot when he came home. It was all she could think to do for him.

Once again she sat down, her body so rigid it didn't touch the back of the chair, her face blank with a kind of terror unknown to her before this night. He was dead, she knew it with a certainty that sent cold and then heat racing in waves over her skin. He would not come back, she would never see him again.

H E   H A D   L E F T just after sundown. The clearing sky, still streaked with thin streamers of clouds, had provided a fiery sunset that faded swiftly into the soft blue dimness of twilight. The condition of the road was worse than he expected for a number of military vehicles heading north toward Fredericksburg had passed during the afternoon and churned it into a gluey swamp. His horse picked its way carefully and he guided it toward the solider ground at the edge of the road.

Then, abruptly, it was night, a dark night before moon-rise and that was lucky. He had learned long ago what few civilians realized—if he could see he could also be seen. It would take longer but he knew the way well, having made the trip to the Rees farm many times since first going there with Angela to meet her taciturn, volatile father.

He turned off the narrow side road and rode down the slope to the house where a single lamp showed in the small front window. As he dismounted a dog came quietly into the light and offered a sleek head to be stroked. David opened the door. The gun, as always, was in his hand although he had seen from the window who was on his land talking to his dog.

Inside, Chase unrolled a tiny piece of oiled silk and read the cipher aloud as he always did. Generals liked to see a cipher themselves, he had told David at the start, it seemed to give them more confidence in the information, but better to destroy it and carry it in your head if you were about to be caught.

"Longstreet's south of the river, huh," David said with a humorless grin. "Too bad for Lee, the old son of a bitch. What d'you think of this new man, Hooker?"

"Fighting Joe? He's a good strategist and he did well at Williamsburg last year but he wasn't the commanding general then. He was promoted for bravery in the Mexican War and nobody ever bragged about it more than he did."

David turned that over in his mind. It was not that his brain was slow but rather that he liked to consider all possibilities before rendering judgment. Finally he said without emotion, "I hate a braggart. Man who blows his own horn usually isn't worth shit." He tucked away the tiny roll of oiled silk, shoved bread and dried meat into his pockets, turned out the lamp and without another word went to the barn and began to hitch his mule to the wagon.

Just like that, without notice or warning, Chase thought. David Rees was an odd mixture of virtues and flaws, odder even than most humans. He could be cold, unkind, even brutal, but he also had insight and cool judgment in a crisis and was ready to go at the risk of his life anytime, anywhere that it would hurt the Rebels. That made him a jewel beyond price. Chase mounted his horse as David rolled off without a goodbye, and headed back toward town.

The moon had risen and was playing hide-and-seek among the few thin clouds, dimly illuminating horse and rider but leaving the muddy, rutted road in shadow. Ahead the road curved sharply to the right. He could not see beyond that curve yet he heard or sensed something that caused him to move quickly off the road.

Scarcely had he reached the first line of trees than a group of at least twenty horsemen came into view, moving carefully as he had done, cavalry with rifles slung across their saddles. Directly behind them came another group of perhaps fifty. And there would be more. The road was impossible now. He would have to go back to Richmond through the woods or be discovered out here at daybreak. He dismounted and led the horse deeper into the trees.

It was rolling country and the pines were often only a foot or two apart. In between were bushes, brambles, dry sticks of trees impeding his way, forcing him to search for the few wider paths. The woods were dotted with streams, the trees thick over his head. He could not see the stars but he knew that by following the direction of the water he could find his way through this maze.

Wet branches slapped at his face and caught on his clothes. He and the horse frequently stumbled over surface roots and underbrush and the slick muddy soil clung to his boots. He found a stream shallow enough to ford, mounted the reluctant horse and forced it down the slippery bank into water it could not see. It trembled as the current caught it and battled across, going in the only direction its rider would allow, and then struggled up the opposite bank, still blind in the dark night, still obeying the will of the man.

On the other side Chase dismounted, started forward with the reins in his hand when an owl hooted suddenly and flapped downward on heavy wings within inches, it seemed, of his face. The horse gave a startled whinny and danced sideways to avoid this unknown danger, caught a hoof on a curling root and went down with a shriek. It tried to get up, failed, and lay back gasping.

Chase knelt down and cautiously ran his hands down each slender leg. It was impossible to tell if there were breaks but the horse had tried frantically to get up and could not. He pulled the pistol from his inside coat pocket, located the vulnerable part of the head and fired, hoping there was no one close by on the road at this moment. There was nothing on the saddle to identify the horse as his, nothing distinctive about the animal itself. The easiest path would be to go back to the road and hope it was clear but that was a risk he could not take. He pocketed the gun and continued along the steep streambank.

M OURNING DOVES WERE beginning to call and the sky was growing light when she heard footsteps on the brick path. He came into the kitchen, dropped his wet coat on the floor, and she flew to him, running her hands over his face and chest, convincing herself that he was here and alive and all in one piece. His face, his lips were cold.

"Sit down," she said, "—here, by the fire." With shaking hands she poured coffee into the biggest mug she could find and he took it in both hands, drank it all, then looked up at her, his face inexpressibly tired.

She pulled her chair close. "What was it? Patrols?"

"Cavalry, heading north. If I hadn't heard them coming I'd have run straight into them in the dark." He took her hand and ran his own hand over it absently. "So I went off the road and came back through the woods."

The woods, a confusing, trackless wilderness even in daylight where the myriad little streams became dangerous traps that were almost impossible to ford in the dark. "Let me pull off your boots," she said gently. They were caked with mud so slippery that it was hard to maintain a grip but she got them off, wiped her hands on a towel and said, "Come. Let's go upstairs."

She closed the windows against the morning light and he stripped off his wet clothes, fell into bed without a word and was almost instantly asleep. It always amazed her, his ability to sleep and wake so quickly. She had decided it was discipline rather than a gift and gave thanks for it now.

She eased into bed beside him but instead of lying down she sat for a while gazing at his face in the lamplight, a face familiar and dear and unlike any other. Heavy brows, strong jawline, skin dark against the white pillowcase. For a long time she had believed his eyes were nearly black but in recent weeks she looked closer and saw blue in them. No one had ever told him that, he said, and she thought with satisfaction, Before me no one ever looked so close. He wasn't easy to know and there was much about him that she did not know. Perhaps it was as well—he didn't know all of her either. She touched him lightly. How terrible if all this vitality, intelligence, and beauty had been destroyed tonight. One rifle shot could have done it.

She sat a while longer, then turned out the lamp, slid down under the covers carefully so as not to wake him, and slept too.

CHAPTER 19

TO KEEP UP APPEARANCES Laura gave two dinner parties in April although her heart wasn't in it. Chase would come after the party and it strained her patience when her guests didn't leave promptly. She also made frequent visits home, an unpleasant duty.

Millie did not speak; the silent treatment was her standard punishment for anyone who displeased her as deeply as Laura had. Paige's moods were odd, ranging from determined cheerfulness to sudden depressions so deep that everyone in the house avoided her. She made halfhearted efforts to be pleasant about Becca's expected baby but her envy was plain to see. She worried constantly that Alex was wounded or dead even though there had been no battle since his last letter.

When on one rainy morning Becca started to read Doug's latest letter aloud, Paige screamed that she was torturing her, burst into tears and ran from the room. A memory came back to Laura—acerbic, observant Ellen Mercer remarking on Paige's mercurial nature and saying "I always did believe the Hamptons married too many of their own first cousins." Millie and Edward were first cousins.

Most people did not come to Laura's house without an invitation but one afternoon Jewel stopped by with a peace offering from Millie—a precious turkey sent up from Pine Hill. She came into the small back garden, took in the patch of grass, the blooming dogwood, the old roses rambling over the high brick walls, and Laura and Chase lounging in lawn chairs with Elvina sitting on the grass beside them. The three of them were drinking lemonade made from Angela Flynn's imported lemons and reading the New York papers. Laura had begun to teach Elvina to read the moment they moved into the house and the girl had turned out to be a bright and willing pupil. This morning she had struggled through the *New York Herald*'s editorial and was now mulling over Laura's explanation of the word "emancipation." She had heard it before, had caught much muttered excitement about it among the servants, but it became real to her only when she saw it in print. It was a long and difficult word which she had sounded out carefully. Its meaning was stupefying.

Laura got up to exclaim over the turkey, saw Jewel's bland face and the sparkle in her eyes, and thought, She knows, damn it. But it didn't matter. Jewel wouldn't talk. She was probably pleased.

But Byron Rollins did matter. He, too, was an uninvited guest who knocked on her door late one afternoon, a courteous man who normally never presumed but a man convinced he held such a special place in her affections that he would be welcome at any time. He, Matt Riley, and Jason Hood, very different men, had one thing in common—the conviction that any woman they wanted must, of course, want them. It was a peculiarly masculine vanity unlike the vanity of women, who might be overly fond of their looks but were always hardheaded about where they stood with men.

Byron's ardor had reached the point where he was no longer content to see Laura only at parties or pretend to run into her accidentally on the street when he had been following her. Luckily the two men who had worried him most were no longer in the running. It was widely known that Colonel Girard was only a friend and General Riley, away with the army most of the time, was no competition at all.

So he arrived, unwelcome, on her doorstep. He left chastened. Laura was pleasant but cool, didn't offer refreshment and didn't encourage him to stay. He went away puzzled, a little downhearted, and then his robust self-esteem came to his rescue. Women were flighty creatures, victims of their emotions, and a man had to make allowances. Probably it was that time of the month and she was really not herself. He would wait a week or so and try again.

Laura watched him go with a frown. "I hated to do that," she said, more to herself than Elvina, "but I can't have him hanging around."

"No, ma'am!" Elvina agreed. She understood the hazards of unexpected guests. White folks didn't expect servants to be married to their men but they punished white ladies severely for the same behavior. If someone walked in at an odd hour when Mr. Chase was here and realized what was going on, Miss Laura would never again be received in polite society. On the other hand it was somehow acceptable for the two of them to travel together. Why this was so Elvina did not know; she had yet to fathom the white mind. Today she had packed her mistress's bags. The passports had come through and Mr. Chase was taking Miss Laura north to her sick relative, into a prospect of danger that frightened Elvina and thrilled her to her soul.

T HE TRAIN THAT carried them northward was a long one—many freight cars carrying troops and supplies and one passenger car, pulled by an ancient engine that puffed and snorted its way toward Fredericksburg like an asthmatic bull. Southern trains were slow and old-fashioned at best and this one had been assembled from equipment hauled out of storage at the beginning of the war.

The passenger car was as old as the engine. The backs of seats were stained from years of contact with gentlemen's hair oil and in some places cotton stuffing was coming through the soiled, worn cloth, but Laura was with Chase, crossing a war zone, heading into the perilous unknown, and she had never been happier.

Within five minutes of taking his seat Chase made friends with the passenger in the seat across the aisle, a red-faced man, tending to fat, and talkative.

"Owen Roper, sir—glad to make your acquaintance," he replied when Chase introduced himself. He shook hands vigorously and tipped his hat to Laura. "I happen to be the sole proprietor of Roper's Hardware Emporium up here in Fredricksburg—perhaps you've heard of it?"

"Everyone knows Roper's Hardware," Chase said respectfully.

"Yes. Saddles, bits, hand-forged tools, the finest ploughs in Virginia—every need you have and nothing but the best. Well, that's the way it used to be. These times good merchandise is hard come by, but I have—so to speak—other irons in the fire. Been down in Richmond for just that reason. The Roper family isn't going hungry anytime soon." Owen Roper went on to discuss his wife, his children, his mother-in-law, and the scoundrel snuffling around his eldest daughter whom he had just run off.

Through it all Chase's attention never wavered. Laura thought, That's why he's so good at what he does. It was that quality of deep interest that drew people out. They talked on while he occasionally asked a question, expressed concern or amazement—and listened. I'm glad we're on the same side, she thought and smiled to herself.

Noon came. She stood up in the swaying car to reach for the lunch Elvina had packed and the train suddenly jolted and threw her toward the aisle. Chase caught her and lowered her into her seat.

"Are you hurt?"

"I'm fine," she whispered. "What is it?" The train was shuddering and squealing its way to a fast stop. She glanced out the window. They weren't in the Fredricksburg station, they were in a wild area near some woods.

The young man sitting alone at the front of the car stepped outside, looked ahead past the engine and came rapidly back. "There's some kind of barricade on the track," he announced and took his seat quickly as other passengers leaned out their windows and strained to see.

Laura looked at Chase.

He said, "We'll be all right," and squeezed her hand.

They came aboard, lean, dirty, hard-eyed men in shabby butternut. One wore a bright blue forage cap and jacket and they all had solid, sturdy shoes, booty stripped from dead Union soldiers. They strode through the car, searching each passenger's face, sending a chill down Laura's spine as the man who seemed to be in charge paused. He had stopped by the seat in front of Chase but he was looking at her, the only woman among so many men. His face and the expression on it were hidden by a long, ragged beard, all but his eyes, the coldest she'd ever seen.

She looked back at him, puzzled, a modest, guileless young woman with nothing to hide. He continued that unblinking stare for the longest minute she had ever lived through, then moved on more slowly. He was no one she knew, at least she didn't think he was—even his mother might not know him behind that beard—but the eyes, she would never have forgotten such eyes.

The men were at the back of the car but they didn't go down the steps. They weren't leaving, they were coming back, stopping at each seat, demanding identification from each person. Under Laura's seat, hidden by her spreading skirt, were two carpetbags. Beneath the false bottoms of those bags were maps of the gun emplacements and defensive structures around Richmond, and details of Executive Mansion conferences and War Department plans. Fighting off the desire to turn and face the enemy, she thought, This must be what it's like when your head's chopped off. You can't see the axe but you know it's coming down.

Except for the four civilians—Laura, Chase, Owen Roper, and the young man at the front—every passenger wore some version of the Confederate uniform and every one was an officer; in the Confederate army, as in all armies, rank brought privilege. Officers rode in the passenger car; ordinary soldiers were stuffed into airless freight cars never intended for humans. But the uniforms and the rank of these officers meant nothing to the men who had stopped the train.

A major seated behind Owen Roper half rose, protesting loudly when challenged. "Who do you think you are, questioning me? I am Major Clement George Alfont, aide to General Lee and your superior officer. Take your hands off me! I've called men out for less."

"Have you indeed? Well, you sit down real quick or you'll never call out another." Major Alfont sat down. "Now let's have some identification."

"I don't know what you mean."

"Where're you from?"

"Surry County, near Elberon."

"Titus, you know any people called Alfont around Elberon?"

"My grandfather was—" Alfont began.

"Now here's one of those fellers with a grandfather, what do you say to that? Us humble folk never did have grandfathers, we just growed like the thistle. Titus, I asked you a question."

Titus, the third man back in the narrow aisle, a young, unbearded boy, pushed his way forward and took a look at the major.

"They was some Alfonts around Elberon, spread all over like horseshit. Yeah, he pro'bly is, Ransom. All them Alfonts is dark like that, nose like a hatchet and beady little eyes."

Ransom gave Major Alfont a lingering look and moved on.

"Afternoon, Mr. Roper. How do you be?"

"Quite well, thank you. Hoping to be home before suppertime. What's this about, Ransom?"

"We have word of spies, Mr. Roper. Yankee agents. There's going to be a big battle around here soon and we don't mean to let any of those customers sneak through."

"But great God, man, look at us! We're all loyal Confederates here. Most of us are in uniform."

"Uniforms don't mean a thing, sir. Nothing means anything except a nose for 'em. Sometimes they stink. Not always but sometimes. This fellow, for instance." Ransom turned suddenly toward Chase. "I don't know him but I don't feel good about him."

"Well, *I* know him," said Owen Roper, who wanted to get home without more delay and after an hour's talk with Chase did feel he knew him well. "This is Colonel Chase Girard, CSA, and his lady." Roper again tipped his hat to Laura and she smiled back warmly. "We're traveling up here from Richmond together. Colonel Girard is on business for the President."

Ransom stared at Chase as if memorizing him and Chase bore it with a pleasant half-smile. Ransom's eyes moved to Laura. "I know you from somewhere. I know your face." Over his shoulder he asked, "You know why that is Mr. Roper?"

Chase said, "My wife's portrait has been in the newspaper many times. She was Mrs. Robert Chandler before the senator's death."

"That a fact?" A trace of interest entered Ransom's voice. "I always liked that man. And now you're married to this feller?" Laura smiled, her lashes fluttered down a little and then she looked up, all the warmth and vulnerability she could muster in her eyes. There was a pause a heartbeat long. He touched his cap. "Ma'am." He moved on, slowly working his way through the car.

Watching him, Laura's mind traveled back to the long-ago summer when she tried to be a belle and thought, Thank you, Valerie.

At the front of the car Ransom stopped and had exchanged only a word or two with the young civilian sitting there when the man leaped up and dived through the door, straight into the arms of the guards. His shouts could be heard for a long time as they dragged him away.

There was complete silence in the car. Even Owen Roper had nothing to say. Five minutes later the engine sounded its thin, piercing whistle and slowly, groaning and straining, the train began once more to move northward. Later Laura told Chase it took almost an hour for her pulse to slow down.

They got off the train at the Fredericksburg station. On the platform Owen Roper said, "Good thing Ransom knew me or we might have been sitting out on that track all night."

"Yes," Chase agreed, "it was a good thing."

Roper laughed. "Ransom Halcot. A decent boy, but hard as a steel nail, had to be. He was orphaned early and brought himself up. I hired him when he was ten years old to sweep out my store. Well, sir . . ." Roper held out his hand and Chase took it. They shook vigorously and then Roper bent over Laura's hand with a gallant flourish. "It's been an honor, ma'am, and a great, great pleasure."

Laura's smile was dazzling. "Mr. Roper, I can't tell you what a pleasure it's been meeting *you*."

They promised to come to the house and meet Mrs. Roper and the girls the next time they were in Fredericksburg and said farewell to Owen Roper. An hour later they climbed back on board and the train lumbered out of the station.

The rest seemed to have revived the antique engine for it picked up speed rapidly, but a short distance out of town, just as it reached top speed, it squealed and clattered its way to a jolting stop. A major of the Alabama cavalry came aboard and ordered the car emptied. The packed freight cars were disgorging their cargo. Young men, suddenly alert after their long, uncomfortable trip, were ignoring orders to simmer down and cut out the horseplay while forming up on the flat ground beside the train in the haphazard but efficient way of seasoned Confederates.

Laura and Chase were taken down a rough trail through woodland so dense it was almost impassable if one stepped off the path. A dashing young captain relieved Chase of one of Elvina's packages of food. He offered to carry Laura's bag as well but she assured him it was not at all heavy. A half mile into the woods they came to an army encampment. The officer responsible had chosen his ground well, Chase said. At least a regiment was camped there and couldn't be seen from the train or even from the trail until suddenly there was a wide clearing before them with tents pitched and fires burning and more tents stretching out between trees that were sparse compared to the thickets behind them.

They had been told only that the general wanted to

interview all civilians before allowing them to travel on. Inside the general's tent a big man, his uniform in somewhat better condition than his men's, was working at a makeshift desk. He looked up. Astonishment and then delight spread over his handsome, sunburned face.

"Laura," he said, rising so rapidly that he almost knocked over the table "by God, I can't believe it. Chase, what the devil are you doing out here?"

Chase pumped Matt Riley's hand. "There's illness in Laura's family and I'm doing my best to see her through to Washington. But we've fallen into the middle of something, haven't we?"

Matt's grin faded. "I'm afraid so. Hooker's out there with more than twice as many men and it's too late to get Longstreet up here. We'll have to fight the bastard—beg pardon, Laura—with what we've got." He looked at her worriedly. "But never mind—this is a great moment and you are a welcome change from the kind of surprises we usually have." He rubbed his hands. "And I believe I can provide a fine surprise for you too, if I can locate a man to carry a message and get back before dark. Orderly, bring a couple of those boxes over here and find me a messenger. Sit down, sit down, both of you. I'm afraid you'll have to stay here overnight. Just a mile beyond us the track's been damaged. We're working on repairs now."

I T WAS NECESSARY to keep the fires small and tend them carefully for the underbrush in the nearby woods was thick and tinder-dry. Supper, such as it was, had been cooked in the few communal frying pans, and utensils and bags of cornmeal were now packed away. A prayer meeting had been held at sunset by the chaplain, John McGruder, who regularly converted the irreligious with his powerful preaching—sometimes he converted the same men several times since they tended to backslide and sin again. Tonight he led them in a hymn. Hundreds of male voices echoed through the woods and across the wide clearing, becoming richer as from other encampments other voices picked up the song.

Amazing grace, how sweet the sound
That saved a wretch like me
I once was lost and now am found
Was blind and now I see.

The melody rolled above the dark treetops, moving Laura as it never had in church. She sang along softly but stopped as the hymn went on.

Through many dangers, toils and snares
I have already come
'Tis grace hath brought me safe thus far
And grace will lead me home.

It seemed somehow wrong for her to sing such words with men who had been through so much and in the next few days would be facing other men no different from themselves, both doing their best to kill each other. So many on both sides would not be led home by grace or any other power. They would die in these woods and be buried in hastily scratched-out graves, and no one who loved them would ever know where or how they died but only that they were gone forever.

More hymns were sung and then someone started "Juanita," a sweetly plaintive love song beloved by both sides. Edward spoke the thought in all their minds. "I suppose the Yankees are singing the same songs tonight—we've sometimes sung together when we were camped close enough."

And then gone out and killed each other the next day, Laura thought. She was still stunned, almost bewildered by Matt Riley's fine surprise. War, it turned out, was not only obscene, it was also wildly irrational, ironic, impossible to predict as Chase had once told her, and sometimes brought great sweetness in the midst of madness. The army was spread out through the woods and neither Doug nor Kirby had been located. But Edward was here, and Alex. Being with them in this tense time before battle was such strange good fortune that it made the war seem even more erratic and senseless.

Alex said, "Old Edward's the hero here—dashing as all hell. You ought to have seen him in our last skirmish. Some Yank pickets held a little bridge over a creek and Edward galloped onto it alone, waving his sword and kiyiing like a wild Indian. They must have thought he was a whole unit of cavalry because they took off fast with him firing after them, laughing like a maniac."

Edward chuckled. "Yes, I'm a hell of a fellow, a god-damned leader of men. This war business is good for me, Chase. Got me off my posterior and into action, got me doing things I never dreamed I could, and before I'm through I'm going to show the world what I am. I'm going out in glory, by God." He stared into the fire, grinning cheerfully and murmured again, "Going out in glory."

Chase exchanged a look with Alex. He picked up a stick that had fallen half-burned from the fire and pulled out his knife. He was good at whittling and rather proud of his efforts, a trait Laura found endearing—he had few boyish qualities. Light and shadow flickered over Edward's face as the low flames moved and she searched it anxiously, remembering from long ago his odd look as he walked over the battlefield at Manassas, wondering if she was now reading more into his expression and his words than was really there.

The desultory conversation between the men went on and in a half hour Chase produced a handsome mule with long ears and a puckish grin. They passed it around, examining it closely and smiling. Matt Riley's orderly brought a request that Edward report to the general and also the news that a tent had been found for Laura—tents were scarce in the Confederate army.

"It's small, ma'am, but it'll keep off the night air," the orderly said.

She wanted to stay by the fire and hear whatever Alex might say now that Edward was out of earshot, but this nice young man was so pleased that she had to go with him. The ragamuffin Confederate army was offering her all it had.

The moment she was gone Chase said, "What was that all about?"

"God knows. He sits around in the evening and talks

about 'atoning' and 'going out in glory.' I don't see much of him but his friends tell me he does it all the time. And he's a crazy man in battle. I don't know what to make of him. Millie would go out of her mind if she knew."

Chase picked up another stick and this time he simply cut the wood aimlessly while he thought aloud. "I knew a man once out West. He intended to be a hero so, of course, he was. Took chances no sane man would, unnecessary, unproductive chances like riding straight across the path of Indian war parties, standing up to fire instead of staying down behind the barricade, generally making a fool of himself. He survived and got promoted. I hear he's now a brigadier general in the Army of the Potomac."

"The Yanks have a lot of high-ranking fools. We have a few ourselves." Alex hesitated. "Paige thinks Edward is the best man who ever drew breath"—he grinned—"except for me. What's eating on him? He's my father-in-law but you've probably spent more time with him than I have."

Chase searched his mind for the exact words he wanted. "He's a good man. He's also unhappy. Honor, chivalry, *noblesse oblige*—he can't always live up to it and I think it haunts him. He wants to be the perfect, gentle knight, something no one can be." He threw the remainder of the stick into the fire and pocketed the knife. "No one except Robert E. Lee."

Alex grinned too. "Don't throw off on Marse Bob. He's already canonized in this army. We'd be scared shitless if we didn't believe God Almighty was in charge. Hell, we're scared shitless anyway." He reached into his shirt pocket, brought out a scrap of paper and a pencil stub, and began to write. When he handed the folded paper to Chase he said, "Give this to Paige the next time you see her. I don't have an envelope. There's a big battle coming up, Chase. Big battle. So many officers have been killed—I don't expect to survive this one."

"I don't believe in premonitions. I've always gone into combat believing I'd be killed and seen men who thought they were immortal shot dead right beside me."

Alex nodded and stared into the fire. "Paige—I love her but she's a funny girl, comes all unstrung over little things. I don't know if she can be strong about the big things."

CHAPTER 20

IT WAS A MOONLESS NIGHT and the river was black in the starlight, lapping quietly at a bank that was hard to see, the midstream current swift and silent. Frank Godwin, the man who owned the boat that would take them across, was a farmer, as devout a Union man as David Rees, and if all had gone according to plan he had been appearing at this bend in the river for the previous three nights. This was the last night he would come.

"He's out there," Chase said.

Laura heard nothing but staring into the dark she thought she saw movement on the water, a shadow not there a moment ago, a few yards from the shore. The boat came in with a rush, the prow lodged on the sandy bank; there were murmured greetings and Chase lifted her in.

It was a little craft but sturdy, and Frank Godwin, a broad, powerful man, pulled his muffled oars with ease. The river was narrow at this point and they headed smoothly toward the farther shore, one more obstacle in their path almost behind them.

THE COURIER WAS an extremely tall man of shocking thinness, with a sharp nose and eyes that never seemed to open fully. He looks as if a light breeze would blow him away, Laura thought, but Chase had said he could move through the countryside like a shadow, unseen if he didn't want to be seen. He was the Godwins' farmhand. They called him Marr.

Chase said, "Get through to Hooker if you can. Does he know you?"

"Not yet."

"Use my name—it may help." Chase handed over his notes, everything he had heard and seen at the army encampment. "Memorize what you can and don't get caught with this. I can't afford to lose you."

Marr's teeth showed. "I can't afford to lose me either."
He unfolded his body from his chair and rose like a dancer.

Mrs. Godwin put her arms around him. "Home safe, now."

"Yes, ma'am."

He left the parlor, as Chase had said, quiet as a shadow.

Food was simple but plentiful on the Godwin farm and Mrs. Godwin provided the kind of meal seldom seen in Richmond these days—pork and chicken, potatoes and onions—delicious food, well cooked. She had been a pretty woman and was still handsome in spite of hard work, a gentle woman who took the pictures of her three sons from the mantel with a smile, named each one and told her guests something of their natures. They had gone off, one by one to join the army. Frank junior, the oldest, went first, then Jeb, the quiet one who wanted to be a school-teacher, and just after Christmas the baby, Alonzo. It was Jeb who was lost to them, Jeb who had died bravely in the last of six charges in the face of withering fire on the open, upward slope at Fredericksburg. He fell in mid-field, they knew that because Frank junior was there and saw it; he died instantly without pain, Frank told them, and was buried where he fell. Frank had dug the grave himself that night among the dead and the wounded still lying helpless in that terrible field. He had found boards and scratched Jeb's name by the light of matches, using his own body to shield the flame from Rebel sharpshooters who would have killed him if they could see him. She and Frank senior hoped to go there, Mrs. Godwin said softly, once this cruel war was over.

She stopped speaking. The only sound in the room was the loud ticktock of the clock by the parlor door. After a little while Frank Godwin said that it was Fredericksburg that caused Alonzo to go. He was just sixteen but he wanted to take his brother's place and fight for the Union. He believed, they all believed, that the Union must be preserved. Later on in the evening Frank mentioned that not all his family felt as he did. His younger brother was a fiery Rebel and the two of them had had many a bitter quarrel and several times almost come to blows. He was probably

in that battle down near Chancellorsville the other day as
Frank junior and Alonzo surely were.

That night Laura lay beside Chase in the Godwins' attic
room, wondering whether anything, even the Union, was
worth so many broken hearts and so much pain. Without a
word she turned to Chase and at the same moment he
reached for her, each knowing what the other felt. Once
she had believed it was wrong to make love in the midst of
tragedy. Now she knew better. It was one of the few
ways—sometimes it seemed to her the only way—humans
had of holding off the cold, enduring dark. It was always a
celebration of life.

B Y   T H E   T I M E they crossed the Potomac and came
into Washington the city knew what had happened at
Chancellorsville. Fighting Joe Hooker, outnumbering the
Rebels by more than two to one, had managed with staggering incompetence and loss of nerve to give the Union
another bitter defeat. He had swaggered across the Rappa-
hannock River announcing that victory was in his grasp,
but when Lee's Confederates stood and fought he overrode
the protests of his able commanders and quickly ordered a
retreat, wasting the bloody sacrifice of thousands of brave
men. The only good news for the North was that Stonewall
Jackson, the daring Rebel who had outmaneuvered and
outfought their own generals so many times, was dead—
killed accidentally, rumor said, by his own men.

This time the capital city did not reel in shock at the
number of casualties. A certain hardness of heart had developed among those not directly affected. You could get used
to anything, given enough time. The families of the lost
young men wept and suffered but other people were
making money. Factories were humming, no one was out
of work, businessmen were pocketing enormous profits, the
stock market was sky-high, and government contracts were
lucrative in a way one could only dream about in peace-
time. It was easy to sell shoddy military equipment to the
government. Soldiers died because of the failure of such
equipment but no manufacturer was pursued and punished,
no one even thought of such a thing. It was the business of
business to make its owners rich; it was the business of the

army to fight with whatever it had. Many a father gladly took home his pay never realizing that his son's feet were soaked and cold because of inferior boots or that he had died because a faulty shell exploded in his face.

A casual walk down Pennsylvania Avenue revealed how freely the money was flowing. Washington's women, unlike the increasingly deprived women of Richmond, greeted spring dressed in the height of French fashion, the colors brilliant, the flower-laden bonnets stylishly extreme. Soldiers and sailors thronged the streets and the officers of both services added glamour with the extravagance of their uniforms. Restaurants were full, balls were given regularly, and parties thrown by Washington hostesses were lavish and frequent.

Caroline Merritt, once one of those hostesses, no longer entertained large crowds and seldom even gave small dinner parties, but tonight was not a party, it was a homecoming. Laura, the child her brother had married, the daughter she had never had, was seated at her dinner table after a journey that made Caroline tremble to think about. It had been foolish, unnecessary, dangerous beyond belief, and—now that she was here and safe—wonderful. The men at the table were welcome too—her old friend Ted Harper, intent on business, looking like a pale clerk and dealing with matters that could affect the fate of the nation; Chase Girard, a man whose warmth and intelligence she enjoyed immensely, a man she was not at all sure was right for Laura.

Laura had started the evening in high spirits too. She loved Caroline and in this house she was as much at home as anywhere in the world. Chase was here with her and that would have made everything perfect but for Ted Harper. He said they had met and maybe they had—she had met a lot of people. He was so nondescript as to be almost memorable for it, but if they had met she'd done right to forget him. She would like to forget him now but it wasn't possible. He controlled Chase's future and, so, hers too.

After dinner the ladies left the men to talk, but instead of going into the drawing room as was usual, Caroline took Laura to her upstairs sitting room, arranged herself on the

sofa and looked up in a speculative way that made Laura
feel much younger than she was.

"How did you get into it?"

"I had to, Caroline, once I opened up my eyes and
looked."

"I didn't ask why, I asked how. He drew you in,
didn't he."

Laura sat down beside her. "Don't make it sound as if he
somehow cajoled me. He asked me to help, I thought it
over and decided I would."

"Was it before or after?"

Laura looked up quickly, said, "After what?", and turned
deep red as Caroline's eyebrows rose. "Lord," she muttered, "is it that obvious?"

"Well, neither of you has been on guard tonight. But if
you don't want people to guess, don't look at each other
like that."

Laura took a breath. "He didn't seduce me into it, I had
already decided. I suppose you're terribly shocked." Then
she added formally, "I would hate to lose your regard,
Caroline."

Laughter started in Caroline's chest and bubbled up,
filled with loving amusement. "Oh, honey, you couldn't
lose my regard if you robbed the U.S. Treasury! I'm not
shocked, I understand quite well."

"Then be happy for me. I was so miserable for so long.
There was a time when I could scarcely face each day—and
then there he was and everything changed. It's not as if I
were putting him in Robert's place. He's different in so
many ways."

"Younger, for one thing," Caroline remarked dryly.

Laura looked down at her tightly clasped hands. Her
voice was a whisper. "Please. Don't begrudge me this."

Caroline laid a hand lightly on her arm. "Dear child, I
don't. I loved Robert and I miss him but he's dead and you
are alive and young. If it were a different man you would
have my blessing, but this man—I have misgivings. No
doubt you love him deeply but I fear he won't be there
when you need him. That's a terrible thing for a woman.
You should be building a life together that will last and it
may not last with him."

Laura's head came up. Her face had an odd closed look. "He's an uncommon man, I trust him completely, but nothing lasts. He'll leave, of course, and it's good for me that he will. Only a few weeks ago he had to take information to a courier who lives a distance out of town. I begged him not to go—troops were moving on every road that night—but he had to, I knew that. He should have been home in two or three hours but he wasn't." Her eyes were wide, looking back into a night of raw terror. "Caroline, I thought he was dead that night and I remembered what I'd almost forgotten—how dangerous it is, loving someone. Too dangerous for me. I'm fond of him, very fond, but that's all. Maybe someday I'll marry though I can't imagine it. If I ever do it won't be for love."

Caroline sank back against the sofa, nonplussed. She had believed she knew this young woman well—not completely, but well—and she had just shown an undreamed-of side of her nature, a side Caroline would rather not have seen. It didn't bode well for her happiness in the long run. At last she said, "What you're doing—this 'work,' as you call it . . . you realize what will happen if you're caught."

"I realize. I don't take it lightly. But"—Laura hesitated, searching for the right words—"I've learned a lot about myself. Every day I pretend to feelings I don't have, I look people who trust me straight in the eye and tell them outrageous lies. I do it even to people I love. I'm not happy about that part but I do it. This trip—I needn't have come but I wanted to. I like the danger, the never knowing what will come next—it's terrifying but thrilling too. This time with Chase . . . it's only for a little while. It will be over soon. He'll go away and I'll go back to the life I had before, following the rules, not feeling much. That's the way I want it."

"You're willing to risk your life for a cause but not your heart even for someone worth loving."

"That's right." Laura's eyes were thoughtful. "Causes don't destroy you the way people do."

Later, thinking it over, she realized she hadn't quite told Caroline all the truth. She hadn't mentioned the joy of having him beside her in the night, of beginning each morning with kisses, or the bone-deep comfort of being utterly at home with one man. It was a private treasure, something to be appreciated for what it was and to let go when the time came. And not to be worried about in the meantime.

Instead, she turned her mind away from the personal and while Chase was in his interminable meetings walked through the town she hadn't seen in four years. The change astonished her. A sleepy Southern village had become a booming wartime city, the nerve center of the nation. The Old Flag flew proudly from the Capitol with all its stars intact, a symbol for a Union that did not intend to be dissolved, and the new tiered iron dome of the Capitol building was being worked on energetically.

Armed Liberty, the huge bronze statue that would be placed at the top when the dome was completed, now rested on the Capitol grounds where people could see and admire it. The great goddess and the continued rebuilding spoke louder than any government statistics of the difference in riches and resources between North and South. The North could afford to fight a great war while indulging in luxuries like bronze goddesses and marble buildings— helpful to morale but not essential. The South, tattered, impoverished, was barely able to feed its people and its fighting men.

But with all Washington's fierce prosecution of the war it was still Southern in manners, attitudes, even accents. People with the harder accents of the North now swarmed through the town but Laura's slow Southern speech was not remarked on or even noticed. Society's most exalted leaders had always been Southerners and many of them had chosen to stay on when war came.

Ted Harper, speaking bitterly of the highborn Southern ladies caught with messages rolled in their chignons or medicines and other scarce items found under their wide skirts, had advised Laura to be careful anytime she passed through the lines.

"Don't depend on chivalry to save you. We've found several prominent women carrying ciphers that damned them. A year ago neither side would have forced a lady to lift her skirts. Now we do if we're suspicious enough and so do the Rebels. You wouldn't believe what we've found—

cans of meat, rolls of cloth, big bags of coffee. One woman
had seven pairs of cavalry boots attached to her hoops. No
one could figure out how she managed to walk."

She said, "Yes," and, "I'll be careful," and got away
from him as soon as she could. Like Fiona he cared only for
his cause. Because she had come to understand Fiona she
knew that Ted would sacrifice anyone for it.

Chase wasn't fond of him either. After a long session
with Ted on this, their last day in town, he came back to
the hotel in a black mood but not until they were almost in
Richmond did he tell her why.

This time they traveled by a different route, north from
Washington to Baltimore, embarking there down Chesa-
peake Bay for Fortress Monroe at the tip of the Virginia
peninsula. Their ship left Baltimore at night and the next
day anchored in Hampton Roads. Most Federal forts in the
South had been taken by the Confederates at the beginning
of the war, but Fortress Monroe still proudly flew the Stars
and Stripes and ruled this portion of the bay with its guns.
The Roads bustled with shipping, the wharves were
swamped with arrivals and departures, and disembarking
passengers had to wait on board until afternoon.

Laura said, "For all the years I lived in Richmond I've
never seen the fort before, never been south of Yorktown.
It looks fierce, like a medieval castle."

"It's fierce enough," Chase replied. "There used to be a
hotel just below the wall but they tore it down about six
months ago. We'll have to stay on the mainland tonight.
Ted arranged it."

"You don't like Ted, do you? What happened at that last
meeting?"

"What makes you think something happened?"

"When you came back you looked just like you look
now—dark as a thundercloud."

He smiled at that and shook his head. "I'd better get out
of the business I'm in if I can be read that easily. He broke
a promise. Ted does that when it suits him."

"What was the promise?"

"That I could go back into uniform." She said nothing.
"Does that surprise you?"

"No." She was looking out at the fort, not at him. "I

was surprised when you came back with me. I could have come home alone, you know. I'm quite capable."

"You could but I wouldn't sleep nights if you did. I wanted to bring you back and then leave—that was his promise, but he said 'Later, not now.' Same thing he said the last time. The damned war will be over before I get into it."

Her eyes flashed up. "You sound like Kirby at the beginning, like Doug, and there's no excuse for you. You know better!" Her voice was swift and cold. "Isn't what you're doing dangerous enough? Do you want to have to kill and kill, do you want to be blown apart by some fool who thinks he's shooting you for his country and you just as big a fool?"

"I want to do what I was trained for. I'm an engineer, Laura. I build things—like bridges. Do you know how many rivers and streams and unfordable creeks there are in Virginia? Our men have to get across them somehow. I also know explosives and I blow up things like fortress walls, like bridges—so they can't come across and get at us."

"Don't patronize me. I know what engineers do." Army engineers, she thought with a chill, men who build bridges under enemy fire or lay explosives while expert riflemen try to kill them, men with one of the riskiest jobs and highest casualty rates in the army. She kept her voice low but fear hardened it. "I thought you were different but you're just like all the rest—afraid of what people will think if you're not in the fighting. How can you be so *stupid*!"

He gave her a long, grave look and said at last, "I'm sorry you see it that way. Before I left I talked to a man with more power than Ted—Grenville Dodge. He's a military man too, and he sees it my way. I won't go now but before long I will."

That night in the large and pleasant room Ted Harper had arranged for them they lay beside each other in the moonlight that filtered through gauzy curtains. He didn't fall asleep as quickly as usual but lay a little distance from her, thinking that nothing was ever as easy or simple as it seemed, certainly not a love affair. He had never seen her angry before, never thought she could look at him with such cold contempt. The sudden swiftness of the quarrel, seeming to come out of nowhere, had stunned him and yet as soon as it happened he knew it had been brewing for some time. Finally he fell into a doze but a little while later was awake again, his sleep disturbed by dreams he didn't like.

She knew it when he woke. She hadn't slept herself but had been lying quietly, thinking over what she had said. She didn't regret a word, it was all true, she was right and he was wrong. She heard him sigh slightly and turn his face toward the window and her hand moved out and then stopped. More than anything she wanted to put her arms around him, to apologize, to say that whatever he did she would still love him, but she couldn't. As she had known all along, it did not do to give your heart completely and she was glad she hadn't done it. He would go, not after the war as she had expected, but into the midst of it . . . into the madness that was destroying everything worth keeping. There was no help for it, she couldn't stop him. All she could do was save herself.

CHAPTER 21

ON THE FIRST DAY OF JULY just before the noon hour word spread through the house that Becca had begun having faint, fleeting labor pains. Laura got the message at the War Department. She finished reading the latest dispatches flying in over the wires from the north and then rushed out into the scorching summer day. Climbing the hill, her pace slowed. June had been miserable, July gave promise of being worse, and there was no real reason to hurry. Byron Rollins had told her he expected this birth to be long and difficult—Becca was so small. At that thought she began to hurry again.

No one answered the chimes at the front door but as usual it was not locked. In the upper hallway she met Jewel.

"How is she?"

"Sleeping now. Come on in here."

They went into Laura's old bedroom, sat down on the

charming canopied bed she had loved in childhood, and looked at each other.

"What do you think?"

Jewel's smooth brow wrinkled. "Dr. Rollins might be wrong. Sometimes wide-hipped women go on for days and little things like Miss Becca just pop their babies out, Lord knows why. So far, she's doing well."

Laura relaxed a little. Jewel was an experienced midwife who had delivered many babies, black and white. She had saved two women, both of them ladies Laura knew well, when their doctors had given up.

"Miss Laura." Laura looked up. She knew that tone. "Miss Laura, what do you hear? They're out there, aren't they?"

Yes, thought Laura, the fear that had been drumming at her all morning returning. Lee the masterful, Lee the great and good had invaded Pennsylvania and they were out there with him. The loved faces were so clear she could almost touch them.

To Jewel she said, "All I know is that they're with Lee and Lee is in Pennsylvania doing his best to start another battle."

"He's a great general, isn't he?"

"So they say. He's certainly better than anything the Yankees have. Every time they get into a fight he wipes the floor with them. The last dispatch I saw said that yesterday he was on the Cashtown road heading toward Gettysburg. I looked on the map and it's mostly farm country but there are a lot of little towns I never heard of around there."

"If we win—" Jewel hesitated, looking not at Laura but out the open window at the hot, blue day. "If we win this battle will the war be over?"

"I don't know. Sometimes I think our children and our grandchildren will be fighting in it someday, like a family quarrel that never ends." It occurred to Laura, watching Jewel's unrevealing face, to wonder which side she meant when she said "if we win." It was not a question that could ever be asked.

"Miss Paige is fit to be tied—she's been throwing up ever since she heard the army is over in Pennsylvania, just sure Mr. Alex is already dead and the telegram on the way."

Alex had come home after Chancellorsville, the only man in the family to be given leave. By the time Laura was back from Washington he was gone again, and during the last few weeks Paige, who had been convinced she was barren, had suffered the pangs of early pregnancy and, she said with a flash of her old humor, was at last able to hold up her head with her friends in between bouts of vomiting. Then word had come that terrified the Seymours and every other family in Richmond. Lee had boldly taken his hungry, ragged army across the Potomac and carried the battle to the North. There were supplies and food to be found in the rich granary of Pennsylvania and perhaps even victory as well. A successful invasion, it was said, might result in official recognition by the cautious English and French governments and encourage the growing Northern peace movement. At any rate, the general was a natural aggressor and despised a defensive position. Better, he believed, to challenge his powerful opponent on its own soil than wait for it to grow even stronger and attack him again.

So he had moved, taking with him men who were the reason for living for many of the women left behind. Some of them were more bloodthirsty than their men and urged them to die in battle if they must, rather than retreat. Others, like Paige and Millie, hating Yankees and devoutly patriotic, prayed for victory but prayed even harder that their husbands be spared. The Confederacy was all very well, Millie said, and she loved it dearly, but Edward was dearer and she hoped General Lee knew what he was doing.

Twice during that long first day of battle, as Becca struggled with increasing pain, Laura made hurried trips to the War Department for the latest news, but word was sketchy so far. All that was known was that a great battle had begun under a blazing sun in the farmland of Pennsylvania. By evening it appeared that the battle was not over but reports were confused and no one knew which side held the advantage.

As the day ended the first stage of Becca's battle ended too. Jewel had been right. Becca's hard labor had begun in mid-afternoon and three hours later a healthy child—a boy she named William—was safely born before Dr. Rollins, busy at the hospital, could arrive. Now the great threat was the dreaded childbed fever that claimed so many women. So the vigil continued, for the fighting men in the Pennsylvania fields and for Becca.

The battle went on in desperate fury for three days. By July Fourth word was beginning to filter in and what little information there was did not sound encouraging. First came the unsubstantiated, contradictory rumors—it was a great victory, a disastrous defeat, the Union dead were piled three high as far as the eye could see, Lee was wounded and Longstreet dead; no one knew what the truth was. In government offices, where the lamps burned late, only official telegrams and military couriers were given credence and even they were treated warily.

That it was a monumental battle was known almost from the start. In the days that followed it also became clear that for once the great Lee had made more mistakes than the Yankees. The invasion had failed with huge losses on both sides—for the South over twenty thousand fighting men who could not be replaced. The disheartened Confederate army started back toward the Potomac and found that the river had become a muddy torrent, almost impossible to cross while fending off the constant raids of Northern cavalry. It was more than a week before rickety, hastily thrown-up bridges were in place and the wagonloads of wounded and the sodden, barefoot troops could cross over into Virginia.

Even before the wounded began to pour into Richmond's hospitals more bad news arrived. That Yankee general, Grant, the one whose style was to pick away at an enemy and never give up, had finally taken the last Confederate stronghold on the Mississippi. Vicksburg, under siege, had surrendered and the Federals now controlled every inch of the great river from its source to the Gulf of Mexico just as they controlled access to almost every Southern port. The Confederacy was now encircled by water. For the South the losses were staggering. The Mississippi was irrevocably gone, the attempt to carry the war northward had failed, they had lost the mighty Stonewall Jackson at Chancellorsville—but, they told each other, they still had Lee.

Lee and his army, gallant and stubborn, would never surrender and, in the end, would save them.

But now the casualty lists from Gettysburg had been revised and updated and the losses were appalling, touching every family in some way. The Mercers had lost their daughter-in-law in childbirth while their son was dying at almost the same time under the Pennsylvania sun. Grace and Lowell Weston's three boys had been killed as they swept up the rising ground of Cemetery Ridge with George Pickett. Grace, all her languid elegance gone, sat in a darkened room recounting to callers again and again the great charge that was already legend.

"I suppose the Yankees must have buried them—don't you think?" she said to Laura. "And said a prayer? They're cruel but they aren't completely uncivilized."

"Of course they did," Laura assured her softly. "I've known many Yankees and any one of them would give your boys a proper burial." She rose to go. Grace murmured again, "Not completely uncivilized . . ." and did not notice when she left.

Alex was one of the wounded who arrived in town during the first week. He came, not walking as many injured men did, but by ambulance because his injury was a leg wound—the same thigh that had sustained the bayonet thrust at Manassas. The prior damage complicated his treatment, Byron Rollins said, and it would take longer to heal but it could have been worse. This was a tearing wound caused by a piece of flying shrapnel, bad enough but not so devastating as a minié bullet which often shattered the bone and required amputation. Paige, listening with huge eyes at Alex's bedside, fainted at that and had to be revived and assured by the doctor many times that no such action was contemplated. But everyone knew that it could still happen if infection or gangrene set in and that more often than not amputation meant death.

From Alex came the only news the family had of their other men. They had all come safely through the battle, he said, but were on sparse rations. Their chief needs were a little broader diet, blankets and overcoats for the winter that was coming, and, above all, boots. Lying on a cot under the trees in the side yard, nursing the wound that was healing well, he gave Chase details he would not mention to the women.

"Edward's still a captain—been passed over for promotion twice and I think I know why. He's well liked but he's too damn dashing to be running the regiment. Kirby was sick as a dog with dysentery the last time I saw him but he's young and strong—he may pull through." Dysentery was the scourge of both armies, a vicious infection of the bowels, worsened by bad food, that was killing more men than any other disease. "Doug seems all right—scrabbling for something to eat like all of us. We'll starve to death before the Yanks shoot us or else freeze our feet off this winter. Did you see my boots? They're in good condition compared to some. And so many fellows are barefoot. I saw bloody footprints in the snow last winter and I'll see them this winter if I last that long. We're almost out of powder and ammunition is low. Whenever we need something we have to go capture a U.S. Army supply depot. When are you going north again?"

"Soon," Chase told him.

Alex grinned. "I forgot. You always did play your cards close to the vest. Well, for God's sake bring back some boots. And uniforms—some kind of warm clothing. Guns and ammunition would be a big help too."

From the house came voices—Joseph loudly ordering Bella out of his way and Bella, in a shriek, saying, "I guess I knows how to serve gent'men better'n you. And you was all ginned up last night, you old fool. Takin' advantage 'cause Mr. Edward ain' here!"

"That's enough, Bella. Joseph knows he was wrong. Give me the tray, Joseph—no, give it to me, and Bella, you go see if Miss Paige needs anything."

Laura came down the path from the house carrying a tray, a little smile on her lips, and looking up, Chase had the odd sensation that his heart was turning in his chest. It did that, especially when she came into view unexpectedly—or, sometimes, his breath simply stopped. Maybe he should ask Byron Rollins, who suffered from the same disease, to look him over, but what ailed him was nothing a doctor could find. She was wearing a dress made of a thin white material with green flowers sprinkled over it, a dress he had seen many times and never tired of. The day was hot and she looked so cool and fresh.

She set the tray on the little table. "This is berry juice and ice, and here are peaches from Pine Hill just in this morning! What would we do without Pine Hill?" She took a peach from the bowl, bit into it and licked the juice from her lips with a grin.

Alex asked, "How is Paige?"

"Better—she's lying down. Now don't look so worried. She hasn't thrown up in two weeks and Byron says the sick feeling will stop soon." She touched his shoulder, said, "You're the one we have to take care of," and went back to the house, eating her peach, her pretty skirts trailing over the grass.

The men watched her go, their eyes met and Chase was the first to look away.

"Hell, ain't it," Alex observed. "Paige drove me crazy. I never intended to get married, you know."

"I'm not so sure it's going to last, and I didn't think it could ever end."

"That was kind of . . ."

Chase smiled. " 'Dumb' is the word you're searching for."

" 'Optimistic' is what I was going to say. Do you want to marry her?"

"She wouldn't have me, Alex. I can go only so far with Laura and then I come to a solid wall—no way over or around it. She won't let anyone come too close, including me. She says she won't take the risk, and the hell of it is, she means it."

Alex looked at the door Laura had closed as she went into the house, and then at Chase. "It's better to marry them—you don't suffer as much. At least, I don't. I wouldn't be back in your shoes for all the tea in China." He laughed. "Not even for all the coffee in Brazil."

He finished his drink and lay back on the piled-up pillows, thinking of Paige upstairs, miserable in her pregnancy, and wondering what the odds were of his ever seeing the baby. His leg ached less every day. If it continued to heal without incident he would be back on the line by fall. He fell into a doze and began to snore gently.

Chase set his own drink on the grass, tilted back in his chair, and placed his boots on the low table. The trip into Maryland would have to be made soon. Judah Benjamin had been noticeably less friendly in recent weeks and was pressing him for supplies he would never deliver. In the gloom and bitterness that followed Gettysburg, spies and their nefarious activities had become an obsession in Richmond. Several friends had informed him that spies were responsible for the defeat at Gettysburg and when he mildly suggested that perhaps the Union army had something to do with it they were shocked. There had been countless accusations and many arrests. Three men who as far as he knew were completely innocent were presently facing trial and might well be convicted and hung. Suspicion, searching for a place to rest, could easily fall next on him.

He would delay the Maryland trip as long as he dared and once away from this town would simply travel on north. It meant never seeing Richmond again unless he came back with the invading army, and God alone knew what would have to be done to take the city. She could be gone when he got back—if he got back—or she could be dead. He would not see her again and how could he bear that? How had this happened to him? He had seen the danger clearly and yet had fallen as hard as a man could fall. With her he had let down his guard, allowed himself to be vulnerable, revealed much of his true self. He believed she had done the same and yet here she was, on the verge of ending the affair; he could feel it coming. Probably in the infinite scales of justice he deserved it for he had done the same so many times himself.

N OT ONLY THE WOUNDED and the sick came back to Richmond after Gettysburg. Whole young men came into town too, and they did what soldiers always did, especially when they had survived a battle. They looked for ways to rejoice in the fact that they still lived. Some were taken up by patriotic hostesses who introduced them to nice young ladies, but these men were usually officers with family names that were familiar. Some sought the comfort of the churches, for religion was a powerful force among the men of the Confederate army. But the great majority looked for release in liquor, gambling, and whatever woman they could find. One young soldier, as poor and ragged as any, appeared on the doorstep of the most expensive parlor house in Richmond and asked for the proprietor.

Venita, the black maid who opened the door, lifted her silky brows. She wasn't used to disreputable men—that is, she told a friend later, disreputable-*looking* men—appearing on the Daisychain's doorstep. (A religious girl, she considered all the customers despicable and prayed for them daily.) But Miss Angela was a kindly owner, entitled to good service, and sometimes the scruffiest-looking sort had money to spend. She never turned away a potential patron without investigation, and this black-haired boy, thin to the point of scrawniness and none too clean, was turning his battered hat in nervous hands and looking at her with such haunted eyes. Nice eyes too. She allowed him to step inside.

"Whom shall I tell Miss Angela is calling?" she inquired as she had been instructed and the boy replied, "Her brother."

Venita flew from the entry hall and rushed to her mistress, but Angela, after hearing her news, came slowly and stopped in the doorway.

"Sammy?" she said uncertainly. And then, "My God, Sam! Oh, come in, come in! Let me look at you."

Upstairs in her private three-room suite, a place no man before Sam had entered, she sat him down to a huge dinner and watched with worried eyes as he ate it all. "More?" she asked when he was finished. "There's plenty where that came from."

He spoke slowly, like his father. "It was first-rate, Sis, but I'm full to the brim."

He was so thin and worn it tore her heart. She searched for something to say and finally observed, "You're a good bit taller than when I saw you last."

"Yes, ma'am."

She did a quick calculation. He had been seven on that night she climbed out the window, heading for New Orleans, and promised to come back for him. Now he was twenty-four. "What do you think of my place?"

He thought her question over and said finally, "It's mighty grand. I never saw such finery."

Pleased, she smiled. The Daisychain was her great achievement. "Yes, it is grand. Sam, I want you to have a hot bath and I'll find you a better uniform and boots and some good things to take back with you. I suppose you do have to go back?"

"Day after tomorrow."

"Would you consider . . . I could help you, Sam. Maybe get you out of the country if you wanted to desert."

He didn't seem shocked or even disturbed but said simply, "I couldn't do that, Angie. Some are running away, I guess, but not me. We've got to throw off the oppressor's heel, you know."

"Yeah, I've heard about the oppressor's heel." She patted his hand. "You sleep here tonight. The bed is pure down-filled and those are real silk sheets."

"I do appreciate a place to lay my head." He reached out and fingered the cloth. "Real silk. I believe I never saw such a thing before."

She wanted to feed him another meal, she wanted to cradle him in her arms as if he were still the baby he had been. "You strip while I have hot water brought up. Pick whoever you want for the night. You can have any girl in the house."

"Well now, I'll pass on the girl. I'm saving myself for marriage . . ." He groaned as he pulled off boots with soles that were almost gone and wiggled his toes through the holes in his socks. "But I surely would be pleased to have that bath."

CHAPTER 22

ADAM ALMOST MISSED HIM. He was not at Mr. Benjamin's office as Miss Laura had said, but he had been there. Adam bounded down the stairs and on the street caught a glimpse of him, then lost him in the crowd around Capitol Square. Adam broke into a run. At the corner of Franklin and Twelfth Street, Chase paused to speak to an acquaintance, and when he walked on, Adam, out of breath, sauntered up to him.

"Morning, Mr. Chase. You're a hard man to catch up with." Now fourteen, he was beginning to look like the man he would become rather than the boy he had been, but he still had the irresistible grin that made everyone love him.

"I try to be, Adam. What's the hurry?"

"Miss Laura says come quick to her house."

"Did she say why?"

"No, suh. She was packin' her clothes and things when I left."

Chase came in the house by the back way as he always did except when on an official visit and took the stairs two at a time. Her bedroom door was open and three bags and a small trunk sat beside the bed. She was standing before her mirror putting on a charming straw bonnet trimmed with crimson ribbons.

One part of his mind noted the way the bonnet brim framed her face; another part saw her smile, which meant the network had not been destroyed, Frederick, Fiona, and the others had not been found out, they were all still safe. That receding fear was immediately replaced by another, even darker. She was going away.

She tied the bonnet ribbons under her chin. "I'm glad you're here. I didn't want to leave without seeing you."

He came in and closed the door. "Where are you going?"

"To Malvern with Becca. Her mother is dying, they think, and her father wants her to come and bring the baby." Becca had recovered well from her son's birth, but her mother, ill since last fall, hadn't yet been able to come to Richmond. "She asked me to go with her so . . ." At the expression on his face her voice trailed off and she finished with less certainty, "So of course I am."

"Of course. You didn't mention it this morning."

"I didn't know! I only heard about it an hour ago. She just got the message at breakfast."

"When will you be back?"

She turned to pick up a hairbrush from her dressing table and dropped it into her small, impractical reticule. "I can't say. I suppose it depends on what happens." Her face was half hidden by the bonnet.

He took her by the arm and jerked her around. "You can't say. Can you say what this means? Can you be honest for a change?"

The sudden violence in his hands, in his face, frightened her. Until now she had received only gentleness from him.

"Please," she whispered. He still held her so that she couldn't turn aside but the pressure of his hands eased. "I need—I need time away from you, time to think. You don't have to kiss me or make love to me or even touch me—you just walk into a room and I can't think straight. Somehow I've got to think straight."

He let her go but stared at her so long and hard that she bit her lip and looked away.

He said, "Benjamin gave me an ultimatum this morning. Go into Maryland as soon as possible and bring back rifles, powder, and uniforms or, since the army needs men with my training, join up. If I'm not careful I'll find myself building bridges for the Rebels or in jail waiting to be hung. So I'm going, but when I get to Maryland I'll continue north." She looked up with a sharp intake of breath and he went on. "I can't come back this time. He's suspicious. I doubt I can last here another month. Come with me, Laura. I can get you out now. If we wait it will be impossible."

His voice was calm, almost matter-of-fact, but she knew this, too, was an ultimatum. She looked down at her hands, then at her dressing table, bare now that everything was packed, then at her hands again. She couldn't look at him. "You're really going to do it, aren't you? You're going back into uniform, into combat."

"I don't think they'll have me at headquarters running errands for some general."

"You could get passage on a blockade runner—it could be arranged—and go away, maybe to Europe. If you'd do that I'd . . . I'd come with you."

"That's not the most enthusiastic offer I ever got. I wouldn't consider running out, Laura, not even for you."

"Well, then, maybe it's best you go back. It's what you want." Her hand went up in a desperate gesture. "You see how painful this is? I told you it would be, I *knew* it! It just doesn't do to get too—too entangled." She took a breath. "I can't come with you, Chase. Becca needs me right now."

He went to the window and stood for a while, his hands shoved deep in his trouser pockets, looking down into the yard. At last he said, "Do you know how hard it is to find someone you can love who loves you too? Do you know how many people search and search and never have a chance at what we've got? It's not commonplace, Laura, it's rare and you're throwing it away." He turned and looked at her. "You're a coward, you know. In spite of all you've done, you're a coward. It's true life is painful but there are good things. You and I are a good thing. I can't promise you I'll live forever, you can't promise me that either, but I'm willing to take the risk of getting hurt. I love you enough for that. You don't."

Her jaw was clenched and her eyes shining with tears.

He said, "I'll have to go soon. If you're not home by the time I leave I won't see you until, perhaps, after the war."

She nodded, said, "Yes, you mustn't stay," and then, softly, "I'll miss you."

"I'll miss you too."

He went quickly out of the room and down the stairs. She could hear him say farewell to Elvina, hear the kitchen door shut. In her mind she saw him go through the woods and out into another part of the city, where everyone he passed was an enemy. Perhaps, after the war, he had said. *Perhaps.*

Thoughts began tumbling frantically through her head. Why had she let him leave believing she didn't really love him? What had made her think the battlefield was more dangerous than what he had been doing here these past years? He would be gone before she got back, he had to go—this place was a snakepit. She could run after him, beg him to take her with him and he would do it. She could live in Washington, see him off to his damnable war and let him go with a smile as other women were doing. It would be easy to find him in town . . . she could see clearly the look that would be in his eyes when she told him she wasn't such a coward after all.

From the foot of the stairs Elvina caroled, "Miss Laura, Miss Becca's out front in the ca'ridge an' Joseph's here for the bags."

She looked around the room, the wonderful, safe, private room that had contained so much love. Then she went to the door.

"Send Joseph up, Elvina, and tell Miss Becca I'll be there directly."

M ALVERN WAS A huge establishment, a three-story colonnaded building of sixty-nine rooms including one upstairs room seventy feet long. Its pristine white eminence could be seen from the river road and in ordinary times the road and the curving drive were busy with traffic, for its owner, Hale McCauley, transported his crops on the river and gave parties and received company constantly. Today both the road and the drive were empty and Becca was almost certain why even before she climbed the steps, her month-old baby in her arms, and saw the black wreath with its trailing black ribbon on the great front door.

That evening she and Laura ate with her father in the dining room at a table that even reduced to its smallest size could have seated twenty. They sat together at one end, attended by two maids and a young, light-skinned man named Knox who served smoothly and silently and came and went on quiet feet.

When Laura had walked into the large drawing room that afternoon she knew immediately whom Becca favored. Her mother's portrait dominated the room, not by its size so much as by the intensity of the eyes in the thin, sharp-featured face. She was seated with hands in her lap in a peaceful pose, yet those hands were not at rest and her large eyes, looking out directly at the observer, were filled with pain. The artist had told volumes about Mary Ann McCauley, and Hale McCauley did not know it. He was proud of the portrait and assured Laura that in seeing it she was seeing his wife before illness had devastated her.

"She was a fine woman, fine," he said quietly. "Her only deficiency was poor health." He put his arm around Becca. "That's why this little girl is our only chick. But she was a good wife, good neighbor, good mother. Wasn't she, Becca?"

"Yes, Father."

Again at dinner he said, "Mary Ann was the best a man could ask for and brave to the end. It will be terribly hard, living here in this big pile alone." He swallowed, and repeated softly, "Terribly hard."

The outpouring of people, many from as far away as Charleston and Savannah and even Alabama and Mississippi, testified to the regard in which the McCauleys were held. Or at least testified to the power and wealth of Hale McCauley. The burial took place in the family burying ground—Hale had built Malvern "from scratch" as he liked to say, set aside this land for the McCauleys, and Mary Ann would be the first occupant. It was in a quiet, pleasant spot, level land near a meadow, surrounded by trees and with many shrubs planted nearby that would flower in the spring. The day was warm, the breeze cool, the sky so blue and trimmed with soft, white clouds that it reminded Laura for one bittersweet moment of the picnic beside the river with Chase, that golden day when he took her out in his new buggy, fed her fried chicken and peaches and angel food cake, gave her a lesson in military strategy, and took the first step toward a love affair that could not last.

The rector of the small Episcopal church Mary Ann had faithfully attended cleared his throat. "Have mercy upon us miserable sinners," he began.

When his voice died away on the final amen the mourners remained in their places, waiting while he murmured to the lady's husband and daughter.

Even Malvern's enormous upstairs room, built for large gatherings, was barely able to accommodate the number of people present. There was no shortage of food on this plantation and long tables covered with white linen cloths were loaded with hams from the smokehouse, roast turkeys swimming in rich sauce, great racks of lamb, sugar-soaked yams, candied fruits. One large table held nothing but an assortment of pies dripping with juice and tall, creamy cakes. The four silver punch bowls were kept constantly replenished and straight bourbon, preferred by many, was poured with a lavish hand. By late afternoon it was clear that some of the guests would have to be helped to bed before evening.

Laura had never met Becca's mother and no one expected her to grieve deeply, yet the day had been harder than she was prepared for. At the burying ground she had experienced sudden vivid pictures of another funeral—the coffin, the flowers, the child she had been looking with surpassing fear at the hole in the ground where they were going to put her mother. Every emotion she had felt on that day came back with chilling force and fused into one—a sense of hideous, numbing loss. The man who now had her trapped between the refreshment table and the grand piano was still talking—she could see his mouth moving but could not hear the words. She muttered an excuse and walked away while his mouth was still moving.

Swiftly she went downstairs, through doors that were half glass—an expensive innovation—and out into the last light of the setting sun. There was a pergola in the garden, fountains and statues of Greek and Roman gods, and a view of the river that could be glimpsed through the trees. No other guest had come into this loveliest part of the garden. She was alone. For a time she sat on a marble bench but as twilight came on she walked down through the arbor, past the peach and walnut trees and then back again.

It must be the sadness of the day and the memories of her own mother that had caused this overpowering sense of losing everything that mattered. The air was still warm but she hugged herself as if chilled, sat down once more on the bench and stayed there until it was completely dark.

BEFORE BREAKFAST WAS over the next morning Becca suddenly announced that she was going down to the stables and asked Laura to come with her. Becca was in a dark mood, giving brief, barely courteous answers when anyone spoke to her, ignoring whenever possible the guests at the table. The gentlemen scarcely noticed her. The ladies, who did notice, remarked to each other that Mary Ann's daughter was taking it hard and must be supported in her grief. As Becca was rising from the table one woman caught her hand and held it.

"She was virtuous and pure-minded, an example to us

all. Take comfort, dear, knowing she has traveled on to a better world."

Becca detached her hand. "It wouldn't have to be much to be better than this one, would it, Mrs. Griffin?" She left the lady sitting with her mouth open.

Outside she looked at Laura. "Rude, wasn't I? Did I embarrass you?"

"Not me—but I don't mind hearing the truth."

"Do you know how much I care what they think?"

"Very little, I'd say. Is this the way to the stables?"

Becca shrugged. "I only said that. I had to get out of the house." Marriage and motherhood had changed her. She had come into the Seymour family so uncertain and diffident that she seemed like a shy young girl. Now she had a husband who loved her and a beautiful new son and looked at the world with cool, confident eyes. On this morning her face was tense and she appeared more angry than grief-stricken. Or perhaps, Laura thought with a sideways glance, the anger was only another form of grief.

Becca saw the measuring look and her mouth curled into a tight little smile. "What do you think of Malvern?"

"It's the biggest house I've ever seen—enormous for a family of three."

"It's big, all right, but not too big for our family. I'll give you the grand tour."

They came into a different world behind the house. Here were the cookhouse, the smokehouse, the laundry. Beyond were slave quarters extending down toward a ravine. "There are other quarters, of course. We have hundreds of slaves here at Malvern, not counting the ones on our other plantations. Their cabins are scattered all through the fields."

Hundreds, Laura thought, amazed. Pine Hill had ninety, an enormous number. Only the richest planters had more than one or two hundred.

"I don't know why they don't run off," Becca went on as if she were speaking of an ordinary occurrence. "Too far from the border, I suppose. Or rise up. There are so many of them and so few of us."

Slave uprisings were a subject of great delicacy, seldom spoken of by Southern women or mentioned in their presence. After considering several possible replies, Laura said, "Perhaps because your father is a kindly owner?"

Two small slave children raced across the yard followed by an older boy who was gaining on them. He whipped in front of Becca and she caught him by the arm. "Leave those babies be, Rudolph! You march yourself back to the house and tell Cookie I said to give you some floors to clean."

Rudolph, a well-built boy of at least fifteen and a foot taller than Becca, mumbled, "Yas'm," and turned slowly back to the house.

"Get a move on now," Becca called after him and he speeded up a trifle. "He could pick me up and toss me across the yard," she murmured softly. And then, "He's my brother, you know. Or haven't you heard of such things?" She looked into Laura's unbelieving face with bright, amused eyes and watched her struggle for an answer.

"I've heard rumors, of course, but . . ."

"But not anyone you know. Well, now you know someone."

"How can you be so sure? How can you say such a thing about your own father?"

"Because it's true. I was unfortunate enough to walk in on Father and Esther when I was nine years old. I have at least twenty-five brothers and sisters right here at Malvern—some of them were my playmates when I was growing up. I know who they are and who their mothers are. So did my mother but you'd never have guessed it to hear her talk. Did you notice Knox, the man who served dinner the night we came? His eyes are just like Father's. Mother could point out the light-skinned children of every master in this district but she never seemed to see Knox. Like all the ladies Mother never saw a thing . . . she just took opium."

Laura said nothing. There was nothing to say. She had always known that light-skinned servants like Jewel must have white ancestry. Every Southerner knew that. She had assumed without thinking deeply that it must have all taken place in times long past and that the white men involved must have been slave traders, dealers, or perhaps even over-seers of the lower type. Looking around the dusty yard at the babies playing in the dirt, at the women hanging clothes outside the laundry, she thought, They are owned body and soul, there is no excuse, and a sense of shame rolled over her and made her feel sick.

In a calm, considering way Becca said, "It's a filthy system we live in, vile for women, black and white." She glanced back at the house. "Those ladies up there are just like Mother—required to be so mealymouthed and proper and utterly chaste themselves, waited on by their husband's mistresses, everywhere they look seeing the servants' children looking so much like their own. Never allowed to *do* anything except sew or paint and run the house. And just as much owned by their husbands as the slave women are! No wonder they have headaches and drink and take opium. Father made my life a hell for not accepting any of the proposals he arranged, but I had decided not to marry. I wouldn't have but for Doug. He's not like most men—I know his heart. He doesn't expect me to be a fool and he could never act like Father. I tell you, Laura, I can't stand Yankees but that man Lincoln did one good thing. Even if we win this war we won't be able to hang on to our slaves. He's accomplished that for us and a good job too!"

THAT NIGHT SLEEP came hard for Laura. In this strange room miles from home, in this sprawling house surrounded by all manner of filth and ugliness, she saw again the long, intense look Chase had given her before he walked out of her bedroom—their bedroom—and a terrible sense of loss and longing swamped her. How could she have sent him away, how could she have been such a fool? It was rare, what they had together, and she had to get it back or die.

She would go home tomorrow—alone if Becca wasn't ready to come. It had taken three days to get here but she could get back in less than that if she tried. She'd been gone only a week and he had said something about not leaving for a month—she couldn't remember his exact words but surely he would still be there. *Perhaps after the war* was not good enough. She had to find him and they would go north together. If it meant never seeing her family again she could bear it. Not seeing him again was what she could not bear. And if he went to war and did not come back—she shrank from it but forced herself to think the thought—*if he died*, she would face it in such a way that in the end he would not be ashamed of her.

CHAPTER 23

EVERYONE CAME TO the Arlington Hotel. Many in the top echelon of Confederate politics had moved there from the Spotswood and it was a good place to be if you wished to see and be seen, something which ordinarily Laura wouldn't have wanted at all. Today she didn't care. She rushed through the lobby, ignoring the greetings and waves of people she knew well. Ellen Mercer got no further than "Good afternoon, dear, how pleasant to—" and Laura was past her without even a glance.

The head desk clerk, beseiged by out-of-towners begging for a room, was turning away anyone without a reservation except for the most important or influential. Experience told him that the lady who stood before him asking for Colonel Girard might be both and he gave her his full attention.

"Colonel Girard is not here, ma'am."

"Then I'll leave a message."

"I regret, ma'am, but he has left the city." He did regret it too. She was so lovely and had suddenly gone so pale.

"When did he leave?"

"Ah, let me see. It was Monday, quite early Monday morning." In an effort to take that look off her face the clerk added information he was not supposed to hand out. "But he held his room as he always does—paid three months in advance so he'll certainly be back."

She nodded and walked away. He watched her all the way to the door and then turned to the next would-be patron of the Arlington Hotel and snarled, "There is nothing available," before he heard what the man had to say.

Just outside the door she stopped, not noticing the

people pushing past her on the crowded street. It was too late, it had been too late even before she fully realized what she'd done. She had lost him and it need not have been— she had done it to herself.

Slowly she became aware of noise and bustle around her—a detachment of soldiers marching down the middle of the road without regard for the carts, drays, and heavy wagons rumbling past or the furious shouts of the drivers, a circle of men on their knees beside the building rolling dice, a black child darting through the traffic carrying a precious load of firewood, people everywhere hurrying toward important business—and all of it meaningless because he was not here. Becca, the baby, the maid, the coachman were waiting in the carriage, and what explanation could she give for insisting on so fast a trip, for coming directly to this hotel without even stopping at home, for the tears that were so hard to hold back?

She climbed into the carriage without a word and Becca, who had been watching since she came out of the hotel, said to the coachman, "Let's go home, Enoch."

LAURA HAD BEEN BACK in town less than a week when a scandal broke that for a few days pushed even the war out of the minds of many people. Women who didn't like Valerie Hood found it tragic but interesting. Jason Hood had added another name to the list of those he had killed for honor's sake—an engineer who worked at the Tredegar Iron Works, Hugh Kellogg.

Susan Armistead made an unannounced morning call to tell Laura the details. "Terribly sad—he left a wife and two or three children, I believe—but nobody's ever heard of him, no one can figure out how he even met her. Anyway, all the gentlemen say that the duel was completely fair, so I'm sure it was. Jason doesn't seem to be a bit mad at her, just wants it known that anyone who accosts his wife will answer to him. Although"—Susan lowered her voice— "some people say there was a good deal more there than meets the eye and he doesn't care to see it. They say Mr. Kellogg didn't just grab her . . . she already knew him pretty well."

"Who says it?"

"Oh . . . people."

"Don't tell that to anyone else, Suzie. She'd be in worse trouble if it got back to him, especially if he thought people were laughing."

"I wouldn't mention it to a soul! I only told you because after all you are her best friend."

Laura watched her drive off, a pretty young woman, not so much malicious as stupid. Without doubt she was hurrying on to the next acquaintance to repeat everything and the story would grow worse with each retelling.

That afternoon another unexpected caller appeared on her doorstep. She had finally faced up to unpacking and was in her bedroom giving Elvina items to press when the door chimes rang. On the front drive stood the Hoods' magnificent carriage and the matched chestnuts that were Jason's pride.

"It's Miss Valerie, Elvina. Put her in the parlor and tell her . . . tell her I'll be right down. Do we have anything sweet in the house—I don't suppose we do. Well, rustle up whatever you can."

Standing in the upper hall she heard the front door open, then Elvina's murmured greeting. At the sound of Valerie's familiar drawl she thought, I won't go down there—I can't listen to her, I can't sympathize, I can't even be civil.

She went down the stairs.

Valerie was at the front window peeking past the heavy draperies. She whispered, "Can you imagine! He's even poking behind the bushes and the other one's gone round to the back." She looked at Laura in sudden alarm. "There's no one back there, I hope. No men, that is?"

"Of course not." Laura peered past her. "That's not Micah."

"Do tell," Valerie said bitterly and sank down on the brocade settee, meant for two, that was barely wide enough to accommodate her huge skirt. "I suppose you've heard."

"Suzie told me. She says there are some nasty rumors but Jason doesn't believe them."

"Maybe he doesn't, maybe he does. He's taken Micah away from me—doesn't think Micah can protect me, he says—and set those two watchdogs on my trail. I never get

away from them." Valerie passed her hand over her forehead. "I had it all so well worked out. We'd meet at the
shop of a dressmaker I've been patronizing . . ."

"Not Addie?"

"No chance of that—Addie wouldn't risk her business.
Rosemary Malone. She's finally gone out on her own and
when I paid the earth for a couple of dresses she let us use
her back room on the occasional afternoon."

"That was dangerous."

Valerie shrugged. "It would have been fine but that
poor crazy man came to the house one day. Jason was out
of town—anyway I thought he was—we were down at the
far end of the garden and something told me . . . honestly,
I'm getting so I can sense when Jason's around. I screamed
and slapped Hugh as hard as I could just as he came
through the trees. Well, I ran to him and he could have
killed Hugh on the spot but he didn't. He asked his name,
said his seconds would call, and took me back to the house.
They fought day before yesterday though it wasn't much of
a fight, I guess. He shot Hugh in the lung, came home and
ate a big breakfast. Never spoke a cross word to me but
since then I haven't been alone for a minute. Those two
oafs follow me everywhere."

She began nervously folding her skirt in tiny pleats,
unaware that she was doing it. "Hugh was from New York.
He didn't know much about guns, he'd never held a
dueling pistol in his hand before. He died last night—two
days lingering. They say lung wounds are very painful
because after all you have to breathe. And he had a family—
oh, Laura, I never meant for anyone to get hurt!" She
searched helplessly for a handkerchief as tears streamed
down her face. Laura handed over her own without a word.

Valerie mopped her face, blew her nose, and took a
deep, shaky breath. "I must seem awful to you, a truly
fallen woman, but I've only done this with two men—three
if you count Kirby but that was just one time. I thought I
wouldn't mind being married to a man I didn't love as long
as he was rich but I do mind. I keep looking for something
more, something else." Great tears slid down her cheeks,
splashed on her dress and left round wet spots on the silk.

Two days with a lung wound, Laura thought. Two days. It could have been Chase, it could have been Kirby.

Elvina came in, put the tea tray on the small table, and slipped out with the same blank expression she had seen and admired on Jewel's face. It reassured the white folks that you were really deaf as a post and allowed you to think your own thoughts undisturbed.

When she was gone Laura said, "Elvina's got another concoction she calls tea. Try a cup, Val. She claims it soothes the nerves."

Valerie wiped her wet face. "My nerves could do with some soothing. Oh, I brought you something." She dug into her carryall. "French chocolates from Hugh. I can't keep them but with sugar so hard to get it isn't right to throw them away." She held out an enormous box of candy wrapped in a lush satin ribbon, a box that must have cost poor dazzled Hugh Kellogg a fortune.

Laura almost said, If Elvina doesn't want it I'll burn it. What a pleasure it would be to rake her nails across that perfect face until the blood ran. So many times she'd told herself that of course there had been others before her, that she didn't mind about Valerie—but it was one thing to acknowledge other women in a theoretical way and another to have one of them sitting in her parlor asking her for comfort.

How could he even for a moment have been attracted to this foolish, tawdry woman with the beautiful body and blond curls and teary-eyed smile, this woman who could so easily have gotten him killed? How could he have believed that she, Laura, meant it when she refused to go with him? Why hadn't he insisted, kissed her into submission, dragged her off by the hair? Why had he left her behind when she loved him better than her own life?

She took the candy and set it on the table. In a voice so steely that Valerie looked up, startled, she said, "There's one thing I require of you and I'm going to say it only once. No matter how you feel, no matter what you think you need, if Kirby ever comes home on leave again don't speak to him, don't so much as glance his way—or I'll wait until he's gone and then tell Jason. I swear I will!"

Early the next morning she went back to work, the only

solace she had for the bitter regret that sometimes overwhelmed her. Loss was all around, the daily experience of most people, and in an odd way it helped. She along with everyone else was part of a community of suffering.

Both armies were resting and regrouping after Gettysburg, there was no action on the battlefields near the Potomac and little news coming in over the wires from the armies in Tennessee, but Laura never missed a day of work and passed on to Fiona any information that might be of the slightest use. But there were problems. Fiona, still quivering, described the quarrel she'd had with David Rees, a quarrel she was determined would not interfere with the flow of intelligence.

"He was *rude* to Maria, and all because of her black skin! I won't subject her to that again or Bessie either—she's too old for this business. So I will go and if I can't it will have to be you, Laura."

So it was often Laura who made the long ride out to the farm. The second time she came she was invited into David's house to share a refreshing drink of well water. David had battled down the lure of whiskey. He now drank liquor only to seal bargains and acknowledge triumphs and made sure the triumphs didn't come along too often. But he hadn't renounced the pleasures of outrage, hostility, and hate. Laura listened to long harangues about the war, the Negroes, the slaveholders who were driving out the hardworking small farmer, and the son who was fighting for the Confederacy. She didn't mind the time spent. David interested her, he gave her insight into a kind of thinking foreign to her own and helped her understand why some people did the kind of things they did. And every trip gave her a sense of *doing* something.

The city was filled to bursting with the sick and wounded and maimed. Federal prisoners captured at Gettysburg crammed the cold, filthy prisons, but in spite of pervasive misery, skyrocketing prices, and the severe shortages of almost everything, especially food, people found ways to enjoy themselves. Millie was one of many hostesses who continued to entertain even though the punch was plain water and no food was served.

Danceables were Millie's favorite entertainment. They

cheered her up, she told friends, and Joseph, a man of many talents, had turned out to be a fine musician. Without ever taking a lesson, he understood the mysteries of the piano keyboard in a way Millie had not mastered after years of instruction. He could pound out music that made the foot tap and the heart merry. Who needed an orchestra when they had Joseph?

He was already performing when Laura arrived at Millie's from an afternoon spent at the Rees farm. She changed her dress and was hurrying downstairs when a late-comer walked in the front door. He looked up and his face was transformed.

"Matt!" She ran down the stairs and embraced him. "Oh, this is grand. When did you get in?"

"This evening. Headed straight here." He was laughing, too, with the pleasure of seeing her, but as they went into the ballroom she saw that he limped a little.

In this room where the guests were gathered Millie had set out more candles than she really could afford to make the evening festive, and the brighter light revealed too much. He looked years older than when they last crossed paths in the woods just before Chancellorsville, somehow smaller and less imposing. Each day of war had ground away a little more of him. He was gaunt with the thinness that had become the hallmark of the ill-fed Confederate soldier, his hair was completely gray, his face haggard. But his mustache was still gold and luxuriant and his smile brilliant when he looked at her.

She said, "I don't want to dance. Come, let's sit over here where we can really talk."

They sat down on a bench in the same alcove off the ballroom where she had once had a chat with another soldier. That long-ago evening came back with stunning force—the gaiety, the music, the richness and beauty of the night Paige married Alex, the night she talked to Chase Girard and her life changed.

Unexpected tears stung her eyes. She blinked and asked, "How are you really, Matt?"

"Oh, I'm well, very well."

His large hands were resting on his knees. She laid her hand over his. "Tell me about it."

He stared at the floor. As though speaking only to himself, he said, "We thought we might win it all that day."

Only a few feet away two girls were dancing with each other—there were never enough men to go around. One stepped on the other's skirt and they parted in a fit of giggles, glancing at the alcove. The couple sitting there didn't seem to see or hear them.

"He was wrong," Matt said as if he could scarcely believe it—"he" was Lee. "He thought if we invaded, beat them on their own ground, the North would crack and England would recognize us." He laughed shortly, bitterly, and then brightened. "We held good position on South Mountain but you know what did us in? Boots! Yes, boots." This time he laughed with genuine amusement. "We heard there were boots over in Gettysburg so Hill's corps went to look for them. What we found were Yankees. We didn't want to fight there and neither did they, but once we got started—we were itching for battle, Laura. Both sides. I got this thing"—he gestured toward his wounded leg—"the third day. Strange, that day. I never before had such a powerful sense of fighting old comrades, but I looked up at that hill we were trying to take. I knew Joe Waring was up there and Johnny Gordon and other men who were my classmates, men I served with. We roared up under their artillery fire and they whipped us—just about wiped out Pickett's men."

The great charge that had caused Grace Weston's grief and Lowell Weston's bitterness, the charge that had destroyed their sons. So many men had died, brave men on both sides.

"Can you imagine how hard it is, Laura—fighting against people you know and love?"

Her eyes were so sweet and steady. "Yes," she said, "it must be very sad," and he knew she did understand.

They talked for almost an hour. War had changed him—he was less abrasive, less certain that he had the answer to everything. A good, decent man. She couldn't love him but she did like him. At the end of the evening she let him take her home and agreed to see him as often as possible while he was in town. She went upstairs with a lighter heart. Millie was right. Parties did lift the spirits.

Much later, in her bed, she came suddenly awake, reached out drowsily in the old way and found only an empty place beside her. It was the blackest part of the night when memories were so vivid and the future seemed most bleak. She lay with eyes wide, listening for the sound of the kitchen door and then his footsteps on the stairs. In her mind she could see him coming in with bags of food and ridiculous stories that made her laugh, smell the outdoor fragrance of his skin, feel his arms around her and the firm, sweet touch of his lips. This time she didn't cry as she had on other nights but thought, I cannot bear it, and lay for a long time staring into the dark.

M RS. JAMES DAVENPORT was another hostess still determined to maintain as best she could the old Richmond ways. Her parties, concerts, and amateur theatricals were less lavish than in the golden past but musicales were always popular and there were still good musicians in town. She sent her maid with messages to her friends. Paper was now so scarce that written invitations were out of the question.

Matt had somehow acquired gold braid and a length of gray wool and tonight stood taller in a magnificent new uniform. His silvery hair fell just below his collar and in three weeks' time he had grown a short, trim beard in addition to the mustache. He looked, Laura told him, the way a Confederate general ought to but seldom did these days.

He inspected her red velvet dress, worn many times but still lush, still vivid. "And you, ma'am, look like a Southern lady should but *never* does." He was rewarded with her musical laugh. She was happy tonight and he took some of the credit for himself. She had been so wan when he first saw her that night at Millie Seymour's, full of determined gaiety and behind it a sadness that worried him. War was wearing them all down. He had devoted himself to cheering her up and it had done the impossible—cheered him up too.

He handed her coat to a servant, wishing he could touch her smooth white shoulders. By God, he did appreciate these plunging necklines. They entered the long room where Mrs. Davenport's little concerts were always performed.

It was the largest in the house, built to accommodate forty guests. Tonight they were in extraordinary luck. The flutist was a Frenchman from the Paris Opera, one of many Europeans attracted to the Confederate cause and now residing in the city; the cellist was an accomplished local musician; the two violinists had performed with great orchestras in New York and Philadelphia before the war.

They tuned their instruments as gentlemen assisted ladies to dainty chairs and the ladies compressed their skirts to make room for others. The rustling and coughing quieted and when the room was silent the concert began. Everyone present was a music lover—Mrs. Davenport did not invite the artistically illiterate to her salons—and tonight the musicians were suberb. Mozart's complex melodies soared, came together, interwove, parted, returned again, the instruments spoke to each other and for a little while it was possible to pretend that the world outside these walls was civilized too.

At the end the audience applauded furiously. The musicians, happy to be appreciated, arranged their music for the next offering.

Laura turned to Matt with the beginning of a smile. Her face went blank, a white line appeared around her mouth, and reaching out he whispered, "My dear, are you ill?"

She rested her hand for a moment on his outstretched arm and whispered back, "Just a touch of vertigo—I should have eaten before we came."

"Let me make our excuses and I'll take you home."

Her eyes came back to him. "I wouldn't think of it. Truly, I'm fine."

Color had returned to her face. She was watching the musicians with great concentration. Glancing over his shoulder in the direction she had been staring, Matt saw only two latecomers, Secretary Benjamin and Chase Girard, standing in the archway. While he watched, Lowell Weston, recently commissioned a colonel in the army, came up and shook hands with them. As she said, it was probably just a momentary faintness—ladies were subject to such weaknesses. He, too, turned his attention to the music.

There was a buffet afterward, not the lavish feast of times past but more food than guests usually saw at parties these days, including, as an astonishing treat that would be talked about for days, small slices of cherry pie.

Matt patted Laura's hand. "Stay right here and I'll bring your supper."

At the buffet table he looked back and saw that instead of waiting for him she was making her way through the press of people to the other side of the room. He picked up a plate for each of them and followed.

P RIDE SWEPT OVER HER as she walked toward him. Of all the women in the world he wanted her, he had come back for her. How astonished and vengeful this crowd of good Confederates would be if she turned and announced, You are fools, all of you, worshiping a country and a cause. This man is my cause, the only country I have.

He looked so good standing there beside suave, roly-poly Judah and that cold fish Lowell Weston, with the slight smile and the wonderful dark eyes that told her nothing. She wanted to throw her arms around him, feel him against her again, tell him she was ready to go any-where with him.

Judah Benjamin's perpetual smile widened. He leaned forward to kiss her cheek, an effusive gesture for him. No one was certain if he liked women nearly as much as he liked food—he didn't seem to mind at all that his glam-orous, extravagant Creole wife lived permanently in Paris—but he was fond of Laura and in an especially cheerful mood tonight.

She lifted her face for his kiss and then gave her hand to Lowell Weston as her eyes flickered toward Chase. Did it mean anything that these two clever, dangerous men were with him? Was it safe for him to come back to this city? He seemed unworried, not like a man about to be dragged off to hang, but that meant nothing. She probably looked as always too, and her insides had turned to water.

She said, "What a surprise to see you. I thought your trip would take longer."

"I had to bring Alex his boots."

What did that mean?

"Yes, he's brought boots," Judah said, "fine leather boots with tough soles, and more on the way." He was a man who could truly be said to beam when he was pleased. "I assure you, dear lady, those boots will save some of our soldiers when the snow falls and they'll have guns and powder to fight with because of this man."

An odd expression passed over Lowell Weston's heavy features. The deaths of his sons had changed him. While his wife, Grace, sat and wept in a darkened room he had pressured an army commission out of Jefferson Davis and pulled every string he could to influence government policy. He and Jason Hood together had prompted the provost marshal to arrest several possible spies although there was no real evidence against the men. They were Yankees, and all were untrustworthy. Northerners had killed his boys and he intended to kill any one of them he could lay hands on. It had been his cold logic that first aroused suspicions of the Yankee Chase Girard, and his insistent demands that had finally caused Secretary Benjamin to send his protégé into Maryland. "Let him fish or cut bait," Lowell had said. Benjamin's conviction that the arrival of a few boots and blankets proved this outsider's loyalty infuriated him. Where were the goddamned guns and powder? he wanted to shout.

But he pulled his face into a pleasant expression. "Yes, it will be a fine day when we deliver those rifles—breechloaders, I'm told—and fuses and mortars. This time, we'll bring it off."

His smile was only a showing of teeth. Laura said, "That's wonderful. I hope you'll find time to call, Chase, and tell me about it."

I'd like nothing better but we're leaving tomorrow."

"Oh. So soon." She looked at the supper plate just deposited in her hand and said, "Thank you, Matt . . ." There was no chance for them to talk, not with Matt and Judah there and Lowell Weston ever present, no chance to tell him that she would go anywhere with him now . . . but didn't he know it anyway, didn't the truth always shine through to someone who loved you?

*   *   *

THERE CAME A CHANCE to speak though, just a
moment when everyone was distracted. Captain
Dunbar, the Bostonian who had given a leg for the South
at Gettysburg, stumbled over the cellist's instrument case
and fell with a crash, his crutches and the plate of food he
had been trying to balance flying into the front row of
chairs. Two men lifted him instantly, retrieved the crutches
and helped him to a chair. Someone brought a cup of
punch but he waved it away, his face flaming with rage at
his own infirmity. Without a word he struggled up and
hobbled out.

The room was silent, a sense of pity and grief so strong it
was almost visible, and then everybody began to talk at
once. Under the sudden buzz Chase murmured a few quick
words. Before she could answer Matt was back with plates
of pie, his eyes on the empty doorway.

"Poor bastard," he said, and then cheerfully, "but
luckier than some—most of the amputees in my brigade
died of gangrene. Here's your pie, Laura."

It was easy to get Matt to take her home early and then
leave him at the door. All she had to do was plead fatigue—
he liked to think of her as a fragile creature, needing his
tender care. A lamp still burned in the entry hall but the
house was silent. Elvina had gone to bed as instructed, a
more obedient girl then Jewel who disobeyed whenever it
suited her.

She waited until buggy wheels crunched down the
gravel drive and then flew up the stairs. He was there in her
room. She flung herself into his arms and he laughed and
swung her off her feet.

She ran her hands over his face. "Let me see you, let me
just look at you! When you walked in tonight I almost
fainted and gave us both away. Oh, darling, after you left I
felt so bad. I came straight back to tell you I was wrong but
you were already gone . . . I can be ready in ten minutes—
five! What do I need? Not a thing except you."

He lowered her to the floor. "Laura, I can't take you
with me now. It isn't possible."

Her exhilaration drained away. "You haven't forgiven
me . . . you think I'm a coward. And now when I—oh, why
did you come back?"

"You're not a coward, I didn't mean that. The last time I saw you I was so damn mad . . . I wanted you to risk everything for me or at least be willing to and when you wouldn't I said some very hard words. I was on the other side of the Potomac when I remembered I hadn't kissed you goodbye so I had to come back."

"That's why you brought the boots?"

"And a few blankets. I had to have some excuse."

"You shouldn't have done it."

"No, I shouldn't have but I do fool things like that sometimes. I figured it wouldn't help the cause all that much, but it's true, some Rebels are going to have a warmer winter. Maybe someone who doesn't die of pneumonia this December will kill a Federal next spring—maybe me." His eyes gleamed as if the unknown, the danger, even the possibility of death brought with it a kind of pleasurable excitement. "Weston intends to go back to Maryland with me tomorrow and he's bringing the ugliest gang of thugs I ever saw to make sure I deliver what I promised." He smiled. "Southern cavaliers make New York cutthroats look kindly by comparison. So I don't plan to keep them company. I'm going to leave before morning and meet some friends up near Woodford. They can get me across the river."

Near Woodford, north of Fredericksburg. A long, dangerous journey through a maze of woods, open fields, creeks and streams, home territory for Rebel cavalry and troops, where every civilian was a loyal Confederate and strangers were always suspect. He had left her in anger and come back to make it up, a foolish, foolish risk taken because he loved her. He needn't have, he needn't have, she thought, triumphant and terrified.

Her voice dropped to a panicked whisper. "You've got to get out of here!" Lowell Weston, the provost guard, *somebody* who meant him harm might even now be on the way, coming up the drive, on the other side of the wall listening to everything he said.

"I'll leave before dawn."

"I don't want you to stay. They could have followed you, they could be outside right now. Please—it isn't worth it."

"Laura darling, they are not outside. I came here at great expense and difficulty to tell you goodbye like a gentleman and that is what I intend to do."

And then he was kissing her, sending waves of feeling through her. Feeling that could trap him and cause his death. She knew his body so well and every inch was precious, his arms so strong, his muscles so hard it seemed he must be immortal, but all this strength could be wiped out in an instant.

Her arms went around his neck in a desperate grip. "Don't leave me . . ." and then she tried to take it back, "I didn't mean it. Go right now, before they find you . . . don't do that, Chase."

He undid the last of the hooks on the crimson dress, untied the tapes, and the entire construction of hoops, petticoats, and velvet slid to the floor. "My God, the things women wear. Hold still." The tight iron cage of her stays came off and she took a full, deep breath. "I can always feel the indentations"—he ran his hands around her waist— "and someday when I have more time I'm going to give you a lecture about it but for now . . ."

"I think," she said tenderly, "that you are completely crazy."

He took her long dark hair out of its net and arranged it carefully on her shoulders. "You are the prettiest thing I ever saw. And you taste like cherry pie."

THE CLOCK IN THE hall gave a single soft chime, the mark of the quarter hour. It was an exquisite clock bequeathed by her grandmother and had been her treasure. She considered running downstairs and smothering the sound that marked the passing of the night or even tearing out the delicate works. But earth and stars would continue to move in their appointed way and morning would come no matter what she did.

He had to wake no later than four o'clock—another forty-five minutes. She sat wrapped in a blanket in an uncomfortable chair near the bed. There was no danger of falling asleep; never had she felt more alert. The clock chimed again and he opened his eyes and reached out. She got into bed beside him, rested her head against his chest, and they lay holding each other, saying nothing.

Another soft chime. She said, "I love you absolutely. Did I tell you that?"

"Yes, you did."

"It seems as if everyone else has faded away and only you are left."

He kissed her bare shoulder and the hollow of her throat. "I know."

"If you should decide not to come back when this is over it's all right. I didn't expect it to last forever. I want you to be free."

"Thank you very much. You know I'll come back if I'm alive."

The room was still dark and she ran her hand over his face, trying to remember it in her fingers. It was so close to morning. She reached for her wrapper and pulled it on.

"I'll fix something to eat."

When he left it was perilously close to daybreak. She walked with him into the backyard and beyond the stable to the beginning of the woods. He mounted the horse, a first-rate stallion he had borrowed from Lowell Weston, and chuckled.

"Lowell's going to be sore as hell at me for a lot of reasons." She smiled, too, and he took her hand and held it. "Goodbye, sweetheart."

He rode into the woods and was almost instantly out of her sight. She stood for a long time in the predawn light watching the space between the trees where she had last seen him, the wrapper pulled around her throat. When she grew so cold that she began to shiver, she turned and went back into the house.

CHAPTER 24

WHEN NEWS OF the bitter battle in the woods and ravines of Tennessee flew in over the wires, hearts lifted for it was a Southern victory—or so it seemed at first. The Yankees had been beaten at

Chickamauga Creek and were now holed up in Chatta-nooga, under siege themselves for a change. But the victory was equivocal. People with relatives or friends serving with Longstreet waited anxiously for the casualty lists. The word was that battle losses were especially heavy in his divisions. They also knew that Chattanooga was the prize the Union army was after anyway and that more Federals were being rushed in to lift the siege.

That was the problem. No matter how many Yankees their men killed in one struggle, there always seemed to be just as many facing them in the next, as if those Union sol-diers were able to rise from the battlefields they had died on to fight again.

To make matters worse, the Yankee general who according to Northern newspapers had "stood like a rock" at Chickamauga and prevented the Union army from being destroyed, was none other than George Thomas, the Vir-ginian who had put the Union ahead of his own people and stayed in the U.S. Army instead of coming home.

Fear and frustration grew even more intense in Rich-mond as word spread that their own Yankee, the likable man they had taken to their hearts more than two years ago, the man who had many times been a guest at Varina Davis's dinner table and was welcome everywhere, was almost certainly a spy. It was stunning, incomprehensible, outrageous—another one of Benjamin's mistakes, his ene-mies said, for he had sponsored the man.

"He *trusted* the son of a bitch!" Lowell Weston ground out when he had reached a point where he could speak at all. "He's gone, vanished, nobody's seen him, and how is that possible when the provost guard was supposed to watch him night and day? That's what I told Benjamin to do and I thought he'd done it. I tell you, sometimes I wonder about Judah—you can't trust those people, you know. They have no real loyalty to anyone but themselves. And he's got Blackie too, the—" He stopped but it was already too late, for President Davis was wearing that look of intense hauteur that meant he had shut his mind to any-thing you had to say. He never swore and did not like to hear it from others, especially in front of his wife. More-over, Judah Benjamin was his most valued advisor.

"In addition to his other sins Judah has taken your *horse*?" Varina inquired with the biting humor she was famous for. She turned to Judah Benjamin for comfort and support more often than any other friend and bitterly resented attacks on him or the Jewish religion.

"Of course not, ma'am—forgive me. I meant Girard."

"Word has gone out," said the President. "He has to cross our lines and without a pass he won't get far. We must take care not to quarrel among ourselves, Lowell—we need all our strength to fight the enemy. We'll find him and give him swift justice. We may even find your animal."

When Matt Riley returned to the army a week after Chase disappeared, he assured Laura that if he ever laid hands on him, the scoundrel would never get back to Richmond alive.

"But there could be so many explanations besides the one Lowell Weston is spreading. I still can't believe—"

Matt took her hand and held it. "Laura, you don't understand the way of the world and your woman's heart is too kind. I liked him, too, and came to trust him—I don't claim I always suspected the way some are doing—but by hindsight I can see, we all can. If he runs afoul of me he'll regret it."

"Would you deny him a trial?"

Matt's face went bleak. "You've seen something of war—the results of war—here in the hospitals, but you don't know what it does to men's souls. We've all done unspeakable things and we'll continue to, things I would never describe to you or any lady, things we never talk about even among ourselves. None of us are what we were before. We are killers, dear, all of us. I promise you, if he crosses my path I won't take him prisoner." He left her, behind her goodbye smile, more frightened than she had been since Chase went away.

But harder to endure than Matt Riley's quiet threat or Millie's hand-wringing and moans was Valerie Hood. She came as always with her vigilant bodyguards, sat in Laura's parlor and poured out her most intimate thoughts. Eyes wide, cheeks flushed, suffused with a peculiar energy, she recited every piece of gossip, rumor, and speculation she had heard and then said, "I am so excited I'm quivering.

Just think, Laura, I've made love with a *spy* and I didn't
know it. Imagine what it would have been like if I'd
known!"

After she left Laura walked to the mantel, picked up an
expensive figurine, and in the kitchen Elvina heard the
shatter of china. She ran to the parlor with a dustpan and
broom, and one look at her mistress told her the delicate
china lady hadn't been broken by accident. Miss Laura
often stalked around with that expression on her face after
Miss Valerie visited. Carefully, she picked up every shard
and brushed hearth and rug with vigor, her mind running
over all she had heard in the past few days and had seen in
this house since she moved into it. She thought of Frederick, whom she loved, and Mr. Rees, who said so little and
took so long to say it, and the others who came to the back
door at odd hours, and remembered her vow to herself
long ago—she would do anything for Miss Laura. One day
soon she might have to make good on her promise.

Valerie's visit taught Laura something about dealing
with fear—anger helped. If she could get mad, really mad
at Chase, think of things he had done that outraged her,
mull over Valerie's every word until she was ready to put
her fist through the wall, her fear for him lessened a little
and she did not hurt as much. The relief lasted for perhaps
half an hour.

That evening she sat in the kitchen watching Elvina cook
dinner, then got up to set a place for herself.

Elvina brought the hot platter to the table and made the
little speech she had planned. "I heard what they's saying,
Miss Laura, and I hope it ain' true, but whether or no, Mr.
Chase always acted kin'ly toward me. I do believe he's a
good man."

"Yes, he is." Laura looked at the food. "Here we are,
just the two of us, and I can't think of a single reason why
you should stand there while I eat. Get a plate, Elvina, and
sit down." She glanced at the maid's astonished face. "I
think Frederick is a fine man too."

They smiled at each other and Elvina, who took life as it
came, got a plate, sat down, and they ate supper together.

*　　　*　　　*

Days AND THEN WEEKS passed and neither the man nor the splendid black stallion that Lowell Weston had paid fifteen hundred dollars for was seen. After three weeks Laura began to sleep through the nights again. Anything could have happened to him, she knew it in the deepest part of her mind. He could be lying dead in a ditch or a bramble in the woods, shot by a sharpshooter or some nervous picket and never recognized, the fact never reported to anyone; that expensive stallion could have lost its footing on some muddy streambank and hurled him to his death—the ugly possibilities were endless and she might live the rest of her years never knowing. But there was a chance that he was out, safe for the present, and that was what she chose to believe. If he died it would be in battle as he wished it and not here in Richmond at the end of a rope.

During this time it took all her discipline and experience to deceive her friends, for they talked of little else and expected her to join in. No one blamed the Seymours although Alex had brought him to town and vouched for him and Edward had introduced him to Benjamin and other high government officials. Probably, Laura thought, because they had all been taken in and could not blame others without blaming themselves. She got an even deeper insight into the question of blame and responsibility one evening at Millie's dinner table where the conversation still was bitter and still concerned betrayal. A month had passed and Millie's shock and disappointment in Chase had not lessened. She turned to Secretary Benjamin. "I declare, Judah, the whole affair gives me a headache. How could he have fooled me so? With all the judgments you have to make every day, how do you bear it when you are mistaken?"

"Ma'am, I am a fatalist. I make a decision and then cease worrying. It is wrong and useless to disturb oneself and thus weaken one's energy to bear what is foreordained. Of course our enemies will send spies into our midst as we send our spies to them. Some of those spies will be found out, some we will fail to detect because we are human and it is our nature to make mistakes. So, you see, it was foreordained."

Laura, who had recently begun drinking a glass of wine

at bedtime to calm her nerves, had had three glasses of sherry before dinner and was in remarkably good spirits. She lifted the glass she was working on. "Judah, you're probably the smartest man in the whole Confederacy and I salute you. If we catch anybody worrying about what they've done, we'll take 'em out and hang 'em like the traitors they are!"

The other guests smiled uncertainly, someone mentioned a new medical theory that claimed worry caused gout and thickening of the blood, and Laura decided that her drinking career had just ended. Alcohol was a bad idea if you had secrets to keep.

After dinner several ladies read poems including a daring one by Lord Byron, and then Millie said, "Judah, do one of your recitations for us. Perhaps *Henry the Fifth*?"

Everyone agreed it was a marvelous idea. Judah, who loved to do dramatic presentations and was very good at it, rose, bowed, and in his appealing, resonant voice began:

The hum of either army stilly sounds,
That the fix'd sentinels almost receive
The secret whispers of each other's watch:
Fire answers fire, and through their paly flames
Each battle sees the other's umber'd face.

November brought days of hard, cold rain and with it illness. Medical science could do little for so many of the plagues that beset humans, particularly those scourges, scarlet fever and typhoid fever. They attacked and killed adults regularly and were even more dangerous for children. Four children in families close to the Seymours came down with fever and three of them died. Ellen Mercer's twenty-one-year-old nephew Bobby, home on leave after surviving Gettysburg unharmed, was diagnosed with typhoid on one day and was dead the next. Measles was a constant danger and severe cases of *la grippe* assaulted many households.

But November brought one gift to Millie that the illness and death around her could not spoil. Almost a year and a half after the spring day he had ridden away to defend his city, Edward was home on leave. Everyone wore smiles and Laura, who had helped nurse Paige through a vicious attack of *la grippe* and now had symptoms herself, decided to stay on a little longer.

Because Edward would be gone again long before Christmas, Millie gathered socks, gloves, a knit blanket she had labored over—any item she could think of that would keep him safe and warm—and presented them on the day before he was to leave. Everyone else did the same but Millie's gifts seemed to please him most. He kissed her tenderly in front of family and servants and she glowed like a bride.

Paige, in her sixth month of pregnancy, was now feeling well but had been ordered by Byron Rollins to stay in her room for another week. On most afternoons Laura kept her company. Two more servants were down, she told Paige, ". . . and I'm not so brisk myself."

Paige scrambled off her chaise longue. "This house is a hospital—here, lie down, lie down. I could perfectly well go downstairs if Dr. Rollins wasn't such an old maid."

"She's right," said Jewel as she brought in the snack Paige was required to eat every afternoon. "Lie down before you fall down, Miss Laura. And you march around the room a few times, Miss Paige. You need the exercise."

Paige paced to the window and Laura stretched out on the curving couch and sighed. "I'm fine, really, but Edward and I talked till two-thirty last night and Millie woke me up at six this morning to tell me she was going to give him his Christmas presents at breakfast. I could have killed her."

Paige smiled too, but said, "Mama's an example to me of what I'm not going to be. She just clings so and men don't like it."

"Sometimes it's hard not to when you know they're in danger." Laura lay back and closed her eyes, listening to Jewel take the covers off the dishes.

Jewel sniffed. "I don't know what that man Rollins is thinking of. You don't have to eat this, Miss Paige. You're fat enough."

"I surely am. You're thin as a rail, Laura. You eat it and we'll lie to Rollins and say I did—ah, cream sauce and pork."

Laura sat up. "Don't say that."

"Why not? You are thin, you're downright skinny . . . Laura?"

Paige started to move but Jewel was already there with the chamber pot and in one smooth motion had Laura's head supported and an arm around her. She looked over her shoulder and saw Becca's questioning face in the doorway. "Miss Becca, take that tray out in the hall and close the door. Don't let anyone else in here, not even Miss Millie."

Becca did as she was told and then stood against the closed, locked door while Laura retched.

Finally she lay back, exhausted, and gave a long shuddering sigh. "I thought it wasn't going to stop that time."

Paige sat down on the edge of the bed. "You've done this before? Reminds me of me this summer—" She stopped and sent a wild look at Becca, who lifted one shoulder and shrugged delicately.

Jewel smoothed back Laura's hair. "How often, honey? Just in the morning?"

"Oh, anytime."

"Have you seen a doctor?"

"Who could I go to in this town? Yes, I've seen a doctor. I went all the way to Petersburg. When he got through he said, 'Do you know what we call ladies like you—mothers.' A doctor joke," she added with some bitterness and then gave a little gulping laugh.

"I don't think that's a bit funny," Paige muttered.

Becca said, "Might as well laugh as cry," and sat down beside her on the bed. There was silence in the room while Jewel washed Laura's face and the enormity of it all sank in.

At last Paige, unable to bear inaction, jumped up and began to stride around the room. "I can't understand, I just can't. Why on earth would you *do* such a thing, Laura?"

"Of all the stupid things you've ever said that is the silliest," Becca observed with cold disgust, and before Paige could answer back Jewel stood up, hands on her hips, and glared at them.

"You hush right now, both of you, or you can leave."

Laura put her hand to her head as if to make certain it

was still there. "I was married for nine years, Paige, and there were no children. I thought I was a barren woman."

The reasonableness of this could not be questioned. They sat, each busy with her own thoughts. It was absolute disaster, the worst ill fortune that could befall a woman, and there was no way to hide it or make it simply go away.

Paige spoke into the silence. "One thing's certain— you'll have to marry him even if you don't really like him quite that much. There's one nice thing about being a general, he can give himself leave for long enough to get married." She looked at the others. "What's the matter with that?"

"If you mean Matt Riley," Laura said wearily, "you're wrong and I don't want to talk about it."

"Oh. Well, then write to . . . uh . . . whoever it is. Don't just sit there and look stubborn—you've got to do something."

"I can't. I have no idea where he is."

After an appalled moment Paige inquired almost timidly, "Do you think he . . . well, considered this possibility?"

"I don't suppose he ever thought of it."

"They never do, do they?" Becca remarked with such gloomy resignation that Laura looked up, their eyes met, and then all four women collapsed into laughter. They laughed until tears ran down their cheeks and they were gasping, quieted a little, looked at each other and burst into laughter again, peal after peal of helpless laughter at the differences between men's and women's lives and the impossible necessity of dealing with them.

For the rest of the afternoon they sat together discussing, as women before them had done for millennia, various ways of coping, and when they parted Becca walked with Laura to her room and at the door kissed her and whispered, "Consider what Jewel said. It may be the best solution."

Jewel's solution. It was the simplest way and, if Jewel was right, the safest. She said Mama Carrie had much experience and had done it for more white women than black, many of them married, all of them desperate. Becca had made an offer too. If Laura decided to have the child, she could go to Malvern and have it there. It was far from

Richmond and Hale McCauley might cooperate if it was put to him in the right way.

"I'll go with you," she had said, throwing away any chance of seeing Doug if he got leave. It was a selfless offer impossible to accept in wartime. And how could she endure months alone in that luxurious, depressing brothel? The Daisychain was honorable by comparison.

She had supper sent to her room, ate as much as she could, and then curled up on the window seat as she had always done when troubled, taking out memories and examining them with care. He was the best man God ever made and she loved him with all her heart. Would those women who had held her hand and comforted her today be shocked if they knew that she didn't regret a thing? Maybe not. Every one of them knew what it was to love greatly. Her mind ran on, back and forth, weighing the actions open to her on a finely balanced scale.

She could get out of this quietly, walk away from it and no one would ever know, yet it excited her—the prospect of a baby, a mysterious package, new and unknown, who might look like him and be like—who could tell? What an adventure, coming to know your own child. And yet, and yet . . . one way or another the South was going down and her own fortune would go with it. This child might have a mother without money, reputation, or status and possibly no father at all. Bringing it into this world would be a stupid, blind, supremely selfish thing to do to her own little baby that she loved as much as if she had already held it in her arms . . . oh, why go on like this?

She had always wanted children, had given up hope long ago and blamed herself for her failure. For years she had admired, exclaimed over, cuddled other women's babies while telling herself that her fulfilling life with Robert was enough. Now she had discovered that with another man she was not barren and she knew exactly what she was going to do. For once in her life she would risk everything, and if people talked, if they despised her and turned away from her forever, let them. If Chase did not come back she would go north after the war to a place where no one knew her. She was no helpless, frightened girl, she was a grown woman, smart and capable. She would find a way to take care of them both.

It was a little past midnight, but only a little. She was going to need Jewel's help to bring it off and she would go upstairs right now and talk it over with her.

SHORTLY AFTER SUPPER MILLIE had told everyone good night and gone to her room. Once there she searched through her dresser drawers for the loveliest nightgown she owned, the one she had been saving for this occasion, and laid it on the bed. Bella set up her bath—a project involving two strong male servants to carry up the quantity of hot water she required—and once the tub was filled and only Bella in the room she took her precious bottle of French perfume, Edward's Christmas gift three years ago, and poured a few drops in the water.

"Stir it and see what you think, Bella."

Bella stirred and they both sniffed. "Needs more than that, Miss Millie. I don' smell a thing."

"Yes, I think so too." A few more drops went in, Millie muttered, "The hell with it," and emptied the entire bottle. Bella stirred vigorously once again and said, "Ah," as a flowery fragrance filled the dressing room.

"Now get me out of this dress, Bella. I want to soak." A half hour later she was bathed, toweled until her rosy skin glowed, and into the pale blue silk nightgown with its plunging neckline and wide panels of cobweb lace. Bella brushed her brown waist-length hair until it gleamed, plucked out the few silver hairs, and looked her over. Millie looked back from the mirror, eyes dark blue and shining in the lamplight.

"Well? How do I look?"

"Like my pretty little girl that came here all those long years back."

"Really? Do you think so?" Millie gave Bella a loving smile and then said in a different, almost motherly way, "You've been very good to me, Bella, always. Go on now. I won't need you again tonight."

Bella ducked her head, murmured good night, and at the door looked back for just a moment before she went out and closed it quietly.

Alone, Millie piled her pillows high, climbed into bed and waited with confidence, knowing he would come to her. He had been home two weeks and had not been in this room once but it hadn't surprised her. From the indirect, roundabout comments of other women she had gathered that soldiers who had been in fierce combat were often strange and distant at first, disinterested in their wives and civilian life in general. But he was leaving tomorrow, going back to that other world which she could not enter, and that was why she knew he would come tonight. It might, after all, be for the last time.

EDWARD HAD WATCHED her kiss the girls good night, watched her leave the room and climb the stairs, knowing with fair certainty what she would do when she got to her bedroom. It would shame him to his bones if he had any sense of shame left. But he didn't. There was only the wild exhilaration of battle to sustain him now, only the driving desire that had finally forced him to come home.

At ten he went upstairs too. The door was not locked; he had known it wouldn't be. All the lamps were out but he could see her at the window, slim and tall and beautiful in the blue moonlight—the only woman he had ever truly desired in his life.

"May I come in?"

"Ah, Edward, what a question. It's your house."

"Don't say that. I'd give it all to you if I could." He closed the door and came across the room but stopped a little distance from her. "Would you rather I left?" She said nothing. The cotton flannel under his hands was thick—he would like to dress her in the flimsiest silk but she wouldn't wear it. He unbuttoned each button carefully, taking pleasure in doing it with slow deliberation. She could stop him at any time. He had never forced her. She could tell him to go and he would. He lifted the nightgown over her head and pressed his face against her breasts.

LAURA RAN UPSTAIRS to the third floor, energized now that the decision was made. Down the hall four small tables, each bearing a lamp, sat against the wall. A lamp flared a few feet from the door she wanted. As she came down the hall the door opened, the man pulled the woman to him for one last deep kiss, and she stopped, cold with dread.

They stared at each other, she and the brother she had revered all her life. He started to speak, shook his head and moved past her down the stairs.

B ELOW WAS THE RIVER, busy with traffic, and beyond it the lovely rolling valley, but on this dark winter day low-lying fog blotted out everything and turned the world into mystery.

How was it possible to know someone intimately from your birth, love him deeply and not know him at all? Were you merely stupid, had you deliberately chosen not to see, or were humans forever separate—their natures such that they could never understand the complexities of another mind and heart?

Edward was leaving today. She must tell him good-bye . . . take care, go with God . . . and how could she do it? Millie was ill this morning and in a way it was a blessing for how could she look into her eyes? The irony was so bitter and yet, considered in a certain way, funny. Edward, the man of rectitude, the man his brothers had patterned their lives on, the kindly master who disapproved of slavery even though he owned slaves—no wonder he had never freed Jewel!

She huddled deeper into her heavy coat against the chill of the damp air. Malvern to her had been a harem and Becca's father a keeper of concubines, but Edward was, perhaps, worse because he knew better. From somewhere out of past religious training the phrase "all manner of uncleanness" swam into her mind. The Bible contained such hard and savage truths.

Behind her the gate squeaked open on rusty hinges. The grounds were not so well kept since two of the gardeners had run away. She did not turn or look but she knew who it was coming down the path. Jewel sat down on the rock beside her.

After a while Laura said, "I've decided to go to Pine Hill before I begin to show and stay till after the baby's born. Becca says she'll come with me."

"The house is rundown, not like you remember it from the old days. You'd be more comfortable at Malvern."

"No I wouldn't. Anyway, it's too far. If Doug comes home Becca can be back here from Pine Hill in half a day." From the river came the hoot of a boat cautiously heading downstream, the sound so hollow in the heavy air that it seemed miles away. "Would you be willing to stay with me toward the end? Would you deliver my baby? It's a lot to ask, I know."

"Miss Becca was easy but you never can tell. You might be better off with a doctor."

"Will you do it?"

Jewel smiled. "I'll do my best." She added, almost to herself, "The other way, with Mama Carrie—that's hard too."

"You've done it?"

"Twice. I couldn't do that to Miss Millie—make her look at my children. It's bad enough as it is."

"Oh, my God. Did Edward know you did it?"

"We never talked about it. Sure . . . he knew."

"When did he start . . . you don't have to tell me if you—"

"I was almost fifteen."

Laura stared at the ground. "What about Ishmael?"

"I loved that man, oh, yes I did. He was tall and so strong and *funny*." Jewel smiled at the memory that was with her yet. "We had a plan that we'd live out at Pine Hill but . . . Mr. Edward tried to buy him. I never saw him madder than he was at Mr. Armistead that day. He said, 'A promise is a promise,' but Ishmael was gone."

Laura thought, Does she have to call him "Mr. Edward" when they're in bed? She took a breath and forced herself to look squarely at Jewel. "I'm sorry for the whole horrible mess—sorrier than I can say. I should have seen and I didn't, I should have insisted . . ."

"Don't feel bad. It's worse for Miss Millie than for me."

Millie, with her headaches and tempers, her shopping and parties and girlish attempts to seduce her own husband, watching the little black child she had mothered so generously grow up into a beauty that her husband couldn't or wouldn't resist. On that day at Malvern, Becca had said, *It's a filthy system we live in, vile for women, black and white.* Laura ached with outrage for Jewel and pity for Millie. Perhaps one day when she had grown more charitable she could pity Edward too.

He left in mid-morning. It was a different leave-taking than the last time. Today only Joseph was there, bowing in his stately way as he opened the door, the faultless, unsurpassable servant. Millie was not able to leave her bed, Paige had said goodbye to her father in her room, Cookie was working in the smokehouse, Adam was on an errand in town. No grooms and gardeners, fewer now since the recent defections, waited outside to bid the master farewell. In the entrance hall there were only Becca with baby William in her arms, Laura, and a few paces behind them, Jewel.

His uniform was battered now, a section of brighter gray on the sleeve where it had been torn and patched, the gold braid tarnished. Millie had tried for months to find a length of gray wool for a new uniform but even she had had no luck. His wide-brimmed felt hat was battered too, but in such a way as to give him an insouciant air. His face was not happy though. It was almost gray this morning and haggard from lack of sleep.

I can't do it, Laura thought, but she looked into his eyes as she said goodbye and then brushed his cheek with her lips. He kissed Becca and her pretty red-haired son and then gazed past her. Jewel stood beside the closed door of the library, her hands clasped before her, her head bent a little.

His eyes grew bright and burning—it seemed he didn't care if Becca saw—then the light diminished. He spoke a word to Joseph and went out into the dark, icy day.

Into Laura's mind came the picture she tried to hold off—Edward, who had given up his youth and ambitions for the sake of three frightened children, who had loved, guided, and protected her for so many years, Edward the gentle, honorable man, sneaking into the bedroom of a fourteen-year-old girl who could not tell him no. Even if he hadn't wrestled her down she had been forced—by his legal power, his status, and the society they both lived in.

He mounted his horse beside the porch but fog had

moved in across the front yard, thick and obscuring, and before he reached the gate he was only a shadow in the mist.

CHAPTER 25

ALL BUT TWO of the horses were sold before Christmas. Edward had made the decision before he left. The cost of feed was now so exorbitant that even President Davis sold most of his horses and Varina Davis gave up both her carriage and the matched bays that pulled it. A group of Richmond gentlemen, shocked by her sacrifice, retrieved them for her and this made the problem worse. She told Ellen Mercer that since they were now a gift she couldn't resell them and how in the name of all that was good could she afford to feed them?

Feeding horses was the least of most people's worries. Feeding themselves was a much greater problem because the shortage of food, apparent since just after the beginning of the war, had grown so great and prices so high that even the rich were suffering. Just before Christmas, Cookie came to Millie and announced that she could not provide a decent meal, let alone a feast, if her budget were not increased.

"Pine Hill ain' sent no turkeys nor no vegetables or butter. Whatever dey got dey ain' givin' us."

Millie went to Laura with tears in her eyes. "I can't give Cookie a penny more—I don't have it. Pine Hill has always produced plenty. How can I make that man disgorge—he wouldn't dare do this if Edward were here!"

"That man" was Rufus Nelson, a New Yorker who had been the overseer at Pine Hill for fifteen years. He was uncouth and untidy and any man who hired himself out to run another man's slaves instead of acquiring his own could not be worth much in Millie's opinion.

Laura listened to her moans and tried to hide her own growing anxiety. Since the day she learned that she was pregnant her attitude toward finance had changed drastically. Now when she would have a child to protect she was faced with the prospect of no money, a necessity as available as fresh air in the past.

Since the first Seymour had come to Virginia the family's wealth had increased with each generation. After a painstaking examination of the investments Edward had made for her, she discovered that shortly after the war began he, like most wealthy Southerners, had staked everything on the Southern cause. He had pulled the family's money and Laura's own fortune out of profitable Northern investments and plunged it all into Confederate bonds.

That left the *Courier* and Pine Hill. In three years of war the newspaper's circulation was down and newsprint so expensive and hard to get that it now published only once a week and was deeply in debt. And Pine Hill was not producing well. Runaways had left Rufus Nelson with a quarter of the manpower he could rely on before the war. Those who stayed, he complained to Millie in a letter she threw angrily to the floor, were the lazy, incompetent ones. Laura noticed that Fiona Rutledge, canny as a banker when it came to money, had held on to her Northern railroad stocks while Edward watched the Southern economy crumble, paper money dwindle in value as inflation escalated, and the cost of all commodities rise to stunning heights. She didn't blame Edward—almost everyone she knew was in the same predicament. But if all her inheritance from Robert was to be lost, she would have preferred to do it herself. It occurred to her that Confederate money even looked worthless—cheap paper, poorly printed, often blank on one side, testifying to the poverty of the economic system that stood behind it. At times when she handed over a bundle of fifty-dollar bills to a merchant for very little in return, she saw ahead a life of destitution for them all.

Cookie finally paid forty dollars for a tough old gobbler and produced two pies with the last of the flour, so that it was possible to pretend things had not changed too much. Laura brought the last of the sherry from her house. But memories of past Christmases came crowding back, Christmases when the men—the troublesome, irritating, essential men—had been home and life was good. The four women ate Christmas dinner together, talked cheerfully of the better days that must surely lie ahead, and wondered if their men were cold and hungry and if they would ever see them again.

LAURA STILL WENT to the War Department on most days and even spent some hours every week at Byron Rollin's hospital up on Church Hill, but she did not sleep well and her dreams were strange and frightening. For the first time in her life she experienced alarming swings of unjustified elation and dark depression. Even though Jewel insisted that volatile emotions were common in the early months just as nausea was and that as time went on she would become phlegmatic as a cow, she wondered if she was strong enough for the task she had set herself and if, perhaps, she was going to fail.

She would try to cheer herself by imagining Chase miraculously here and the way he would smile and embrace her when she told him about the baby. Then the terrible thought occurred. Suppose he wasn't happy at all? He loved her but he had always been a wanderer. Suppose he didn't want a wife and child? What if, when it came down to it, she could not earn her own living—she never had before—what if she got sick, what if she died? Who would feed, clothe, love her baby? With great clarity she saw now why it took, at the least, two adults to raise a child. It was a monumental job for a man and woman working together. Facing it alone was terrifying.

Then morning would come and with it optimism. He had said, *You know I'll come back if I'm alive.* He would love their child, of course he would. And if, at the worst, he could not come back she would do it all herself, somehow.

BELLE ISLE, ONE OF the loveliest islands in the James River, had always been a favorite spot for picnics. It was green and hilly, surrounded by picturesque falls and swirling ripples caused by the fast current—from the Southern point of view a perfect place for a prison. But Northern prisoners—enlisted men all—suffered greatly. It was impossible to escape from the island; every one of the strong swimmers who had tried it drowned. There was no shelter, few tents or blankets, and the marshy ground was cold and wet even in summer. On almost every winter morning daylight revealed the frozen corpses of prisoners who had died in the night. Even young, strong men often could not survive such conditions when they were sick and half-starved but Richmonders, struggling with exorbitant prices and severe shortages, felt little compassion for them.

As always, officers fared better than enlisted men even when prisoners, though not by much. Captured Northern officers, warehoused in cold, drafty Libby Prison, also subsisted on moldy bread, spoiled bacon, and filthy river water, but they did have floors, walls, and a roof. They also had a better chance to escape. A group of them, with agonizing effort, had been digging a tunnel for more than two months through the bottom floor and had finally surfaced on the other side of the street at a spot hidden by a low building. The escape was planned for mid-January.

One cold afternoon just before sunset Elvina answered an urgent knock at the kitchen door. Frederick came in— walking so lightly for a big man, she thought with possessive pleasure—and she knew by his face that something was wrong. He lifted her up and hugged her, forgetting as usual how strong he was, then asked for Miss Laura. She recovered her breath and trotted upstairs. Laura was just taking off her coat. The War Department, all the government offices, had been in turmoil since early morning when it was first realized that over a hundred prisoners were missing, and she had spent the afternoon commiserating with Varina Davis.

Elvina leaned in the doorway. "Frederick be here, ma'am. He don' look happy."

Laura sped down the stairs.

In the parlor, behind closed doors, Frederick said quickly, "Well, dey's out and scattered but four of dem is still at Miss Fiona's. Her an' Bessie is down with fever— Maria cain' leave 'em an' Miss Varina's gonna be lookin' for me. Will you do it?"

Laura said, "You go back now. I'll get my coat."

"Take blankets. It's gonna freeze tonight."

Elvina had stayed near the parlor door, more strongly tempted than she had ever been to listen, but it seemed just a moment before Frederick was rushing out with only a pat on her fanny as he passed and Miss Laura was hurrying up the stairs, her lips compressed with anxiety or tension. Elvina followed.

"Find every extra blanket you can," Laura ordered, and then stopped and looked into the girl's face. "Would you be willing to do something dangerous? You don't have to."

Elvina's eyes shone. "Yes, ma'am!"

"It may not be easy. You could get into a lot of trouble."

"If you can do it, Miss Laura, I can too."

"Get the blankets and your coat and something to put over your head. I'll meet you in the stable."

They had become adept at harnessing the horse; it showed, Laura had once informed Elvina with considerable satisfaction, that women could do perfectly well on their own if they had to. On this night she gave special thanks that she had sacrificed some little extras in order to buy feed for the horse. She flicked the reins and they rolled out to the street. The sky was silver-blue, as icy as the snow-drifts at the side of the road, and traffic was light. She touched up the horse and they trotted briskly into town.

M ARIA LET THEM in by the side door. "How is Miss Fiona?" Laura whispered as they climbed the stairs. She kept her coat on, the house was so cold.

"Better, thank you kin'ly, though weak as a kitten. But Bessie been porely all day and that Joelle been hiding under de bed, she so scared. Don' want her talking to Con-fed'rates. I got 'em all in the same room so's I can keep a sharp eye." A fat woman, Maria began to puff. "We gots to go another flight. Deys four of 'em, nice genl'mens."

In the attic above the third floor she led them down a narrow passageway and stopped at the end where the roof sloped sharply. The wall was paneled wood. She pressed the edge of the last panel and Laura, peering past her, saw it slide open. It was a tiny room and with four men in it barely space enough for her to squeeze inside.

"Good evening, gentlemen. I'm Laura Chandler. Elvina and I are going to get you out of here." She gestured toward the open panel and Elvina grinned and curtsied.

"We hope to have you in safe territory by tomorrow evening."

They crowded around to shake her hand, courteous, well-spoken men with Eastern or Midwestern accents. Their leader was Colonel Elroy, who had organized the escape. The three others were much younger. Boys, really, Laura thought. They were thin, ragged, and one young man had a racking cough.

From outside came the sound of horses pounding up the drive, shouts and loud hammering on the front door. There was no time for hesitation or even an instant of fear. Everyone acted, almost as if by agreement or plan.

Laura was out of the room and in the hallway, her hand urgent on Maria's arm. "Where is Miss Fiona?"

"Second floor, end of the hall." The men had huddled back into the little room and as Maria spoke she closed the panel.

Laura and Elvina flew down two flights, stripping off gloves and bonnets as they went. At the end of the hall Laura opened the wide double doors.

"Get your coat off, Elvina. Sit down and try to look as if you've been here for hours." She threw off her own coat and pulled a chair close to the high canopied bed.

Fiona lay against piled-up pillows, her angular face drawn from days of illness, her pale blue eyes alert and almost amused. Bessie, on the couch near the fire, turned over, pushed the blanket away, and muttered in her sleep. Elvina tucked the blanket back around her. In the corner on the other side of Fiona's bed, Joelle, who had never seemed quite right in the head, crouched with her apron over her face.

Loud voices below, the slamming of doors and then a series of crashes.

"I believe they are breaking my furniture," Fiona remarked in a mild tone. "I hope they roast in hell."

Heavy boots cracked on the stairs and the wide double doors flew open.

"Stay out of dere, you. Dat's Miss Fiona's bedroom an' she's a sick lady!"

Maria was shoved aside.

If they were provost guard they had no uniforms but

that meant nothing; even the guard had been reduced to odd bits of clothing in recent months. Whoever they were, these men with the unkempt beards and hard eyes couldn't be easily fooled. They stared at the occupants of the room and the women stared at them. Joelle lowered her apron enough to look and quickly pulled it back over her head.

Laura rose from her chair. "Maria is quite right. Miss Rutledge is ill. Please leave, sirs, without disturbing us further."

The men turned from her without reply, opened the wardrobe and threw down Fiona's dresses, pulled out dresser drawers and flung stockings, underdrawers, and other intimate articles of clothing on the floor. A fourth man, neater than the others and wearing a butternut uniform, stopped in the doorway and glanced in.

"Captain Warren?" Laura said tentatively. "Is it you, Rob?" His face had changed so that she wasn't certain until she saw the flash of recognition in his eyes. Rob Warren had gone hunting with her brothers, had been at the house many times in the days before war had scattered everyone.

"What are you doing here, Laura? This is a disloyal house."

"Visiting a friend of my mother's. She's been very ill with typhoid. It would be a kindness if you all would keep your voices down." She came toward him. "May I ask what this is about?"

"Over a hundred prisoners escaped from Libby last night. We're searching every questionable house in the area."

She cast an eye toward the jumble of clothes on the floor. "Surely you don't expect to find them in this poor old lady's dresser drawers."

From Fiona's dressing room came the sound of glass or china being smashed. Laura said nothing but gave Captain Warren a look. He called out, "All right, boys, that's enough." And then, "Family friend or not, she's a traitor. You have no business here."

Laura made a little moue, a plea just between the two of them for his understanding. "She's old and sick, Rob"— she lowered her voice—"and a little cracked, you know. No one takes her seriously."

"I do. I want those men." He looked down at the empty sleeve pinned across his chest. "I'm no good for combat now—I can't handle a rifle. But I'll find those bastards. Don't leave this room." He went out and his men followed.

Shaking in her thin slippers, Laura sank down on the chest at the foot of Fiona's bed. Elvina crept to her side and Maria slipped into the room, light as a girl in spite of her size. They listened as the men went through every room and closet down the hall, then did the same on the floor above, their boots overhead sounding, Fiona muttered, "like a herd of bull elephants." Bessie moaned in her sleep but did not wake.

The invaders thundered up the stairs to the attic and in the silent room on the second floor the women scarcely breathed. Over their heads the ceiling shook so violently that plaster dust showered down. The door-slamming, the crashing of furniture, the curses continued for some time, then stopped abruptly.

If they've found them, Laura thought, what do we do?

Above them a voice unrecognizable as Rob Warren's bellowed an order. The men came down, bypassing Fiona's bedroom, but at her door their captain paused. "We're going, Laura." He hurried down the wide stairs into the night.

Laura went to the window and without disturbing the curtain looked down into the front yard. "They're leaving," she said. "All of them."

UNDER THE FALSE BOTTOM, the space in the wagon was about a foot and a half deep. The wagon looked as if it had been in use for years; it actually had been made only two years ago by an escaped slave whom Fiona then drove out of the city. In four more risky trips, she had carried eleven people out of captivity to a meeting point with a friend who had a boat and was willing to take them across the Potomac.

"A round dozen," she crowed to Laura, "right under the noses of their ham-handed provost guard!"

Laura wasn't as convinced that the guard were fools. Luck had had something to do with it. From the stable she gave the signal. Watching those Union officers slip from the house and move silently along the shadowed path, she gave thanks that the moon had not yet risen and wondered if she would be as lucky as Fiona on this night.

The lantern, dim and flaring, cast monstrous moving shadows, briefly lighting the men's faces as they came in. The colonel reminded her of Chase. He was about the same age and had the same cool resolution in his eyes. The three young men with him were lucky, she thought, to have such a commanding officer.

"Get in, lie flat," she whispered, "three behind the seat, one of you here at their feet." She put a warning hand on the lieutenant with the wheezing cough. "Be completely silent, all of you must be silent if we're stopped." The young man nodded and climbed in quickly.

Two wide, thin boards had to be lifted from the stable floor and lowered into place. Maria took one side, Elvina the other, and Laura, leaning from the driver's seat, guided it into the ridge it was meant to rest on, just above the four men. Then the second board, enclosing them. Just as the board came down Elvina whispered, "I hates to do this," and the soldier beneath, so young, so gaunt, looked up and grinned.

"Perfect fit." Laura picked up the reins. "Load the cages—no, right here behind the seat. Get in, Elvina."

Maria stepped back with her particular light, dancing movement and watched with anxious eyes as Laura snapped the reins and the wagon rolled out, pulled by Fiona's two remaining horses.

Four men, two women, five hens, and a rooster. It was dangerous, exhilarating—it was crazy. Laura almost laughed. She touched up the horses and they jounced down the dark, rutted road that would take them to David Rees's farm.

Twice, horsemen passed, going the other way. None called a greeting or even glanced at them. Everyone on the road on this dark, cold night seemed absorbed in his own business. The army and the provost guard were scouring the city; they would surely be watching the roads out of town, but so far no patrols and no questions.

The road narrowed. Above their heads black trees towered, giving a feeling of enclosure and safety, and that meant a time for increased alertness. She was aware in all her senses—of the cold that clawed through her coat, the smell of the pines, the rhythmic clop of hooves and the groan and squeak of the wagon, the faint wheezing of the boy under the board, the rustle as the chickens moved in their cages. Those five hens meant eggs for Fiona and her little household, precious eggs that might help bring her back to health and were so hard for even a rich woman to buy. And the rooster—beady eyes, ruby-red comb, magnificent iridescent tailfeathers, always spoiling for a fight. Fiona loved that creature. She had added her treasures to tonight's game with the nonchalance of a high-stakes gambler laying all his chips on the table.

They rounded a curve and far down the road horsemen appeared, dim shapes coming toward them. To the side of the road was a ditch and snow-covered brambles. There was nowhere to go but straight ahead.

"Halt there!"

She pulled on the reins. They came up, two men, slouch hats, country voices. It was all she could make out. One struck a match, fumbled at the lantern hanging from his pack and held it high. His breath was like smoke in the frosty air. "It's a girl. And look what we got back here." Elvina tried to make herself small under her bulky coat, but the men were laughing. "Chickens, by God." The rooster stepped nervously around his cage and the hens in response produced a riffle of clucking. "Where'd you get these beauties, lady? Where're you headed?"

"Just down the road a ways, to Miz Parteger's. You know her?" Without conscious thought, Laura moved into their speech, the kind she had heard all her life, the soft twang of the hardworking, uneducated Virginia small farmer.

An unspoken tension eased. The man lowered the lantern a little. "You from around here?"

"Over to Carleton way. I work for Miz Linder in town. Miz Parteger's her sister. She's a real sick lady so Miz Linder sent me to bring these chickens and her to help out." Laura jerked her head at Elvina who smiled timidly.

"Well, who's this Miz Linder think she is, sending a girl

like you out alone on a night like this? There's prisoners loose."

Laura's eyes widened. "From Belle Isle?"

"Hell, no. Don't nobody get off Belle Isle. These be officers out of Libby. Damn officers. Nothing but trouble in any man's army. We got to go now." He turned out the lantern. "You take care . . ."

There was an odd whistling sound from somewhere in the back. Laura froze. Elvina pulled hard at one of the rooster's long tailfeathers drooping through the bars of his cage. He gave a huge squawk and leaped forward.

The men roared. They kicked their horses' sides and as they leaped off one of them said, "Chickens!"

THE WAGON ROLLED DOWN the slope and across the yard without slowing. They were past the house before Laura began to haul on the reins. In the dark barn they came to a jolting stop.

Laura climbed down and clutched David Rees's arm. "Cavalry passed on the main road just after we turned off. I can't be sure they didn't see us."

"Get to the house. Go the back way. I'll take care of this."

"Where will you hide them?"

"Go!"

Laura grabbed Elvina's hand and they ran. Down the icy slope, behind the brush, behind the privy, into the house through the open window. There was a narrow bed and a chair in this room. The other, larger room was kitchen, dining room, parlor. No niches or attics where David's children might once have played or where hunted prisoners might hide on this dangerous night.

Horsemen rode into the yard, lit now by a white moon. There were about ten, much too many.

Lanternlight spilled from the open barn door. In the yard the cavalry captain called, "Dismount!" and then, "Let's go in."

David sat on his stool, working on the right front wagonwheel. The horses had been unhitched and were lodged in a stall.

He looked up and remarked mildly, "You again."

"Yes, Mr. Rees. I see you've got yourself another wagon."

"That's right. Looked like a good buy but the bastard diddled me—this wheel's been trouble ever since I got it."

The young captain snorted. "You've never been diddled in your life."

David looked the man up and down. "What bee you got in your bonnet tonight, sonny? State your business and get out of here."

The captain flushed. If he had been a little older or more experienced he might have thought further, but he was only nineteen, he hadn't yet been in real combat, and was always worried that his men were laughing behind his back. "My business is escaped prisoners, sir. Out of Libby. Have you seen anything suspicious?"

"Have I seen Yankees this night? No, I have not, son."

"You willing to swear to that, Mr. Rees? On the Bible?"

"You got one handy?"

"Well . . ."

"I got mine, Cap'n."

"Get it, Darcy."

Darcy was seventeen, a deeply religious boy who was convinced that his Bible had already saved his life twice. He dug it from his pack and hurried back.

The captain handed it to David. The others shuffled a little. All religious men of one stripe or another, they took their Bible seriously. They knew Mr. Rees hated the Confederacy—he'd shouted around about it enough and still wasn't speaking to his son—but they also knew his passionate Methodism. At one time or another David Rees had tried to convert every one of them.

David took the worn, grimy book. He looked at each man, his face austere. The words came out slowly. "I swear by Almighty God I have not seen Yankees on this night." He handed back the book. "Does that do you?"

The captain said, "All, right boys. Mount up."

Unlike his captain, Alton Begley had been in every big battle since Bull Run and had lost some of his illusions. His eyes had been moving around the barn while all the talk was going on. "Cap'n," he said, "we haven't even looked in the loft."

The captain looked up. A few strands of straw were hanging at the edge of the loft next to the ladder. It was true, he hadn't searched the loft, hadn't even thought of it. If he sent someone up there now it would be the same as calling David Rees a liar before God. Yet with every eye on him how could he leave without looking?

"All right, Alton, go on up. And you two." Alton's two closest friends scrambled swiftly up the ladder after him.

It didn't take long. The loft was small.

Alton called down, "Nothin' here, Cap'n. Hardly a teaspoon of straw to hide under."

They came sliding down the ladder and the captain, his young face burning, saluted David without looking at him and muttered, "Let's get out of here."

DAVID WALKED IN HIS front door and looked at the women.

"How did you get rid of them?" Laura whispered.

He sat down at the table. "Said I hadn't seen Yankees tonight and they asked me to swear to it. So I did."

She sat down, too, and stared at him. "You swore?"

"I hadn't seen 'em, not then. They were still in the wagon. Couldn't swear to it now. They're in the loft."

He smiled, the first smile she'd ever seen on his face.

She began to smile too. "Well, you do beat all."

"I'll be up there with them tonight. You can use that bed in there if you want." David glanced at Elvina. "Don't know what you want to do with her."

"David, she's been very brave. Without her we never would have gotten here."

He made some sound, more a grunt than a word. As he left he said, "She can stay in the house."

ON THE SUNDAY FOLLOWING the escape Paige woke with pains that spread alarm through the house. The baby wasn't due for another month. Dr. Rollins left his hospital, something he seldom did since the burden of wounded and sick had grown so great, and after his examination ordered her body tilted so that gravity could hold the child in place. Pillows were piled under her knees, the room was darkened, and everyone tiptoed and whispered.

Paige wept a little, holding her mother's hand, the pains quieted, and after a time she fell asleep.

In the hallway Jewel said, "Sometimes it settles down. Not much to do but wait," and left Laura to her thoughts.

She herself was four months along and had expected to go to Pine Hill before this, but she didn't show yet. Elvina had let out the waists of her dresses so she could wear them without the compression of stays and she was still so slim that only with all clothes off was a slight outward curve of abdomen apparent. Jewel, her authority on all matters obstetrical, said that yes, most women were a little bigger by now but everyone was different, it was probably due to the position of the child. And yet, Laura worried. Under pressure Jewel had admitted the possibility that the baby wasn't developing properly and that was the fear that sometimes kept her awake nights.

Adam loped past the open library door and she jumped up and went into the hall.

"What is it?"

He barely paused in his onward rush. "Miss Paige," he called back as he jumped off the porch. "She's got pains bad and Mama says get the doctor here if I have to drag him."

All during the long night Paige struggled. Dr. Rollins, arriving two hours after he was sent for, told them there was now no hope of preventing a premature birth. He could only do his best to help Paige through it and then pray that the child was strong enough to live. At slightly past eight months it was possible.

Sometimes the pain was so great that they all thought she would die of it; at other times it stopped completely and she slept. That was the problem, the doctor said. The contractions should not start and stop but continue, become more frequent and intense. "This diddling around," he muttered more to himself than the others, "is getting us nowhere."

At one point Becca whispered to Jewel, "Look at Laura—she's like a ghost. She shouldn't have to see this mess just now."

"She's strong—she won't faint," Jewel whispered back, and hoped it was true.

In everyone's mind were the many young, strong wives, women they all knew well, who had died in childbirth recently.

The flirtatious beauty Serena Wynn had finally stuck to a decision, married her young hero, Mason Campbell, and died the day after her child was born. Three days later the baby died. Mason never knew. He had lost a leg at Chickamauga and was dead of gangrene when the long, slow train pulled into the Richmond station. The worst of it was that it was not an uncommon tragedy, it was a frequent one.

Through the rest of the night Paige thrashed about, calling for Alex, and early the next morning her "trouble," as labor was politely referred to, began in earnest. Just after the noon hour her child was born, small, thin, but crying lustily, a boy she named Alexander just before she fell asleep. In mid-afternoon she woke and told her mother that Alex was dead.

"Oh, not so, dear, not so." Millie turned to Laura for support.

Laura, on her knees beside the bed, said quickly, "Of course not, Paige. We'd have heard."

"I have heard. I've got the letter right here—it's from a friend"—she dug at her pillow—". . . under here somewhere."

Laura passed her hand under the pillow. "There's nothing, honey. You've been dreaming."

"Here it is!" Paige began to read the letter no one else could see. " 'He picked up the flag when it fell and rallied the men for one last charge. They ran straight into the canister and grape . . . cannon were lined up on the hill, sharpshooters everywhere and the bullets cracking past our ears. None of it touched him until we were at the crest and then that Yank bayoneted him right in the chest . . .' " Tears were running down her face and Millie murmured, "Hush, hush," and stroked her hair.

Becca whispered to Laura, "A soldier we nursed in the hospital told us that story . . . I swear, it's word for word . . ." and Laura nodded, helpless and afraid.

The doctor had left immediately after the birth and there was disagreement throughout the afternoon as to whether he should be called back. He wouldn't come if he thought they were just a pack of nervous women, but Paige was still out of her head, sometimes talking to Alex as if he were by her side, sometimes sitting up and declaring to the room that she was now a widow. The baby had to be taken from her because she couldn't be made to understand that she was clutching the little thing too tightly. She sobbed for a while as they carried him out but then seemed to forget and fell asleep.

Jewel came to Laura. "You, too, missy. You haven't slept since yesterday morning."

"I'm all right," Laura mumbled but allowed herself to be led to her own room. She lay down on top of the coverlet. "I'll just rest for a few minutes. Call if you need me."

Jewel spread a blanket over her. "Yes, ma'am," she said, and tiptoed out.

Toward morning the steady rain slowed and then stopped. The clouds cracked open and Laura woke to see sunlight streaming across the bed. It was almost ten o'clock. Why had they let her sleep so long? She scrambled up and hurried into the hallway. They were gathered outside Paige's door, the women who had nursed her through the night and Dr. Rollins.

Swept by the cold certainty that Paige was dead, Laura moved forward, almost stumbling in her haste, and heard Byron Rollins and Millie, tears fresh on her cheeks, discussing the gentlest way to tell Paige that her baby had been too frail to survive and that it was really all for the best.

A LEX GOT THE PAINFUL news—his son was born and had died, Paige had gone through a bad patch but was recovering—and understood why so many men under his command had deserted. He read Millie's letter again and wondered what kept him from doing the same. Duty, honor, country—he had been taught well. The short pathetic note from Paige, apologizing for her failure, brought him even lower. He was certain in his heart that the war was lost, he knew Paige needed him, and he knew that, like a fool, he would stay here until the end.

Millie was skilled at using letters to put the best face on troubles and she had done her best when she wrote to Alex.

It was true that Paige, after giving them a terrible fright, was recovering—she no longer read invisible letters that told her Alex was dead—yet Millie knew that her daughter had crossed over into a faraway place and had not yet found her way home. She lay awake nights yearning for Edward. If he were here, he would know what to say to Paige. If he were here, she, Millie, would not feel so desperately alone.

CHAPTER 26

PINE HILL PLANTATION—the land itself—had been granted to the first Edward Seymour only ten years after Englishmen came ashore at Jamestown in 1607 and had remained in the family's control through Indian attacks, revolution, secession, and civil war, when those less tenacious were going bankrupt and losing everything.

The cottage, the first structure built at Pine Hill and now used by the overseer, was a modest dwelling that had sheltered Seymours in the early, uncertain years. Then the superb main house had been built, a red-brick, white-columned Georgian mansion now almost a hundred and fifty years old, dominant on its hill with the sweeping vista of the river. Several rooms had been added as the Seymours grew richer and their land holdings increased and then an entire wing. By the time Laura's father inherited it the house had expanded to include little rooms and oddly shaped acloves on the top floor where young children could imagine themselves almost anywhere doing almost anything. For Laura and her little brothers the narrow winding back stairway to the attic, intended for use by servants, became a castle turret, the dark eight-sided room under the eaves a dungeon, the balcony a pirate ship.

Laura walked through each room, remembering. She hadn't been to Pine Hill since war began and it was shocking to see the house beginning to deteriorate. Doors stuck, the building needed paint inside and out, a banister on the stairs leading to the third floor was broken. Worst of all, there was a leak in the roof. Pine Hill had never been a mansion that could match the size and magnificence of Malvern—few plantation houses were—but a leaking roof?

She went out onto the veranda. The marble under her feet was as solid and lustrous as ever, if in need of cleaning, but the stately columns, the shutters, the white trim, so striking a contrast to the dark red brick, were shabby and peeling. Still, it might be the time of year that brought this oppressive sense of sadness. The sky was a dark, ominous pewter and every tree along the drive bare against the wintry sky. This summer those majestic trees would provide leafy shade all the way to the main road.

The overseer's cottage, the barn, the laundry, the stables were out of sight behind the house. Before her, down a rolling incline where the well-kept lawn once had been, was a field of rich green weeds that in the spring would glow with wildflowers, then a darker line of pines and cedars and beyond them the river, a wide lazy tributary of the James. She took a deep breath of the fragrant air. In spite of war and neglect Pine Hill was still beautiful and whatever came later her baby would get its start in this lush, lovely place.

Jewel said she should take a long walk every day and so, since they wouldn't let her do anything in the house, she decided to walk to the river. She found the old path, somewhat overgrown but passable, and swung down the hill, energy and hope rising. Here she felt freer and happier than in Richmond. Here it seemed possible that she would go through the next months without incident and deliver a healthy child as summer came on. It didn't have to end as it had with Paige—grief, despair, and everything gone wrong.

When told that her baby was dead Paige had cried in wild, raging abandon, asking again and again what she had done to deserve such punishment. Then after a day and night during which even the doctor feared for her mind, a cold calm settled over her. As soon as she was able she wrote to Alex and Byron Rollins pronounced it a sign that she had accepted her loss and was on the way to full recovery. When she was allowed out of bed she assembled the diapers, the blankets, the little clothes she had made and tried to give them to Laura.

"Take them, I want you to have them."

"Paige, there will be other children. You'll need them yourself."

An expression so bleak passed across Paige's face that she looked almost old. "No I won't. Take them. You'll be doing me a favor."

"Well, then—thank you," Laura said, thinking that she would give them to Millie and tell her to store them away.

They had sat together for a little longer on that cold February afternoon, Paige wearing the same odd, empty look, Laura with a growing sense of unease.

Then, out of nowhere: "Chase Girard. How could you, Laura? Well, don't look so surprised. Did you really think I couldn't guess?"

Never had Laura said who the father was, but Jewel and Becca, each for reasons of her own, had come to the same accurate conclusion. Now Paige had seen the truth, though not all of it. Laura said, "I loved him. Is that so hard to understand?"

"I don't mean not being married. Who cares? I'd have run off with Alex if Papa hadn't let me marry him. I mean how could you with a Yankee, a vile, filthy, spying *Yankee*."

"I didn't know. He was Alex's friend—I met him at your wedding."

"Don't throw that up to me."

"He was attractive and I was lonely. I fell in love. As far as Yankees are concerned I've known many. Some of them are very good people."

"That's what comes of traveling and getting broad-minded. You lose your standards. Personally, I'd as soon go to bed with a colored."

Laura bit back the rising anger. It was a harsh attack from one whose ties of blood and love were so close and she would have slammed back bitterly if she hadn't had so much to hide. It might be best, all things considered, if she went to Pine Hill sooner than she planned and that meant doing the one thing she had managed to avoid thus far. She would have to tell Millie about the baby.

Millie made it surprisingly easy. She seemed more stunned by who the man was than the fact of pregnancy itself, muttered something about deceiving men who came into one's life only long enough to cause trouble, and then turned practical.

"Pine Hill is the very thing. Jewel must go with you and stay the whole time. You'll have Elvina too, so Becca can come back after she's helped get the house set up. I expect it's a mess. Take Adam—he can drive your buggy. Enoch will drive our carriage and bring Becca back. Between the buggy and the carriage we can load in everything you'll need."

"Ah, Millie . . ." Laura swallowed and turned her head away. "You don't even scold me."

Tears burned in Millie's eyes but she smiled. "Well, of course not. You're still my little girl." She put out her arms and they sat for a while, Millie holding Laura against her breast.

In a muffled voice Laura said, "I don't know if you'll understand but the truth is . . . I'm not sorry for anything."

Millie stroked the dark head. "You still love him, don't you, dear. I understand loving in spite of everything. I understand it very well."

So they had trooped out of Richmond, the six of them, and arrived at Pine Hill without warning, throwing the overseer and his wife into complete disarray. Rufus Nelson moaned over his problems with his disappearing labor force and described the mansion as a casualty of war, but Laura noticed that his own comfortable cottage was in excellent condition. As soon as she was settled in she would have a talk with Mr. Nelson. But for the present she was content to sit here on the riverbank and watch the dark green water flow. Perhaps Jewel was right. She was becoming passionless as a cow and would soon be disturbed by nothing.

They had ordered her out of the house and were up there now, Adam and Enoch pulling covers off the furniture, sweeping, and cleaning windows so dirty they could barely be seen through. Becca and Jewel were doing what Jewel said was always the first task when you moved in—making beds. "That way you've got someplace to fall down when you run out of steam." Elvina was in the kitchen searching cupboards for the utensils needed to cook supper and Laura looked forward to this first evening with pleasure. Tonight she would sit by the fire out here in the country quiet, somnolent and at ease in a place where there was no one to whisper or judge her and no risks to be taken, except for the risk of childbirth.

It was three days before she was able to pin down the elusive Rufus Nelson and have a serious talk about the condition of the house. Surely he was not so short of men that he couldn't repair the roof.

But it soon became apparent that he was. Most of his skilled men, including the roofers, had taken off and the workers who remained lacked the skills to replace such craftsmen, their primary work being to labor in the gardens and tend livestock. Laura knew Rufus was right. Vegetables and fruit brought high prices in the marketplace, as did turkeys and chickens and the eggs the laying hens produced.

He had talked it over with Mr. Seymour when he came home last fall and they had decided that tobacco production on a big scale was impossible with so many slaves gone over the border. Even if a fair-sized crop could be brought in, it would rot in a warehouse, unsalable because of the warships blockading the harbors. "I hope you'll bear with me, ma'am, and I'll have my boys work on the house whenever they've got a spare minute."

That night he told his wife, Emma, "I was hoping she'd say she wasn't staying long but it looks like they're settling in. That Elvina was in the kitchen complaining that there weren't enough pots and where were the good dishes. You may have to take some things back. Oh, she was looking for tablecloths too."

Emma continued to sew. She was a serene woman, rarely disturbed about anything, and usually could find a way to get at least part of what she wanted. "I'll give back a set or two of dishes and some of the pots and tell her the darkies stole the rest." She clipped the thread and squinted while she threaded the needle again. "I must say, I don't think she'll be leaving anytime soon." They both understood "she" meant Laura. In spite of themselves, they were awed by Mrs. Chandler and often referred to her simply as "she."

"Why not? Nothing here for her to do and it isn't the pleasantest time of year."

"There you are."

"There I'm where? What have you got in your head?"

"She hasn't been out here in years. Why now, with only the two maids and the boy staying on and with the roof falling in? Only one reason I can think of—she doesn't want to be seen."

Rufus turned that over in his mind. "She's slim as a willow, Emma."

"Not so slim as she was when we went to see Mr. Seymour last fall. You could've put two hands around her waist then. You couldn't now."

"She's a lady, Emma."

"Ladies fall from grace too. Maybe I'm wrong but wait and see—maybe I'm right."

Rufus edged forward in his chair. They were sitting beside a great blazing fire on a night that was cold even for February. There was plenty of firewood, there was plenty of everything in this comfortable cottage a half mile from the big house. "You listen to me, wife. She's not just a lady, she's a great lady, she's Mrs. Chandler, so even if you're right you're wrong. You keep your mouth shut, not a word to anyone. Whatever she's doing here is her business. Our business is to run this farm the best we can so we live the best we can. If we mind our business we'll survive in the long run. Understand me now?"

"Don't lecture me, Rufus. I understand as well as you. She's always been nice to me but I wouldn't want to get on the wrong side of her. You can't be a senator's wife without learning how to do in someone you don't like. I intend to keep my nose out of it and help her any way I can."

B ECCA BEGAN TO SNIFF as she waited on the veranda with her bags piled high. By the time Enoch brought the carriage around she had to dig for her handkerchief and blow her nose.

"Laura, I'll be here when you need me, I promise."

"Don't worry, I'm fine and I have the best midwife in the world." Laura gave Jewel a fond glance and Jewel rolled her eyes. Becca knew very well that Jewel didn't have the confidence in herself that Laura had.

"The truth is, I'm scared to death," she had told Becca during one of their anxious whispered conferences. "It's always harder when it's someone you care about."

"Do you think something's wrong?"

"Like I told her, I think she's still so small because of the position but I really don't know."

"Should she stay in town and go to some doctor there? I can't bear to think about it."

"They'd barbecue her on a spit in Richmond. But we might find some little village far enough away with a decent doctor . . ." Becca looked skeptical. "I know. Word travels."

"I don't know any doctor we can trust. You'll do fine, Jewel, and you'll have Elvina and me to help. I wonder—I haven't had the nerve to ask. What will she do with the baby?"

Jewel gave a helpless shrug. "I know one thing—that child is all she's got. And I'll tell you something else, Miss Becca. Down deep she believes he'll come back to her."

ON A COLD WET morning in mid-April Laura appraised herself before the cheval glass in her bedroom. "I'm really quite huge. We're going to have to make over every dress."

Jewel agreed with deep relief. "You are a tad plump." The house was damp and drafty and they were always cold away from the fires, sometimes what they faced in the immediate future terrified them, yet they looked at each other and began to giggle as they had when they were little girls subject to laughing fits for no reason except that they were young and life was good.

Downstairs Adam heard them laughing and smiled. Miss Laura was better, Mama said, and that was good. He turned his mind to his own responsibilities. On days it didn't rain he worked on the roof and it was now patched over all the rooms in use. Only one patch had failed in yesterday's heavy downpour and he had repaired it early this morning before rain began again. He had with no instruction figured out how to set a pane of glass in a window and seal it, using tools found in the barn and glass from windows in an unused room in the attic. He moved furniture, fixed everything that broke, and was, in general, indispensable. He was nearly fifteen, a man in reality. The thought sent a thrill through him and made his chest expand. It was a good thing, being a man. He didn't know what to do with the sense of power it gave him.

JEWEL HAD BEEN proven right. The walks Laura took every day it did not rain had strengthened muscles she hadn't used for serious excercise since childhood and as winter moved into spring and the wet days diminished she walked greater and greater distances. As a child she had been as athletic and daring as any boy, run races, climbed trees, and at six galloped her pony toward a hedge, crouched forward as she'd seen her father do, and sailed up as the land dropped away. She had fallen, being too little to hang on, and landed in a bramble. She still had a scar on her leg to prove it and the memory of freedom too.

At fourteen freedom ended. She was required to lower her skirts and be cinched in by stays that compressed her organs and nearly asphyxiated her. At first she thought she would die or at least never eat again but gradually the stays became part of her and she would have felt undressed without them.

She said aloud, "Baby, I promise, if you are a girl I'll never make you wear a corset." Then she laughed. She was talking out loud to her unborn child, making plans for a fourteen-year-old daughter who might turn out to be a son instead.

Behind her Adam called, "I saw a rabbit, Miss Laura. You stay right there. I'm going after him."

She stopped to wait for him in the shade of a tall pine. Adam, unlike most slaves, was allowed to own a gun and he was a good shot. Edward himself had taught him. Since he'd been at Pine Hill his marksmanship had won him a supply of hard-to-get ammunition and his task was to add to the pot with any game he could scare up.

The sun slanting through the trees was warm, the air cool, and the road drew her on. She continued a little farther, slowing her pace so as not to leave him too far behind. On either side the fields were the rich green of spring and wildflowers flamed in the grass. A clump of daisies caught her attention and she stopped to pick a few. Around her was a deep stillness, yet in the country hush there were multitudes of creatures pursuing their own destinies, creatures and systems she and her baby were connected to. Everything was worthy of notice because everything affected her child. It was an entirely new view of the world that had come to her the moment she found out she was pregnant.

She stretched on tiptoe to reach the lowest branch of a cherry tree, broke off a twig and fastened the blossoms above her waist. Adam was not in sight. Ahead in the middle distance a dogcart moved toward her with a drunken, erratic motion. The wobbling wheel fell off and the cart lurched to a halt. The woman walking beside it gave a cry of exasperation and plopped down in the road. As Laura came up to her she grabbed at the child who was beating on the dog.

"Cut that out, Binny, you rotten brat! That ain't gonna make him move."

The girl twisted away from her mother, then stopped in mid-shriek. Her baby brother crawled out of the cart and the two of them stared while Laura looked at the wheel.

"We can fix that. My servant's just down the road."

The woman gazed at the wheel with disgust. "You think so? The wood's splintered."

"It's not too bad. If Adam can't do something maybe we can find you a new one—there are lots of odds and ends in our barn." A fallen tree, one of many victims of the winter's storms, lay beside the road and frogs sang in the puddles around it. Laura stepped over the wet places and sat down. There was instant silence from the frogs.

The woman, still sitting in the dirt, looked up from under straw-colored hair that had come loose from its knot. She pushed it out of her face and stared with open curiosity. "You live around here?"

"Pine Hill. I walked farther than usual today."

"Oh." Pine Hill was a name to be reckoned with. "You one of those Seymours?"

"I was. I'm a Chandler now."

"My husband doesn't like the Seymours. They put us small farmers out of business, he says, but I say, that's because they're rich, Walter, and we're not. It's always been so."

Laura thought that over. Walter and his wife called a

spade a spade, much like David Rees. She said, "My name is Laura," with such a bright, inquiring look that the woman felt obliged to respond politely.

"I'm Mary Louisa Hardin, pleased to meet you." Then, in an altogether different tone, "You chirrin cut that out or I'll find a switch!"

The accent was similar to a Virginian's yet a Virginian born and bred could hear a difference. Laura said, "You're not from around here, originally, that is?"

"We had a farm near Knoxville, over in Tennessee. Walter thought we'd do better here but we ain't. He's down there right now with old Joe Johnston." The boy was climbing his mother's back, his arms around her throat in a strangling grip. She pulled him onto her lap such as it was—she was enormous with child and appeared about to deliver at any moment—and went on speaking in the way people, especially women, sometimes talked to strangers, confiding problems they might never mention to those they know well.

"He was at Chickamauga. I couldn't stop him though I told him he's a fool. I said, 'All you're doing is fighting so's the rich man can hold on to his slaves which we don't have any of. Let 'em fight for themselves.' But he said, 'Mary, they're on our soil. I got to go,' as if all by hisself he could stop 'em. He came home last summer just long enough to give me this"—she looked at her stomach with fore-boding—"and went right off to Tennessee again."

"Yes," Laura said, "they do that."

Binny, Mary's daughter, looked to be about six or seven. She had been edging toward Laura while her mother talked and now was almost leaning against her, shy but curious. She had large violet eyes and Mary's turned-up nose. Laura offered her the bouquet of daisies. She drew back a little and dimples appeared around the pretty lady's mouth. Reassured, she took one flower from the bunch, sat down beside Laura on the log, and began methodically pulling off the petals whispering, "He loves me, he loves me not." Triumphantly she held up the last one and crowed, "He loves me!" and then wondered why her mother and the lady laughed.

"I'm due in June," Laura said with satisfaction. After

being on the outside for so many years while other women boasted or complained about pregnancies, it was mightily pleasing to be a member of the club herself.

"Miss Laura, you was supposed to wait!" Adam caught sight of her as he came around the bend of the road. He trotted up, the carcasses of two fat rabbits tied to his pack, and stopped before her, his voice sharp with annoyance. "You had me bothered—you was supposed to wait."

Laura hopped up. "I'm sorry Adam, I didn't mean to worry you."

Mary got to her feet, bemused by the humble apology. To Laura she said, "You think he can fix it?"

Laura pushed at the wheel with her shoe. "What do you think, Adam?"

"Maybe." Disdain for the woman and the children clinging to her skirt was plain in his face. He didn't like white trash and felt superior to them. He belonged to the Seymours of Pine Hill, a great and powerful family, and their status was his. This scrawny white woman with the callused hands and aversion in her eyes had no business even speaking to Miss Laura. He picked up the wheel. "The pin's come loose, that's all. I can fix it, Miss Laura, but Mama won't like you staying out in the sun so long."

"We'll go sit in the shade and not stir till you're done." Laura picked up Mary's toddler, who was plump and soft and no doubt sweet-smelling when he was clean.

"Your boy don't want to fix it," Mary said as they settled under the tree.

"Oh, he's glad to." Laura looked back. Adam was bending down, scratching the dog's ears. In fact, he was considerably put out and would lecture her about the worthlessness of white trash and the foolishness of trying to help them all the way home. At times like this it seemed to her that black and white were indeed like oil and water and would never forget or forgive each other, not until hell froze over.

CHAPTER 27

MARY HARDIN'S BABY, another son, was born on the first of May. Emma Nelson mentioned it in passing a week later and Laura, over Jewel's objections, told Adam to bring the buggy around.

"Mama says you ought not to go." He looked down disapprovingly from the buggy.

"Adam, put this basket on the seat and help me up." She still moved lightly but the step was high. More importantly, she had to assert herself or he might turn around and go back to the stable. They stared at each other and his eyes wavered. It was impossible to disobey Miss Laura when she looked like that.

On the way he remarked, "Doesn't do any good trying to help no-accounts," but it was said softly to the passing countryside and she chose to ignore it. Then, to soothe his feelings, she told him to drive on to Claremore after he left her with Mary. Claremore, five miles to the south, was a tiny village of board sidewalks and dirt streets, with a half-dozen shops and a church on the main thoroughfare. It was their closest connection to the outside world. There was a telegraph office which brought instant news except for the frequent times when the lines were down, and mail was sporadically delivered to the post office next door.

"Ask if there are any letters for Mrs. Hardin too, and be back by mid-afternoon."

"Yes'm." He struggled to keep the delight out of his face. A good two hours in town. After the country quiet of Pine Hill little Claremore seemed like a bustling metropolis. All sorts of information could be picked up while drifting around, scarcely noticed.

He left the buggy in front of the feed store and without conscious thought slouched along slowly, his eyes on the plank sidewalk. In Richmond he walked with head high. Here, he knew better. In the telegraph office he hung back until the man behind the counter noticed him.

"You, boy," the man called. "Adam. Got a letter here for Mrs. Chandler."

Adam moved over and glanced at the envelope as he stuffed it in his pocket. It was from Miss Millie. He turned on the full power of his smile but at the same time ducked his head a little and said in an accent that would have given his mother fits, "Miz Chandler say does you have anythin' for Miz Hardin?"

"Mary Hardin? Nothing yet and probably ain't goin' to, not for a time." The man didn't chat much with coloreds but Adam was likable. He added, "They's a powerful big battle on down in Georgia and Walt Hardin's likely to be in the middle of it."

A large well-dressed man with a hurried but purposeful manner strode in from the street and Adam was out of his path before he was two steps inside the door.

"Any news?" The man leaned big hands on the counter.

"They're moving down toward Dalton over in Georgia but Old Joe Johnston'll take care of that. It's up by the Rapidan we got to worry. The last dispatch I saw go in to Richmond said it's a killing match up there."

They launched into a debate over military strategy that went on for some time while Adam leaned against the wall staring vacantly. When they began repeating themselves he slipped out and went directly to the buggy. It was only the noon hour but he drove back to Mary Hardin's little farm as fast as was consistent with the welfare of the horse and the kind of news he carried.

That night Laura and Jewel sat up late, talking. The Yankee general, Sherman, had jumped off from Chattanooga in Tennessee and was now attacking Joe Johnston at Dalton with the obvious intent of driving deep into Georgia, astounding news that opened up possibilities good or bad depending on one's point of view. But of more immediate concern to them was the fighting in the dense forest just south of the Rapidan River. The battle that had been raging there for two days could easily spread and engulf Pine Hill. The question was, Should they leave while they could?

"We might wake up smack in the middle of a battle with the shells flying in the window."

"How do you vote?"

"I go where you go, Miss Laura."

"Jewel."

"Oh, all right. I think we should stay. After all, where can we go—back to Richmond? Anywhere we jump they're liable to show up, the whole lunatic crew. Sometimes I wonder if all men are crazy. You wouldn't find women running around in the mud taking potshots at each other."

"True, but on the whole I prefer them to women, present company and a few others excepted. Why do I have to hide here? Because of what people, mostly women, would do to me if they found out. I do believe no one can be crueler to a woman than another woman—they have such an exquisite way of slipping in the knife. I hate having to hide, I truly hate it because I'm not one bit ashamed. What do you say to that?"

Jewel grinned. "I say hooray." After a little while she inquired, "So we stay?"

"We stay and if they show up we'll go out and ask them to kindly keep down the noise." They giggled. Although there was nothing funny about their situation, they had laughed together recently more than they had done since they were girls. It was not foolishness or a lack of understanding or bravado, it was that in such circumstances, when the world was out of control and there was nothing they could do about it, laughter was the only sane response.

CHAPTER 28

THE FIRST INTIMATION of trouble approaching was a low rumble echoing so softly over the trees that at first Laura wasn't sure she heard anything. She paused on the porch and listened. In the field the long grass bent in glimmering waves under a light breeze, a welcome breeze because the bright May sun was hot. In the trees near the river a woodpecker was hammering, mourning doves gave their throaty three-note call, and the owl who hunted in the day as well as night answered them, but beyond that there was another sound.

She shaded her eyes and gazed toward the road and Emma
Nelson, coming up the path, stopped and looked back too.
The rumble was unmistakable—many wagons coming
down the road from the north.

A horseman turned into the drive, galloped up to the
house under the avenue of trees, and came to such a
sudden halt before the women that his horse reared and
had to be battled into submission.

"Ladies, Major Cole, Fifty-first Alabama Cavalry, at your
service." He swept off his hat, his manner rushed but punc-
tilious. "We're escorting a wagon train of our wounded
back to Richmond and some are so ill they are sorely tried
by the jolting of the ambulances. Would you be so kind as
to take them in?"

"Emma, get Jewel and Elvina." Laura came down the
steps. "What battle, Major?"

"The Wilderness, ma'am—a great battle. They did not
break through."

"Where are they now?"

"Moving southeast. Never fear, ma'am, they won't take
Richmond. We won't let them pass."

Jewel came out on the porch, and Elvina, drying her
hands on her apron.

"We have guests," Laura told them. "How many,
Major?"

"As many as you can handle."

They took nineteen, placing them on beds, cots, and
pallets throughout the house. The one burn victim, a
Yankee prisoner, was taken to the small room off the parlor,
and the doctor explained, "His pain is great, as you must
know. I'll leave some carbolic acid. A one-percent solution
on lint frequently renewed may relieve him somewhat and
use the laudanum, but sparingly. Our own men will need it
too. He was caught in the fire as were many of them, poor
fellows. We could hear them screaming." The doctor
looked at her with hard, unsmiling eyes. "It's good of you
to take him in, ma'am. So far we've found two other houses
willing to accept our wounded but they both turned down
the prisoners, even this one."

Laura looked at the sleeping soldier. He was very young

and had blond hair that curled to his shoulders. "Do you expect—"

"I expect him to die. He'll suffer here but less than if we had to haul him onward. Taking him is an act of Christian charity."

"No, Doctor, it's selfish. I have . . . I have someone in this war. If he were hurt I hope some woman would try to help him even if he were her enemy."

The doctor clapped on his hat. "The carbolic solution can be applied to gangrenous and ill-smelling sores as well. You may have a lot of those."

They did. Four men developed gangrene in the stumps of legs that had been hacked off in a filthy field hospital and another had a wound in his thigh where a broken bone had torn through it. The bone had been set by the doctor but the wound was suppurating and had begun to stink. The thigh wound—Jewel, Elvina, and Emma referred to all the men by their wounds when out of their hearing—was the other Yankee in the group. His name was Benjamin Hobson and Laura thought of him as Benjie, the name he said his mother called him. It was the anguish of watching, so often helplessly, while the men suffered that drove the other women to think of them with detachment, but so far she hadn't been able to do it.

She had discovered Benjie just as the ambulances were about to roll out and insisted on taking him in too. He asked often for his mother and sometimes wept for her—he was only seventeen—but there were times when the older men in their pain also cried out for their mothers with the same bewilderment. Benjie was a farm boy from Indiana, talkative in a way that reminded her of Adam, and as she washed his face he asked if her husband had been in the Wilderness too.

Her hand stopped. She dipped the cloth in the basin to give herself a moment and then said, "It could be—I'm not sure. I haven't heard from him in a while."

"Don't worry, ma'am. I reckon your mail is as slow as ourn and we don't none of us get time to write much. It was as fierce a battle as I've seen and I been in a few."

Cuts and bruises covered his arms and hands. As she washed them gently his voice began to rise with remembered fear. "The brush and leaves in them piney woods caught fire from the shot—that's where old Norman got his." He glanced at the savagely burned boy on the bed across the room. "And the wind was tossing fire through the air—seemed like the ground itself was burning. Then I got this leg . . . fell over old bones from last year's fight . . . a skull was right there, grinning at me. . . ."

His voice slowed and stopped. He fell into a doze and she moved on from bed to bed, bending, lifting, changing bandages, comforting, and all the time she was seeing Chase lying on the ground in the midst of hell, his hair and clothes on fire, screaming to her to help him. And next year his charred bones would lie exposed to wind and sun and rain, next year some other poor soldier would stumble over them, and so it would go year after year until every man was dead and every woman mourned.

Jewel came to her and whispered, "It's after midnight—get to bed before I take a stick to you. I don't want to deal with that child before its time."

Laura whispered back, "All right, all right, I'm going." She passed each bed slowly, hating to leave them, knowing she must; she was very tired and her back ached viciously tonight.

Nothing must jeopardize the baby, not even these tragic men, because it might well be all of Chase that was left to her.

TWO DAYS LATER, quite early, something woke her from a deep sleep. She got out of bed and padded barefoot to the window. Early as it was the breeze blowing back the curtains was hot. There was no traffic on the road, no rumble in the distance. Whatever had woken her, it was not more ambulances heading for Richmond. The struggle and the dying had not paused during these last weeks but civilians in the neighborhood had taken all the injured men they could handle and the stream of wounded was being carried home on other roads.

She leaned her elbows on the windowsill and let the warm air flow over her. Strange that she couldn't hear gunfire violating the country hush. The armies were sure to be out there somewhere tearing at each other on this last day of May. All civilians were living in ignorance these days, so close to the fighting and yet with almost no knowledge except that the Union army, in spite of bloody losses, would not quit. They assaulted Lee's army again and again, and the weary Confederates, equally stubborn, were steadily losing men. One cavalry officer had told her last week that many Yankee prisoners now were men fresh off the boat speaking with foreign accents, many babbling German or French or unidentifiable Middle European languages.

"We can't replace our men—they have all of Europe to draw on," he said. "Although," he added after a moment of reflection, "I don't know why the immigrants keep coming. Word ought to have spread by now that if you come to New York you'll be dragged into the Yankee army."

Three days ago a letter from Becca had brought bad news and was eloquent for what it didn't say. She could not be with Laura during her trouble because Doug was home, his arm torn by a minié ball, but she would come as soon as he was better for she couldn't wait to see her new niece or nephew. That was the gist of it. No mention of what a minié ball did when it tore into a human being, no mention of the amputation that such a wound usually led to or what amputation meant. There was also no mention of Edward or Kirby or Alex. Either Doug didn't know where they were or he had brought news Becca didn't want her to hear.

She turned away from the window, stripped off her nightgown and began to dress, feeling strong and optimistic, ready to face any pain that childbirth might bring. The downright drudgery of the past weeks, the grief for the five men they had buried so far, the two deaths yesterday, none of it had fazed her. So far in her life the only pain she had suffered had been of the mind and heart, not the body; childbirth meant physical discomfort but she could bear it. After all, women were designed for it.

She buttoned her basque, tucked her hair into a net, and as she did every morning examined her figure in the long mirror on her wardrobe door. She hadn't grown huge like Mary Hardin, thank God, but she looked satisfactorily pregnant. Halfway down the stairs she almost stumbled in surprise as a grinding sensation struck deep inside her. Her hand flew to the banister and she clung to it, knowing now that her own body had woken her this morning. She opened her mouth but no sound came. The pain left her breathless. She gulped in air but before she could cry out for help the world went dark.

They found her on the stairs. It was Adam who carried her to her room and placed her on the bed. She came back to consciousness to hear Jewel issuing orders like a general.

"Miss Emma, you'll have to see to the other patients the rest of this day. Bathe the right stump in what's left of that solution. I doubt the lung wound will last the day and no-legs may go anytime too, but you can't tell. Be careful with that laudanum 'cause it's close to being gone. Adam, you do whatever Miss Emma says. Run tell Elvina I need her *right now.*"

Emma scuttled away, so glad to get out of the room she didn't even resent being ordered about by Jewel, who tended to uppitiness. Emma had never borne a child, had never been around when it was happening, and didn't intend to extend her education now.

Laura's eyes fluttered open and she saw Jewel smile.

"Back in the land of the living?" Jewel sat down on the bed.

"I was thinking about us sitting out on my rock years ago, talking about men. Never thought we'd be going through this together. Lord, we were ignorant."

"Remember, some boy kissed you on the back of the neck when you were ten and you asked me, all worried, if I thought you'd have a baby. I said no, you had to swallow a watermelon seed and even then you had to be married."

Laura laughed and Jewel was relieved to see color come back into her cheeks. "Sit up a little—here, let me fix those pillows. Are you dizzy?"

"Not a bit. I don't know what came over me."

"It happens sometimes. Rest a bit and pretty soon I'll walk you around the room. You're going to keep moving today."

She walked, it seemed, miles during that morning. The pain was fierce when it came, but intermittent. It would be closer and more regular before it was over but she could stand it quite handily. By early afternoon she was not so sure.

"This is . . . this is really uncomfortable, Jewel."

"Um. It's only junior labor but don't worry, we'll get there. Elvina, come with me. Be right back, Miss Laura."

Outside in the hall Jewel whispered, "This is going to be a long haul. I wish to God I'd asked that doctor for some chloroform—I didn't think. Go see if you can help Miss Emma but don't let her send you out of the house on any errands. I want you close by if I need you."

Elvina, scared, whispered back, "I'd just as soon Miss Laura didn't do this."

"Once you start down this trail you can't decide you'd rather not and turn around. No such thing as being a little bit pregnant. Remember that, Elvina, next time Frederick drops by."

Elvina's eyes went round, wondering if there was something about being a mother that gave women the second sight. She started down the stairs with a twist of her bottom, her lower lip stuck out resentfully.

Laura heard the whispering in the hall but not the words. She recalled thinking comfortably that women were designed for childbirth, but perhaps the design had flaws. If this pain was "only junior," what lay ahead? Surely nothing could be worse.

"I heard horses come up the drive," she said as soon as Jewel returned. "Is Rufus back from Claremore?"

"Yes'm. Big battle over near the Chickahominy, started before morning and still going on."

"It seems like we ought to hear the guns . . . Chase told me once it depends on the way the wind blows." She passed a hand over her forehead in a distracted way. "I didn't expect Benjie to die, did you? I thought he was getting better. Last night he told me to go rest and got so upset about it that I did just to quiet him. When I came back he was dead. I try not to care too much but . . ."

"Come on," said Jewel. "Let's walk for a while."

By day's end the breeze cooled a little but heat had built up in the attic and all the upstairs rooms were stifling, adding to Laura's misery. Slowly through the endless night and the day that followed the pains grew fiercer and by evening she gasped, "When you said 'junior labor' I thought you were joking. How do women face this more than once?" She was standing, clinging to the bedpost while Jewel straightened the bed.

"We forget. It doesn't seem possible at the time but we do. Ask most women just a little while after they've got hold of their baby how it went and they'll say 'Oh, not so bad.' Give them a few weeks and they'll half believe it's true. Nature's way, I guess."

"What a dirty trick," Laura said with a little laugh.

"Yes, but they're worth it."

"The babies or the men?"

Jewel's mouth curved up in a smile. "Both."

Laura smiled too, and pain, the worst so far, struck with blinding force. She clung to the bedpost, swaying as if tossed by a powerful wind, clamping her lips and trying not to scream. She had promised herself not to scream. The men in nearby rooms were suffering greatly too, and some might soon be dead. They should not have to hear this.

Jewel lowered her to the bed. "Now you've gone and bit your lip all bloody. You scream if it helps. You're not going to get through this without a little noise."

Laura rocked back and forth, hugging herself. "If I ruled the world it wouldn't be like this. Babies wouldn't come with such pain, Varina's little boy wouldn't have died last month, good men wouldn't be hacked up for no reason except that someone wanted to have a splendid little war. All the disease and death in the world and for what? Where is God anyway? If He can't do a better job we ought to fire him!"

"Good for you, honey, tell Him off. We may get kicked but we don't have to say thank you."

The pain was ebbing. Very low, Laura said, "I think of Chase every minute of the day, I see his face. Is he safe, is he still alive? I want to put my arms around him and protect him and I can't."

"I know." Jewel smoothed the hair away from Laura's sweaty forehead.

Another pain struck. Laura reached out desperately for Jewel's hand and held it in a tight, twisting grip. "Do you ever think of Edward? Do you hate him?" It was a question that on this night of all nights could be asked.

"Don't think about such things, missy. It's not good for you."

"I have to know! You must hate us all, you must hate me. I should have seen, I should have done something."

"Don't talk nonsense. How could I hate you?" Jewel looked out the open balcony doors into the dark, back down the years into what her life had been. Outside the night was hot, humid, alive with creatures singing in the grass. "In the beginning I was just a little girl, really, and he was Master."

Laura turned her head away.

In a reflective voice Jewel went on. "When he let me marry Ishmael I thought . . . I had hopes of a real life, but it wasn't to be. Time went by like it always does and I got older. I began to understand things. There's a lot of good in him. He hates himself more than anybody else could— bad men do whatever they want, you know, and never doubt themselves at all. His trouble is all the power he's had. It was too much and it's just about destroyed him." After a little space of time she added softly, "I think of him. I'd bring him home safe if I could."

J EWEL WENT OUT onto the balcony. A thousand stars shone in the clear night sky. Her back ached and her legs trembled with fatigue but a sense of peace such as she had not felt in years encompassed her. In the dim lamplight of Laura's room she could see Elvina moving about quietly, tidying up. Elvina was deeply pleased with herself and was entitled to be. Although, as she had said several times, she'd never seen such a business before, she hadn't panicked even during the worst of it and might make a good midwife one day if she worked hard.

Laura's daughter had been born at ten minutes before midnight—Jewel had written down the hour as she always did—a good-sized, healthy child, already beautiful—and why not when she had such handsome parents. It had been a long labor and a hard one, but not unusually so for a first child. Jewel thought that she had never been so happy at a birth as when she watched Laura examine her child with that triumphant look on her face.

"Fingernails and toenails and eyelashes too. It doesn't seem possible but here she is. I wish I could talk to Chase about it but since I can't"—Laura kissed the damp, dark curls on the baby's head—"her name is Rosalie."

CHAPTER 29

FIVE WEEKS AFTER he came home Doug's arm was taken off just above the elbow in Byron Rollins's hilltop hospital. Becca's hasty note said that the doctor had tried his best to save it but an elbow shattered by a minié bullet was beyond the skill of medical science. She did not use the word "amputation"—somehow "taken off" seemed easier to bear—but it came to the same thing. Swamped by fear, Laura didn't even think about the loss of his arm. It was minor compared to the threat to Doug's life. Seven of the new graves at Pine Hill contained young men with missing arms or legs.

She read the letter once more, thinking of the gentle, earnest little boy Doug had been and the good man he had grown up to be. Probably she would never speak to or touch him again. She couldn't go back to Richmond with a baby in her arms and Rosalie was too tiny to leave. She wrote, telling him exactly what her circumstances were, promising to come as soon as the baby was old enough to leave behind, and in her heart said goodbye.

Then she went searching for Adam and found him in the stable where he spent every spare moment. He loved the horse and cared for it as a mother would, fed it, groomed it, cleaned its stall every day, observed and applied Rufus Nelson's veterinary techniques, and Jewel couldn't say a critical word. The horse was a treasure, the only transportation the women had. Rufus Nelson had managed to hide two geldings and a mule when the army's procurement officer confiscated all the others, but he maintained he needed them full time for the farm and Laura didn't dare challenge him. All of them were living on food the farm produced.

In recent weeks Adam had been in a noticeably odd mood, staying to himself as much as possible, following the war news on the maps Edward had given him with close attention, maps worn from much folding and refolding. Jewel said, "He thinks he knows so much and he hasn't got a notion what it's like for colored folks outside this family. I've told him and told him but he won't listen and he's too big to use a switch on." She didn't quite say it but Laura knew her fear was that some morning they would wake to find him gone. The thing to do was keep him occupied.

She gave him the letter to Doug. "Take it straight to the hospital, then stop by the house with the vegetables. Tell Miss Millie I'll see her soon."

"She's gonna ask me what's soon, Miss Laura."

"Say before the end of summer. Tell her I'll write."

She sat on the low fence rail watching while he loaded the wagon. As he climbed onto the seat she said, "I don't know what we'd do without you, Adam."

His old grin flashed. "Me neither."

He slapped the reins and she called after him, "Stop by the house and say goodbye to your mama."

He didn't look back but lifted his hand and waved.

She walked down to the river, thinking how knowledgeable she had once believed herself to be and how little she had understood about herself, the world, and what was really important. Like Adam, she had thought she knew it all. Carrying a child and bearing it alone, looking into her daughter's face for the first time, had given her a glimpse of how much she still had to learn. Every day Rosalie taught her something new. From her she had already learned what it was to love in a way almost impossible between adults no matter how dear—a desire to give, always, rather than take, a fierce need to protect, and since nothing was ever unalloyed joy, a willingness to accept pain in the process of loving. Now she understood Jewel's fear for Adam with her heart as well as her mind because her own desire to protect Rosalie was so intense.

Whenever she looked at her child she was stunned, astonished, overwhelmed by love. In her arms was an entirely new person, a miracle, the product surely of something more than the joining of her two parents. She loved to kiss the soft indentation in the baby's neck and smell the sweetness of her skin, she loved the silky round arms and legs and the revelations that each day brought. Jewel thought Rosalie's mouth and chin were very like Laura's and they both agreed that her eyes were turning dark. Chase's eyes were dark and wide-set too. Her nose was still a question and that was the excitement of it—every day brought changes that Laura would miss if she went to Richmond even for a short stay.

Two letters came from Becca during July, each one opened with apprehension so great that her hands trembled but each one bringing encouraging news. Either Byron Rollins was as good a doctor as he thought he was or Doug had been blessed by Fortune, for at the end of the month came a third letter saying he was still in the hospital but healing well. The letter also brought the happy news that Kirby was home, in good health and expected to be in town for at least a week. That afternoon Laura went to see Mary Hardin.

"It would mean living at Pine Hill while I'm gone but you'd have help with your own children. Would you consider it and let me know?"

Mary was standing at the window looking down the path to the road as if she were expecting someone. She stood there, just looking, whenever she had a free moment. No word of her husband had come since the battle of Chickamauga last September. It seemed he could have found a way to get a letter to her in the time since then, but maybe not. His name had never appeared on a casualty list and she placed her hope in that.

"It's not a lot to ask and I don't want to be paid. Help with the chirren is enough." Mary turned away from the window. Her thin, angular face was pretty when she smiled. "You ought to go see your brothers, for God only knows . . . You go. I've got plenty after my own is done. I'll be glad to feed the little thing."

In Laura's world it was commonplace for other women, usually slaves, to nurse the babies of the family, but she went home low in her mind. She felt driven to go to Rich-

mond. Doug was recovering so well that he might even
have to go back to the army; the Confederacy, desperate for
replacements for their thinning ranks, were dragging in
many men with severe mutilations. And it could be her last
chance to see Kirby. If she went it meant not only giving up
nursing the baby but bathing and cuddling and watching
her grow. No one else could love her as much or be quite
as careful with her, and yet in war so much that was good
was lost; she would have to give up a little of her baby in
order to see her brothers, perhaps for the last time.

B YRON ROLLINS'S HOSPITAL was not the fresh,
clean place it once had been. The wards were crammed
with beds and the sick and injured could be found almost
anywhere—in hallways, cubicles once meant for offices, any
space with four walls and a roof. Nurses were of all descrip-
tions, farm women and society women working side by
side through the long hours, men too old to serve in the
army but determined to help, convalescent soldiers still
unfit for active service but able to do light chores. The
wards smelled of sickness and the distinctive odor of gangrene was pervasive. Even here high above the river the
smothering heat made sick men worse and all windows and
doors stood open to catch the breeze that usually rose as
evening came on.

Outside the air was a little cooler. They had told her
Captain Seymour could probably be found near the pas-
ture; he liked to go out there at the end of the day. She
walked down the path. He was there sitting on one of Dr.
Rollins's strategically placed benches. In the quiet her footsteps were loud on the gravel but he didn't move or look
around.

"Doug?"

At her voice he turned and light came into his face.
"Well," he said slowly, starting to rise. "Laura."

"Don't get up, just let me hug you."

He was shockingly thin, he looked forty, not twenty-
seven, one sleeve was empty and his bright hair had dulled,
but he was here, he was alive, and his somber face had
broken into a smile at the sight of her. She sat beside him
on the bench and they talked for almost an hour, picking

up the threads of their lives as if they had been separated only days, not years.

He said, "Have you seen my boy?"

"I saw him the minute he was born. He's like you"— Doug screwed up his face—"or don't you think so?"

"He may look like me but I'll try to teach him to be smarter. This war was a mistake, Laura. I don't plan to be patriotic ever again."

On the other side of the split-rail fence a cow wandered up and gazed at them with large sad eyes. Laura smiled. "What do you suppose she's thinking?"

"Probably 'Look at that damn fool who was going to be a hero. Better to be a cow.' "

"As long as no one decides to eat her. We're living mostly on vegetables at Pine Hill and lucky to have them."

"I just might eat her if I had the chance. I've almost forgotten what beef tastes like. Remember the thick, juicy roasts and the pork chops and the hams—we took them for granted, we took every damned thing for granted and now we have to pay. I never dreamed I'd hand on such a world to my children."

"Neither did I."

They looked at each other. He said, "Tell me about Rosalie."

"She's beautiful, she's perfect, I don't know how I lived without her so long. Do you think less of me, Doug? Are you shocked?"

"I worry for you—what will happen to you, how you'll manage, but . . . I've seen things, Laura, and I've done things I can't tell you or anyone. I'll never judge another human soul again because I'm not fit to, nobody is. I won't even judge him although if I ever meet up with him—well, never mind. Have you heard from him? Does he know?"

"There's no way to let him know. But when the war is over . . . 'When the war is over' . . . doesn't that have a ring to it? When it's over he'll come back."

There was love and pity in his eyes, she could see it, but Doug didn't know him as she did. He had said he would come back and he would. If he were alive.

She said, "You mustn't worry—Rosalie and I are doing very well. Tell me about Kirby. He's at the house, at least he was this afternoon. All the time I was with him I had the oddest feeling . . . as if I were talking to a complete stranger."

"You were. War changes everybody, it changed me, but Kirby—we managed to stay together most of the time but even I don't know what all's happened to him. The thing is, Laura, two people can go through pretty much the same experience and come out different. I think at bottom I'm just older and tireder. Kirby . . ."—he hesitated, either groping for words or reluctant to say them—"Kirby isn't like he was and I don't think he ever will be again."

D ESPERATION HAD TAKEN final hold in Richmond, she could sense it in the clamorous streets, feel it in the air. Just a few miles south, the Yankee army was besieging the little town of Petersburg and everyone knew that Petersburg was the key to Richmond, everyone knew that the Confederacy was now surrounded.

As always, the heat of August fell with the subtlety of a sledgehammer, but this year, with the capital faced by imminent capture, it went almost unnoticed. People on the street wore makeshift, ragged clothing and many were carrying to the auction houses family heirlooms stubbornly held onto all through the hard years. Confederate money was close to worthless, it took bundles of paper dollars to buy even a few potatoes, and anything that could be turned into cash had to go, sentiment be damned.

There were soldiers who had forgotten why they were fighting, who stayed with General Lee only because they didn't know what else to do. Others knew exactly what to do; they deserted. Lee's ranks, holding the breastworks before Petersburg, thinned daily as more and more men went home to desperate, starving families and tried to begin life anew. The politicians, with their world crashing around them, were preparing to hold out to the last and go down with colors flying, all except Jefferson Davis who did not intend to go down at all. With every passing day he sank deeper into his private dream, insisting that Richmond would hold forever and the Confederacy ultimately prevail. Some of the men closest to him quietly expressed doubts about his sanity.

On the porch of the Executive Mansion Laura hesitated, not wanting to go in, knowing she must. Inside the hushed house there was a pervasive sense of dread and depression. No couriers dashed in with dispatches, no servants bustled through the halls preparing for official entertainments, and if the children were at home they were very quiet in their play. Grief added to the air of despair. Varina had lost little five-year-old Joe in April, only two months later she had borne another daughter, and in the midst of her personal travail the cause she had given her heart to was collapsing. Unlike her husband she was too realistic not to know it.

She came down the stairs with a smile but in the months since Laura had seen her she had aged years. "Come up to the nursery," she said. "The first thing you must do is meet my new little rosebud. We named her Varina Anne but everyone calls her Winnie, everyone but me. I call her Piecake."

Laura took the baby from the nurse and held her with newfound expertness. "Ah, she's adorable, Varina. You must be so proud."

"Proud of her but not so proud as I used to be about a lot of other things. It's been kicked out of me. I've listened to the dead march so many times in the last years but I tell you, Laura, I never expected to hear it for my little boy. Ladies call—I had to lose my child for some people to decide to like me—but they won't let me talk about my Joe." She took the baby and handed her back to the nurse. "I suppose they think they're being kind."

Laura had been told all the horrifying details. She said, "I've only heard he fell. Do you want to tell me how it happened?"

Varina moved to the window overlooking the back garden and stood looking down at the long portico with the wrought-iron railing that ran the entire width of the building. The land dropped sharply away from the street and here at the rear of the house one could step out onto the portico from the first-floor rooms and still be fifteen feet above the ground. As Laura had heard the story, Catherine, the children's Irish nurse, had taken her eyes off Joe for too long; Varina had said she didn't blame her but two days later Catherine had been replaced.

"Banny hadn't been well—he couldn't sleep and sometimes forgot to eat so I had been taking his lunch to his office. The children were playing inside but Joe went out on the balcony. He climbed onto the banister and . . . and slipped." She pointed. "Down there. It's so high and the brick path is just below. Catherine loved him, of course. Everybody did, you know, especially Banny. For a while it seemed to unhinge his mind."

This woman, "Queen Varina," some called her, had outraged people with her ostentation, her pride, her loudly voiced opinions, her influence over her husband. At this moment she was only a mother bearing sorrow as best she could.

Laura said gently, "Is the President still so ill?"

"He rides every day and I read to him at night. It helps him sleep but still he's so tired. He says we will win even if we have to take to the hills and as you know he is a military genius, but it looks very dark to me. There are so many dead and we have only old men and little boys to replace them. Those devils are still battering away at us. If Petersburg falls . . ."—Varina looked around distractedly—"I don't know . . . I just don't know. Yes, Frederick, what is it?"

Frederick still managed to appear dapper even though the uniform Varina had given him was now shabby and worn. "Madam, a message for Mrs. Chandler." He bowed before Laura with a look in his eyes that caused a chill to prickle up her spine. "Mrs. Seymour says come home immediately. It's your brother, ma'am, Mr. Kirby."

K IRBY HAD GONE OUT that afternoon on a private mission. The naïve and eager boy Laura had watched walk away from the house almost two years ago had died at Gettysburg, and in his place was a cold-eyed man, a killer like all combat soldiers, who intended to outlast the war and unlike Doug had no regrets over what he had done to survive. One of the many realities war had taught him was to keep his own counsel. He never mentioned his actions or revealed his thoughts to anyone.

His plan was to buy a sidearm to replace the one with the broken firing pin, then play monte at one of the better gambling hells, get thoroughly drunk and end the evening upstairs with a good-looking whore. But first he had to find a pawnshop. He had considerable cash on him but a fine handgun would cost plenty and this was going to be a prodigious, monumental, rip-roaring evening; he needed more money to finance it. The cash he had found in the pockets of dead Yankees. The rings and pocket watches, all solid gold, were from the same source, as were the boots on his feet and the warm coat back at the house that would help him through the coming winter. Confederates always stripped Yankee bodies after a battle if they could get to them—the unlucky suckers were their only source for supplies—but even though in their minds war justified almost anything, many balked at taking jewelry from the dead and those who did sometimes felt a momentary twinge of guilt as they tore rings from stiff fingers. Kirby felt nothing at all. He had done so much that was worse than taking jewelry that he'd had to stop feeling in order not to go mad.

The pawnshop owner, a nervous little man who constantly rubbed his hands together as if he were washing them, bargained hard over the five watches and the dozen rings. He offered more for the six rings that had small diamonds in them and when Kirby left the shop he was satisfied. At the gun shop, across the street from the Exchange Hotel, he saw the handgun he wanted the moment he looked in the case, an English double-action revolver that could be fired accurately and rapidly by the trigger action alone. It cost more than he wanted to pay but since it might one day save his life he handed over the cash and loaded it before he left the shop. There was no reason to carry a gun unless it was ready to use and no telling when you might need to. He stuck it in his belt, feeling properly dressed now, and walked across the street to the hotel.

As always in high summer the town was somnolent during the heat of the day and the lobby was hushed and empty except for the clerk behind the desk. But liquor could be had and Kirby took his drink and headed toward the back of the room.

"Kirby Seymour! Well, I just can't believe it."

He turned and there was Valerie Hood, luscious, lascivious Valerie, looking like a welcoming goddess. There had been many women for Kirby since her, most of them whores of one degree or another, but none like her.

"Mrs. Hood." His eyes crinkled in the boyish smile he had learned women loved. "Valerie."

She came closer, extended her hand, and as he bowed he allowed his lips to touch it, then turned it over and kissed her fingertips.

"My goodness," she murmured huskily, "how I've missed you."

They found a table in the darkest corner of the room and she sat down gracefully, saying, "No, I don't want a thing but please do have your drink and catch me up on what you've been doing."

He lifted his glass to her, took a swallow and said with a smile, "Killing people. What have you been doing?"

Her eyes widened a little. His smile was so sweet, his words so blunt, but then he had always been unpredictable.

"Oh, uh, this and that. Nothing to speak of. Everything is so dreadful now, hopeless really. I don't have any expectation of good things."

"You're right. They've beaten us and we're just too stupid to give up." His voice softened. "But I can think of a few good things in the immediate future if you'd care to join me upstairs."

They were sitting together on a leather-covered bench and he had moved so close that only inches separated their lips. She leaned toward him and he kissed her, slowly and then with increasing passion, his hand caressing her face in such a way that her bonnet was pushed to one side and hairpins fell from her hair.

He pulled away just a little and whispered, "Delicious." In the next instant he was jerked up by the collar and dragged away from her as the table crashed over. He whipped around, his hand going instinctively to the gun in his belt, and looked into Jason Hood's deadly eyes.

Valerie had been thrown to the floor as the table went over and she scrambled up and backed against the velvet hangings that covered the wall as if she would like to hide herself in them. "Jason, I can explain . . ."

He didn't take his eyes from Kirby's face. "My seconds will call."

"Go to hell, Hood. I don't fight duels."

For an instant Jason seemed confounded. No man had ever before refused to face him. Then, with contempt he said, "You can't refuse, boy, and if you do—"

His hand appeared to move toward his coat. Kirby pulled his gun, fired twice in rapid succession and Jason flew backward as if punched by a powerful blow. Valerie screamed and the desk clerk dived behind the front counter, waited, and when there was no more firing crawled out and got to his feet. The hotel's janitor, a small elderly black man, came from the back room with his broom held out like a weapon and together he and the clerk approached cautiously. Jason was sprawled out, his head thrown back, his mouth open. His tall hat had slid across the floor and come to rest against a spittoon.

The janitor said, "Look like he daid."

The clerk felt for a pulse. "I think so but we'd better get a doctor all the same." He looked up, met Kirby's eyes and immediately looked down again. The gun was back in the young man's belt but in his present unpleasant mood he might take it out again. These days soldiers were capable of anything.

Valerie had sunk down on the floor again and was rocking back and forth moaning softly, her hands covering her eyes, her bonnet tilted drunkenly over one ear.

"See to it that Mrs. Hood gets home," Kirby said to the clerk. "Goodbye, Valerie."

The clerk's eyes followed him as he strode out to the street.

The janitor watched too. "Does we have to call de police?"

"You go for the doctor and I'll find someone to take the lady home." The clerk looked at Jason, his coat flung open, his waistcoat and white frilled shirt stained bright crimson. "Then I'll call the police."

L AURA SAT ON THE bed watching Kirby pack his few possessions, wishing she could load him down with blankets, warm clothing, and all the food in the pantry. But he said he preferred to travel light and she knew he was right.

When she raced into the house and discovered that he wasn't dead in some insane accident, relief was so great that at first she hadn't grasped just how much trouble he was in. Then reality fell on her. He had killed the undersecretary of war, a man with powerful connections if few true friends, after being caught in compromising circumstances with the man's wife. He had fought no duel, which would have been perfectly acceptable, but instead had simply killed before he could be shot, which might be counted as self-defense but more likely as murder. Jason hadn't quite pulled out his pistol—he didn't have time—and he had been, one could say, defending his home. Almost all gentlemen believed in the right of a husband to kill any man who made improper overtures to his wife (although wives were not accorded the same privilege.) In any case, murder was still punished by hanging in Richmond.

Laura's first thought when she heard that Jason was dead had been *Now that snake can't kill any more good men.* Then all her protective instincts rose up. "Get out of town, Kirby, don't waste a minute. Go back to the army as fast as you can. They need men too much to ask questions."

He raised an ironical eyebrow. "You think I'm in less danger fighting Yankees?"

"Maybe, for the time being. Just go and we'll let you know when it's safe to come back. If Richmond falls—"

"When Richmond falls."

"All right, when it falls maybe all the records will be destroyed, maybe . . . well, God knows what will happen. They'll be so busy they'll forget about you."

He touched her cheek with one finger. "My sweet sister. You haven't even told me what a fool I am."

"As far as I'm concerned that man's death was overdue and richly deserved. I'm sorry you're in trouble but I'm glad you had sense enough not to fight a duel. He'd have killed you sure."

"Oh, I learned a long time ago never to give the other fellow a crack at you if you can help it. There are no fair fights, Laura, just winners and losers, and I don't propose to be one of the losers. Give me a kiss goodbye, sweetie."

She watched him slip quietly out the back way, so devastated that she could scarcely think.

It was a miserable evening. Paige refused to eat and went to bed early with a sick headache. Immediately after dinner Becca went upstairs to put little William to bed, leaving Laura and Millie together in the front parlor, the only one they used now, reluctant to say good night and face their thoughts alone.

The doors stood open to the normal scents and sounds of a Southern summer night—the fragrance of roses still stubbornly blooming in spite of neglect, the cries of night birds in the dark trees, the singing of insects in the grass. And, loud in the imagination, the boom of the great guns just beyond their hearing, crashing constantly, eternal as ocean waves, killing everything they cared about. There was so much they could not say to each other, these two who were sometimes like mother and daughter, sometimes like sisters, and yet they understood each other very well.

Into the silence Millie said, "There's something I must tell you . . ." and Laura's heart sank. What new catastrophe was falling on them? Millie smiled a little. "Don't look like that—it's not so terrible. Just the usual thing these days. Bella went to town yesterday afternoon. She hasn't come home. I believe she's run away."

Bella gone? Not only Millie's maid since childhood, but her confidante, her friend. How could such a thing be? "Are you sure? Maybe something's happened to her, maybe we should—"

"Joseph scoured the town all morning, talked to her friends—the ones who are still left—she wasn't in any of the usual places. He even checked at the jail, isn't that ridiculous . . . imagine my Bella in jail! No, she's gone to the Yanks, I know it. Every dress in my wardrobe is clean and mended, all the darning done. She plaited a new hat for me from palmetto—it's decorated with dyed chicken feathers and new ribbons, very pretty. Lord knows where she got those ribbons. She even left my bed with fresh sheets so I won't have to change it for a while. Wasn't that thoughtful!" Millie put her hands to her temples as if they ached.

"I'm so sorry, Millie. I know how you'll miss her. Strange, Bella gone and Joseph, of all people, still here. I expected he'd be the first to take off."

"Oh, him." Millie shrugged. "He can go anytime and I won't care. But Bella . . . Oh, I do worry for Bella."

Proper, respectable, devoted Bella a runaway to freedom. Laura thought, I'd be less surprised if it were Jewel. And maybe someday she will go too.

CHAPTER 30

ALEX AND EDWARD HAD been together through most of the recent fighting, part of the few troops committed to defending this section of the line. The day was burning hot and so humid that although the sun was barely up Alex's shirt was soaked and clinging. They were coming again, the bastards, with their damned bands and bugles, even though blazing artillery fire the day before had broken their charge and driven them off—rather remarkable since the artillery rarely seemed to do anything right. But Yankees never gave up—nothing you could do discouraged them and an entire brigade of scared Confederates, trying to stay alive, were running to the rear in the face of this new onslaught.

Alex mounted his horse and glanced around swiftly. Edward was not in sight. He drew his pistol and with other officers shouted the standard rallying cries, orders, and threats.

"All right, men, to the flag and forward! Goddammit, color-bearer, pick up that banner! Back in line, back in line—I'll shoot the first man who runs!" About as much use as trying to stop a hurricane by blowing on it, he thought, waving his pistol. They were less afraid of him than of the Yankees. Crowds of panicked soldiers rolled toward him, parted around his rearing horse like stampeding cattle and hurtled past, determined to save their own lives if nothing else.

He rode toward General Field and shouted, "We can't turn them around, sir!"

"I don't understand it. They're Hill's men, brave men. Well, nothing to do but fall back until we get reinforcements—I'm told there may be forty thousand Yanks out there. Wyatt, you bring up Law's Alabama and Binning's Georgians and then we'll give them a tussle!"

Alex wheeled his horse, slammed in his heels, and leaped off at full gallop. Just over the ridge was Law's brigade and Binning's lining up behind. His little horse stumbled, regained its stride, and then suddenly was down, shrieking in pain; it had taken a ball in the chest from a panic-stricken Confederate running to safety who had glanced back and seen a horseman bearing down on him.

Alex was thrown from the saddle and landed hard. When he came back to consciousness he was in a field hospital tent. "Lie still, sir. You took a bad bump."

Gingerly, Alex touched his head and tried to sit up. "Feels as big as the earth."

"Yes, sir. A stroke of good fortune. You'll be going back to Richmond in the next ambulance." Lieutenant Hatch, temporarily the general's aide since the adjutant was killed, lowered Alex to the cot.

Alex pushed away his hand and tried again to sit up. "Ambulance, hell," he said, "I've got . . ." and the world went black.

AMBULANCES WERE ANY VEHICLE that came to hand—wagons, carts, drays—few with springs of any kind, the best cruelly uncomfortable, most giving such a painful, jolting ride on the rutted roads that injured men screamed in pain and those who did not faint often begged to be left on the roadside rather than go on.

Alex said several times that he wanted to get out and then began to tell the others about his beautiful wife and young son. "Big, healthy boy—named after me," he announced distinctly. "You all never saw such a fine baby."

Lieutenant Hatch, returning to Richmond with dispatches, murmured to the driver, "His boy only lived a day. He never saw him."

The driver shook his head. "Damn shame." A man in the back of the wagon moaned loudly and he added, "The whole shitty war is a damn shame."

The two of them, the only whole men in the ambulance, began to talk about what they would do when they got to the city to shut out the sounds of suffering behind them.

They once again became aware of Alex when behind them he said in a tone that did not allow for disagreement, "Stop this goddamned go-cart and let me out."

They turned. Lieutenant Hatch looked into the iron face of his superior officer, apparently in full control of his faculties, giving him a direct order with a gun pointed at his chest. "Stop the wagon," he muttered to the driver, who gladly hauled on the reins. He, unlike Lieutenant Hatch, had seen many injured men go completely crazy and do horrendous deeds. He wanted no part of this colonel with the wild look and the loaded gun.

They lurched to a sudden stop. Alex climbed out and waved his pistol. "Many thanks. Now get the hell out of here. I'm going to walk."

The wagon moved off with a jolt and he strode purposefully down the road, passing other walking wounded making their way back to Richmond, but when he saw a flat boulder a little distance off the road he stumbled to it over the rough ground and sat down. Aloud he said, "Paige, I'm home and I'm not going back—you don't have to worry anymore," and slid backward into the weeds behind the rock.

JOSEPH LISTENED TO THE young officer at the door, allowed him to step into the entrance hall, and then hurried to the member of the family he considered to have the most sense.

"He say he lef' Mistah Alex by de side of de road but it been two days an' he ought to be here by now."

Laura said, "Don't tell Miss Paige until I talk to this man," and hurried down the stairs.

Lieutenant Hatch's ruddy young face wore a look of strain. In addition to the awful suspicion that he had made a mistake of gigantic proportions that could bring him a great deal of trouble, he honestly liked Colonel Wyatt or, rather, respected him as a competent officer who took good care of his men. For both reasons he was concerned for Alex's safety. When a pretty young woman came rushing toward him, her hands clasped tight and her eyes wide with anxiety, he assumed she must be the colonel's wife.

"Mrs. Wyatt—" he began, wondering how in hell he was going to explain this to her, and she cut him off.

"I'm Mrs. Wyatt's aunt. What happened? Why didn't he come into town with you?"

"Ma'am, his horse was shot from under him and he sustained a sharp blow to the head. Our ambulances are, well, not the most comfortable and only a few miles out of town he insisted on getting out. Said he wanted to walk."

"To walk?" Laura looked stunned. "How bad is his wound, Lieutenant? Tell me the truth because I'm going to have to tell Mrs. Wyatt."

"Well, ma'am, there was a fairly deep gash"—palm flat he drew a line across the back of his head—"here. I think he must have struck a rock. We took him to the field hospital but the doctors were very busy." At the expression on her face he went on quickly. "Men were bleeding to death, you see. One doctor took a look and said he might have a brain concussion or some other damage—he'd been unconscious for quite some time. So the doctor said bring him to Richmond and see what the hospital here can do for him."

"And you let him get out and walk."

Her eyes were pale as clear water and at the moment expressionless but her tone said everything. Lieutenant Hatch squirmed inwardly. "He ordered us at gunpoint, ma'am. Looking back, I fear I made the wrong decision."

Her gaze went past him. "Yes," she whispered, "yes." Then, "Take me to the spot where you last saw him."

"I've already looked but found nothing. I regret I can't do more but I am ordered to report to General Field immediately. I carry a message from the President."

And what a treasure the President's advice will be, Laura thought bitterly. She said, "Then tell me, if you can take the time, what road you were on, how far out of town you were, and any landmarks you can remember."

L AURA AND PAIGE were not the only civilians searching along the road for those they loved. People in carriages, landaus, buggies, and wagons who still possessed a horse to pull them came out from the city in great numbers after each battle, toiling through a swirling, erratic tide of traffic moving both toward and away from the battlefield.

Laura slowed the Seymour carriage as a few bedraggled, exhausted soldiers hobbled toward them. Paige clutched her arm. "For pity's sake, can't you drive faster? Those men don't look so bad hurt. Just bear down on them and they'll scatter." Her jaw was clenched and she spoke in quick little gasps.

The carriage lurched as it rolled into a deep rut. "Let go of me, Paige, before we turn over. I'd be glad to run over those men for you except we'd end up in a ditch and be stranded out here. We can't do Alex much good if we are." Paige snatched back her hand as if she'd been stung and Laura's lips turned down in grim amusement. Sarcasm had no more effect on Paige then appeals to common sense but mention Alex and she would agree to anything.

Millie had been right. It was madness for them to come out here alone in this big clumsy carriage pulled by two half-starved, temperamental horses when she was used to handling only her buggy and the docile mare, but the coachman, Enoch, had not been in the stable, and Paige refused to wait. Laura knew they were considerably farther out of town than seven miles, the distance Lieutenant Hatch had given her as a guide. She pulled to the side of the road.

"Keep going, keep going!" Paige muttered in wild anxiety. She tried to grab the reins and the horses danced nervously.

"Try that again," said Laura in a hard voice, "and I'll slap you silly. We'll be wasting time if we go any farther. We've already passed the spot where they let him out. He was heading toward town."

"But he was hurt! He could have got confused, he could have headed the wrong way." Her eyes begged to be told that it wasn't true, that solutions were simple, Alex would be found well and safe, the worst could not happen, not to her.

There was not a sign of sympathy from Laura. "That's right, he could have headed back to the battlefield or he could have wandered in that direction or over there." She pointed to the fields, brambles, and dark stands of trees on either side of the road. "He could be anywhere, Paige. *We don't know.* So we have to choose the most likely places, we have to do the best we can."

She waited until the traffic thinned a little and began to turn the carriage, a difficult maneuver that took an eye for distance and precise control of the horses, and for a panicked moment she thought they were going to roll off the road into the ditch.

A group of mounted men came in sight just at the instant the carriage completely blocked the road. There were shouts and orders to clear the way and she muttered between clenched teeth, "They can goddamn well wait," causing Paige to stare in astonishment.

The horses shied in confusion. She battled them into obedience, and then they were around, too close to the edge of the road for comfort but headed in the direction of the city. The cavalry flowed past in a cloud of dust.

Laura said, "Now—" She stopped to catch her breath. "Now we drive as slow as they'll let us. You watch on the left, I'll watch on this side. If we see anything at all we'll get out and look."

IT WAS GROWING DARK. They had stopped many times, and Paige had finally fallen silent, her hands knotted and her knuckles white. Off the road, on a stretch of level ground, the shape of a large canvas-covered wagon loomed in the twilight. An ambulance. The driver was standing beside the horses, smoking.

Laura pulled up beside him. "Please, would you help me?" She scrambled to the ground before he could turn away. "I only need information. We're searching for an injured soldier . . ." Another man came out of the brush, buttoning his pants. He climbed on the wagon seat and she directed her appeal to him. "Wyatt is his name, Colonel Alex Wyatt, with General Field's division. We're told he had a head wound and got out of an ambulance somewhere around here."

"Sometimes they do that, ma'am—these old wagons give a rough ride. I never heard of any Colonel Wyatt."

Paige climbed down and hurried over to him. "He's a very handsome man, sir. You couldn't forget him if you saw

him. Dark blue eyes and curly brown hair . . . his head may
be bandaged."

He looked at her, not unkindly but with great fatigue in
his face. "Every so often we find 'em beside the road and
bury 'em. Or it could be he made it into town."

The other man, silent all this time, dropped the tiny butt
of his cigar in the dirt and ground it out. "You check with
the hospitals before you give up." He climbed on the seat,
lifted his hat and gave the horses a smart slap of the reins.
The ambulance moved off with a lurch, leaving them
standing in the settling dust.

Laura took Paige by the hand and said, "Let's go
home."

THEY SPENT A WEEK searching the city's hospitals
and put a notice in every newspaper asking if some private home had taken in a patient answering Colonel
Wyatt's description; long columns of such desperate notices
appeared in the papers every day.

The week went by and there was no word. At the end of
the second week Byron Rollins took time from his hospital
to come to the house. When he saw Laura his eyes brightened momentarily and he almost smiled. Then he turned to
Paige.

"Honey," he said, and Laura's heart sank—Byron never
called anyone "honey." "My news isn't good. One of my
patients, Captain Greenfield, said he was in an ambulance
that stopped to bury an officer found by the side of the
road. He said it was Alex—" Except for a quick inhalation
of breath Paige made no sound. "He served under Alex and
knew him well."

Millie braced herself to catch Paige if she fainted but she
did not and there was only a slight tremor in her voice.

"Where is he buried?"

"Apparently there were no particular landmarks. Perhaps
five miles out of town. I'm sorry I can't tell you more but
young Greenfield took a turn for the worse and died this
afternoon."

"The ambulance driver . . ."

"I'll make inquiries, but I don't know his name."

In the silence the ticktock of the hall clock fell like repeated hammer blows.

"Well. Thank you, Doctor, for taking—taking the trouble."

"Not at all, dear girl."

She went into the hall and up the stairs, her shoulders squared, her slight body straight, almost rigid. At the top of the flight she paused, her hand on the newel post, then went on to her room and closed the door.

CHAPTER 31

THEY SEARCHED BUT NEVER found the grave. As the days went by Paige grew a little paler, a little thinner, but she downed at least a portion of every meal and came to the kitchen to watch while Cookie stirred her dresses in the dye pot. She had wanted to look her best if Alex should come home unexpectedly and so had not worn mourning for her child, but now she said that black became her. She received condolence callers, she made plans for the future, she even talked of going back to nursing at the hospital, all healthy signs.

Laura agreed with this cheering opinion, kept her real thoughts to herself, and watched her niece with worried eyes. To her Paige's thin sweet face was a mask and every smile, every word, intended to deceive. The fate of Sarah Cunningham came often to her mind. Sarah was a vivacious Charleston girl, a distant cousin of the Seymours, who had taken her husband's death as bravely as Paige. She had received callers, talked philosophically of her loss, and one day smilingly said goodbye to her visitors, closed the door and hanged herself.

Byron Rollins visited and gave an optimistic report, but shortly after Laura remarked casually that Paige needed company and perhaps, for a while, should not be left alone. Millie instantly agreed and the flash of fear in her eyes, swiftly hidden, said louder than any words that she was thinking of Sarah too.

To Mary Hardin, Laura wrote:

"Things are so sad just now and my family so alone that I can't come back yet. Would you be willing to come to Richmond with the children? You could leave word at the post office in Claremore that your husband can reach you here. I would be forever grateful."

Her letter to Jewel was more blunt:

"We are in a desperate pass, afraid to leave Paige for a moment. Becca is working ten to twelve hours a day, five days a week at the hospital but helps on her days off. Of the staff only Joseph and Enoch are left. Cookie went to the market one morning and didn't come back. We haven't seen her since and don't expect to. You would laugh to see Millie and me in the kitchen crashing about, trying to produce meals. And we keep William with us whatever we're doing—afraid to leave him alone for a second, God help us. I hope Byron Rollins is right and we are starting at shadows but he doesn't know Paige the way we do.

"As for me, I miss Rosalie so much I ache even in my sleep. We have few visitors so it's possible no one will even know there's another baby in the house, or if Mary comes they may believe it's hers. I no longer care. Please come, bring Rosalie, Adam and Elvina, and Mary and the children if she will do it. Rather than trust to the crazy postal service I am sending this with Joseph. Enoch is too old and frail now to make the trip and I figure the chance to see you will outweigh even the attraction of freedom!"

T HE WHITE FOLKS, as Joseph thought of his owners, were fools to turn him loose with two fine horses and a first-class carriage that would bring big money in Washington City. But he wasn't going to sell them, he was going to set up a chauffeuring business. After he picked his way around the part of the country where those dumb white men were shooting each other, he could get up to Washington in a couple or three days and be hauling in money by the end of the week. First, however, he was going to Pine Hill and get Jewel.

He drove horses well, he thought, considering it wasn't his speciality, and he negotiated the heavily trafficked roads with relative ease, only twice required to show the pass Miss

Laura had given him. He reached the cutoff to Pine Hill at twilight and drove the rest of the way in the dark.

Light from a lamp in a back window fell across the yard. Joseph peeked in. It was the kitchen and that girl, Elvina, was rocking by the banked fire with a sleek cat in her lap. She was pretty enough—he liked deep dimples and fine breasts and believed he had been getting somewhere with her until she went to live with Miss Laura—but she was not Jewel. Jewel was perfection.

The door was unlocked. He went in.

Elvina leaped to her feet with fear in her eyes and the cat jumped from her lap and flew out of the room as if demons were after it.

"What . . . Joseph? Oh, Lordy, you gave me a scare! I thought you was the Yankees."

"Yankees'll come in louder'n that. You gonna know when they coming." He shut the door and smiled his most seductive smile. "How is you doing, little lamb? Been missing me?"

Elvina scowled. "You're full of wind, Joseph. What you doin' here?" Her eyes sharpened. "Something wrong at home?"

"Yes, ma'am, plenty. I got to talk to Jewel. Well, make tracks, girl!"

Elvina knew Joseph for what he was but when he spoke in his butler's voice she moved. He heard her footsteps pattering on the stairs and in less time than he expected Jewel was standing in the doorway gazing at him in all her grace and beauty. She was wearing an old flannel wrapper which did not conceal her splendid figure and her glossy black hair was as he had glimpsed it only a few times before, hanging loose below her shoulders. It was her white blood that gave her that soft, wavy hair. The sight made him want to smash something.

He took off his hat. "Evenin', Jewel. Fine hot weather we been having."

"You got a message, you give it to me, Joseph."

He came closer. "Ain't you even gonna say you's glad to see me?"

She gave him a cold stare. "The message, Joseph."

He fumbled in his pocket, pulled out two badly crumpled envelopes, and she snatched them from him.

He leaned forward to peer at them. Jewel doubted he could read but for safety's sake put Mary Hardin's letter in her own pocket and moved to the lamp to read the one addressed to her.

He followed, hat in hand, and she muttered fiercely, "Back off!"

When he retreated to a point that satisfied her, she smoothed the wrinkled paper on the lamp table and read it swiftly.

"Elvina," she said in her general's voice, "we're going home tomorrow. Here, give this to Mrs. Hardin—yes, wake her if you have to."

Elvina raced from the room and once again Joseph heard her quick, obedient footsteps on the stairs. The sound enraged him. "You two is the best little slaves I ever did see. Don't you know you doesn't have to do what the white folks says no more?"

"Yes, I heard that," Jewel said absently. "You can sleep in the barn, Joseph, and be up by sunrise. I want to get an early start."

At her ignorance, her grand ways, her disregard of his manhood, his rage boiled over. He was big and had always used his size to intimidate. He came close and breathed in her ear, "You a fool, Jewel, but this time you ain' gonna do what the fine lady says, you gonna come with me. We goin' to Washington City. I'm gonna make you lots of money, big money driving rich white folks dyin' to swank around town. I got a carriage, I got two horses, and I brought along my livery that looks just as high-toned as a chaffeur's uniform. *Look at me!* I'm a fine-lookin' man, honey, I'm strong, I can pertec' you. You gonna leave this place behind an' come with me."

She looked into his eyes. He was handsome, physically powerful, black as Ishmael had been, capable of taking care of her. She whispered, "I love Miss Laura and I've got to take her baby to her, but if you help me do that I'll go with you."

* * *

IT WAS A HARROWING trip back to Richmond, although Adam, driving the buggy, didn't seem to mind at all. He was needed and he liked that. There were so many of them that both the carriage and the buggy were crammed and a second driver was essential. Mary Hardin and her children rode with him and he didn't really object. She took good care of Miss Laura's baby, she worked hard and never interfered with him, she was honest. He dismissed her from his mind and went back to his own private thoughts.

The city had grown more desperate in the months he had been gone. It showed in the deteriorating buildings and shabby clothes, in the expressions on faces, even in the hunched posture of people as they hurried along the littered streets. It was an interesting observation and he filed it away, to be thought over later.

For Jewel it was a homecoming. Everything she had had to do to get here became worthwhile when she laid Rosalie in Laura's arms and saw the radiance of her smile. The huge house itself seemed strange. Her sharp eyes noted dusty floors and furniture, stains on rich brocades, a trace of mildew on a section of wallpaper. But, she thought, that's the way it is without many hands to do the work. The glory days are truly gone.

But Paige was the greatest shock. In the quiet of Laura's bedroom Jewel said, "I wouldn't leave her alone for a minute."

"I was half hoping you'd say we were wrong. I could have kissed Mary's feet when I saw her—she won't let those babies out of her sight. Between you, me, Millie, and Elvina we can keep an eye on Paige and still do the cooking, the laundry, and the gardening. We have a pretty good vegetable garden—wait till you see. Becca helps when she can but she's about to drop. Once Doug is home I think she'll quit the hospital."

Jewel looked down at her hands. "How is Miss Millie?"

"Pretty well, considering she's worried sick about Paige. Not a word from Edward since the Wilderness but we'd surely hear if anything happened. I asked her once if she thought he'd changed since he went in the army and she said no, but . . ." Laura's voice trailed off.

"I can't imagine him being anything but what he's always been."

"Neither can I. Sometimes, though, I have a terrible feeling. The one thing I always trusted in was this family. I knew we'd get older, the boys would find wives, there'd be new babies—but that just meant additions, not . . . not loss. I never dreamed we would change but that's what's happened. Only Doug, for all he's gone through, seems the same—battered and bloody but still Doug, like a rock. But Kirby isn't just Kirby grown older. Somehow, in his mind, he's gone away to a far country."

" 'Gone to a far country.' That surely describes Miss Paige."

"If Edward comes home still the same man underneath maybe we can hold together but I think he's gone away too, and if he has there'll be nothing left. The Seymours will dry up and blow away."

J EWEL CLIMBED THE STAIRS to her room by candlelight. Lamp oil was precious but so were candles, even a stub of tallow like this, and she planned to put it out as soon as she reached her bedroom. Miss Laura had a bad case of the dismals and no wonder. Her family was disintegrating before her eyes and every day came word of another ferocious battle. If her brothers died she would at least be told. If it were Chase Girard all she would ever know was that he didn't come back. Jewel knew what it meant to lose a man that way. As for family, the only real family she'd ever known was this one. For her, too, the props of her life were falling away.

She blew out the candle and opened her door. Moonlight fell through the open window and a faint warm breeze stirred the curtains. Then arms slid around her from behind and if she hadn't been, at some deep level, expecting it she couldn't have jerked away and spun around.

"Joseph, what're you up to!" she whispered furiously. "You weren't invited here."

"No, ma'am. I just come to inquire where's my engraved invitation?"

"I don't want to talk to you now."

"Well, I wants to talk to you. I is leavin' tonight and you is coming too."

"Maybe later. I can't leave now—they need me."

"Where's your head, girl? Whut they need don't count no more. The carriage is ready and we goin' tonight."

"Go if you want but not with me."

She could hear his breathing quicken. "You never was gonna come. Using me to get back here, wasn't you?" He grabbed for her and she backed away.

"I wouldn't go to the corner store with you!"

In the dim light she could see his eyes glitter and she drew tight inside herself, waiting.

His voice shook. "Whut you think? Think *he's* comin' back to you? You just his whore, honey. He don' love you an' he ain' gonna do nothin' for you. White folks *cain'* love, don' you know that? You comin' with me!"

He lunged and she slipped away. Metal gleamed in her hand and she hissed, low and guttural, "You come aftah me you gwine be one daid niggah!"

It was the accent of the brutal world she had lived in before the Seymour family bought her, speech Joseph had never heard her use. The shock of it brought him up short. Three thoughts occurred simultaneously: I can take her. She can cut me. They will catch me.

He straightened and said slowly, "You gonna cry for me one day. Marster ain' gonna do for you, he gonna be too busy tryin' to feed hisself. Don' matter whut they calls you, you gonna be a slave all your life."

He slipped out into the dark corridor and she flew across the room and bolted the door. Hers was the only servant's room in the house that had the dignity of a lock; it was Edward's way of telling himself that she could indeed refuse him. She leaned against the door for a few moments, trembling, and then began to pace, the knife still in her hand. Something had told her to take that knife from the kitchen, something had told her. Through the open window came faint creaking sounds and she pulled back the curtain just enough to peer out.

Below, the dark bulk of the carriage was moving away, the horses' hooves making only a muffled clop-clop. Clever Joseph. He had tied rags around each hoof. Well, let him go and find freedom if he could. The horses and carriage were a great loss but—let him go. She sat for some time beside the window, finally moved to her bed and lay down on top of the coverlet, thinking that soon she would get up and undress. The warm night closed around her and sooner than she expected she fell asleep.

I N T H E M O R N I N G S H E woke with a sense of having rested well. Already Elvina was singing in the kitchen; that meant there would be some kind of hot breakfast. There was water in the pitcher too. Elvina had done that last night, bless her. She changed from the dress she had slept in, brushed her hair, twisted it into its knot, and splashed water on her face. It was cool, of course, and that was fine for the September morning was already hot. She went downstairs ready to take on the day.

"Elvina, that smells good." She looked in the pot on the big woodstove. "What is it?"

"You asts me no questions an' I tells you no lies."

"You're getting impudent."

Elvina grinned. "Yes, ma'am. I looked and looked but I don' know where that Adam's got to."

"Out in the quarters, I expect." Jewel took a long spoon and stirred the contents of the pot.

"No, he ain'. The wood was all chopped but I cain' find him nowhere and Miss Millie wants him to go to town."

Jewel looked up. Then she was flying out the door and down the path. He wasn't in his bed. She ran to the stables and grabbed old Enoch by the shirt collar just as he was trying to fasten a feedbag over the head of Laura's mare, the only horse they had now.

"Adam!" Speech was almost impossible. "Have you seen him?"

Enoch tried to pull away in self-defense and couldn't. "Loose your hold, Missy Jewel, iffen you don' mind."

She let go, ashamed in spite of her fear, and the old man adjusted his shirt and hitched up his pants. "Now," he said. "He gone."

"What do you mean, 'He gone'?"

"No need to screech. I kin hear you. He gone las' night, wid dat uppity Joseph. Oh, disyere's for you." There were

two words written on the folded paper and he peered at it.
"Least he said it was for you—I don' read, myself."

The words were "for Mama." Jewel opened the paper
with shaking hands and the carefully formed letters seemed
to dance before her eyes.

> Dear Mama,
>   I am going with Joseph like you said. I would kiss
> you goodbye but Joseph says not to wake you up. We
> will be waiting for you in Washington. Tell Miss
> Laura and Miss Millie I love them and will see them
> again someday after I have found freedom.
>   Love from your boy Adam

She was sitting on the stable floor, the tears streaming
down her face, hugging herself and rocking back and forth
when Laura came.

"Thank you for calling me, Enoch." Laura sat down on
the floor beside her. Jewel pushed the letter at her and she
read it unbelieving. "Gone to Washington? With *Joseph*?
How can such a thing be?"

"He stole my child, he stole him to punish me," Jewel
muttered, so low that she could hardly be heard.

Laura put her arm around her. "Lean on me. I've
leaned on you so many times. Come dear, tell me what
happened."

H E C O U L D B E A N Y W H E R E, he might be nowhere.
Would Joseph look out for him, would he harm him,
abandon him, drag him into some fight or thievery that
would get him killed? Would they get through the area of
combat safely, would someone murder them both for possession of the valuable horses and carriage?

Jewel described every horrible possibility and Laura,
having thought of each one herself, tried to reassure her.
Joseph was strong enough to fend off attackers and too
smart not to look out for a young man who could be
useful. And while Adam was trusting and inexperienced he
was no fool. He was clever and capable and learned fast; he
would see himself through this crisis. She didn't mention

what they both knew—free blacks were swarming on the roads to the North, pouring into Washington in a frenzy of jubilation, and the word was that they were not much more popular there than in the South.

They had been stoned in the streets of the capital by Northern troops. They were constantly attacked by soldiers and street bullies and beaten for no reason but that they had dark faces. And it was well-known that the camps around Washington were cesspools of sickness and violence. Rumor said that the smallpox in those miserable, crowded camps had killed hundreds. So far, freedom had for most of them turned out to be a bitter, empty promise.

Jewel gave a great shuddering sigh. "No use to cry, no use. I learned that a long time ago. But I never thought of this and I should have. I know Joseph."

"What did you mean, 'He's punishing me'? What for?"

"Doesn't matter." Jewel wiped her face. "That boy never should have believed that low-down snake. He knew how I felt about going North. I have told him and told him they hate us up there, they don't want us for all their talk. I told him the best thing for us was to stay right here where we have some friends. Up North we're just strangers in a foreign land. Up there we don't have any friends at all."

E VERY MEMBER OF THE household was stunned by the news and grieved for Jewel, even Paige came back to herself long enough to express her sorrow, but it was Millie, not Jewel, who sat in her bedroom, gray with distress, and mourned. She never spoke of the serious consequences of losing the carriage and horses. The loss of Adam was all she could think of.

"If only I'd sent Joseph away a long time ago, just let him go, this wouldn't have happened." There were tears on her cheeks. "Oh, I don't know what Edward will say."

Laura was sitting across from her, her hands busy with the mending. At the break in Millie's voice she looked up and suddenly blinders fell away. Her hands sank to her lap and were still. Even knowing what Edward had done, Laura had continued to assume that Adam was Ishmael's child, but Ishmael had been a black man, without a trace of white in him. Adam was even lighter than Jewel and his eyes were hazel, not brown. How many times had some part of her noticed the familiar tilt of his head when he laughed, the stockiness of his body and his way of swinging one arm as he walked? How many times had she shut her mind against a fact she didn't want to face—Adam looked like Edward. He was as much a Seymour as any of them.

Now Adam was gone, not knowing he belonged with them, and there was nothing any of them could do to help him or bring him back. What, indeed, would Edward say? How could she ever forgive him?

CHAPTER 32

AS THE GLOOMY WET DAYS of November passed, hopelessness settled over the city. The enemy was so close that the constant growl of cannon had become part of life; everyone knew that this time they were not going to be driven away.

But Valerie Hood's despair was more personal. She had never loved Jason, not even at the beginning, but now that he was gone she missed him bitterly. In a nightmare session with his lawyer she had discovered that like her father, her husband had left his widow and child impoverished. Like many others, he had staked his fortune on the Confederacy. And lost.

Valerie alternated between helpless crying fits and spasms of fury at Jason for his blind faith in the idiot Confederacy, his jealousy, his getting himself killed. Prospects for remarriage were bleak. Most of the men were gone and many would never come back; those who did survive would be stone broke.

During all her love affairs she had lived with the awareness of danger—if Jason caught her she would be punished. But never had she thought he would die and leave her alone. Never had she expected to be poor.

Since fuel was so scarce and expensive she and her son lived in three rooms, with the rest of the huge house closed off and Hallie her only companion. Some women were still giving "starvation" parties but Valerie did not attend.

Other women might wear ugly clothes as a badge of honor but not she! Instead she sat in her great cold mansion, dreamed of the old days, raged at Jason, and wept.

F ROM THE FROZEN, muddy trenches surrounding the city came men so grievously wounded that case-hardened doctors were shaken. It was waste piled upon waste and brought tears to the eyes of those who recognized how useless their sacrifice was.

Doug Seymour was one of those who survived. He was leaving the hospital at last and Becca informed the head nurse that she was resigning to care for her husband.

Miss Hodge drew down her thin lips. "There are others at home to do that, Mrs. Seymour. You are needed here."

Becca flushed. "Even so, Miss Hodge. I'll be here only till the end of the week." Guiltily, stubbornly, she went through the remaining days, ignoring the lady's reproachful glances. Doug came first, tragic though her patients were.

But she couldn't entirely harden her heart or shut them all out of her mind. One man even entered her dreams. He was young and sweet-faced and for many days lay in a morphine-induced stupor. Then Miss Hodge discovered how much of the drug was being used for this one soldier and that was the end of the boy's peace. So Becca broke her rule of not caring too much and searched for other ways to help him. She blandished Byron Rollins into examining him, something the doctor, swamped by surgeries and administrative work, now left to others.

As he walked away she followed him. "Doctor, is there something more I should be doing?"

"You're easing his way out of this, Becca," he said, kind but matter-of-fact. "That's all anyone can do."

"He has a sister here in town. Mrs. Flynn, Angela Flynn. He can't recall her address. If I could reach her . . ."

"Ah," said Dr. Rollins. "I believe I've met the lady. I'll try to locate her."

A NGELA FLYNN, WHO HAD thought she'd seen and smelled the worst life had to offer, almost reeled back against the door when she entered the hospital ward. Outside she had picked her way over the bloody bodies of men still lying on the steps and porch in the wet, freezing air, some of whom she suspected were already dead, and now that she was inside this hellhole she needed someone in authority.

The young woman who had stopped at a bedside with her basin and washcloth was almost girlish in appearance, but seemed to know what she was doing. As she began to bathe the silent man in the bed he looked up and smiled.

Angela watched until she was finished and then said, "Pardon me, miss. I'm looking for Dr. Rollins."

Becca glanced up. "He's in surgery, probably for the rest of the morning."

"Oh." Angela bit her lip. "I had a message from him. My brother is here."

Becca rose, smiling. "You're Mrs. Flynn? Well, I am glad to meet you." She dried her hands. "I'll take you to him but be very quiet. Don't hug him, don't even speak unless we can be sure he's awake."

"He's hurt bad?"

"Come," said Becca.

Sam's eyes were closed. With his long silky lashes resting against pale cheeks and the pain wiped from his face by the morphine Becca had sneaked to him, he looked like a boy too young to be involved in adult madness.

Angela made a small sound and sank into the chair Becca offered her.

His eyes fluttered open. "Well, Angie." He smiled, unsurprised. Every event seemed reasonable when he had the morphine.

"Sammie," Angela said, and the tremor in her voice was alarming. Becca hoped she wouldn't cry in front of him.

Angela didn't cry, quite. She sat beside him all morning, talking in a low voice when he seemed to want it, remaining silent while he slept, sometimes stroking his hand. She asked if she could wash his face and Becca brought her a basin and cloth. She combed his hair, too, and smoothed it gently from his forehead.

Becca, watching them when she had a free moment, noted the coal-black hair of brother and sister and the similarity in their faces, although there was, well, a hardness in the lady's expression that was not there in his—but of course he was so young.

By noontime he was sleeping again, and as Becca passed by, Angela rose and touched her arm. "Tell me true. Is he very bad?"

"I can't give an opinion, Mrs. Flynn. I'm not a doctor."

"But you know."

"No, ma'am. I'll try to find the doctor, though. You're a personal friend of his, I believe."

"We know each other," Angela said.

"Just stay close by. I'll be back."

It was more than an hour before Byron came. Sam was asleep and Angela in her chair had almost drifted off. The doctor laid a light hand on her shoulder and she jerked into wakefulness.

He gestured her away from the bed.

"Where is he hurt, Byron? I can't see a thing wrong."

"It's an abdominal wound."

"Oh, my God."

"Yes. But he's not gone yet and sometimes—"

"No bunkum, please."

"Sometimes, with good nursing, they do come through. We are trying."

Angela ducked her head. "I'm sure you are. Byron, I want you to be his personal doctor. I'll pay the bills."

"I'm already doing all I can for him. Good nursing really is the only hope now and he has that." Sam moved restlessly and the doctor glanced at his sleeping face. "If he lives it will be a long recovery. Can he come to you?"

"God, yes! He's my family."

"Of course. How are things with you otherwise? You're looking fit."

Angela's lips curled down. "Oh, I'm fit all right but I'm sure not easy in my mind, I'm scared. My money, well, if it were prettier I'd use it to paper the walls. At least there's one comfort—my business'll never go out of style."

"The times are indeed uncertain," Byron remarked, suddenly anxious to be away. "And now I must be off. Come by often—I'm sure it will help our patient."

He strode down the aisle, a powerful man as confident and authoritative as God Himself, Angela thought. He had said Sam had a chance and seemed to believe it, which gave a faint gleam of hope. He had also said the times were uncertain, and she would laugh at that if she could laugh at anything. The truth was, no matter which side they had been on, for Southerners very soon now there was going to be a terrible price to pay.

CHRISTMAS PASSED, SCARCELY noticed. Kirby hadn't been heard from in months. They assumed he was freezing in the trenches near Petersburg, Virginia. A letter came from Edward that spoke of all being well again when the war was over. For herself Laura thought that was hard to believe but Millie seemed satisfied and so she put it out of her mind.

Overriding everything was fear for Chase. It was as if she were two people functioning on two levels which never met. One part of her worked in the kitchen and the vegetable garden that was now sustaining them, helped with the children, washed clothes and swept floors, laughed over her struggles with work she'd never done before. The other part of her was rigid with dread. At times she was convinced that he was dead. So many, many men had died—why would God spare him? When she visited Doug at the hospital the desperately wounded scorched her mind and she was driven to volunteer one day a week. No matter how badly needed she was at home she had to do it, for perhaps Chase was lying blind or armless or legless in a Northern hospital and some other woman was doing for him what she could not.

One young Arkansas soldier with a minié ball wound in his thigh, a boy plagued by dark visions, could talk only of war. His captain, he told her, had sent him out with a burial party and in a ditch they found the contorted body of a Yankee officer, his gun still in his hand, struck in the head by a shell fragment. They passed on for they had come out only to bury their own. Four months later the armies fought over the same ground again and when the firing ceased the young soldier came across the skeleton of that officer, his gun rusted, his uniform rotting, still in the position of violent death.

"It makes me think, ma'am," the boy said. "Someplace

some lady's waiting for that man and all she'll ever know is that he's missing. There must be hundreds and hundreds of bones out there on both sides that nobody knows who they are and never will." He had told her nothing she didn't already know yet the story haunted her.

She thought of writing to Chase's parents. They might know where he was and if he was well. They ought to be told of their beautiful granddaughter with the dark eyes so like his and the smile that caught at her heart. Then she tore up the letter just begun. How had she expected to send it from Richmond to Philadelphia in this time of chaos, and even if she could, what would they think of an unknown Southern woman making such a claim?

She must be losing her mind.

She was sure of it when the dreams started. In every one he came to her, whole and healthy, and said he was going away to a far place and might be gone forever. In each dream his destination changed—South America, China, India—but when she begged to come with him he told her she could not; when she cried he said she was making a great fuss over nothing and then disappeared. The meaning of the dream itself was simple but there was nothing simple at all about the way it made her feel.

Sometimes instead of dreaming she would wake suddenly at two or three o'clock, the most vulnerable time of the night, and monstrous fear for him would dive on her out of the dark like a huge black bird, tearing great chunks from her body, leaving her bleeding inside. On the day following one of the bad nights the others would notice that she looked especially tired but nothing would be said. They were all struggling with private devils, they were all enduring—waiting for the end.

CHAPTER 33

SOMETHING WILL GIVE before long, Edward thought. It had been a vicious winter and now that the world was warming, the frozen ground had turned to mud so deep that men sank to their

knees and horses sometimes could not be pulled out and
had to be shot. Men without shoes hobbled in from picket
duty with tears of pain running down their cheeks and sat
near smoky fires of green pine branches, held their frost-
bitten feet and shivered.

There was no doubt that the army would soon evacuate
Petersburg. The lowliest private had observed the moving
out of artillery and supplies and could understand what it
meant. When Petersburg fell Richmond was gone and
then, no matter how long Lee continued to duck and
dodge, it would all be over. Soldiers on picket duty had
orders to shoot deserters but although they would fire at
men seen fading into the brush the bullets somehow never
struck their mark. Edward didn't blame deserters either. At
this point they were committing an act of sanity.

He drank another cup of the hot bitter brew that passed
for coffee but he did it automatically, not really feeling the
early morning cold. In his mind he was taking inventory of
his life.

Until this spring when his country was dying, until this
very day he had told himself that after the war, no matter
how devastated the land, no matter how much he lost in
possessions and power, he could somehow go back to his
women, both of them, and continue to live with dignity
and satisfaction. But just beneath that lie he had always
known the truth. George Armistead, Ishmael's owner, had
not casually or without knowledge sold the man south. He
had sold him at Edward's request. He had done a favor for
a friend.

It was the ultimate dishonor, worse than taking Jewel in
the first place, for he had used his unlimited power to get
rid of the rival with whom she could have lived happily,
sent him to certain death, and maintained the lie all these
years. Like King David sending the beautiful Bathsheba's
husband into the forefront of battle. God, he recalled, had
forgiven David. Then he laughed. He was no ancient king,
he was a paltry little man with chilblains on his hands and
rags on his feet, a man who had lost everything, even his
honor. He didn't think God would forgive him.

He threw the liquid that remained in his cup on the
ground and walked over to his horse, a tired old fellow

who had brought him this far. Yankee sharpshooters hidden in ditches and coverts, in trees and behind rocks, had been making mincemeat of his men and it was time to do something about it. He dug in rusty spurs and the horse leaped off.

Several startled soldiers rose to watch their commander, his sword held above his head, gallop toward an area they had been warned about. There had been no order to form up or prepare to move, and he was alone. They liked and admired Colonel Seymour although they didn't understand him. They thought he was astonishingly brave, sometimes a little mad, and that he had deserved his recent promotion long ago. As they watched, the short, sharp crack of rifle shots echoed on the cold air and Edward flew backward as if hurled out of the saddle by a giant's hand. The horse raced on toward the Yankee lines.

I T WAS A LARGE gathering considering that funerals went on every hour of the day, every day of the week, but Edward had been much admired. Even President Davis and his wife had taken time to attend.

The widow carried herself with great dignity, everyone noticed, her eyes dry, her face calm as her husband was eulogized as a hero of the Confederacy. Poor young Paige, who had lost her husband, her baby, and now her father, was an object of great sympathy too. It seemed, one mourner murmured to a friend, as if all of life had come down to funerals, and if the war didn't end soon every Southern man above the age of ten would be dead.

Kirby hadn't been located but Doug was there, his empty sleeve pinned to his jacket, strong, responsible Doug who was now the head of the family. Elvina and Enoch stood directly behind Laura but if she turned her head a little she could see Jewel, just a pace apart from the family, her face impassive. She had closed her eyes when she was told Edward was dead and laid her head on Laura's shoulder for a moment. It was only a flicker of feeling, instantly suppressed, but her voice had wavered when she asked if there was anything Miss Millie needed.

Millie carried with her everywhere the letter the young officer had brought from General Wise, clinging to it as if it were her hope of life. She insisted on reading it to the family several times and to every visitor who called, and now knew it by heart. " 'He fell while charging the enemy in as gallant an action as I ever witnessed,' " she would recite. " 'He was shot in the shoulder, the chest, and both legs, severing an artery in the right thigh, a total of eight shots, any one of them, the doctor says, probably fatal. I assure you that he died instantly and suffered no pain. He was the finest of men, beloved by all'—'beloved by all,' " she would repeat softly, " 'a splendid soldier and faithful friend, a gentleman, a patriot, devoted to his family, his country, and his God. Always remember, dear madam, he died as he would have wished, attacking the enemy in the service of his nation.' "

When Doug came home he had read it silently, then put his arm around Millie and held her for some time. "You must not weep too much," he had whispered, "you must be proud." But that night in their bedroom when Becca said, "It was a wonderful letter, wasn't it," she was astonished by his cool reply.

"Not to me. I've written too many of 'em. Every man killed in this war died instantly and suffered no pain, they were all splendid and beloved—it's standard stuff. Hell, every shirker in the army died that way if you believe the letters home. I'm sick of the war, I'm sick of the goddamned lies. Don't ever repeat this, Becca, but there was a lot more wrong with Edward than eight bullet holes. I don't believe he ever intended to come home."

CHURCH BELLS PEALED ACROSS the city on the first Sunday in April, calling the faithful to services, giving some a sense that life was continuing as it always had, but no one in the Seymour house intended to go. If they were to eat, the garden had to be tended, Sunday or no. As Becca said with calm irreverence, God would just have to get along without them.

Not until late afternoon did they begin to sense that something was different. The downtown streets were always busy but today they were chaotic and there was a desperation in the air that had not been there the day before. Wagons, carriages, vehicles of all kinds overflowing

with baggage and household goods were moving through
the city as fast as the clogged traffic would allow and people
scurried along the streets with frightened faces. The word
was everywhere—Lee said he could no longer hold the city
and people were scrambling to get out of town. The only
way out for civilians was over the bridge to the roads
heading south. The army prevented them from boarding
the trains; only government officials and the military had
access to the railroads.

Boxes and bags filled with papers were being hauled out
of government buildings to the Danville Depot, the one
rail line still open. In Capitol Square great heaps of paper
money were burning; at the same time gold bullion was
quietly hauled out back doors to the depot. There were
long lines of depositors in front of every bank, drawing out
all the hard currency they could lay hands on.

Over Becca's protests Doug went out to reconnoiter and
when he returned three hours later Paige pounced on him.

"Have you seen any Yankees?"

"No, but they're close, I guarantee it. Everyone's gone
crazy out there so we're going to stay put."

"Crazy?" Millie quavered. "How so?"

"The mob's taken over. They're looting every store in
town. The guards at the penitentiary have disappeared and
the prisoners are on the loose too. The damn fools on the
city council decided to get rid of the liquor so they poured
it in the streets and the looters are scooping it out of the
gutters. They're all drunk."

"Well, then, I'd better bury the silver and—and—"

"Forget the silver, Millie. I want you all in the attic. We
can keep watch from there."

In the attic room they laid out blankets and pillows and
settled the babies to sleep. Rosalie and William obligingly
drifted off. Mary Hardin's older children sat wide-eyed and
silent, watching every move the grown-ups made, but her
baby fussed and wailed intermittently and she walked the
floor, humming softly, pretending her only worry was for
the cranky child.

Rosalie stirred and whimpered in her sleep and Laura
turned her on her stomach and patted her until she was
quiet again. Mary's baby finally slept and she sank down

beside Laura and sighed. They sat, not speaking, their backs braced against the wall, listening for sounds in the wild and dangerous night.

At sometime after midnight Jewel called, "Come look. There's fire!"

They all rushed to the window. A south wind had sprung up and great tongues of flames were leaping skyward down in the commercial district.

Paige moaned, "Oh, my God, the Yankees are here! They'll kill us all."

Staring out over her head, Doug said grimly, "It's not the Yankees, it's our idiots. I heard the army had orders from Davis to burn all the military supplies and the tobacco warehouses but somebody said the mayor was trying to stop it. The pinheaded army's gone and done it anyway."

As they watched the fire flew onward, out of control, attacking more warehouses, store buildings, mills, banks, forcing evacuation of the wounded from hospitals. The houses on their hill appeared to be safe, at least for the present, but closer to town people were being burned out of their homes. The night sky turned crimson and then liver-colored, then crimson again as new flames shot upward. At dawn four enormous explosions shattered windows and shook the huge house to its foundations. Doug said they were blowing up the gunboats on the river but Paige was convinced it was Yankee cannon bombarding the city. She sat on the floor in a corner, cursing so vividly that Millie whispered, "Where did she ever hear such language? Not in this house!"

"Sounds like the army to me," Doug replied. "Leave her be. Maybe it makes her feel better."

Vandals had destroyed all the fire hoses and there was no way to fight the giant conflagration. It gobbled up more structures while the city was looted, growing deadlier as the hours passed. The earth continued to shake with repeated explosions and the fierce heat, the deafening noise, the blinding, suffocating smoke made it seem to some that the world at last must be ending. President Davis and most of his cabinet had escaped. Whistles shrieking, their train pulled out at midnight and government wagons filled with official papers and supplies jammed the bridges out of town. But some official documents never left the city. Before closing his office door for the last time, Judah Benjamin destroyed every paper containing the names of those who had spied against the North for the Confederacy (unknown to Benjamin, General Grenville Dodge in Washington had decided that now the end was in sight all lists of Northern intelligence agents would disappear).

The bridges, including the railroad bridges, were burning and people were taking desperate chances to get out. On the river, ships of the Confederate navy were blazing at the docks or drifting erratically downstream, outlined in fire, a sight of weird beauty in the night. Flames reached the arsenal and once again the world was torn by terrific explosions. Shells exploded in all directions, eight hundred thousand of them, ripping up streets, destroying houses and killing the people inside.

The sun rose but towering columns of fire spread smoke so thick that the shining April sky turned a dark, sullen gray. The breeze, fragrant with spring blossoms only the day before, now carried an acrid stink of many odd substances burning and the sweet-rotten smell of scorched flesh; people had died in their blazing houses last night and some who tried to run with their clothes on fire had fallen on the street and were now charred bodies still lying uncollected. Frantic refugees stepped over them, scarcely noticing, looking ahead toward the great wall of flame that seemed to be eating the city alive, searching for a way out. Looters, unmindful of danger, trundled past with wheelbarrows filled with stolen foodstuffs, tools, fabrics, furniture, anything movable that might somehow be usable or worth money. The last of the rear guard had moved out of town at daybreak and no longer were those left behind members of an organized society; they were, each of them, on their own now, pursuing survival any way they could.

On the street someone shouted, "The Yankees are here!", and this time it was true. A detachment of Massachusetts cavalry rode into town past the raging fires, went directly to the capitol building and hauled down the Stars and Bars. In its place the Old Flag rose, and as the fire they had set upon themselves devoured their city, the people of Richmond heard a hauntingly familiar melody, at first so

soft that some thought they might be imagining it. Somewhere a military band was playing "The Star Spangled
Banner."

The family gathered in the attic room heard it too, and
Paige said, "To think, that once made me feel patriotic!",
and she said it with such profound bitterness that Laura
turned away from the window to look at the girl huddled
on the floor. Doug sat down beside Paige, took her hand
and said, "Yeah, me too."

It was night before the last of the shells in the arsenal
exploded. Then a hush spread over the city and behind
bolted doors people lay awake through the long dark hours
and listened for sounds of rape and pillage that never came.

The next morning Doug and Laura walked down into
the rubble of their beaten, battered hometown. Blue uniforms were everywhere and even the most dedicated Rebels
had to admit that the conquerors were behaving themselves. They had driven away the drunken looters, fought
the fires and put them out. No acts of violence were taking
place and nervous ladies alone in their homes were given
Federal guards if they requested it. The invading troops
were also offering help to people whom the fires had left
destitute.

The business section of town was destroyed and of all
the government buildings only the Custom House still
stood. Cavalry horses were tethered on the lawn of Capital
Square. Any grass that had not burned had been crushed
and torn by their hoofs. Crowds of people burned out of
their homes milled around the square, uncertain what to do
next, and many, including the haughtiest aristocrats in the
city, went to the headquarters of the Yankee general to beg
for food.

Local blacks, no longer afraid of their former masters,
had congregated on the street and cheered every blue-
coated soldier they saw, hugged them, wept and called,
"God bless you!" and "Thank God the Yankees has come!"
Many fell to their knees and one woman cried out, "Bless
God, mah sufferin' is over!" so loudly that Mrs. James Davenport turned to stare. Once such a cold glance had struck
terror into her servants' hearts. This noisy woman did not
even notice. The elegant Mrs. Davenport, now homeless,

pushed past her and prepared to be polite to the first Yankee officer she saw.

In many places, Laura thought, the streets looked oddly like stage sets, only the front walls still standing with nothing behind them. Two soldiers on horseback clattered past and she looked at them searchingly. They were strangers. None of these young, vigorous Federal officers moving through town so confidently had the right eyes, the right smile, the right soul. They were the lucky ones, they were survivors too.

T HERE WERE MANY SOUTHERNERS who had be-lieved that their defenses and protections were firmly in place and no matter what calamities befell the rest of humankind they would remain comfortable and reasonably safe. No one had built the barricades higher than Angela Flynn. She had thought she was in a disasterproof business but standing in the ruins of the Daisychain, she changed her mind. There were only three chimneys and one wavering wall still standing. The French furniture, the Persian rugs, the brocade draperies and silk sheets all were destroyed; every costly, gleaming mirror that had not shattered under the force of the explosions was cracked and blackened.

The fine china was broken and every bottle of liquor, every piece of silver had disappeared. She suspected Teddy, the piano player, perhaps in league with Venita, the maid. Why she suspected them she did not know except that she had been fond of them both and people she was fond of always let her down. Just as her mother had let her down when she died all those many years ago, just as Sam had let her down four days ago when he up and died after seeming to be getting better. She brushed away tears and walked back to the respectable residential district and the perfect house she had struggled so hard to acquire, the house that had contained all the possessions she loved most.

In the wreckage of what had once been her home her eyes moved again over her belongings. She had come back here three times in the hope that somehow things weren't as bad as they seemed or that something had been overlooked. Everything that wasn't ashes was badly damaged; her valuable paintings, her heavy silver pieces, her jewelry, all the cherished possessions she had accumulated not only for her own pleasure but as a hedge against misfortune were burned, twisted, or melted. None was in condition to be pawned.

Her sharp eye caught a gleam of something on the scorched rug at her feet. She knelt and brushed away the ashes. It was a gold bracelet, a thin bracelet, not worth as much as she could wish, but still it was something. Why wasn't it ruined like everything else? She took it as a sign of an upward rise in her fortunes and slipped it on her wrist. The good-sized diamond she had luckily been wearing at the time the world exploded had already been pawned and was paying for her hotel room. Unfortunately, the market for diamonds was not at its peak and although it tore her heart she had sold cheap, something she didn't intend to do again if she could help it.

She made the long walk back to her hotel once again and by the time she got there she was beginning to limp. It was bad luck that she had been wearing shoes that pinched when the fire started. It was good luck that her gown, the only one she now possessed, was attractive but subdued, quite ladylike.

The front window of her hotel was cracked but not shattered. At the desk, a Union officer with the insignia of a major of artillery was talking to the clerk. Angela, an expert at appraising men, watched him through the window for only a few moments and came to a conclusion.

He would be interested.

From the beginning of her business life she had hated her work and loathed her customers. Never once had she slept with a man she could admire or respect for they had been, without exception, unworthy of either. And they were such fools! Every man, it seemed, had an unwarranted high opinion of himself, every man found it easy to believe that she really liked him.

She drew in a long breath. There was no help for it. With a graceful swish of skirts she walked into the lobby and stopped at the end of the desk.

The clerk turned to her with sympathy in his voice. He

and Angela had an arrangement. "Mrs. Flynn, were you able to rescue anything?"

Angela raised blue eyes. Her brave smile included the officer. "Everything is gone—the furniture, my mother's jewelry, the house itself, all gone. It's hard to believe." That was true enough.

The clerk shook his head. "I'm sorry." In a low voice he told the major, "That dear lady has lost everything. She's a widow and her little brother died just a couple of days ago. Poor thing, I don't know what she'll do. I doubt the management will let her stay here much longer."

The major looked her over carefully. There was no lack of available women in this town, although the general's orders had chased them off the main streets, but he had never gone to prostitutes and didn't intend to. It was a point of honor. This woman was obviously a lady and attractive Southern ladies interested him. He had heard they could charm in a way Northern women never dreamed of and, although hard to get, were tigers if you could lure them into bed.

"I'm sorry to hear that." He removed his hat and said courteously, "I am Major Kendrick, ma'am, presently on General Shepley's staff. If you are in need you might apply at headquarters. We're trying to do all we can to help civilians."

When he first began to speak, alarm was plain in Angela's face but his gentlemanly manner calmed her and she smiled timidly. "I've heard of General Shepley. He's issued an order protecting citizens from insult and attack, has he not? It greatly reassured me. The sooner we put this dreadful war behind us the better."

"Indeed." Major Kendrick moved down the counter. "I'm told your little brother has recently passed over, ma'am. May I offer my condolences."

"Thank you." She looked away.

"I apologize if I've mentioned too tender a subject. It's very hard when a child dies."

"Sam wasn't a child but he was young, too young to realize what he was doing. I tried to stop him, tried to keep him from going back to the army but he wouldn't listen. So he died for nothing."

The pain in her voice, the sudden heartfelt passion, wiped out of his mind for the moment the desire to get her into bed. "I'm truly sorry, ma'am. Could I ask—would it be too forward of me to invite you to join me at supper? I was just going into the hotel restaurant and I hate to eat alone. Please don't hesitate to refuse, if you prefer. I won't take it amiss."

Angela looked up, her mind back on business. Although she had intended not to settle for less than a colonel, a major might do very well.

"I . . . I suppose we have been introduced"— she smiled hesitantly and glanced at the clerk—". . . in a way. You are very kind, Major Kendrick. I'd be pleased to join you."

CHAPTER 34

IN LAURA'S MIND the war was over but Doug said, "You don't know Marse Robert. He still has the army and the word is he's moving west. That means he thinks he can get to Lynchburg or Danville, join up with Joe Johnston and head for the hills."

"That's vile, Doug. More death, more misery, more lives ruined, and for what? It will all be the same in the end." She rarely dared speak her real thoughts to anyone but at that moment she didn't care.

They were sitting on the side porch in the early April dusk. Doug's stump had been aching all day and he put his hand above it as if by force he could stop the pain from traveling upward. He stared into the twilight for some time and finally remarked with quiet bitterness, "Sister, I couldn't agree with you more."

Doug's guess was right. Lee was moving along the Appomattox River, hoping to get rations for his starving army at Amelia Court House, meet with Johnston and take to the hills with their combined force. But on the other side of the river Grant was hurtling after him, and the rations, as had happened so often, were not where they were supposed to be. The Army of Northern Virginia was slowly disappearing as men decided for themselves that they had had enough and walked away. Only an enduring few of the most fiercely loyal refused to give up. After four days without food, staggering with hunger but still following Lee, they crossed the river and ran straight into more Federals. It was, finally, the end.

Millie wept when the news came, not for the lost cause but for her lost husband. No one else cried but the house was very quiet and every face was somber. In a way it was a relief, a final resolution of what they all had known was coming, a relief for everyone but Paige.

"I can't be like the rest of you, I can't be polite to those blue-bellies," she said one night when the family was gathered around the small fire they allowed themselves.

Millie looked up from her knitting. She had taken on the task of providing new blankets for the babies and worked on them every evening, patiently unraveling old sweaters, socks, and blankets and knitting them into colorful new patchwork covers. "Honey," she said, "they're here. We have to accept it and go on."

"I don't accept it, I can't stand the sight of them lording it over us, swaggering around town as if they'd done something to be proud of."

"They won," said Doug.

Laura was only half listening. For the last hour she had been trying to rock her fretful baby to sleep. William had a cold and she suspected Rosalie was coming down with it too. Without thinking she said, "It could be worse. They put out the fire and they're handing out food. Ellen Mercer asked for a guard and she got one."

Paige gave her a hard look. "Yes, they're just dandy and I'll bet you like seeing them here. You're hoping your Yankee will show up soon, we all know that. But he's not coming back. You were just another conquest, Laura, one of many. He's probably found somebody else by now."

Laura stopped rocking and Rosalie began to whimper. Before she could say anything Millie spoke in a voice of steel. "Go to your room, Paige, and think over what you have said. When you've got yourself under control, make your apology."

Paige jumped up, bright spots of red in her cheeks. "I'm not a child to be sent to my room, I'm a grown woman, a widow with a dead baby in case you've forgotten! Yankees killed my husband and I don't feel kindly toward them." She pointed a trembling finger. "As for her and that—that baby, I only said what we all think."

Millie's eyes never wavered. "No, that's not what we all think. We don't insult our own, Paige, we take care of each other and hold together always. It's the only way we'll survive."

Paige started to answer back, changed her mind and walked out of the room. Her footsteps on the stairs echoed in the quiet house.

"She'll apologize, Laura," Millie said in the same steely voice, "and I apologize too. She's suffered but so have we all. There is no excuse."

"It's all right," Laura answered in a suffocated voice. "It's nothing to do with you, Millie."

Becca sat with her hand in Doug's and stared at the floor and Mary Hardin, who didn't know Paige well, was so embarrassed at being present at this family fight that she wondered if she should go home soon and how she would feed her children if she did.

After a few minutes of uncomfortable silence Laura said good night and took Rosalie up to bed. She kept the baby with her at night in a crib near her own bed so she could reach out to her in the dark, pat her into sleep if she was restless, hear her soft, regular breathing and know that she was really there.

She undressed, took down her hair and brushed it, but did not go to bed. Instead, she put on her worn wool wrapper and sat for a time beside her sleeping daughter, the light of one small candle throwing shadows against the wall.

A conquest. One of many. At dark moments similar thoughts had slid into her mind. He could have found someone else. He could be hurt or dead. It was the uncertainty, the hope that rose and fell, then rose again that drove her crazy. Better to know even the worst truth than live like this. Paige would be sorry in the morning, but the unhappy scene tonight had reminded her of what she'd always known—she and Rosalie would have to leave soon. When the first shock of defeat and surrender passed, people who knew her would lift their heads, look around and begin to notice things. It wasn't possible to go on living in town. She would have to go back to Pine Hill.

T HE NEXT MORNING SHE told Becca. "I know Mary will come with me—she's wild to get home. So I won't be alone." They were on hands and knees pulling away weeds that threatened to choke the new green shoots sprouting in the vegetable garden. Tending the roses that had once bloomed there hadn't prepared them for this kind of work, hard stoop labor such as none of the Seymour women had ever done or ever expected to do. Several paces in front of them Elvina stopped and passed a hand across her damp forehead; already the sun was high and hot and this kind of outdoor work was new to her too.

Becca gave Laura one of her sharp, direct looks. "It's the right thing to do." She rubbed the spot in her back that always ached these days. "After we went to bed last night Doug and I talked till almost midnight. He's not happy— well, how could he be? He doesn't want to stay here. We decided to move to Pine Hill. He thinks he can make a go of it—not a big plantation, we won't have the workers— but a living. What do you think?"

Laura smiled, a bright, glowing smile such as Becca hadn't seen on her face in a long time. "It's wonderful. I thought it would be just Mary and me and the babies. Truth to tell, I was feeling pretty sorry for myself." The kitchen door banged and Millie came down the path from the back of the house. She mourned for her roses and hated vegetables, both to grow and to eat, but determinedly worked alongside everyone else every day. Laura's brows rose. "We have to tell her."

"Um," said Becca. "I don't look forward to that."

I T WASN'T AS BAD as they feared. Millie wept a little, then wiped her eyes, blew her nose and, almost as if she had been expecting this latest calamity, began to help plan the move. They must take plenty of linens and whatever furniture they could use since most of the house was closed off anyway. And they couldn't get along without Jewel.

But in the end, after much discussion, it was Elvina, not Jewel, who went with them.

"I have to stay here," Jewel said, not quite looking at Laura. "This is where Adam left me, it's where he'll expect to find me. Besides, I can't leave Miss Millie to cope with Miss Paige alone and only Enoch to help her."

Laura started to point out that Elvina could be talked into staying with Millie, then decided not to. Every time she had left home, years ago when she went to Washington and again when she moved to her own house, Jewel had refused to come with her for reasons she never quite expressed. Jewel was free now to go hunting for Adam, to go anywhere she wished, yet she chose to stay here.

In sudden realization Laura thought, This is home for her, more, even, than it is for me. This was where Jewel had grown up, where Adam was born, where everything important in her life, good or bad, had happened. There were bonds of loyalty and affection between her and home that even war and emancipation could not break.

Elvina didn't intend to strike out on her own either. "I doesn't have no other job nor likely to get one," she told Laura. "Why, everybody and his dog is out there in the streets tryin' for work and ain' nobody got enough money to hire 'em."

"I don't have much in the way of cash either, not right now, but you will have food and a roof over your head."

"And family. I got you all."

While she was helping pack the baby's things Elvina suddenly inquired, "Miss Laura, does you think men lies when they says they loves you or does they jus' get busy and forget?"

"Why, Elvina, haven't you heard from Frederick?"

Elvina's lower lip pushed out. "No, ma'am. He lef' before the white gent'mens give up—said he was coming right back but he ain'."

"Yes, well—men do that sometimes."

"I'd druther, iffen they ain' coming back they'd jus' say so . . . but it wouldn't sound so good when theys sayin' goodbye, would it?" A sudden grin lit Elvina'a face and she looked around, but Laura was in the alcove sorting books and hadn't heard her.

They arrived at Pine Hill on a Sunday. The house was shuttered—dank and cold but untouched by any assaults worse than the cruel winter just past. The closest fighting in the district had been ten miles away and although stragglers had passed this way no one had broken into the house and most of the chickens and geese had survived, as well as four cows and the mule.

"I never thought I'd be so glad to see cows," Doug said with a laugh, surveying them safely pastured in the meadow behind the barn. He turned to Laura, who had just come up the path from Rufus and Emma Nelson's cottage. "Did you find them?"

"Nope. They've cleared out."

He looked around. "That's a solid fence. The barn's been reroofed and the door is new. The place is in pretty good shape, considering."

"No thanks to them. They left before Christmas"—her eyes gleamed with the news she had to impart—"but we have workers, Doug. Eleven good strong hands! They haven't all run away."

IN FACT, THERE WERE TWELVE, one more coming in from the woods when he saw who the white folks were. Twelve left out of almost a hundred. But among them were two skilled craftsmen—a carpenter and a blacksmith. Doug told them what to expect in as straightforward a talk as they had ever heard from a white man. They were free to leave, to seek work where they pleased. If they chose to stay there would be no pay until there was a crop to sell and buyers with cash, but meanwhile they would have a home and food from the produce of the farm. In a destitute land it was a fair offer.

As they walked back to the house Laura asked, "What do you think?"

"I think they'll stay."

THE FAMILY SETTLED INTO a routine, working harder than they ever had in their lives except for Mary Hardin, who had labored in the fields since childhood, first beside her parents and then her husband. For her the job of caring for the children was easy, a pleasure that absorbed her, but part of her was always looking outward toward the road, hoping that any day now the man she was waiting for would come home.

June arrived and with it Rosalie's first birthday. She had grown into a sturdy child, dark-haired, dark-eyed, and opinionated, with a habit of observing others with a frown that said she was assessing them thoroughly and forming judgments. She had begun walking at ten months and now talked incessantly, making sounds which strangers might take for babble but which those who knew her well understood clearly as her names for them, the objects around her, and the firm expression of her desires. When Rosalie wanted something everyone knew it.

"I don't understand," Laura said, watching her daughter with a smile. "*I* was always so docile."

Doug gave a shout of laughter. "Sure you were. You were the sweetest little tyrant I ever saw, hard as stone once you got your mind set."

"I was not!" Laura thought a moment. "Of course I wasn't about to be run over."

"No danger of that. Come here, Rosalie, let me see." Doug scooped the child onto his knee. "Yes, the same stubborn glint in the eye. Face it, Laura, you're going to have your hands full with this one and serves you right."

The family sat down to a birthday dinner of ham, yams, and greens, lavish food compared to what people in Richmond had to eat, and then Elvina brought in the dessert, a cake made with precious flour and sugar, eggs from Pine Hill's own hens, and butter churned from milk the farm's cows had produced. Everyone applauded its beauty and the fat tallow candle on it.

Rosalie, worn out by excitement, fell asleep in her chair and was carried upstairs and put to bed with frosting still smeared around her mouth. When Laura went out on the porch the twilight of early summer still lingered and the air itself had a blue translucent quality. A letter had come from Millie along with a blanket she had knitted for Rosalie. The streets of Richmond were blue with Yankees, she wrote— thousands of them, pouring in from everywhere, overrunning the town since Lincoln was killed, and black soldiers, an astonishing sight, were present in large numbers too.

She leaned against one of the chipped, peeling columns and gazed down toward the river ploughing its silent way into the James and then to the sea. There were thousands of Yankees in Richmond. He would be there, too, by now, he would be with her at this moment if he were still alive. She had to give up the foolish hope that one day he would ride up the drive and she could fling herself into his arms as Mary had done when Walt Hardin finally, unbelievably, came home last week. There were women all over the South hoping for the luck Mary had had, women who were going to spend the rest of their lives waiting for men who would never come, and she must not be like them. She must face reality and go on as he would want her to.

She would not feel his arms around her again, ever. She would not see his face when he looked at Rosalie, but when their daughter was old enough she would hear about her father and understand what a fine man he had been and how much her mother loved him. Tomorrow the sneaking, insidious hope would return like an unwanted guest and she would start looking down the drive again, but right now she felt strong enough to believe she could go on without him.

S UMMER HAD COME EARLY that year. On the day Chase rode into Richmond it was sultrier than usual for mid-May, with a tropical intensity that Northerners never grew used to. He tilted his hat against the sun.

John Gibson, the young major recently made his executive officer, rode beside him. John ran his finger beneath his tight collar in a futile attempt to loosen it, looking at the blackened ruins around him in amazement. "Why did they do this? Before God, I'll never understand these Rebels."

They had arrived by train a half hour earlier, acquired horses at the army corral, and were seeing for the first time what stupidity and fire had done to Richmond. It was much worse than they had heard.

"Some fools must have thought it was better to fall on their swords than surrender," Chase said absently. "John, I'll report in later." He turned the horse south and dug in his spurs. John called after him but he was already halfway down Broad Street.

The house where he had lived with her had a deserted, unkempt look and he knew the moment he saw it that no one had been there for a long time. Every door was locked and many windows shattered. He went into the backyard, into the little garden she loved. Vines had overgrown the flower beds and the lawn was dead. Slowly he walked back to his horse, tethered to the railing of the front porch, and as he untied the reins there was a rustle in the hedge that separated the property from its neighbor.

"Looking for the lady?"

The man skillfully sidled through a gap in the hedge, handling his crutches with ease. Wisps of dirty black hair hung around his shoulders and his scraggled beard reached to the middle of his chest. His eyes had the wild look that Chase had seen before in men who had been through more battles than they could bear.

"Yes," he said, "Mrs. Chandler. Do you know where she is?"

"Dark-haired and uncommon pretty? I always remember the pretty ones." He smiled and looked around vaguely. "I recall her from far, far back. Haven't seen her in a long while."

"What are you saying, George?" A young woman pushed through the hedge, then stopped when she saw Chase's uniform. "Come home," she murmured to the man, who watched her like a child waiting to find out what it must do. "We don't have to talk to those people." She took his arm and pulled him gently through the hedge.

Chase mounted his horse and headed back through town and up the hill to the Seymour house.

At the gate he stopped. The mansion was no longer perfection—it needed paint as did every building, small and large, in town; the gate sagged badly, several front windows were shattered, and there were more weeds than grass in the front lawn. But it hadn't been attacked by fire and there were unmistakable signs that people still lived here. He went up the front steps and rang the chimes. They no longer worked. He pounded on the door and no one came.

Like the savage-eyed man on the crutches, he had seen many battles, had smashed men, equipment, and other obstacles that barred his way, and his tolerance for any hindrance had long ago worn thin. He was about to attempt kicking in the massive front door when a lock was turned and the door opened a crack. It was Paige, her face gaunt in its thinness, her eyes narrow and suspicious.

"What do you want? We're not to be bothered—we have an order from the Yankee general."

"Paige, don't you know me?"

Something moved in her eyes. She opened the door a fraction more and peered at him. "Chase Girard." She looked about to close the door, then changed her mind and opened it wider. "I suppose you might as well come in."

He walked into the cool entrance hall as he had so many times before and followed her into the front parlor, the one always kept ready for guests.

"Please," she said, "sit down."

The house was in no worse condition than most he had seen in the past months and seemed, in fact, better than many. He wondered what the rest of it looked like. He wondered where Laura was and how soon he could ask.

"We've been very lucky," Paige said. "We're a little out of the way and the general took a big house nearer town for his headquarters. You're the first Yankee that's been inside—that is, since *you* left."

"I'm sorry I had to mislead you, Paige. I was always on duty."

"I know about duty. Alex talked about it a lot—duty and honor. So did Papa. I've never rightly understood what men mean when they talk about honor but then, being a woman, I don't have to, do I?"

"Paige—"

"I must catch you up on the family. My baby was a boy—I named him Alexander Thomas Wyatt, Junior. He lived almost two days. Alex was wounded at Petersburg last summer. They were bringing him home but the hurt was in his head and it made him a little mad. He decided to get out of the ambulance and walk home but he never got here. We couldn't find his grave." She looked into his face. "Papa was killed this spring. He was charging the enemy gallantly, his general said."

The list of her sorrows was harrowing, the more so for her matter-of-fact tone. He said, "I am so sorry for everything. I admired your father. Alex was the best friend I had."

"Yes. Doug lost an arm. He and Becca and little William are living out of town now. Kirby—we haven't heard a word. I doubt we ever will."

He was silent, recalling the joyous girl she had been on the night of her wedding. This woman looked as though she would never smile again. He said, "I'd like to pay my respects to your mother, if I may."

"It's not a good idea. She was so fond of you and feels you took unfair advantage of us. I told her that's the way war is, but she feels—well, Mama can be unreasonable, you know. Just now she's lying down with a sick headache. She's had them so often since Papa died. We're alone, just Mama and me and Jewel. Everyone else has run off, even Adam is gone, but with Jewel we manage. She's out trying to find some flour and meat for us right now."

It was the opening he needed. He said, "Where is Laura? I went to her house but it appears she hasn't been there in some time."

"No. She came home when she discovered that she was—uh—with child. What else could she do?" Paige's eyes widened. "I regret telling you so bluntly but I don't know how else to say it. It was a very bad situation for her, for all of us."

He took a sudden deep breath. "Where is she now? How is she?"

"Quite well, I believe, although the birth was difficult—having a baby is never easy. As to where she is, I really can't tell you. We expected to hear before now. She promised faithfully to write and let us know but I'm sure she's been busy getting settled."

"She's gone away?"

"Gone north to New York—or was it Chicago? I don't rightly recall. They may have mentioned both and, as I say, we expected to hear before now. Matt Riley had some kind of job offer and jobs aren't too plentiful down here just now. They left not long after the surrender." At the expression on his face she gently twisted the knife. "Laura was terribly fond of you, she must have been to take such a risk, but a woman with a child has to have a husband, you know, and Matt always adored her. So much so that he was willing to accept the baby. He's a decent man and I'm sure he'll take good care of both of them."

She watched him walk to the window and stare out into what had been the rose garden. After a little while she asked, "Perhaps you'd like to hear something about the baby?"

He turned and looked at her as if he didn't know who she was. Then he sat down opposite her again and said, "Yes. Please."

"Her name is Rosalie. A lovely child—of course she would be with such good-looking parents. Her first birthday is just two weeks away. The first of June. Her hair is almost black and curls in the prettiest ringlets around her little face. Her chin and her smile are like Laura's, I think, but her eyes are exactly like yours—dark and with that same mischievous twinkle. And such a will of her own, oh, my! It's going to be interesting watching her grow up."

A wave of pain passed across his face and when he finally found words his voice was hoarse. "I would have married her gladly, *gladly*, anytime she wanted it."

"Oh, I'm sure you would!" She leaned toward him, her eyes intense. "Don't feel too bad. It's all the fault of the war. If she could have reached you, if you could have come back, things would have been different, but it could be so much worse. Look at me. I loved greatly, maybe even more than you, but Alex is dead and our child too. You are alive and even though you'll never see Laura again she's alive and she has her baby too." She sank back against the sofa cushion and murmured, "You are lucky."

She wasn't sure that he heard her. After a while he rose and picked up his hat. At the door he said, "Thank you for receiving me. Considering everything, many people wouldn't."

"It was my pleasure."

"I am sorrier than I can say about all you've lost. I may be sent on to New Orleans soon—in any case, I won't bother you again—but if I can arrange it may I send you some supplies from our commissary? We're one country again and the army wants to help where it can."

Her eyes glistened. "Mama and I would be very grateful."

When Millie came downstairs an hour later Jewel had just arrived home triumphant. She had acquired a pound of bacon and a small bag of flour and they chortled over it together.

Jewel got out the big knife, newly sharpened that morning, and began to cut thin slices from the slab of bacon. Paige was standing at the stove stirring a pot of the vegetables they were all growing to hate.

"We'll add just one strip of bacon—maybe two—to that stew," Millie said. "It'll make all the difference. Paige, did you hear me?"

"Yes, Mama. That sounds good."

"Paige, did we have visitors this afternoon? I thought I heard voices but I was just too sleepy to get up."

Paige glanced over her shoulder. Rested and rosy with sleep, Millie looked almost young at that moment. In spite of her tragedies there was still an innocence in her, a view of the world that said, *I know quite well you're a vicious old place but I will look for the best and perhaps I'll find it.* It was, Paige supposed, a noble quality. It always irritated her beyond bearing.

"Yes, Mama, we did. I hate to talk about it."

Millie sat down at the kitchen table. "More bad news?"

"I'm afraid so. I didn't wake you because—well, because I didn't think you'd want to see him. It was Laura's Yankee."

Millie put her hands to her face.

Jewel laid down the knife and it made a sharp cracking sound on the marble-topped table. "Where is he? Did you tell him?"

Paige turned from the stove and looked at the two women. "I told him. He'd hoped to catch Laura here, he said—but he's on his way to New Orleans. Orders, I guess. He said he'd like to see the baby and would stop by the next time he's in town."

Slowly Millie said, "In spite of everything I never thought he was that cold."

"He wasn't really cold, Mama. He seemed quite touched when I described Rosalie to him. I guess he just didn't have the time." Millie gave her a look and Paige said with some asperity, "Well, what did you expect from a man like that? I told you all, didn't I? I warned you and you got mad at me."

Jewel picked up a towel and carefully wiped the grease from her hands. "She's got to be told."

"I'll write." Millie's voice was soft and cool. "I'll tell her the best way I can."

Paige turned back to the stove. "Oh, by the way, he said he'd send something over from the commissary if I'd be so kind as to accept. I guess that was to sort of make up for it."

S ITTING ON THE FRONT STEPS, Laura raced through Millie's letter, let it rest on her lap for a time and then, although she didn't want to, read it again more slowly, stopping to reread certain passages to make sure she understood.

"He had just got to town but went straight to your house and when he didn't find you came directly here. He seemed very sorry to have missed you and was most interested to hear about Rosalie. Paige described her as best she could, told him how much she resembles him, especially the eyes, and he seemed quite moved. He would come out to see you, he said, but for having to go on to New Orleans and will surely do so the next time he's in town. Remember, dear, he's under orders. As a soldier's wife I know how the army can be. I'm sure he'll come to see you and the baby the moment he can."

He was sorry to have missed her. He was interested in Rosalie. He might even come out to see them someday when he could find the time. Even one of Millie's artful letters couldn't fix this up. It was what, beneath her hope, Laura had always feared. She crumpled the letter and threw it to the ground, then picked it up and stuffed it in her pocket.

For a week she moved about the house in such a contained fury that the others could only wonder and speculate. They knew a letter had come from Richmond. Doug, who picked it up at the Claremore post office, said Millie's handwriting was on the envelope. What could gentle Millie have written to spark such awe-inspiring rage?

No one could guess and Laura didn't enlighten them. For Becca her behavior was a revelation. Almost from the beginning she had liked, admired, and trusted Laura more than anyone else in the family she had married into; she believed she understood her sister-in-law well. Now she saw a side to her that she never dreamed was there. Laura, with all her tenderness, was a tough, determined woman, and whether it was Millie or someone else she was mad at, Becca did not envy that person at all.

CHAPTER 35

AFTER THE EXPLOSIONS ENDED, the fires were put out and it appeared that this was not Armageddon, after listening to Hallie's vivid description of the destruction everywhere and how the Yankee soldiers were swarming all over town, Valerie's curiosity got the better of her and she decided to go out and see for herself.

She located the best dress in her wardrobe, twice-turned but not bad if you didn't look too close, had Hallie dress her hair, still as gleaming a gold as it had ever been, cinch in her stays until she could barely breathe, and she ventured out into the charred city.

It was as bad as Hallie said. The once-lovely shade trees that lined the streets were singed and unhealthy, some of them burned to cinders. In some places she hardly recognized where she was for the familiar landmarks were gone. And everywhere were bluecoats, the Yankees of everyone's nightmares. If you looked closely you saw that they were men, not monsters, men who but for their uniforms looked exactly like Southern men. But they didn't sound like Southerners; they spoke with clipped nasal twangs or flat Midwestern drawls, attacking consonants as if they meant to bludgeon them to death and completing sentences in half the time a Southerner would take to say the same thing.

And of course, some of them were monsters. They must be for everyone knew what had happened down in Georgia. That devil Sherman had devastated countryside and towns, his soldiers had burned and pillaged and, it was whispered, even raped, although Valerie didn't know if that were true, and had a hard time even imagining such a thing. Nevertheless she kept her eyes modestly down as she made her way through the downtown crowds, careful never to directly meet the eyes of any stranger. And so it was with surprise that one day as she was making her way past a hotel that had escaped the fire, she realized a soldier was speaking to her, addressing her by name.

"Valerie."

She looked up. "Chase?" she said in flat astonishment. War had not changed him, it seemed to her. He was perhaps a little thinner but with the same smile, the same intense maleness that had taken her breath away on that memorable day four years ago when Alex Wyatt introduced him.

Someone in the crowd bumped into her from behind, muttered, "Your pardon, ma'am," and Chase took her gloved hand and said, "Come."

The hotel lobby was filled with men in blue uniforms. Every Northern officer in town must be staying here. They found a table in the hotel restaurant and sat down.

She pulled off each glove finger by finger and looked at him with a smile. "It's wonderful to see you."

"You too. Have you had lunch?"

"Yes," she said, although she hadn't. "But I've heard you Yankees brought real coffee with you. I'd love some of that, if it's possible."

It was rich, black, and fragrant. "Scrumptious," she said with a sigh. "I can't even think how long it's been since I tasted anything so good."

She was, he thought, prettier now than he'd ever seen her. Her shabby dress was becoming and the faint lines around her mouth and shadowed eyes added a maturity he'd never expected to see. And then Laura's face replaced hers and he wondered if the child, the war, the turmoil that her life must have been after he left had changed her too. She was lost now in some great Northern city and he would never know.

Valerie looked up from under her lashes in the old flirtatious way. "I shouldn't even be talking to you—we don't speak to Yankees if we can help it, especially spies. Were you really a spy, Chase? That's what everyone said after you disappeared so suddenly."

"Do I look like a spy?"

"You look like a man who might do anything. If you were, though, you made up for it when you took Lowell Weston's precious horse. It was the funniest sight I ever saw, watching him jump up and down in sheer frustration, threatening to draw and quarter you once he dragged you back here. I thought to myself, 'But you'll never catch him—not Chase.' "

"Thanks. I wasn't so sure myself." He leaned back in his chair. "How are you, Valerie? How is your son?"

"I'm well. Henry, too, although I think he misses his father, Lord knows why. Jason never paid him much mind. But you can't know. Jason was killed last summer—I've been a widow almost a year now."

He hesitated and then said, "Somehow I never thought he'd go in the army."

"He didn't. I was—I was sitting with a man at a table in a hotel"—she glanced around—"a lot like this. He stormed in and issued one of his famous challenges. Kirby said he didn't fight duels and shot him dead on the spot."

Good for Kirby, Chase thought.

She seemed not to expect condolences or indeed any comment at all for she went right on. "He killed so many men for no good reason—but it took some getting used to, his being gone."

"Yes, it must have."

At the gentleness in his voice she looked up and he was surprised to see tears in her eyes. Valerie had never been a crier. Hurriedly she fished out a handkerchief and dabbed at her face almost surreptitiously. "Aren't I foolish! It's just that you always were the most understanding man. Not many are." She put the handkerchief away. "What about you? Are you well? Are you happy?"

"Yes, I'm well. As for happy, who is?"

She leaned forward, her eyes suddenly blazing, and he knew what she was going to say. "I could make you happy, Chase, I certainly used to. I never got over you or forgot you. I'm not even sure what pulled us apart but—"

"What pulled us apart was someone else." He said it quickly before she could go on.

She gazed at him dumbfounded, her mouth a little open. "Who?"

"It doesn't matter."

"It matters to me! Who is she? Some Northern woman?"

"She lives up North."

Silence fell. The waiter poured more coffee from a tall silver pot. When he was gone Valerie murmured in her soft, husky voice, "I can make you forget her."

"No. You can't."

"Of course I can! What do you need that I can't give you? Just tell me and I'll change."

"It isn't possible, Valerie. I love her. She's the part of me I value most."

Valerie seemed to shrink a little. There was something very final in the way he said that. "And she loves you too?"

"I think so."

A stunned look came over Valerie's face. "You aren't already married, are you?"

"Things were very difficult for her. She married someone else while I was away."

"How can you love someone who wouldn't wait?" she demanded so loudly and passionately that the two young lieutenants at the table across the room turned to inspect her with interest. "If I thought you really loved me I would have waited forever! Just give me a chance and I'll—"

"Valerie, no."

She wanted to walk around to his side of the table, put her arms around him and convince him right there in front of everyone but even if she tried it would do no good. He meant what he said.

The coffee in her cup was cold. She didn't want it anyway. There was a hunting print on the wall above his head and she stared at it, uncertain what to say next. In a voice so low it was almost a whisper she asked, "If you don't want me what are you going to do? Give up women entirely for this—this lady?"

"I have no idea what I'm going to do. I still have to figure that out."

As ABRUPTLY AS IT came on, Laura's dark mood disappeared. She came to breakfast smiling and cheerful one morning and asked, "Could you all spare me for a day or two? I want to go into town and find out how things really are with Millie. I'll work twice as hard when I get back."

They urged her to go and stay as long as she liked. It was time somebody went; Pine Hill was so isolated, real news was scarce. There might be merchandise in the shops now, little things they could afford, and Laura was certainly the right one to go shopping for them.

She left the next morning with butter and eggs for Millie and orders for ribbons and pins and lengths of cotton fabric if it could be found and wasn't too dear. Becca and Doug stood on the porch and watched the buggy roll down the drive with relief but no idea what had caused the sharp rise in her spirits.

Doug said, "What do you think?"

"Don't ask me. She's your sister. All I can say is she seems better and let's hope it lasts."

The truth was that Laura had come to much the same conclusion as Valerie—she was too young to despair and had lived in seclusion long enough. Out in the world there were great events in the making and she intended to see and maybe even be a part of them.

After TIM O'HALLORAN SAW the wounded come in from Gettysburg, he had closed his bookshop, stored his inventory of books, maps, and manuscripts, and gone off to fight for a cause he only half believed in. His reading of history told him that the Confederates were engaged in a mad enterprise, they could not win and probably didn't deserve to, and yet once they were close to being on their knees he enlisted. Never had he been able to resist lost causes, he told an acquaintance just before leaving. " 'Tis a weakness that comes of being Irish. Besides, I want to keep me friends company."

He had done just that. Now most of his friends were dead and he had a bullet fragment lodged in his ankle that had left him with a limp and would always cause pain in wet weather. He didn't regret the wound too much except on rainy days, but the loss of friends and certain remnants of idealism had been a high price to pay. As for the burning of the city he was one of the lucky ones. His precious books had survived—he was now one of the few booksellers in town with merchandise to sell—and his shop still stood. His landlord, a once-wealthy man who like everyone else had fallen on hard times, was willing to accept the rent he could pay. So far sales were slow because people with any cash at all used it for food and other absolute necessities. Relatively few Southerners considered books almost as important as food but one who did was now crossing the street and heading directly for his door.

Like a breath of spring, he thought as she came in with her wonderful smile.

Laura hugged him. She used to do it every time she came into the shop as a child but had stopped after becoming a young lady. He could still see her, a girl of eleven or twelve, eyes shining like a child in a candy shop as she looked over his latest books, sometimes following his guidance when she bought, sometimes ignoring him and taking home novels, usually French, that he considered beyond her capacity to understand, then returning to debate whether the heroine was truly immoral or only misunderstood.

"Tim, how are you? I heard you were wounded this spring."

"A scratch only but it took me out of the army. Sure, you're bloomin' like a rose. Are you back in town to stay?"

"Only to shop. Look. A box of pins, two papers of needles, and a half-dozen ribbons—what do you think of that? No cloth at all, though. The speculators have plenty but the prices! I'd rather buy a book."

She followed him as he moved down each aisle, searching for something she hadn't read, his limp pronounced. It worried her, the slowness of his movements, but she knew better than to mention it—veterans didn't like prying questions.

The bell announced another customer and he left her to browse. When she came to the front counter the customer had left.

"No sale," Tim said with a grin. "He only wanted directions."

"Never mind. You have a sale here. My *Vanity Fair* has disappeared and I never get tired of Thackeray. I—" Her voice went ragged and stopped. She was staring out the window, her face paper-white. All Tim saw were Yankee officers, some with women, coming out of the hotel across the street. There were, it seemed, thousands of blue-coated soldiers everywhere, not a startling sight these days.

She saw only one soldier, the set of his shoulders and the way he moved as familiar as her own body and her own mind. The woman with him smiled, said something and reached up to touch his cheek with a gloved hand. He smiled too. In a moment they were lost in the crowd.

And I loved him so, she thought.

Tim had to strain to hear when after a long period of silence she said, "Do you know what it's like to love someone who doesn't love you, who is terribly kind but doesn't really care that you exist?"

She was still staring out the window with that foreshortened gaze and he could see her only in profile—the classic nose, the sweet, full lips, the gracious curve of throat. "Yes," he said, "I know about that."

She turned to him. "I'll take this book and come back next month if there's a chance you might have something new by then."

He had trouble writing up the sale but finally got it right. "Yes," he said, "come back next month," and watched her leave. He caught the door before it swung shut and stood on the pavement in front of his shop, watching until she was beyond his sight.

The calm did not desert her on the ride home. After the letter from Millie, in spite of hurt and anger, she had held on to the secret hope that perhaps, written down, his words sounded colder than they had been, perhaps he really did have to leave immediately—the army was like that—and would come to her the moment he could. But four weeks had passed and now she knew he was still in town. He had no time to make the short trip to Pine Hill yet somehow had found Valerie. It was the intimacy in their pose that struck her most—his dark head bent, looking down, Valerie's smile and the touch of her hand on his cheek.

The truth stared her in the face and there was no avoiding it. He had loved her once, she still believed that, but not enough and not forever. On that last night she had said she wanted him to be free and she meant it. Now she, too, was free—from romantic dreams, from the impossible hope of a life with him, from the hurt that such useless hope could bring. It was, in a way, liberation.

ONCE BACK AT PINE Hill she discovered that philosophy, however wise and sensible, didn't help much when the immediate crisis was over. There was still every hour of every day to be gotten through. Although she worked hard, physical tasks left her free to think—not a good thing—but during the days there were times when she was so busy or so tired that she forgot for a little while. Such moments didn't come often or last long but they did come. The late-night hours were the worst time, the hours just before sleep when her guard was down and memory made its cruelest assault. At such times she would tell herself that the last years were not true, it was all a bad dream. She would wake in the morning to find that Edward was not dead, Kirby had not vanished, probably buried in some unknown grave, Doug had not lost his arm, and even if all those horrors had really happened Chase would be there beside her, loving her and kissing away the sadness. The picture was so clear in the dark hours of the night that she sometimes felt his arms around her. He'll be here, she would think, he'll be here in the morning . . . and then, of course, he wasn't.

The whirling, frantic quality of her thoughts began to worry her. Children were allowed to pretend reality wasn't real. Grown women were not. Such thinking had led some women to strange treatments by puzzled doctors, had even led to locked attic rooms. She didn't intend to end up that way. She began rising before sunup, working furiously all day at any task she could find, and if there was time left at the end of the day, going for long walks to tire herself even more so that she would, she hoped, sleep and not be prey to strange fantasies.

She didn't tell anyone that she welcomed the mundane fear that assailed her every time she came to milk the cows. It was good, healthy, sensible fear that any normal person would feel so close to those huge, ill-tempered beasts, not the dark dread of the future that could destroy her if she allowed it to take over. She welcomed the hours it took to collect the eggs and feed the chickens and geese, to keep the barnyard passably clean, to deal with the pig, who turned out to be a good-natured creature given to rolling ecstatically in the mud and manure and quite friendly. Even the stink of the manure was not displeasing. There was a gritty reality about it that kept her mind in the here and now.

As the weeks went by she began to feel herself regain balance. She still could not remember him without crying in her heart so whenever his face rose before her and she saw his eyes crinkle with laughter, whenever she recalled something he'd said that had opened her mind to a new idea or made her laugh or, most dangerous of all, the ways in which he had loved her, she immediately distracted herself with work, with talk, with anything that was of the present moment. And gradually she began to see that a meaningful life could go on without him if she was strong and brave and determined enough.

CHAPTER 36

WHEN HE MOVED his family to Pine Hill, Doug thought he understood the job he was taking on. He quickly discovered he didn't. Pine Hill was in a state of collapse. It was no longer a plantation, it was a small farm able at best to feed the people who lived there. His hope was that eventually they could produce crops of grain and tobacco that would bring in some cash on the open market. Of the twelve former slaves still on the place after the surrender, four more had left for points north, but among the eight remaining workers were the carpenter and the blacksmith, a stroke of luck Doug gave thanks for. And in the beginning he was grateful for a hard worker like Walt Hardin too.

Walt did work hard but it soon became apparent that he was not happy. He had returned from a long, bitter war to find his farm taken over by brush and woodland and his wife and children living at Pine Hill with the high-and-mighty Seymour family. "I depended on you, Mary," he told her. They were whispering in their bedroom, a large room given to her because it was next door to the children's nursery. "You should have stayed home and held the farm, not gone traipsing off with them people."

"The chirren was hungry! I couldn't've plowed and planted and harvested enough to feed us even if I didn't have a baby coming. When Laura took me in I didn't have a twig of food in the house. She's been a good friend, Walter."

It was the wrong thing to say. His rage flared so violently that his face went dark red. "She's a Seymour and no friend to us. You're just a servant here, a servant that don't cost very damn much, just like the niggers!"

He had always hated wealthy white planters just as he hated the black slaves. The slaves had become what he feared most, free and in competition with him. And the planters even in poverty and defeat still managed to control the land and have the say about who worked and who didn't, just as they always had. He stayed on at Pine Hill, working for Doug because for the present he had to, polite to the ladies because he knew he had better be, ignoring Elvina because outright courtesy to a smart-mouthed colored was beyond him.

Before the month was out Doug knew what he had in Walt Hardin. Becca also knew. She had overheard several short, sharp exchanges between Walt and his wife, and she and Laura talked it over and agreed that before long the Hardins would have to leave.

August fell with the scorching sun and humid air that could drive tempers past the breaking point. Everyone at Pine Hill, black and white, understood the wet, suffocating heat. Without conscious thought they slowed their pace, drank more water, poured it over themselves by the bucketful and worked on. By September the worst of the heat seemed to be over.

The hands always cooked their supper over open fires near the old slave quarters and after eating played the one harmonica and the only banjo with unbroken strings that they possessed, sang the old songs, and danced. The white folks would come out of the house, sit on the steps to listen and sometimes wander down to join them. Only Walt Hardin and his family never came.

"Look at them," he told Mary, "sitting right there with the coloreds. Look at *her*." In a circle around the fire whites and blacks were clapping and singing as Laura, outlined in the firelight, danced the high, prancing cakewalk she had learned in childhood, tilting back, laughing and swinging her hair.

Mary said, "I think she dances real pretty. It does my heart good to hear her laugh like that."

"You don't understand at all. That's a nigger dance, Mary. Only rich white folks fool around like that because they can do anything they damned well please, even nigger stuff. But they oughten to. It's wrong."

Mary stood and straightened her dress. "It looks like a good time to me." She marched down the steps, heading for the campfire, her very back defiant, while Walt stared after her, disbelieving.

"You come back here, Mary!"

She ignored him.

"Mary!"

She walked into the circle of firelight, lifted her skirt to her ankles and began a little clumsily at first to follow Laura's steps, leaning back, kicking her feet higher and higher, her cheeks rosy with exertion and unaccustomed fun. She laughed, tilted too far and lost her balance on the uneven ground. With a shriek she fell backward onto Eli, the blacksmith, who caught her with one arm and at the same time swung his banjo out of danger. She sat up, giggling with embarrassment, and in the next moment was hurled aside.

Eli was a compact, powerful man with muscles like hams

and fingers that had twice strangled men imprudent enough to attack him, but when Walt shot out of the dark all the old fears and prohibitions came leaping back. Never in his life had he raised his hand against a white man or touched a white woman and for an instant the man's wife had been sitting on his lap. He hesitated and Walt was on him.

The women scrambled out of the way. As from a great distance Laura heard Mary scream, the only sound in the night except for the grunting men rolling in the dirt, and for the first time in her life she felt a stab of fear at the sight of dark faces, faces that gleamed, unreadable, in the firelight.

They are so many and we are so few, she thought.

But they were only watching—at least so far—transfixed by the sight of one of their own fighting a white man, beginning to wonder what, if anything, they should do if the white man appeared to be winning. The struggling men rolled back toward the fire and Walt's hand, reaching out, found a heavy piece of smoldering wood and slammed it into Eli's face. Doug pulled the gun that was always at his belt, fired one shot and ordered them to stop with all the authority that four years of war had brought him. Walt swung the wood up like a club and Doug fired again. "Don't make me waste more bullets, Walt. The next time I'll put it in you."

Eli lay on the ground dazed and breathing hard. He hadn't put up the fight he could have and everyone knew it. He had been afraid.

Walt got to his feet, wiped his face with his arm and stared at Doug. "You take his part against me?"

"No fighting on my land, no matter who it is. You get along or you leave."

Walt took Mary by the arm and dragged her unresisting back to the house.

JUST BEFORE SUNSET ON an afternoon in late October Laura left the house and walked down the path toward the river. Leaves had begun to fall and scudded across the grass under the pressure of a sharp breeze. The bare trees, the angle of the sun, low on the horizon, the inevitable shortening of the days all brought on a melancholy, a sense that everything was ending. She ought to feel relief that the brutal summer was finally over but just ahead lay cold rain, sleet, snow, and the piercing winds of winter in a house that was drafty and hard to heat. Last winter Rosalie had had two frightening attacks of what she suspected was bronchitis, illnesses that could so easily have become pneumonia. Many children died in the first year or two of life—it had always been so. She did not think she could survive losing her child.

Wind lifted the edge of her shawl and she wrapped it tighter. Far down the drive a man had turned in from the road, a man wearing an assortment of butternut garments, which meant he was an ex-Confederate soldier still struggling toward home all these months after the surrender. She turned to watch. He was a soldier with more optimism and energy than most of these poor souls for he moved up the drive with a quick, springy stride and as he came nearer he waved cheerfully and called, "Hey, Laura!"

At first she simply stood and stared. Then she began to run.

He lifted her off her feet and swung her around and laughing and crying she hugged him. "Oh, my Lord, Kirby, we'd given you up."

He laughed. "Always a mistake, sister. You don't ever want to give up on me."

Looking at his face that night in the firelight she saw that he was not as young and untouched as he first seemed. He'd never been wounded, he told them, not even scratched but his eyes said otherwise. Even when he laughed his eyes never changed; they were as cold as any she had ever seen.

Doug was smiling all over his face this evening, happy that his brother was alive, relieved that at last he would have a two-armed man on the place to help him now that Walt Hardin was gone. His stump had been aching since the colder weather came on and he tired easily. They were sitting before the fire replete with the best meal they'd eaten in months. Doug had killed a chicken that had stopped laying, deciding in Kirby's honor not to wait and see if it would start again.

To Kirby he said, "We've got potential here. Not much tobacco yet, not until we can hire on more hands, but the barley's done well. What do you think about trying oats next spring? In a couple of years we'll be the grain kings of the South!"

"Me, a farmer? I wouldn't know an oat if it walked up and called me brother."

"But you'll learn. It's hard work but it's going to pay off and meantime we eat. I learned a lot in the army—how to run men, how to improvise, how to stick to a job. I'm a damn good farmer now."

Kirby smiled. "Well, I'm glad for you. I learned some things in the war too. Mostly how to use a gun. I'm good at it, Doug, better than anybody I've met so far. A lot of the fellows are traveling out West where there's new land, new opportunity. I hear a man who's quick with a gun does well out there. I plan to go see for myself."

They were all dumbfounded. "West?" Doug repeated, as if he'd never heard the word before. "You're a Southerner, Kirby, a Seymour. There's plenty of opportunity here if you look for it."

"I don't think so. The South, our South, is dead and nobody's going to work any miracles to get it back for us." Kirby leaned forward, his face intense. "Northerners despise us, they whipped us solid and now they're going to run our ass off, wait and see."

"They've treated us pretty well so far, better than I expected. I've still got the land and no one comes around here bothering me."

"I tell you, Doug, it's all over for people like us. The Yankees won't let us ever get our country back. They mean to ram the coloreds down our throats and I don't plan to be here when it happens. I'm going west and make a real life for myself. The only reason I'm here—" his eyes met Laura's stricken eyes and his voice softened a little—"is to say goodbye."

T HERE WAS MORE WRONG for white Southerners than an occupying army or even blacks who were free and on the loose. Not all of the land had been physi-cally devastated by war, in most parts public and private buildings still stood, but for practical purposes the Southern economy had collapsed, and the transportation system was in ruins. There was a steady drain of young, energetic, educated men like Kirby Seymour who had given up on their homeland and were going west or to the great Northern cities seeking employment. Others like Doug Seymour, who might have helped organize a new economic system, were working like field hands simply to feed their families. And so many young men were dead. Many families had lost all their men, with only women and children left to struggle on.

Looking at their shattered land in the dreary spring of 1866, some Southerners, thinking more clearly than they had in years, wondered why it had ever seemed like a good idea to take on the industrial might of the North, but they also saw that in spite of the losses something remained. The land, an eternal source of wealth and power, was still there and still theirs. The work force was still there too. Although many blacks had fled north most remained in their home territories, working for white men as they had before war came. Jeff Davis was locked up in Fortress Monroe at present but no Confederate leader had been hung for treason as had been threatened during the war, and Robert E. Lee had sworn allegiance to the Union. Doug Seymour and thousands of other ex-Confederates, following Lee's example, signed the Oath of Allegiance and so regained the right to vote, took control of state and local governments, and began to govern themselves once more.

All would be well, many whites believed, but for the great fly in the ointment. The Negroes. It was not that white Southerners wanted blacks to disappear or be sent back to Africa as Lincoln had once proposed—workers were needed, great numbers of workers used to hard labor in the fields, willing to work for low wages, but they had to be kept "where they belong," as Andrew Ferguson, Doug's neighbor, said as they sat before the fire on a chilly April evening.

Andrew had been Doug's captain and like Doug he had been wounded on that bloody day near Antietem Creek, then wounded again in the action that cost Doug his arm. Neither of his brothers came home from the war and his

mother had died, he believed, of grief. In the winter following the surrender he buried his father too, and now he
was the owner of Westwood plantation, Pine Hill's nearest
neighbor. Having survived the first desperate struggle to
get his crops started, loneliness had driven him to search
out the few friends left from the past.

His favorite topic of conversation was politics and how
to preserve what was best of the old ways. He had a resonant voice, an attractive manner before audiences, and was
deeply concerned about the future of Southern society. He
was running for the state legislature.

"I need your vote, Doug. As far as slavery is concerned
I'm glad it's gone, but have you read the talk that's going
on in Washington? They mean to push the coloreds on us
and if we don't protect ourselves they'll overwhelm us.
These black codes are the only way to keep them in their
place."

Blacks now had rights they had never had under
slavery—marriages were legal and they were allowed to tes-
tify in court if it were a matter between their own kind—
but the codes, varying in severity in different sections, were
designed to keep them working only in the fields or as
domestic servants. They had no schools, they could not
own any kind of weapon, even a gun to hunt for food in a
country where food was scarce and game plentiful, and in
many places there were tight restrictions that kept them
from freely moving around. Above all, they could not vote.

Doug tilted back his chair, scowling into the fire. "Last
time I was in Richmond I talked to Wade Hampton. He
thinks coloreds with property and a good reputation should
be able to vote just like whites."

"Yes, well, so does the general"—Wade Hampton was a
general too, but "the general" always meant Robert E.
Lee—"good men but they're wrong about this. Look what
happened down in Jamaica when the English tried emancipation. They got a revolt for their trouble and ended up
having to send in troops. We have to keep the blacks under
control or we'll find ourselves fighting another war, something I don't care to do."

Laura was sitting on the other side of the fire, working
on a dress for Rosalie. The fabric had come from an old

dress of her own. "But after all," she said, not lifting her eyes from her sewing, "we have emancipation now and there hasn't been a revolution. Maybe we should try what the general said and see how it goes."

Andrew Ferguson looked at her with a slight smile. She certainly had picked up different ways during her time spent in the North, but in the past weeks he had come to rather enjoy the direct approach.

He knew that most Southerners agreed with him about the codes. They accepted the outcome of the war, came back into the Union in a manner that amazed Europeans, and were functioning according to democratic principles they understood very well. The one matter they refused to yield on was the blacks. Blacks would never be accepted as equals.

This determination was expressed in different ways. Attempts by well-meaning Northern reformers to build schools and teach former slaves how to be citizens were fought with cold social disapproval by the gentry and fire and violence by others; teachers were run out of town and schools burned to the ground. Almost all Southerners found it hard to understand why Northerners wanted to help lift up the blacks who were, by their natures, inferior and meant to be so. The rolling biblical phrases, used so often in the past to defend slavery, were brought out again. Ministers in their pulpits quoted Joshua: "From a very far country thy servants are come . . . let them be hewers of wood and drawers of water."

And never, never anything else.

THE ODD FLICKER OF light across her bedroom wall was the first warning Laura had that something was wrong. Doug and Becca had left that morning with two field hands and a wagonload of produce to sell in the Richmond market, and she and Elvina were alone in the house with the children. It was almost midnight, the end of a long day, and she had just taken down her hair and begun to brush it. She went to the window.

They had ridden silently into the yard, six hooded, white-robed horsemen, two bearing torches that flared yellow-gold in the dark. They started down toward the quarters and in the next instant she was racing down the hall to the childrens' room. Rosalie and William slept, their faces rosy, their breathing steady and peaceful. She locked the door from the inside, went through the connecting door and locked it too.

Elvina was deeply asleep. Laura took her by the shoulders and shook her. "Wake up, Elvina, *night riders!*"

At the words "night riders" Elvina came fully awake and leaped up. "Whut we gonna do?" she whispered, her voice harsh with fear.

"Come with me."

They flew down the stairs to the small room Doug used as his office, the room where every gun in the house was kept except the one always in his belt. She unlocked the case with the key kept hidden behind the table. There were four rifles, all breechloaders captured from the Yankees. She took one, broke it open, slipped in a shell, closed it and took out another. "Look in the bottom drawer of the desk on the left-hand side. There should be a pistol."

"Cain' find nothing . . ." Elvina pulled out a stack of papers. "Here it is!"

Laura loaded it, a long-barreled dueling pistol with a carved walnut handle. Doug had the Colt with him. "Now take this rifle"—Elvina shrank a little—"take it! Hold it so, against your shoulder and sight down the barrel. If you have to fire, squeeze the trigger, don't jerk it."

Suddenly Elvina smiled, completely calm. She had never touched hands to a gun before but the thought of fighting back against night riders made her want to laugh with savage joy.

Laura dropped a handful of shells into her pocket and looked though the curtains. The intruders had Eli and were dragging him roped and bound toward the front of the house. Hammered into the ground only a few feet from the veranda was a crude cross and they poured kerosene over the wood and touched it with one of the blazing torches. Tongues of yellow flame shot upward, outlining a fiery lopsided cross against the dark night. It was a fearsome sight intended to awe and terrify, never to be forgotten by the two women watching inside the house.

The white-robed men stood back in apparent reverence

for their own handiwork. Then they stripped Eli naked and tied him to the stake they set before the burning cross. Their leader, a big, bulky man, unhooked a bullwhip from his saddle and stood contemplating the black man before him as if in reflection or prayer. Then he brought down the whip with all the strength of his powerful arm.

Laura saw and heard everything with great clarity—the arm coming down, the crack of the rawhide whip, Eli's dark, glistening back and his scream pealing out into the night, the brown, sweating, terror-stricken faces of Pine Hill's workers, the armed men who surrounded them, grotesque in their hoods, all lit by the blazing cross. The whip cracked again and Eli's scream seemed to tear the night apart.

"Stay inside, Elvina, stay by the window. If I need help, aim to kill—even if you miss they'll know we mean business."

She walked out on the porch and set the rifles on the table where the family had so often sat with cool drinks on summer evenings. Before her it continued, an eerie, nightmarish scene. No one had seen her. She could have been watching actors on a stage, absorbed in their parts, unaware of the audience. She lifted the dueling pistol and fired in the air, took a rifle and moved out of the shadows.

The men in front of her were still standing as they had been when they first heard the shot. They looked up at her.

"Go back in your house, Miz Chandler," the man with the whip called out. "This here's nothin' to you."

"Get off my land, you varmints! You have no business here."

"You happen to be one of them nigger lovers, ma'am? You got uppity niggers if you don't mind me saying so. We're the invisible empire, the Knights of the White Camellia, and we're doing what has to be done."

" 'Knights' my left hind foot! You're a sniveling, sneaking coward, Walt Hardin. Yes, I know who you are, hiding behind that hood. And you, Jake Crenshaw—I'd know your big feet anywhere. And Toby Foster—my Lord! What are you all doing, riding around the country wrapped up in bedsheets? You all ought to be ashamed, behaving like white trash. Go home, all of you!"

They stirred uneasily. They hadn't bargained on being recognized and she knew at least three of them. But Walt Hardin moved toward her, so close that she could see his eyes blazing through the slits in his hood. His words were slow and distinct and hate-filled.

"*You*, woman." His voice quivered. "I despise you and your kind, always and forever running the show as if you had some God-given right. Well, you don't run me, you don't run anybody anymore. You Seymours—you're on your uppers just like everybody else. It's a wonder how you stayed on top so long when you're too dumb to see plain facts. That nigger"—he jerked his head at Eli—"he laid hands on my woman and that just don't happen. We kill a few like that and the others'll remember their place, by God! Now, you get back inside your house, close your eyes and put your fingers in your ears, and we'll get on with our work."

Laura lifted her gun. "Get off my land now or I'll shoot you where you stand."

He tore off his hood with a cry of fury and leaped upward, reaching for the rifle. With great calmness, her hand steady, she squeezed the trigger as Doug had taught her. The gun roared in the quiet night and, as the recoil knocked her backward, Walt Hardin staggered, went to his knees and fell backward, his head in the dirt, his legs flung out. Almost immediately a crimson stain began to spread on the white sheet that covered his chest. His friends started toward him and there was another blast coming from the house. No one was hit but they stopped and stared.

Laura regained her balance and picked up the second rifle. "This is loaded and you know I can shoot. Toby, you pick him up and get him out of here. All of you, get out. If you plan to come back, remember, we know you now and we'll be ready."

They carried Walt to his horse and slung him across it.

As they rode off Elvina came onto the porch and leaned against the railing. Now that it was over she was suddenly weak in the knees. "Think they's comin' back?"

"No telling." Eli was unconscious, and heavy though he was, Old John, the biggest of the hands, was carrying him toward the quarters. "Elvina, there's some salve in my top dresser drawer. Take it down to him but don't leave it. You put it on real careful. It's all we've got." They looked at each other. Laura said, "You did good tonight."

"Yes, ma'am. You did good too."

When she was gone Laura lowered herself onto the step like a shaky invalid. Had she killed Mary's husband? A chest wound like that meant he would soon be dead if he wasn't already. She had had to do it, she had had to murder to stop a murder. Did that make sense? It seemed to her that it did but she wasn't sure. Perhaps, at some future time, it would all come clearer.

"Mama? What is it?"

Her child was standing in the doorway, her eyes worried and beginning to fill.

"Oh, my God, baby, come here. What are you doing out of bed? How did you get out of your room?"

"Willum climbed out the window an' opened Elvina's door. There was funny noises, Mama."

"William, are you there?"

William leaned around the door. "Um, yes." He looked prepared for a scolding.

Laura put out her arm and he ran to her. She pulled both children onto her lap and held them, their little bodies soft and sweet against her. Young as they were they were strong, adventurous, determined children and precious beyond words. "Ah, I love you, I love you both so much! Now listen close and don't forget what I say. If ever you see or hear funny things again you must stay *put*, stay where it's safe till a grown-up comes for you, understand?"

"Yes'm," said William. "Um . . . where is it safe?"

She kissed the top of their heads. Where indeed?

CHAPTER 37

LIKE FIRE IN TINDER-DRY woods, word raced through the county—Laura Chandler, with only children and a black maid in the house, had stood off a band of night riders and shot Walt Hardin dead in her front yard. There was only a low undercurrent of criticism, quickly suppressed. Laura was a Seymour and Hardin a poor-white trespasser—a hero of the war, it was true, but a bad-tempered man who had been in many fights and had numerous enemies. And it appeared that the black man in the case had done nothing wrong.

Night riders were not popular in this part of Virginia. They set themselves up as judge and jury and butted into the business of others in a way intolerable to independent-minded people. It was up to Doug Seymour to control his workers and administer any needed punishment and not have his women and children jeopardized when his back was turned. A story was floating about that there had been a second shot from the house but no one believed it. The only other adult present was the maid and Laura would never have given a loaded gun to a servant.

In less than two days word reached Richmond. Doug and Becca hastened home without completing their business but Andrew Ferguson, leaving the running of West-wood to the best field hand he had, got there ahead of them.

Before the war Andrew had been a soft-looking man, slightly overweight, indolent of manner and sometimes thoughtless, but war had stripped away most of his illusions as well as the excess weight. He was the officer who had separated Doug and his brothers before the bloody battle near Antietam Creek in the hope that one of them would survive, and he took a proprietary interest in the younger man and his family. Since renewing his friendship with Doug, he had begun to take an interest in Doug's sister too, and after the raid of the night riders he rode home late one evening engrossed in thoughts of her, knowing he was in love in a way he had believed could not happen at this point in his life. Whether or not he was able to win Laura, he admired her enormously and tried to let her know without quite saying it, for there was about her a mystery, a shadow in her eyes, a warning that he must not come too close. At least, not yet.

The only real impediment might be the child and he gave a great deal of thought to little Rosalie, turning and twisting in his mind, trying to think of a good explanation.

Laura's husband had been dead for many years and she had a young child, a fact that led to certain inescapable conclusions, yet how could he ask questions? She didn't try to explain or justify or seem to care what anyone thought, an attitude some would consider brazen. He decided it was courageous, as gallant as facing a pack of armed jackals, and he would not pass judgment. Others would, however, and it could have consequences. He had lost in the last election by only a tiny margin and he wanted to try again, he wanted to be governor of the state one day. But that was in the unknowable future and he needed her now.

He had heard about the raid the morning after it happened and rushed to Pine Hill before the noon hour. He would have done the same for any woman alone and in need of help but it was a special pleasure to do it for Laura. He got the grateful smile he hoped for when he rode up to her door and when Doug arrived home he left certain of what he already knew. He was going to marry her if she would have him.

After that every moment he could spare from his own farm was spent at Pine Hill. He lay awake nights trying to plan ways to be alone with her. For the first time in his life he longed for life in the city where there were places to go and things to do, where you could take a woman to a restaurant or the theater, get her away from her relatives to some spot where you could at least talk privately.

Just after sunset one evening when the sky was still streaked with coral and gold, he and Laura took the long way down to the broad, open place where the river widened and became smooth. It had rained the day before and the air was newly washed and sweet with the scents of spring yet it all seemed dismal to Laura, dismal and sad as the peculiar cry of the nighthawks echoing through the pines, gloomy as the pines, wet and pungent and crowding darkly along the bank downriver. She had come to detest pines and nighthawks and the damned owls that were beginning to hoot. Her life was passing as swiftly as the river and nothing had turned out as she had hoped. That was a childish thought—no one got what they expected from life—and she probably ought to be ashamed. He was gazing at her and saying something about cities and did she find rural life dull? He added, ". . . since you have traveled so much."

She took a guess at what he'd said. "I've never been to Europe but I have been to Boston—very traditional, very stuffy. Philadelphia is just as fond of itself but it's a pleasant place"—her voice softened—"I've known people I liked very much who came from Philadelphia. New York is a different story. They're the hub of the universe, you know, and they'll tell you so when they're feeling impolite."

He was smiling. Her voice had picked up vigor and interest as she talked. "What about Washington?"

"Don't even ask. I'd rather leave you with any illusions you may still have."

"I don't have any—not about the Federals."

They were walking along the bank and he held back the small branch of a tree so she didn't have to step off the path.

He said, "Before the war my father sent me on the Grand Tour—London, Paris, Heidelberg, Rome. I came back never wanting to leave home again. Everything I need is here." She kept walking. "That's why I fought, not for slavery but because I love the land. It's mine and I want to keep it. Laura . . ."

His hand was on her shoulder and she had to stop, she had to turn and face him. The bones of his face were distinct in the fading light, long jaw, narrow eyes, dark blond hair—a good-looking, well-built man. He was a tremendous catch, he would have been even before the war. Such a man could pretty well have his pick these days and in spite of all her many drawbacks he wanted her. His thinking was sometimes wrong but he had a remarkably open mind, willing to at least allow that there might be another point of view, he was honest, he never, as Doug once remarked, dealt from the bottom of the deck. She couldn't imagine ever doubting him or worrying about where he was or what he was doing. And she was not madly in love but felt instead a deep affection that might in the long run be much better.

When he asked, quite formally, "Dear, will you marry me?", she answered, "Yes, Andrew, I will." When he kissed her she kissed him back. After all the lonely years it was wonderful feeling a man's arms around her again, it was wonderful being loved and wanted.

CHAPTER 38

THE BATTERY WAS a uniquely beautiful street of long, narrow houses with graceful three-story galleries overlooking the sea wall and Charleston Harbor. From the rooftops only a few years ago, Charlestonians had watched while cannon bombarded the fort on the tiny man-made island in the harbor and began the war that destroyed their way of life. Now, faced with the reality of defeat the city struggled on, at once insular and sophisticated, willing to allow that others with ideas different from their own might be merely eccentric and mistaken, not intentionally evil. Or so it seemed to Chase as he left the grand, dilapidated house where he had just spent a depressing afternoon visiting the impoverished cousins his mother loved best.

With gracious sincerity Jane and Melva had received their blue-coated guest, expressed regret at his brother Richard's death in battle, and sent him on his way with loving messages for Isabel, not only a cousin but their dear, dear friend.

He came down the steps of the big, shabby house and turned toward Broad Street and a tavern he liked, thinking that he could use a drink or perhaps several, scarcely aware of the three women in inevitable black who averted their heads and pulled their skirts aside to show their disdain for the conquerors.

The tavern, the Bull and Bell, was a town institution. At the long mahogany bar Charlestonians, West Indians, and foreign sailors who spoke no English except the one word "whiskey" had gotten thoroughly drunk for generations and at one time or another most of the male population had lifted a glass there. The wood-paneled room provided a cozy atmosphere that some men considered more homelike than home. At the Bull and Bell it was not uncommon to run into old friends from the distant past and on this evening it happened to Chase.

He saw the other man coming, thought about turning away before he was seen but did not.

"Chase, by all that's holy . . . I can't believe my eyes. How goes it, old man?"

"Fine, Matt. How are you?"

"Very good, very good. In a manner of speaking, that is. Two whiskeys, barkeep—I have a great thirst this evening." Matt Riley sat down at the bar beside Chase and grinned cheerfully. "I'd planned to kill you the next time I saw you. Wouldn't be very practical now, would it? *Salud*." He tossed down the liquor neat and picked up the second glass. "Let's grab that empty table in the back."

Drinks in hand they shouldered their way through the crowd, cut out two other men with the same intent, and when they were settled comfortably Matt said, "Still working for our great republic, I see. Where all have you been since I last saw you?"

"A lot of places I'd rather not have been. After the war I was sent to Arizona for a while. Miserable place. Then Washington. New Orleans until a week ago. What about you? I heard you'd gotten a good job and moved to New York—or was it Chicago?"

"Where'd you hear that?"

"I don't recall."

"Don't know how a story like that got started but I wish it were true. I wouldn't mind working for the Yankees. Hell, they've got all the money." Matt snapped his fingers at the barmaid, a round-faced girl in a low-cut dress, and ordered three more drinks each for himself and his friend. Barmaids at the Bull and Bell were chosen for a good memory and good looks, and Matt followed her with his eyes as she walked away. He turned back to Chase. "What are you up to in this old town?"

"Just passing through. I hope to get home before long. My mother isn't well and it's been a while since I've seen her."

Matt muttered polite regret and looked into the crowd for signs that the drinks were coming. It was the first time Chase had seen him out of his general's uniform and as always civilian dress subtly diminished a man, especially when the clothes were as threadbare as these. He looked years older than he was and had developed the red face and anxious, impatient manner of a man with a real need for the liquor he'd ordered. What kind of life did Laura have with him? What kind of life would the child have? Chase looked past the barmaid as she delivered the drinks. He had to get out of here soon before he kicked over the table and beat this sodden drunk to a pulp.

Matt lined up his three glasses. "That's what I like—adequate reserves. It was our greatest problem, you know. No reserves. It was always make do and do without. I look back and I know it was insanity, mass insanity. We didn't have anything we needed. Not enough cannon, rifles, ammunition, powder, not enough boots—oh, God, how we needed boots! My feet still ache when I think about it. Sometimes I think it was the women egged us into it. They were always hot for the fight. 'Go, my hero, and come home with your laurel wreath.' Easy for them to say." He gulped down the first drink and set the empty glass carefully to one side.

Chase said, "It seems to me that the women on both sides have paid a terrible price. Up North there are so many widows and here every woman I see is wearing black for someone. And starving and working like field hands. Two years ago Richmond was in worse shape than Charleston and I doubt it's much better now. You Southerners misjudged us—you thought we wouldn't fight and you could get off cheap. Now you're reaping the whirlwind and rightly so. You deserve everything you get." He waited, hoping the other man would be enraged enough to make a move, longing for an excuse that would let him smash a fist into Matt Riley's ugly, stupid, bleary-eyed face, even allow him to pull his gun and shoot the goddamned fool dead.

But Matt, who had been well into his cups when he walked in tonight, thought it over and nodded agreeably. "My friend, you have a point." He picked up another glass, took a judicious sip and set it down. "You were in Richmond, huh? Ever hear what happened to Laura Chandler? I think of her often. Sweetest damn—sweetest lady I ever met in my life. I stopped by the house just after the surrender, looking for her. I thought—well, you know. I intended to pay my respects and see how the land lay but she wasn't there and the whole damn family was very close-mouthed. I couldn't find out where she'd gone to. Just as well, I suppose. I have nothing to offer her." He had been staring into his drink, remembering, and when he looked up he was astonished by what he saw.

The man across the table looked utterly blank. And then triumphant. Through a haze of alcohol it occurred to Matt that he'd never seen Chase Girard smile in such a way and had the fleeting thought that he would like to be that happy about something himself.

Chase pushed back his chair and pulled some greenbacks from his pocket. "I have to go, Matt, but let me buy you a round." He laid the cash on the table, enough for several evenings of hard drinking if Matt wanted to spend it that way. He picked up his hat.

Matt struggled uncertainly to his feet. "See here now, don't go just yet. I don't like drinking alone, not a good thing, you know."

Chase looked at him and was able to see again a man he had once liked. "Goodbye, Matt. I wish you well." He pushed his way through the crowd and went into the soft spring night.

I T WAS A WARM DAY and Jewel was on her knees in the garden wishing she'd brought a gourdful of water and her bonnet with her. Both were lying forgotten on the kitchen table. She got up to go back to the house, saw a man coming through the gate, the blue uniform registered, and then she knew him.

He said simply, "Where is she?"

She stared back. "Not here."

"Is she well? Is she safe?"

"She's fine. The last thing she needs is you. Go away before you cause more hurt."

The kitchen door slammed and Paige came swiftly down the path. "Go in the house, Jewel. I'll deal with him." Her narrowed eyes rested on Chase. "I thought we'd seen the last of you."

"Not yet. Paige, you lied to me."

"Jewel, I said go in the house—go *on*. I declare, Colonel Girard, you Yankees need lessons in manners. Can't you tell when you're not wanted?"

"I ran into Matt Riley in Charleston two days ago. She didn't marry him and she hasn't moved north. Why such a fantastic story, Paige? Who do you hate most, me or her?"

Her eyes blazed. "I hate you both and I hope you rot in hell!"

Jewel had started for the house and she turned back. "For shame, Miss Paige. You never want to talk that way . . ."

Paige ignored her. "You killed Alex—yes, one way or another, you did! Why should you be alive when he's dead, why should she have her bastard baby and mine be dead?"

Jewel took her arm with a gentle touch. "Come on, Miss Paige, come in the house. We don't care about him. Let's go inside and get out of this hot old sun." With a soft hand and murmuring voice she urged Paige up the path. At the kitchen door she looked back at Chase and then shut the door with a firm click.

He walked through what had been the rose garden and past the lily pond. The water lilies were long dead and the pond bone-dry. He went on past bushes grown wild, past the crumbling summer house, through the gate to the place where the land dropped away. Below, the powerful river flowed and his mind went back to a day when farther downstream they had in ten hours of maddening, desperate work built the bridge that allowed the army to cross, besiege Petersburg, and finally break the Confederacy.

Behind him the gate creaked. Jewel came down the steep path with her swinging stride, calm and beautiful as ever but with a sad look about her eyes and mouth that gave her a tired, older look. She sat down beside him on Laura's rock.

"I apologize, Mr. Chase. I've known that girl since the day she was born—she was a cranky little baby, always fussing, wanted her own way even then, but I never knew her to flat-out lie before."

"Where is Laura, Jewel?"

"Not so very far. She's been living at Pine Hill with Miss

Becca and Mr. Doug ever since the war ended. She's fine, the baby's fine. Considering everything, that is."

He stood and she thought he was going to leave right then and race out to Pine Hill without even a farewell. She put out her hand. "Miss Paige told us you'd been here— said you were real interested in Rosalie and would come see Miss Laura someday when you had the time. That's what she's believed for a long time now." He sat down again and she went on in a repressed voice. "She thought . . . we all thought you just didn't care. For a while she was pretty low but she's strong. Things got better. You go on out there and tell her what happened. Just don't tell her lies."

"I don't have to lie. Thank you, Jewel. You're a good woman."

"Oh, yes, I'm a honey."

"Why do you stay here? There's more in the world than the Seymours. If you want to go north I could arrange a job." He smiled. "My mother knows a dozen women who'd sell their souls to hire someone like you."

The old gleam came into her eyes. "Truth?" Then she shook her head. "I can't leave, not for a while anyway. Miss Millie—most days she's fine, some days she thinks Mr. Edward's coming back. How can I leave her with only Miss Paige? I don't trust *her* an inch."

"You don't owe Millie your life, Jewel."

She looked up swiftly. "You don't know what I owe."

He considered saying what he thought and decided not to. "Have you ever heard from Adam?"

"Not yet but—maybe soon. You see, I'm as bad as Miss Millie."

After he left she continued to sit for some time, thinking what a kind man he was. He had stayed and talked, inquired after her needs, even offered to find her a job, when all he must have cared for in life was getting to Miss Laura just as fast as he could.

T HE HOUSE ITSELF was much as Laura had described it—a classic Georgian mansion set on a rise of ground at the end of a long shady drive, dilapidated but somehow still handsome, its white columns and shutters accenting the dark red brick. On either side of the house stood the two massive oaks that were, she had said, well over a hundred years old. Indians must have passed under those trees. In front of the house a grassy field sloped to the river and southward was the line of pines that had given the place its name. The grass was growing tall. It rose and dipped in waves under the pressure of a slight but pleasant breeze, and from the corner of his eye Chase saw on the dirt path cutting through the moving green a flash of red or orange. But his mind was on what lay ahead. He took a breath. In this last moment before seeing her, for reasons he could not name, he felt a sudden loss of nerve. He climbed the steep marble steps.

No one answered the door. The house was silent, seemingly empty. In the side yard chickens wandered, clucking and pecking in their jerky, aimless fashion, and beyond them stretched a field of barley, bright green, row after row as far as the eye could see to a point where the rolling land dropped away. Once again, in the direction of the pines, a flash of color appeared and disappeared. He walked down the path.

It was much cooler under the trees and shadowed after the bright sunshine. As his eyes adjusted to the dimmer light he saw her, a dark-haired little girl in a bright red dress. She was carrying a basket and searching the ground, frowning. Occasionally she picked up an object, all the time talking to herself.

He stopped a little distance from the river's edge and watched.

As she worked she glanced in his direction and remarked as if continuing an interrupted conversation, "It's a lot of trouble but worth it." She said it distinctly, in such a weary, adult tone and with a gesture so purely Laura's that he almost laughed. She came closer, her eyes on her latest find. "You see, dis is silver and dis liddle one is gold." She fished another pebble from her basket. "You can have it if you want." She laid the gold in his palm, thought it over and gave him the silver too. Then she moved closer to the riverbank and picked up another rock.

He said, "Come back, Rosalie, you might fall in," and she turned obediently and came to him with her newest treasure, laid it in his palm and dimpled with pleasure at her own generosity. Many times he had tried to picture her according to Paige's description and believed he had done a rather good job, but it was a shock to see his own eyes gazing at him out of that little face. There was much of Laura about her too, but something else as well, something that was Rosalie herself, unique and never seen before on this earth.

She was considering the pebbles she'd given him. One by one she took them back, dropped them in her basket and seemed to feel better about it.

He held out his hand. "Rosalie, come help me find your mother."

She was in the yard behind the house, bending over a galvanized tub. The two of them watched while she poured a pitcher of water over her head, rinsed off the soap and groped for a towel. She ran the towel over her hair, dried her face and opened her eyes.

Color left her cheeks and returned in patches. He was there, right in front of her, and she could not speak. Elvina came scurrying out the back door. "Where you been, Miss Rosalie? I turned this house upside down huntin' for you!" She saw who was with the child, cast her gaze toward Laura and then at her shoes.

Rosalie helped her out. "I was down by the river. I got lots of stuff—gold and silver an' a ruby big as your ear."

"You're full of hooey, missy, an' you ain't supposed to go near that river widout you got a grown-up."

"I had a grown-up." Rosalie looked at Chase. "Him."

There wasn't a good answer to that so Elvina took the little hand, said, "You're full of sass, too," and led her off protesting, "No, Vinie, no nap, no nap," until the door shut behind them.

He said, "She's so much like you."

She smiled a little. "Some people say that but when I look at her I only see you." She passed a comb quickly through her hair. Because it was wet it seemed jet-black in the sun. She said, "I'm so glad to see you. You . . . you're looking well. Please, come in the house and sit down while I tidy myself . . ."

"You look wonderful the way you are." His hand was warm on her arm. "Come walk with me. We have to talk."

Years later he could still call up that afternoon as if it were happening again—the blowing grass, the warmth of the sun, the breeze with the fragrance of May blossoms on its breath, her long lovely hair loose down her back, the chestnut lights and the soft curl returning as it dried. And her face, transparent to him because he loved her, showing every emotion as she listened to what Paige had done.

After a silence she said, "It must be horrible to hate like that."

"Forgive me if I don't feel sorry for her. She tried to ruin our lives." They had climbed to Pine Hill's highest point, higher than the land the house stood on, with a clear view of the river and the distant, rolling countryside. Here the grass was a thick mat, cropped short by the small herd of sheep the farm had lately acquired, and he sat on the soft turf and pulled her down beside him.

He said, "I'm going to resign from the army and go home. That is, if you think you can stand living in Philadelphia." He smiled but his eyes were wary, the eyes of a man who had looked on hell and decided it wasn't going to break him, reminding her in a disquieting way of Kirby. Long ago he had said, "We will all do terrible things before this is over." What terrible things had he seen and done?

She said, "Do you—are you talking about marriage?"

"Of course."

"Chase, I haven't been waiting all this time for you to come back and make an honest woman of me. I am honest already."

"I never thought anything else. I would have been here two years ago if I'd known where you were, that you were free." He laid his hand over hers. "What's wrong, Laura?"

It took only that light touch to bring back the memories. He looked so good, her beautiful man. She wanted to tear off her clothes and hurl herself into his arms right here on the hill on this breezy, summer afternoon with only the blue sky to see. She had loved him so much and waited for him so long. Now he was here and it was two years too late.

Never once since she looked out the fly-specked window of Tim O'Halloran's store had she told a soul what she'd seen on that day just two months after the war ended. She knew what Becca would say, and Elvina, too, if she told them. Never mind, they would tell her, that he'd gone straight to an old mistress and looked perfectly happy with her—after all, he believed Laura was lost to him. Forget Valerie's possessive caress of his face, they would say—it meant nothing that he had held that pretty, foolish woman's hand as tenderly as he was holding hers now. Men did that sort of thing, especially when they couldn't have the woman they loved.

But that little scene, played out before her eyes, had cost so much in pain. She would not reveal it any more than she would tell what she had learned about kind, honorable, loving Robert after he died. To this day she thought it strange that a man of his experience and vulnerability to blackmail had put such words on paper, but intelligent men, when entangled with a woman, sometimes took reckless chances. After that savage disillusion she never entirely believed what any man told her, never was willing to risk her heart until Chase, for a little while, made it impossible not to.

Robert, Edward, Chase. She had loved them all in different ways and all had been promiscuous, cheaters not only with their bodies but their hearts.

He still held her hand, knowing her thoughts were unhappy but unable to guess what they were, thinking that she would drive him crazy if he didn't put an end to this. His arms went around her and as he pushed her gently back onto the grass he whispered, "You're not wearing stays."

As always when he touched her like this her mind went spinning into that other place where the essential part of her lived. Why not? It had been so long and it would be so good. But some instinct for self-preservation overcame even desire and she put her hands on either side of his face.

"I'm sorry, I can't."

"What is it, Laura? Have you stopped loving me?"

She sat up and that brought a measure of control. Lying back, it was too hard to refuse him, too hard to skirt the truth. As soon as mind and body calmed a little she said, "I'll always love you in a way . . . ." She hesitated. He said nothing. "Chase, I know you would have been here if you could, you'd never abandon me because you're not that kind, but the way things were I had to do it alone. I've made a life for myself and Rosalie—it was hard but I've done it." She wished he wouldn't look like that, she wished he'd say something. She stumbled on. "I'm independent now, strong in my mind, and I want to stay that way. You're a good man and I admire you but I don't want to need you or—or depend on you. Can you understand?"

"Oh, I think so. You're scared. You always were."

That nettled her more than an outright insult. "I think I've been pretty brave."

"Well, that makes one of you."

She was silent, wishing she could think of an equally crushing reply. All she could come up with was, "You're angry, aren't you?"

"Not angry, but I can see you don't trust me and I wish I knew why." Almost gently he said, "No one can hold out on life, Laura. It never works. There'll always be someone you care for in spite of yourself. What about Rosalie? Do you say to yourself, 'I'll love her but not too much in case she hurts me later on'? It nearly killed my mother when my brother died." She drew in a sharp breath. "Yes, he died in the Wilderness, no one knows where or how, just that he's gone."

"I'm so sorry," she whispered, her eyes down, "so sorry. It seems there isn't any end to it."

"There isn't. You're afraid I'd hurt you sometime in the future and maybe I would—how can I know? So I'll give up on that for now. But if you mean I can't come here you're out of luck. I don't know my daughter at all but I'm going to and that means you'll have to put up with having me around. Are we clear on that?"

"I wouldn't prevent you from seeing her even if I could. I want her to know you, I just don't want—"

"You don't want me."

"I don't think you're meant for marriage. I'd like us to be friends if that's possible." She looked into his eyes and then away. He was angry, all right, he was furious.

She got to her feet and brushed the grass from her skirt. When she started down the hill he was just behind her.

CHAPTER 39

THE MOCKINGBIRD HOPPED in a drunken, zigzag path across the porch, its left wing dragging. Rosalie followed. When it stopped she stopped, dipped something from her hand and the bird hopped again. "Oh, my *Lord*!" she muttered with Becca's exact inflection. "The durn thing don't stay still."

Chase was sitting on the top step, watching with the bemused smile he often wore when looking at her. "What have you got there, Rosalie?"

"Salt," she replied as if he ought to have known. She added in a determined tone, "Gonna catch this birdie."

Salt was precious. During the war people, in desperation, had taken to boiling out boards from their smokehouses to extract any residue of salt. It was still hard to get and expensive.

"Did Elvina give it to you?"

"Yes." He looked at her and she looked down. "Not ezactly."

He held out his hand. "We'd better give it back."

Already she had learned that he couldn't be moved by either temper or charm. She poured the salt into his hand, her lower lip thrust out only a little. "Willum says you got to put salt on a birdie's tail to catch him."

"Honey, if you can get close enough to a bird to put salt on its tail you can pick it up without the salt."

She thought that over and brightened. The bird had hobbled to the step and was teetering on the edge. She stooped, picked it up with two plump little hands, and chortled, "Got 'im!"

Immediately she looked to Chase for approval. She knew he was the father who had gone away "to the war," the father she had heard about all her short life, because her mother told her so. She was not clear about what "war" was but her imagination pictured an oddly shaped building in a faraway place that had somehow claimed his attention for a while. She was in no doubt at all about what a father was because William had one, and the fact that she now had one herself gave her the greatest satisfaction.

He took her hand and they went into the house to find Elvina and return the salt and then decide how to fix the bird.

Doug leaned back in the old rocker that was kept on the porch for his exclusive use. He liked watching Chase and Rosalie together for he, too, had come home from war to a child he didn't know. He liked to sit out here on Sunday mornings, his only time of rest during the week, and think and plan and worry. At present he was worried about harvesting the huge crop of barley that prospered so mightily in the fields before his eyes, for his supply of workers was uncertain. He appreciated having another man, a man he had once admired and considered a friend, to talk to.

He believed it likely that Chase had sent information North but he never hinted such a thought to anyone, not even Becca. He despised Northern politicians without exception but bore no grudge against the soldiers who had fought him in war—they had all been drawn into the madness by false ideas of patriotism, they had all suffered and died—and he drew no distinctions between the various ways they had served. So he sat often on the porch with Chase in the evenings or on pleasant Sunday mornings like this one, drinking homemade brew and watching the children play.

Unlike Doug the women had no day of rest. On this Sunday morning, as soon as prayers were concluded, they had carried the linens out to the laundry house, the small, hot building that stood between the icehouse and the storage barn. The morning was sunny, breezy, too good a drying day to waste, and they had been laboring for more than two hours over the steaming tubs.

Becca extended her small shapely hands, now fiery red from hot water and rubbing on the washboard. "It's permanent, you know. If I never scrub another sheet in my life they'll still look like this." The kitchen door slammed and she glanced back at the house. Rosalie was climbing down the high steps holding tightly to Chase's hand. "You have to give him credit. He does care about her."

"Yes," Laura said and hauled the last sheet out of the tub. Together they carried it outside and went through the struggle of wringing out the water. In the beginning every sheet had been a wrestling match that led them sometimes to despair and sometimes to helpless laughter. Now they had become so expert that they could think about things other than yards of waterlogged cloth, discuss, disagree, even touch on sensitive subjects and still not drop the sheets.

Becca had a strong opinion about the man who was now walking down the hill with her little niece and didn't hesitate to express it. She harbored no love for Yankees, but she told Laura, "He has tried to do the right thing by you and the baby." Laura didn't reply and they worked for a while in silence. Then, as if launching on an entirely new line of thought, Becca went on. "I ran into Alice Dilworth in Claremore last week. She introduced me to the three girls she was with—every one of them good-looking, perfectly presentable—and you know what she said in complete seriousness? 'We've decided to stick together, all four of us, for the rest of our lives because we're all going to be old maids.' It's so sad and so true. The South is going to be a country of old maids for a generation. Just a bunch of lonely women without a crack at a man, especially a nice, attractive one . . . Oh, don't give me that look. Maybe he was a spy, maybe he wasn't—we'll never know. If he was I don't appreciate it, but he is Rosalie's father and he loves you. As Doug says, the war is over."

Laura said nothing. Her relatives were naïve about people in a way she had not been for years. They couldn't imagine that she, herself, had been disloyal to them or that a man might love a woman and yet betray her.

Becca added in an offhand way, "Did I mention I asked him to stay for dinner?"

"Today? Oh, Becca."

"Yes, Andrew will be here too, and it'll do him good."

"It won't do me good. I guess I should have told you before. I'm going to marry Andrew."

For the first time in months Becca almost dropped her end of the sheet. "When?"

"I told him—I said the end of summer."

Becca drew in a long breath. "Well, yes," she said, "you should have told us."

THERE MIGHT HAVE BEEN evenings more miserable and embarrassing but Laura couldn't recall one. She stole a look at Chase, at Andrew, and then applied herself to chewing food she could hardly swallow.

As well as she knew him it was often impossible to tell what Chase was thinking. Neither anger nor anxiety would show in his face if he didn't want it to. He held Rosalie on his lap and allowed her to eat from his plate—he had done it before when only the family was present but never when there was company. She knew he did it because he loved the child and had so little time with her but she also suspected that on this particular evening he didn't mind annoying Andrew Ferguson. As for Andrew, she didn't yet know him quite well enough to guess his thoughts.

The truth was that Andrew, a politician to his fingertips, knew how to hide his feelings too. But it had come as a terrible shock that Rosalie's father was not a Southern hero, not dead in the war, as he had convinced himself must be the case, but a Yankee colonel, alive and healthy, who sat across the table from him with the child on his lap and was now helpfully passing the wine he had brought—naturally Yankees would have wine, they had every material possession you could want. He had met Chase once before in this house, spent the evening talking with him, and had not put it together until a few moments ago when Rosalie looked up and smiled and the truth struck. How had he missed it when it was plain as day?

He took a swallow of wine and said something about its flavor, he had no idea what, breathed deeply, and turned to Laura. "Would you like to go over to Westwood in the morning and see your new home? If the harvest is as good as I hope, we might be able to make a few changes." He was rewarded with an expression of shock on Chase's face that he thought might last him for some time.

"Why—ah, I don't see how I could just now." Laura, red-faced, looked at Doug, who was pouring the last of the wine into his own glass. Becca was gazing studiously at her plate. "I have so much work . . . it would be a burden on everyone . . ." Oh, she hadn't wanted Chase to find out like this. She had meant to tell him herself in her own time, in her own way.

Becca looked up. "You go, Laura. We can manage just fine. My goodness, Chase, that child's asleep and no wonder. It's nine o'clock. Why don't you take her upstairs? Elvina!"

Elvina was working in the butler's pantry where it was impossible not to hear every word spoken in the dining room. She put her head around the corner.

"Ah, Elvina, there you are. Come help Mr. Chase put the baby to bed."

As soon as he decently could, Andrew got Laura out on the front porch, but before he could speak she said, "That was an awful thing to do. It was my place to tell him, not yours."

"Why is he here all the time?"

"You know perfectly well. He's visiting his child. Don't say one word. I don't intend to explain a thing."

He hated her cool self-possession. It was the only unlikable trait she had. "I saw the way you looked at him. You looked—"

"How did I look?"

"As if you still love him."

"I don't but I did once. You can't expect me not to remember." She went down the steps and he followed.

"You sure will remember if he's around all the time. Get rid of him, Laura. Tell him to go."

"I don't want him here any more than you do but how can I tell him he can't see Rosalie?" Andrew, a fair man, hesitated. She laid a light hand on his arm and her voice softened. "It will be different after we're married. He'll be going away soon and he won't come back often, not if he stays in the army."

"If he stays?"

"He says he may resign and go back home. He's come to hate the military and I think he misses his family. Whatever he does, he won't be around us much."

The shaky feeling in her stomach, a mixture of regret and anger and sheer embarrassment, began to ease. Andrew wasn't quite smiling but the rigid lines around his mouth relaxed, which meant she had him smoothed down, at least for the moment. He put his arms around her possessively and at that moment Chase came out the door and down the front steps. Quickly, guiltily, she moved away from the man she was going to marry, like a wife caught by a husband in a compromising situation. He was going to the stable for his horse.

She gathered herself to smile pleasantly and say good night but he passed her by with a look so forbidding that she was left standing on the brick path, a careful space away from Andrew, cold and trembling with a sense of having done harm to someone she had never wanted to hurt.

T HE FOLLOWING WEEK Chase wrote his letter of resignation, sent it to Washington with army dispatches, began a letter to his parents telling them he was coming home and then stopped and tore it up. Better to wait until he knew exactly when he would be there or his mother would be sitting on the doorstep every day, looking down the street and worrying. She had lost one son and was convinced that she was destined to lose the other in some unforeseen and tragic way.

He had to go home, he had to give his parents something of himself after all these years. Not for a moment did he believe as some veterans did that he had been allowed to survive the war for a reason. It had been pointless, meaningless chance that separated the living from the dead. All he could do now was turn back to those who cared for him and try to find some kind of peace. He told his aide he was leaving.

He walked all afternoon, along the brick paths of Capitol Square where he had once explained the economics of slave breeding to Laura, down street after street of the ruined town. In some places rebuilding was beginning but money was not only tight, it was nonexistent. Only structures that were relatively whole were worth even minor repairs.

He turned down a familiar street. The house he remembered was there, battered, and weather-beaten yet somehow still elegant, like an elderly *grande dame*, beautiful in spite of her age. He pulled the bell and heard distant chimes. There were footsteps on wooden floors and the door opened.

"Good evening, Hallie," he said. "Is Mrs. Hood at home?"

CHAPTER 40

NULA HAGGERTY CAME through the arbor into the garden carrying a tray. This little green space, a hidden city garden, was her favorite of all the grand things about the house on H Street. Here, in hanging pots, were brilliant flowers of a kind she'd never seen before and fish of many colors flashing through the dark water of the pond. The stone floor, mossy and cool in the dappled sunlight, reminded her of home.

Caroline had hired her fresh off the boat three months ago when Ailsa, her maid since girlhood, fell and broke her hip. The hip had healed but the most Caroline now allowed Ailsa to do was sort visitors' calling cards and sit on the bed helping choose her dress for the day. Nula was excessively proud of her long strawberry hair and harbored a look in her eyes that her employer didn't entirely like, but she was strong and willing, never openly impudent; she was an immigrant and must be given a chance. Her white starched apron and cap gave her the appearance of a proper maid but she was not well trained, not yet.

"No, not on the wall," Caroline said in mild exasperation, "set it here by me. Nula, you know I require female servants to restrain their hair."

"Yes, mum."

"Yours is hanging loose. Have it up in a neat bun, not touching your collar, the next time I see you."

"Yes, mum."

Nula gazed with bright attention at Mrs. Merritt's guest. The lady arrived this afternoon and had been pouring out her soul to Mrs. Merritt for over an hour but she talked softly and was hard to hear. The only good thing about working as a maid, other than earning a living, was the gossip and intrigue you sometimes overheard if you faded into your surroundings and had big ears.

"You may go, Nula. Get your hair up and then take a tray to Ailsa." Caroline watched the girl go with a line between her brows. "Here, dear, have another sandwich— you're thin as a rail. I hope . . . I trust the stories of hunger at home are greatly exaggerated."

Laura picked up the sandwich and took a bite to please her. "Meat is still scarce but at Pine Hill we've never gone hungry. For city people it's much worse. Your house, this garden, the whole town . . . I'd forgotten what luxury is like. Imagine fish swimming in a pond and not eating them, imagine keeping a dog as a pet—you don't see many dogs at home except for the hunters who earn their keep. The rat population has diminished too."

"You don't mean—"

Laura shrugged. "You don't see many horses either— oh, some ploughhorses and mules for us farmers who are lucky enough to have them, but not carriage horses. No one can afford to feed them."

Caroline stirred her tea with a thin silver spoon, set it down and abandoned delicacy in favor of directness. "And so, are you going ahead with this marriage?"

"The minute I get home, no matter what he says, I'm going to release him. I should have done it that night. He wants to be the next governor and how can he run for office with me and Rosalie as baggage? I don't know why he ever thought he could."

"Men will do anything when they're in love."

Laura laughed shortly. "So will women but it doesn't last. Nothing lasts."

"Chase's feeling for you has lasted. Or so it sounds to me."

"I told you a long time ago—he's a good man. He feels responsible and he'll do what he thinks is right but he doesn't love me, not the way I need to be loved. He has another woman and I don't want to talk about it."

There was silence.

"It would happen again and again. I wouldn't tolerate it because I couldn't."

Caroline still said nothing and Laura felt pressed to

explain. "You don't understand. It's happened to me before. After Robert died, a woman came to me with letters."

"Ah," said Caroline.

"Robert . . . oh, I hate to tell you this . . ."

"Pauline Johnson. And she wanted money? I wouldn't have expected that."

The air went out of Laura as if she'd been punched. "You knew about her?"

"I met her. Twice."

Laura set down her plate. It hit the teacup with a rattling sound and tea slopped into the saucer. "In God's name, Caroline, why didn't you tell me?"

"How could I? What good would it have done?"

"I'd have known, as no doubt everyone else did, and I would have gone home. Why didn't he marry her if she was what he wanted?"

"He didn't want her for a wife, I suppose. You were his darling, his young beauty, and he was so proud of you. Don't look like that, dear."

"I thought I was his *wife*, not some trinket he picked up to show off. What would have happened when I wasn't pretty anymore, what about when I grew old?"

"You were his wife—he loved you, he relied on you. Laura, you did more to help him than he ever expected. I always thought he was wrong to live as he did. I also think you're wrong to believe Chase would do the same."

"You're the one who told me not to trust him."

Caroline smiled, rueful, almost sad. "Did it ever occur to you that I could be wrong? Perhaps he isn't like Robert at all."

"Perhaps isn't good enough. I can't live with perhaps."

"We live it every moment of our lives. The best things are always chancy, especially marriage and children." Caroline's eyes went down to her slim white hands. She touched the large emerald on her hand and said in a softer voice, "I'll tell you something no one but Ailsa knows. I was in love once, desperately in love with a young man named Charlie Murphy. He was an immigrant with great ambition, as fine and good a man as you could want, but can you imagine me as Mrs. Murphy? I couldn't. I wouldn't take the risk of a life with him so I married Langdon Merritt. I don't know what happened to Charlie, whether he was the grand success he believed he'd be or simply worked hard all his life, but I'll tell you this. There's never been a day that I haven't wished I'd taken the risk with him. I don't want you to be like me—looking back on your life someday and wishing you'd had more courage." Caroline leaned back in the comfortable chair that was brought out now whenever she sat in the garden and closed her eyes. "I had an easy life with Langdon but I wish I'd taken the risk." In the clear light her fine skin seemed almost translucent.

Nula came out and began to clear away the dishes, doing it slowly so as to pick up any stray bit of information floating between the ladies. But the intense talk, whatever it was about, appeared to be over. Mrs. Merritt said she was going upstairs and her guest went to look at the bird that lived in the fancy cage on the other side of the pond. A nasty heathen bird, a *talking* bird from India of all places, that made rude remarks when you least expected it.

She picked up the loaded tray and as she passed through the arbor the bird called after her, "So long, cutie!"

"Sure, I'll never get used to it," she muttered and heard the lady laugh.

"How are you, sweetie?" the bird asked Laura. She opened the cage and offered a palmful of seeds, wondering if she'd ever really known anyone. Caroline, regretting a lost love all her life. Lack of courage, Caroline said. A softer way of saying cowardice. More than once Chase had called her a coward, said it in anger but was it true?

"What do you think, Dilly?" she asked the mynah and he answered, "What do you think, sweetie, what do you think?"

THE FRONT DOOR OPENED. She came down the steps with the two men who had arrived only a few minutes earlier. One of them said something and she laughed, and across the street Chase threw down his cigar and ground it under his heel. He had never felt more like a fool in his life, hanging around watching the house, trying not to be seen. He should have gone up to that door as soon as he got into town this morning, told her that he couldn't give her up, tried this last time. The shorter man with the lean, distinguished face seemed familiar. Some politician she knew or a businessman on the make, the kind that infested this place. The other man, taller, younger, good-looking, seemed to know her well. Better to have stayed home and been a banker as his father wanted, better anything than to have gone out into the world looking for something, met her and loved her and ended up standing here, forever at a distance.

His train left at four o'clock. He had to go. She didn't want him and he couldn't and wouldn't follow her around like a lovesick schoolboy. He began to walk in the direction they had gone.

The city was as great a contrast to Richmond as could be imagined, leaving no doubt as to who had won the "recent conflict," as Washingtonians liked to describe the war that had torn their country apart. People were well dressed and energetic, optimism and wealth were evident on the bustling streets. The town was filled with ambitious, new-rich people trying to break into society and their expensive clothes and swank new carriages added a sense of luxury to the booming town.

Just ahead was the White House and across the street the little park, Lafayette Square, where the Marine Band was forming up under an awning for the afternoon concert. The band's performances, stopped at the request of Mrs. Lincoln after little Willie Lincoln died, had been resumed. Everyone had missed the concerts, everyone loved the vigor and excitement of a military band, and the square was rapidly filling up with prosperous-looking men and women dressed in the latest style. Not one of those women, Chase thought, could compare with Laura in her old-fashioned hoops.

She took Lucius Newton's arm as they picked their way across the busy street, still muddy from last night's rain. Lucius, one of Robert's old friends, was a senator now—the dream of his life. A fiery orator, he had left the Whig party as it sank and jumped to the fast-rising Republicans just before the war. But he was not, he had assured her at dinner last night, one of the radicals who wanted to punish the South; he wanted reconciliation. John Holley, who had invited himself along on this outing, wanted to crush the Rebels with all the punishment the occupying army could arrange. Laura hadn't liked him in the old days when he was an ambitious young man about town and she didn't like him now that he was in Congress.

The colorful awning over the band fluttered in the breeze that had sprung up and for some foolish reason it lifted her heart. This little park was like Capitol Square back home, a lively gathering place of movement and color and optimism. She was at that moment so glad to be there that she gave John Holley a genuine smile.

Chase crossed the street, walked into the square, and stopped beside the great statue of Andrew Jackson on his prancing horse. She was only a few feet from him and he could see her from the side, her face somehow different with that little hat tipped over one eye, a hat that was in the latest mode and seemed to be constructed entirely of tiny white feathers. He wondered if one of the men had bought it for her. An unworthy thought.

Why didn't she turn and look at him, how could she not know that he was here as he would know whenever she was near him?

"My God," he said to Andrew Jackson, "I'm not only a damned fool, I'm a little crazy," and saw the startled glance of a woman standing on the other side of the statue. He walked toward Laura, wanting to come on her suddenly, see her reaction before she had time to think.

At that moment she turned. Was it joy or pleasure or simply surprise that flashed across her face before she smiled and introduced him to her friends? Senator Newton, Congressman Holley. The men shook hands.

There was a pause.

Senator Newton commented on the splendid concert they were about to hear. Congressman Holley spoke of the sudden coolness of the day and the threatening sky. The two men realized that they were talking only to each other, saw other people to greet and excused themselves.

"Your hat is charming," Chase said.

"It's Caroline's. I'm so surprised to see you. I had no idea . . . where did you come from?"

"Right over there. Had an interesting conversation with General Jackson."

Her eyes moved to the statue and back to him. "What did you talk about?"

"You and me."

"I thought you were going home."

"I am but not without you. I came to get you, Laura, I came to take you home."

"How . . . how in the world did you know where I was? They promised—"

"Your relatives didn't tell me anything. Rosalie did. She said you'd gone to see Aunt Caroline. Rosalie is the only sane one in your family. She takes after me."

There were experimental toots on the horns as the band tuned up. Lightning flashed across the dark gray sky, followed by rolling thunder.

"I think it's going to rain," she said, turning away a little.

He caught her arm and turned her back, his eyes unsmiling. "I've tried to do without you, I've tried everything I can think of and nothing seems to work, so I'm going to stay here and follow you everywhere you go. I'll turn up at all the parties, embarrass you, make an idiot of myself, and everyone will feel sorry for me. I'll follow you back to Pine Hill and pitch a tent in the front yard and if Andrew Ferguson or anyone else comes around I'll kill the bastard. I'll even help you clean up after the pig and the chickens if I have to, because you are the love of my life."

He watched every change in her face. She thought of the guarantees he couldn't give, the riskiness of life, the many Valeries to be found anywhere he cared to look. And what it would mean to wake up beside him every morning, see his face across the table every night, and the two of them, together, helping Rosalie grow up. Love could bring hurt but also supreme blessings.

She said, "That is the best proposal there ever was in this world." Her slow smile began. "I've been living without you for a long while now so I know I can do it but, truth to tell, it isn't much of a life."

The band had started to play but onlookers were

glancing upward, unfurling umbrellas. A great bolt of lightning split the sky, followed by a deafening thunderclap and warm rain poured down, a sudden summer deluge.

From under her umbrella a woman said, "Look, there he is kissing her, the man who was talking to the statue. They're getting soaked and the feathers are coming off her hat."

The man with her said, "I don't think they care."

AUTHOR'S NOTE

FIRST OF ALL, my gratitude to my editor, Beverly Lewis, whose interest and faith has carried me this far. Her feel for the story I am trying to tell is always on target. Her expertise is awe-inspiring.

Both the North and the South destroyed records of their spies. Except for those caught during the war (or the few who went on the lecture circuit afterward), most of those who fought in this daring way kept their secrets and lived out their lives unknown, as they must have wanted it. Some of the fictional characters in this story are based on historical figures. In order to develop them fully while weaving together history and fiction, I have given them other names. All recognizable historical figures, their attitudes and actions, are as accurate as I could make them.

I am indebted to the following sources: *Mary Chesnut's Civil War*, edited by C. Vann Woodward; *The Blue and the Gray*, edited by Henry Steele Commager; *Experiment in Rebellion*, by Clifford Dowdey; *Spies for the Blue and Gray*, by Harnett T. Kane; *Slave-Trading in the Old South*, by Frederic Bancroft; *Reveille in Washington*, by Margaret Leech; *The Oxford History of the American People*, by Samuel Eliot Morison; *Jefferson Davis*, by Varina Davis; *Heroines of Dixie*, edited by Katharine M. Jones; *A Southern Woman's Story*, by Phoebe Yates Pember; *First Lady of the South*, by Ishbel Ross; *Judah P. Benjamin*, by Eli Evans.

And my respectful thanks to my great-grandmother who, alone with her children, stood up to night riders, too.

ABOUT THE AUTHOR

DIANE AUSTELL is a native of California. Her ancestors came to America before the Revolutionary War and her family's history is interwoven with the development of the country. Her great-great-grandfather fought for the Union in the Civil War, while other family members fought for the South.

Ms. Austell lives with her husband in southern California. They have two children.